SB

Living the Good Death

By Scott Baron

Curiouser Publishing
1223 Wilshire Blvd. #960
Santa Monica, CA 90403

Living the Good Death
ISBN 978-1-945996-14-6 (Ingram Edition)
ISBN 978-1-945996-13-9 (Cratespace Edition)
ISBN 978-1-945996-12-2 (ebook)

Heartfelt thanks go out to Rachael Levy, my tireless sounding board, Christopher Papastefanou, for endlessly amusing input, my amazing editor Melissa Gray for her eagle eye, Dane Lowe, cover designer extraordinaire, and my family and friends for all their years of support

"Life is pleasant. Death is peaceful. It's the transition that's troublesome." – Isaac Asimov

Traffic flew by in a blur, a speeding deathtrap of rubber and metal buzzing at speeds well above the posted limit. A casual observer might think the deadly machines were almost anxious to turn anyone made of less-sturdy stuff and foolish enough to stumble into their path into grisly roadkill. They may have been inanimate, but they were dangerous as hell nonetheless.

That didn't concern the pale young woman in black one bit as she stood casually on the median of the busy street. No, her gaze and attention were entirely focused upon a doorway across the road as she ignored the buzzing vehicles.

Donny's Happy Hour Bar & Pool Hall really wasn't much to look at. Dingy and run-down, with that ass-end-of-town look that made you wonder just how lighthearted and joyful any happy hour there could really be. Of course, with the sun high in the sky, it wasn't anywhere near happy hour. In fact, by all but the most serious alcoholic's standards, at just past noon, it was still quite early.

Only *serious* day-drinkers would be partaking at this hour.

As if on cue, the disheveled shape of Andy Meade came into view as he was birthed to the sidewalk through the faded red door. He blinked rapidly, wincing as his eyes tried to adjust to the bright afternoon light.

Though a mere fifty-three years of age, Andy, with his thinning hair and ashy complexion, looked closer to a well-worn seventy, the result of a life of hard drinking, chain-smoking, and a diet of questionable nutritional content. He had long ago given up on getting ahead in the world, and that world-weariness bled through into his every movement.

He stood in the doorway a moment longer, squinting until his eyes finally acclimated to the sunlight as the cool breeze lapped uncomfortably at his skin. Andy popped his collar up against the unexpected chill, then turned and staggered slowly toward the parking lot adjacent the bar.

It's only a couple of drinks, he rationalized as he swerved down the sidewalk on wobbly legs. *I'm perfectly fine to drive. Just need to sit down a minute is all.*

The young woman in black followed his progress, her piercing gray eyes watching him as a cat watches a mouse, seemingly disinterested, yet paying close attention nonetheless. Then, as if heeding an invisible call, she abruptly stepped off the median and into traffic, striding purposefully across the street, her long black coat swishing behind her in time with her rapid steps.

She didn't bother to look at the cars hurtling her way. She didn't even spare them so much as a glance, yet somehow, she avoided them all without mussing a single hair or missing a step. In fact, it was as if the drivers didn't see her at all.

The young woman in black's boots crunched to a stop as she reached the curb, eyes narrowing ever so slightly as she focused on her quarry. A slight furrow creased her brow as she slowly raised her left hand, stretching it out toward Andy just as he reached his silver sedan.

Her outstretched fingers gently flexed at him from across the parking lot, as if plucking invisible strings in the ether. The action somehow caused his body to shudder, his grip faltering as the keys slipped from his hand.

Drunk as he was, Andy was startled. Alarmed even. Even through the high-proof haze that clouded his mind, he sensed something was distinctly not-right.

A faint glow became visible from his chest, tugging his very core as his life force seeped from his body, slowly pulling through the very fabric of him, inch by inch. Wide-eyed, he glanced around in shock and disbelief, but no one passing by took notice.

Andy quickly slid into a panic as he clutched at his chest. He sensed that he wasn't just suffering from having too much to drink. No, viscerally, somewhere in the depths of his primitive mind, he *knew* that wasn't the case.

This was something different.

Something horribly wrong.

In a moment of unusual clarity he realized, much to his surprise, and with absolutely no warning, that he was dying.

The young woman in black lowered her hand, casually watching as her victim's life force slowly ebbed out of its meat case.

She just stood there. Calm. Expressionless.

One might say she looked almost bored even, because, hello? For Death, Reaper of Souls, this was just another day at the office.

A beam of light flashed across her eyes, and for just a second her attention faltered. On the sidewalk, a man had stopped and opened his unusually ornate blue enamel antique pocket watch, the sun's reflective blaze playing across its face in a dance of light. Such an out-of-place object caught her attention.

Who still carries a pocket watch nowadays? she found herself wondering.

The man turned to continue his walk, shutting the watch case with a quick flip of his wrist. With the distraction gone, the young woman refocused her attention fully back onto her quarry, but as she did, her expression turned to one of shock.

She had only lost focus for a moment, but despite the immense power at her command, Andy's life force inexplicably, and quite suddenly, snapped back into his body.

"That's not supposed to—" she almost managed let out an utterance of surprise, but she didn't have a chance. Her vision swirled and faded to black as she tumbled to the ground, unconscious.

Waking up on the floor of a grimy, low-end hotel room, dazed and disoriented with a mouthful of sick, really isn't the ideal way to start your day. Most would prefer a simple cup of coffee, but some aren't so lucky.

The young woman in black lay there, facedown on the floor, carpet fibers tickling her lips as she slowly breathed. A thick mental fog weighed her down like a damp blanket, dulling her senses as she tried to free herself from its embrace. That annoying pulsing in her head and chest only made things worse.

Thump-thump. Thump-thump. Thump-thump.

What the hell is that sound? Why can't I see anything? Wait, am I on the floor?

Try as she might, she found it surprisingly difficult to tune out the noise filling her head so she could focus.

Okay, there is something seriously wrong here. She struggled to clear her head. *Slow down, focus. Get your bearings. First things first, see where you are.*

Unfortunately, her eyes weren't giving her any information.

Open your eyes and look around. This isn't rocket science.

Her body had other ideas, at least for the moment, and her vision stubbornly remained at zero as she gingerly tried to open her lids. Try as she might, they remained glued shut in a most uncomfortable manner. It took a moment, but finally, she realized what the problem was.

Eye crud? How can I have eye crud?

Several frustrating seconds passed as she gritted her teeth, ignoring the pain of her lashes pulling out one by one as she strained to open her eyes. Finally, the sticky layer of crud and grime began to loosen, releasing her eyelids with a wet pop and a sting.

What is this place? She looked around with somewhat blurred vision.

Something is really not right, she realized. *And what's that taste?*

Propping herself up on one elbow, she pondered the lingering foulness in her mouth. Spitting out the remnants of Lord knows what and wiping the straggling bits of carpet lint from her lips, she surveyed the scene as best she could from her less-than-ideal vantage point on the floor.

Okay, that's a little better. She could feel her senses slowly sharpening as she shook the cobwebs from her brain.

As her vision cleared, she discovered the room was actually worse than she had thought at first glance, if that was even possible.

The carpet may have been lush and beautiful once, but that was many, many years ago, and all that remained now was a distant memory of its former regality, encrusted with countless years of filth and grime rubbed deep into its fibers.

My face was on that, she thought with a shudder.

The walls were no better. Peeling paint and ancient smoke-stained wallpaper from the 1970s graced them, the sounds of a slow drip echoing from what she imagined must be an equally horrible bathroom. A musty smell permeated the tiny space with a pervasive dampness. The television was the most modern thing in the room by far, and even that marvel of technology was outdated by decades.

I don't understand. I'm in a seedy flophouse hotel, and a low-end one at that, but why? For that matter, how?

The unexpected groan coming from the bed took her by surprise. A sudden, heavy pounding filled her chest as a flush rose quickly to her cheeks. A tingle rushed through her body as a wave of adrenaline surged into her veins. She froze, straining her senses, and listened. The person the noise had originated from didn't seem to be aware of her presence.

At least not yet.

She quietly pushed herself up to her knees and peered over the edge of the bed, shocked that she had failed to even notice there was someone else in the room with her.

Get up. You're not doing yourself any good on the floor.

Unsteady, she cautiously found her way to her feet, wobbling ever so slightly, clutching a rickety chair as she slowly regained her balance. Peering through much less blurry eyes, she discerned that the sound had come from an old man lying on his side on the threadbare comforter, breathing deeply.

He appeared to be sound asleep and totally unaware of her presence.

Propped up against the wall, she noticed an unusual and ornate walking stick, the bird's head pommel well worn, from years of use. The twisting length of the wood rippled with curved lines. For a moment she thought perhaps it might be necessary to use it until her balance evened out, but as she released her white-knuckled grip on the chair, she was pleased to find her equilibrium had returned.

Okay, starting to feel better.

Scoping out the dimly lit room, she noted an old picture of the man and a woman she assumed was his wife on the chipped and faded wooden nightstand next to the bed. It was obviously taken at least a decade ago if not more, the pair of them smiling like a postcard-perfect happy couple.

The room lacked a feminine touch.

She's gone, she thought. *Many animals mate for life. Occasionally humans follow suit, though not so much in this era.*

She glanced at the other items on the table, and noticed that next to the picture sat a small bottle of pills and a bottle of vodka, both quite empty. The man shifted slightly in his bed, and the smell of something acidic and foul wafted to her nostrils.

What is that stench? she wondered. Then she saw it.

The thick stream of the man's sour vomit, consisting mostly of vodka and undigested pills, along with what she guessed to be the remnants of his dinner, had trickled down the side of the comforter. It must have been drying for a while since the pool on the floor had slowly begun caking into yet one more mystery stain in the ancient carpet.

As for the smell, let's just say calling it unpleasant would be an understatement.

The old man's chest continued to rise and fall in a slow but regular rhythm. Apparently, the pills and vodka didn't quite do the trick.

I see, she thought, studying the lines of his face. *A failed suicide.*

She rolled her shoulders and neck, loosening her limbs as she stood upright. Her body stretched and cracked as she rose to her full height, vertebrae swinging into alignment as her back returned to a more familiar and comfortable posture.

Having finally gotten her bearings, though still rather confused by them, she happened to catch a glimpse of herself in the filthy, chipped mirror above the dresser. Her raven hair may have been a bit askew, and her eyes seemed a bit puffy, but she still looked like the same twenty-something girl she'd always been. Pale and lean, clad entirely in black, wearing her ever-present long black coat. Her wardrobe fit just right, and seemed to almost be a part of her.

It's okay. I'm okay, she thought, pleased that at least she still looked like herself. Mostly anyway. Something still seemed *off,* for lack of a better word, and that worried her. Of course, what constitutes *off* when you happen to be the girl who thinks she is Death is a whole other question.

Walking slowly on unsteady legs, she made her way down the smoke-stained halls. The ancient lobby was empty. Speckles of dust hung suspended in the stale air, making bright points of reflected light as they lazily floated through the lone ray of sun that somehow discovered a gap in the ancient blinds.

She stumbled out the front door of the seedy hotel, a blast of riotous sound hammering her ears as she found herself overwhelmed by the sheer volume of the street noise.

"What the hell's going on?" she gasped aloud in shock as she was buffeted by the cacophony of the city.

So noisy today, she marveled. *Unusually so.*

And to her ears, it was indeed louder, but why the change? Perhaps she'd find the answer if she explored the area further.

The neighborhood itself, though one of the older and more run-down in the city, really wasn't all that bad. At least not anymore. Apparently, the dive hotel in which she'd awoken was one of the last raggedy holdouts in what appeared to be an otherwise rapidly gentrifying neighborhood.

There was the smell of ART™ in the air, as creative types pursued their dreams of installation-piece recognition and stencil-graffiti glory. Meanwhile the junkies and drunks who had populated the area for decades were being quickly displaced from their weekly rentals and hobo squats as the buildings were snatched up by out-of-town investors and developed into ridiculously high-priced lofts.

With nowhere cheap to go but the few remaining flophouses, which were full to capacity, a good many of the men and women now slept in boxes in alleys and doorways. Every day, girls in yoga pants, artists with trust funds, and professionals who wished they were artists with trust funds, milled about the street, ignoring the down-and-out camped in their own doorways.

Meanwhile, they failed to notice the world around them, stepping over them like so much trash as they texted on their phones, obliviously engrossed in their own world.

Taking it all in as she slowly walked, the girl in black finally began to feel like herself again, sharpening her focus and forcing the myriad noises to the background. An unexpected gust of cold wind hit her like an icy slap from a scorned lover. It cut through her clothes, chilling her to the bone and making her shudder as goose bumps sprang to life beneath her insufficient garb.

What the—? she thought as she brushed her wind-blown hair from her face. She paused, realizing her hands actually *felt* cold, the tips of her fingers fading to an even paler hue than normal.

How can I feel the cold?

Puzzled, she stared at her hands for a moment, then flexed them into fists a few times, fighting the cold as they began to stiffen from the chill.

Most disconcerting indeed.

With a shudder, she continued down the street, icy hands jammed deep in her pockets against the frigid air. It was only a few blocks until the buildings parted, leaving a gap to the brightening sky, and the girl who thought she was Death felt a sudden flush of glorious warmth flow over her as she stumbled into a sunny patch near the corner of the street.

The welcome heat startled her, bringing her to a full stop as she took her hands out of her pockets and held them up to savor the delicious warmth of the sun.

Stopping suddenly on a busy sidewalk isn't typically a good idea.

"Hey! Watch where you're walking!" a man grumbled as he

brusquely shouldered his way past her.

The impact startled her, but surprise quickly gave way to anger.

He touched me? He actually touched me? She fixed her gaze on the man as he walked away, a furrow forming on her brow as she raised her hand to channel her energy to suck his life and soul from his body.

Her fingers splayed, and a look of calm passed onto her face.

This is what she does. She is Death, and this man's life is now forfeit. Slowly, she moved her fingers, willing his life from his body.

Nothing happened.

Utterly confused, she watched him fade in the distance.

Why didn't it work?

Scanning the crowd, she picked out a man berating his girlfriend. The woman was in tears, while he just yelled louder at her reaction. Yes, that one would do just fine.

Once again she raised her hand, focusing all her energy on the man.

This time it would work. It had to work.

It didn't.

Oh shit! Oh shit—oh shit!

A full-fledged panic was about to set in, and she was the girl who never panicked. Her cheeks flushed from another unfamiliar burst of adrenaline, as the girl who thought she was Death tried once more to take a life, this time selecting a woman sitting on a bus bench.

Again, nothing.

A bike messenger.

Nothing.

A man in an expensive, tailored suit walking past.

Nothing.

She ran over the situation in her head.

Something has happened to me. Has my power left me entirely? And I can feel... people can see me. An unpleasant possibility formed in her mind. *It can't be— am I mortal?* She shuddered at the thought, but all signs pointed to that being a very distinct possibility.

She could feel heat and cold. Then there was the issue of people seeing and even touching her. And the icing on the cake, she was apparently unable to take a life. Something was very wrong indeed.

Standing on the sidewalk, dazed and utterly confused, the girl reluctantly accepted the horrifying realization.

No. This cannot be. I am Death. I am not merely a bag of mortal flesh, but what has changed? A look of concern flashed across her face. *If I am unable to do my job, what happens when people are supposed to die?*

As if the universe heard her query, the piercing sound of skidding tires cut through the air, followed by the screams of bystanders.

They were playing her song.

She turned toward the commotion. Not a random stranger on the street, but an actual traffic collision.

If I can't cross this one over, then… She shuddered at the thought. *Come on, pull yourself together. This is what you do, it's what you are. Go do this.*

The accident had taken place a mere half-block away. A thirty-something man, his full attention focused on the Facebook drama with his possibly soon-to-be ex-girlfriend that was unfolding on his cell phone, had quite obliviously stepped off a curb without seeing or hearing the blue sedan rapidly approaching him.

Who liked what post and unfriended which person apparently took priority over situational awareness, which, in this case, proved a bad idea, especially when a two-ton hunk of metal on wheels was barreling down the road right toward him.

No matter how good your anti-lock brakes may be, no one can force their car to stop on a dime when someone steps in front of it at short range.

Unless, of course, that dime is in that someone's pocket.

The girl who thought she was Death pushed her way through the gathering crowd, making a deliberate line toward the epicenter of the accident, her hand raised, her face showing the strain as she tried to focus her powers and reap the victim's soul.

This is someone who should be dead. This time it will work.

Her confidence was building with every step. She was Death, and she was going to take this person's life.

She finally edged her way through the throng of bystanders, who she noted could still touch her—*how annoying*—and spotted the injured man on the ground, locking him in her sights.

To her dismay, as she attempted to pull his essence free, the would-be corpse simply stood up, dusting himself off, a bit scraped up and dirty, but otherwise unharmed.

Not what she had planned.

Not at all.

No, it has to work! She strained her hand outward toward the man, but he just stood there, brushing the gravel and dirt off of his clothes.

A concerned woman ran up to him, shocked by the accident but equally amazed that he appeared unharmed after such an impact.

"Oh my God, are you okay?" she asked, her breath catching as she looked at his torn clothes, expecting the worst.

"Yeah, I'm fine. It's just a scrape."

"You shouldn't stand up," the woman said. "You might have internal injuries. You should lay back down until an ambulance gets here."

"I feel fine, thanks."

"But... the speed he hit you—how are you not hurt! It's a miracle!"

The driver of the car, who was naturally quite freaked out at the prospect of running a man down on his way to work, hovered close, wringing his hands nervously.

"I'm so sorry. I didn't see you. Are you sure you're all right? Should I call an ambulance?"

"No, really, I'm fine. Don't worry about it."

And the girl in black knew he spoke the truth. He really was okay.

Murmurs of, "He should be dead," and, "How can he be all right?" and even, "It's a miracle!" filtered to the ears of the girl who thought she was Death.

Yes, he should be dead, she thought, grimly. *But for some reason my powers have vanished. This does not bode well.*

Distraught, she turned and started off through the bustling crowd, finding herself quickly overwhelmed by the steady flow of people streaming against her as she struggled forward.

Surging humanity was buffeting her like a salmon swimming upstream, and much to her distress and distraction, there was nothing she could do to stop it.

The girl had been walking down the busy sidewalk for a long while with no sense of time. Her distraction continued to grow as the sheer number of people pressing in around her had become downright overwhelming. She felt drained, swaying on her feet from the sensory overload. She managed to push clear of the throng, pressing her back against a store's façade as she took a moment and regained her equilibrium.

This has got to be a mistake. Someone has to know what's going on. There has to be a way back.

She looked up, a boiling frustration building within her, when a neon sign just down the street caught her eye. It was gaudy thing, flashing pictures of stars, a pyramid, and the all-seeing eye. Her eyes locked on the words "Madame Bavmorda, Psychic" calling to her in bright red.

The bell jingled as the girl entered the dimly lit occult shop. Crystals and tapestries adorned the walls and counters, and new-age music quietly filtered through the incense-tinged air. Watching from a plush chair, decked out in flowing, mystical attire of rich fabric, with what appeared to be very old tarot cards spread in front of her, sat Madame Bavmorda. She gazed casually at her new guest, a hint of a bemused smile on her lips.

To the girl, the psychic appeared to be in her fifties, though with her elaborate outfit and makeup, it was hard to tell for sure in the dim light. For all she knew, the woman could have just as easily been one hundred.

The woman's intense eyes looked at the cards spread on the

table then focused again on the girl, studying her.

"You come seeking answers, yes?" The psychic's accent was notably Eastern European.

"You see me?" asked the girl who thought she was Death. "You can actually see me?"

"I see all," the mystic replied. "Come, sit."

She gestured to a cushioned divan across the table from where she reclined. The young woman hesitated for a moment.

If she can see me… could she help get me home?

She lowered herself onto the cushion.

"You must know, I am not meant to be here. I must cross back."

Madame Bavmorda furrowed her brow as she sized up the girl now seated across from her. With a flourish, she scooped up her deck and shuffled the cards with well-practiced hands, slowly fanning them out in front of her, pausing as the tarot cards' images revealed themselves.

"Ah… yes, yes… You are so very far from home." She watched the girl's reaction closely.

"Yes!"

The psychic turned over a card.

"But there is a way. A way back!"

"Tell me!" The girl slid to the edge of her seat as she anxiously watched the old psychic.

Another card turned, and Madame Bavmorda paused dramatically, then raised an eyebrow as she fixed her piercing gaze on the young customer seated across from her.

"Hmm, interesting," she mused. "Very interesting."

The girl stared at her intently, waiting. "What is it? How do I get back?"

"Madame Bavmorda can help you—for a nominal fee."

"I am Death, Reaper of Souls, and I must return to my rightful place! People must die! It is my purpose!" the young woman blurted.

The cards that had been slowly turning one by one stopped suddenly as Madame Bavmorda gave her an exasperated look.

"You what, now?" she groaned. "Oh God, not another one. Okay, you know what, you need to get out of here, all right? I don't do crazy."

Madame Bavmorda's accent had disappeared, the girl noted, as she started scooping up her cards.

"But you—"

"I said OUT!"

The woman lurched from her seat with surprising spryness for someone who had just moments before appeared so old and wise, and grabbed the young woman by the arm, hustling her to the exit in a rush.

With a yank, she opened the front door and pushed her strange would-be customer out onto the cold sidewalk, slamming the door behind her, the bell chiming an unhappy ding as the door shook in its frame from the impact.

The girl thought to go back inside, but heard the lock slide shut as the Open sign flickered out.

Despondent, she slowly turned from the door and started moving, one foot after the other, distraught and alone. Direction wasn't important, she simply felt compelled to walk and think. Two things she'd be doing for many, many hours.

CHAPTER 2

Darkness had fallen at some point during her walk, though when exactly, she couldn't say. The girl hadn't really paid much attention to the transition from day to night, so deep in thought she had been, placing one foot in front of the other almost mechanically. Now, however, when she paused and looked at her surroundings, she was faced with the uncomfortable realization that she had no idea where she was.

She scanned the area, and noticed the half-lit streets were lacking the hustle and bustle of earlier. In fact, they were rather deserted, for the most part, save for the occasional post-work jogger and a few small ragtag groups of homeless huddled together against the night's chill.

The old-school, high-intensity sodium vapor streetlights that had once illuminated every nook and cranny of the somewhat historic boulevard had recently been replaced with high-tech, low-energy LED fixtures during the neighborhood's transition from seedy slum to hipster haven. While perhaps better for the environment with their lower energy consumption, they were far less efficient at their principal job of actually illuminating the streets and sidewalks. The resulting long shadows and dark patches made the girl's path one that led directly into a murky patchwork of inky-black spots. The type of darkness in which the things that go bump in the night might lurk.

Normally these types of shadowy places would have been inviting to the girl who thought she was Death, but for some reason, on this most unsettling of days, she found herself experiencing a rather foreign sensation; a visceral discomfort tightening her gut. Accompanying it was a slight tingling of the hairs on the back of her neck standing at attention, causing an involuntary quickness to her steps as she walked past the dark alleyways and building entrances.

What is wrong with me? she thought, noticing the chill in the air that accompanied nightfall as she hurried along.

Have I really been walking all day? No wonder my feet are so sore, she mused.

The afternoon sun that had previously warmed her slender body as she wove through the neighborhoods had been pleasant. Now that the sun had slid below the horizon, however, and the evening chill had taken over the streets, she found herself once again experiencing a sharp cold that cut right through her all-too insufficient clothes.

Across the empty street, a shifting flicker from a small mom-and-pop television and audio store caught her eye, the light emanating from the several TV sets on display behind the heavy iron security grating protecting the store's windows.

Huddled in their ratty coats, bundled against the night air, stood a couple of neighborhood winos watching the free entertainment through the glass. The men slowly swayed in their inebriated state, thoroughly enthralled with the flickering screens, laughing drunkenly.

What could possibly be so interesting?

She crossed the street without even looking, as was her habit. It didn't matter; there were no cars for blocks in either direction.

It wasn't until she got within a few feet of the two men that she was hit with the eye-watering smack of alcohol wafting off of them.

Good thing they aren't smoking, she thought. *These two would probably burst into flames with just a spark, though that would at least make things a little warmer.*

The sound was either off on the TVs or just turned too low to be heard through the thick glass, and most were showing cheesy talk show reruns, reality TV, and old action movies (edited for television, of course). It seemed they were all set to one form or another of what could be considered the lowest common denominator entertainment for an undiscerning audience. All but one.

One of the smaller screens was tuned to the news.

Though the sound was inaudible, the closed captioning subtitles provided a running narrative, albeit one with occasional typos from the imperfect speech recognition program accompanying the images in the box offset on screen next to the square-jawed anchor's smiling face.

She watched for a moment, unimpressed, but just as she was beginning to turn away, the anchor wrapped up his 'news' report on some C-list celebritard and the reckless paparazzi drivers stalking her, something made her pause.

The story had shifted to a breaking news event.

The screen was filled with a helicopter shot of an overturned commuter bus, along with several crashed cars piled up around it. Smoke could be seen billowing from the engine compartment as emergency personnel swarmed the site.

The news anchor turned serious as he shifted his gaze from camera one to camera two. He even dialed down his smile from full-toothed and gleaming, to the slightly reserved one saved for tragedies and politics, which were often one and the same.

As his lips moved in silent commentary, the text captioning scrolled at the bottom of the screen;

"...Amazingly, despite both the speed of the accident and the ensuing fire, all passengers managed to escape with only minor injuries. The driver, though in critical condition, is expected to pull through, according to hospital staff."

Oh no, she thought, staring at the screen. This is not good.

She noticed that the drunken men standing beside her had paid no attention to the broadcast whatsoever, so fully enthralled were they in whatever they were watching. She glanced over and caught a glimpse of what her very inebriated viewing companions were so engrossed in, and found herself totally unsurprised.

A really bad 1980s action movie.

Naturally.

Oddly enough, thanks to an unexpected twist of luck, the schlocky movie was actually better without sound, the silence sparing them from truly horrible action film dialogue.

The fight scene underway bordered on ludicrous, but ridiculous as it was, the drunken men seemed to be thoroughly enjoying it. The fight climaxed as the on-screen hero kicked the villain in the groin, the inebriated pair chiming in with a chorus of "Ooooooh!" as they instinctively bent forward to protect their own groins.

Funny that anywhere in the world, men will all have that same reaction, she thought with a smile. *Drunk or sober, it's always the same, although I think this particular pair's reaction time may have been a bit diminished.*

A shiver ran up her back. The nighttime chill was setting in deeper. A discomfort that motivated her to start moving again.

The girl who thought she was Death walked and walked, until she eventually found herself in one of the more historic parts of town. As it hadn't been completely bought up and renovated yet, some of the older restaurants and buildings in the neighborhood still vented their steam to the streets and alleys through gratings and exposed ducts. Welcome warmth.

While the nests of pipes and trash piles were perhaps not the most appetizing of locations to pass the time, the girl had discovered that while her fashionable black coat may have looked good, it was quite ineffective at fending off the night's chill, which was surprisingly adept at burrowing right through whatever layers stood in its way.

In the face of the biting cold, it was a very easy decision. The heat was well worth tolerating the smell.

She hunkered down next to a large dumpster, which provided her some protection from the breeze, and huddled against a warm pipe emerging from the building. It took the edge off, at least a little, as the night grew darker and the air temperature dropped. Fortunately, she had chosen to seek refuge in one of the nicer alleyways in the area, if one could call a dirty alley nice. At least this was one where the garbage was collected regularly, though it nevertheless still had that universal alley smell of rotting refuse and the occasional whiff of old, or not-so-old, urine.

She sat there quietly, grumpy and most certainly non-thrilled by her situation, when out of nowhere, a bag of trash came flying past her, right over her head and into the dumpster with a loud crash.

She jumped to her feet in surprise, the fight-or-flight flush buzzing in her cells an as-of-yet undetermined response.

The sandy-blonde waitress in her early fifties stood in the open alley doorway of the twenty-four-hour diner, likewise startled at the unexpected, and quite sudden, appearance of the young girl dressed in black.

"Oh my God, you scared the shit out of me!" the waitress said, putting her hand over her fluttering heart as she looked closer at the shivering girl. "Hey, are you okay? I'm so sorry about that. Did I hit you? I didn't see you there."

"It-t-t... itsh allll right. I know it wassh unintensshonal" *What the hell? Why can't I speak properly?*

"You must be freezing out here," the waitress said, rubbing her arms briskly against the cold air that had already started to chill her skin.

"I f-f-f-f-eeeeel...I am..." She paused, confused. "I d-d-don't know w-w-why I f-feeel." Standing up had distanced her from the warm pipe, and her teeth had started to chatter from the cold.

Of course, my lips are going numb. That's just great, what next?

"Why you feel?" the woman said with a questioning look. "You mean why you feel sad?"

"N-n-no," she replied. "W-w-why I f-f-feeel."

The waitress looked her over head to toe, and after but a moment's thought, she decided the slender girl in black didn't look like a junkie or crazed vagrant, just a girl down on her luck, much as she'd once been, though that was a long time ago.

"What's your name, hon?"

"I ammm D-d-d-death," she said, shivering.

The waitress arched an eyebrow and flashed an amused smile.

"Death, huh? Ah, you crazy Goth kids. I'm Angela. Come on, let's get you inside and get you warm."

"B-b-but-t-t I—"

"No arguing. Hurry up, before you catch your death of cold."

As she stepped from her nook beside the trash bin and moved toward the light of the open door, the girl could feel the warm air flowing out invitingly.

Well, at least it'll be warmer in there, whatever happens, she thought, then followed the woman through the door.

CHAPTER 3

Walking out of the cold, dark alley and into the warm restaurant sent a wave of comfort over the girl's tired body.

The diner was a fifties-themed throwback, but unlike so many of the ill-conceived and gimmicky failed attempts out there, this establishment was tastefully done. The chrome was polished to an immaculate shine, as were the floors and countertops. The deep-red vinyl seating and cushions in the booths lacked the duct tape repairs so often found in the more greasy spoon variety of all-night establishments.

A modern jukebox played quietly in the background, stocking a mix of both new and older songs, to satisfy a diverse crowd. A few neon signs lit the windows, casting a warm glow from their reflection across the interior spaces.

All in all, it was a cozy place that would be pretty hard not to like. Especially hard if you had been uncomfortably squatting in a dark alley, damn near freezing, just minutes before.

It was getting late, and though it was a twenty-four-hour joint, the diner was mostly empty. An older couple sat together in a booth, sharing a bowl of soup and a sandwich between them, and an attractive, thirtyish, brown-haired man sat by himself at the counter, slowly savoring a plate of pie and nursing a hot cup of coffee as he leisurely worked his way through a crossword puzzle.

The kindly waitress led the chilled young woman to a welcoming spot in the back of the restaurant. The girl slid into the booth and sank back against the cushioned vinyl, almost immediately feeling the muscles in her sore legs slowly start to relax.

"Take a load off. I'll grab you something warm to cut that chill."

The girl who thought she was Death didn't say anything as she simply enjoyed being warm for the first time in hours.

I can't believe how tired my feet feel, she thought as she pondered the aching pulse in her boots.

Angela left the girl to unwind for a moment and collect herself, casually strolling back behind the counter to get the poor girl something warm to drink.

In the full light of the diner, the girl was able to get a better look at the woman whose kindness had given her a much-needed break from what had been a really crap day.

Why did she help me? She doesn't know me. This makes no sense.

In no time at all Angela returned to the booth, a cup of steaming hot coffee in hand. She set it in front of the girl and squatted next to the table.

"Here," she said. "This oughta warm you up. I've gotta warn you, though, we make our coffee pretty strong, so you might want to cut it with some milk. Probably a lot, actually. There's also half & half and sugar if you want."

"Thank you," the girl replied.

"Glad to help. I'll be back in a minute. Gotta check on my regulars," she replied, gesturing to the man at the counter as she stood up.

The girl in black picked up the mug and cradled the warm porcelain in her chilled hands, feeling the heat slowly bring her fingers back to life.

Oh, that is so much better.

Lifting the cup to her lips, she sniffed the aromatic steam wafting up from the mug, then carefully sipped at the murky brew. She quickly recoiled from both the bitterness and heat.

She said to add milk and sugar. Maybe that will help.

Angela had left a good bit of room in the cup for milk, as if she knew it would take a fair amount of doctoring to achieve a palatable mix, so the girl heeded her advice and poured liberally until the formerly black beverage became an appealing caramel color.

As the milk flowed, she found herself staring into the mug, fascinated by the psychedelic, lava lamp patterns it made as it swirled and mixed with the coffee. Watching the whirling patterns as they formed in the cup, she didn't know why, but her body relaxed just a bit.

A caffeinated meditation of sorts.

After a few moments, the milk had blended entirely, and she felt it likely that the temperature was reduced and the bitterness cut enough for another try. She lifted the mug to her lips and took another cautious sip.

Just like Goldilocks, she found the cup now was indeed *just right*, and she savored the warm liquid as it rolled over her tongue before finally swallowing it, feeling the warmth trickle and spread down her throat, heating her from the inside out.

Oh, this is divine. This sensation…

She took another sip. More of a gulp really, quickly followed by another, and in no time she found her cup empty, just as Angela approached with a full pot in hand.

"Hey, let me fill that up for you."

"This is amazing. The sensation, the heat. Thank you!"

"You're welcome, hon. Now you just relax and warm your bones and I'll come check on you in a bit."

Angela walked back behind the counter, stopping for a moment to chat with Randy, the brown-haired fellow, who happened to also be one of her favorite regulars. She topped off his cup of coffee while he happily polished off his last few bites of apple pie.

The pie was an unusual one, a signature dish, as it had a nice Gruyere cheese baked into the crust. One of the pie-maker's assistant's specialties he'd developed a fondness for.

Randy was absentmindedly skimming through an arts magazine while doing his crossword puzzle, scoping out exhibits across the country with a casual flip of the page in between across and down clues.

In addition to his affinity for good pastry, he was also a gallery director, and something of a rising-star in the local art scene. He'd been away for some time, having fallen victim to a drunken depression a few years back, but had finally cleaned up and moved home, returning to the art game he loved.

"Hey, Angie, who's the girl?" he asked, blowing the steam off his freshened cup.

"Stray. I found her curled up out back, looking all cold and miserable. Couldn't just leave the poor thing there."

"She doesn't look homeless."

"Nah, seems like a good enough kid. Probably just down on her luck."

"I know how that can be."

"Don't we all? Still, there's something a little odd about her. Not bad, just something I can't quite put my finger on."

Angela did not fail to notice his repeated glances across the diner.

"You think she's cute? You should go say hi. I'm sure she could use some company, and when's the last time you talked to a girl, anyway?"

He blushed, caught looking. "I don't know, Angie. I'm really not—"

"Hey, you've gotta get back in the saddle someday," she said as she picked up her coffeepot and walked away. "Think about it."

He had made the diner his home away from home since he'd returned to town nearly a year earlier, and spent most evenings there, even if just for coffee and company. He and Angela had developed a particularly sound waitress/regular friendship in that time, one that was solid enough, in fact, that he was inclined to take her advice to heart from time to time.

After Angela headed back to the kitchen, Randy found that, much to his surprise, he was actually considering taking her advice and going over to talk to the girl in black.

For most men the prospect of talking to a pretty girl would find them halfway across the room at the merest hint of an opportunity, but the sad circumstances of his romantic past had left him jaded, reclusive, and mostly disinterested in women. At least, that was, until now.

He glanced over at her again, quietly psyching himself up as he tried to figure how best to make an approach. Butterflies hatched in his stomach, fluttering their wings as he realized just how long it had been since he'd actually chatted up a girl. It was a thought that spurred a bout of approach anxiety he hadn't felt since he was a teenager as he imagined all the things that could go wrong.

"Should I go talk to her?" he muttered under his breath. "Oh, come on Randy, when's the last time you even thought someone was worth approaching? Don't sit here procrastinating. The worst that can happen is she'll say no. Come on, this is stupid. You're a grown man, get off your ass and go talk to the girl!"

His self-pep talk seemed to light at least a small fire of hope in his chest. Quickly, before he could let any doubt build up again, he put his fork down, abandoning the final bite of pie on his plate, and purposefully walked across the polished checkered floor to her booth.

As he had neared her table, he noticed she had absentmindedly arranged the silverware by size, though she didn't seem aware she'd done it. Really, she didn't seem too aware of anything, so deep in thought she appeared.

Too late to turn back now, he realized. With the most confident smile he could manage, he slid into the seat across from her and, despite his nerves, did his best to play it cool.

"Hey, there. I saw you sitting over here by yourself and thought you might like some company. I'm Randy."

The girl seemed to not hear him at first, her eyes unfocused and lost in thought.

So I feel heat, I feel cold, people can touch me. How did this happen? Wait, who is this man talking to me?

Her gaze suddenly focused on him as she snapped out of wherever her mind had been wandering.

"How… why are you talking to me?" she asked, confused.

"Well, I—"

"How can… why can you see me? Can everyone now?" She seemed perplexed. Not by his approach, per se, but by some thought still ricocheting around in her head like a hi-bounce ball

31

dropped from a great height.

"Well, I saw you from across the room…"

He thought she was acting a bit strange, but then a flash of panic hit him as he wondered if he had come on a bit strong. Unsure of the best move, he froze, sitting quietly, flashing his best non-threatening smile while he tried to figure out what damage control he might need to recover from his botched approach.

For all his worrying, the girl in black didn't seem to notice, and simply took another sip of coffee, pondering the warm cup cradled in her hands.

"This is coffee," she said in an almost dreamy tone. "It's so hot. Heat, I mean. Why heat? I can feel heat."

"Well, I know it's really cold out tonight," he said, realizing perhaps he hadn't messed up so badly as he first thought. "Listen, I know we just met, but you seem nice and, um, well, we're both here alone, so, um, can I maybe buy you some dinner?"

She slowly turned her gaze on him, an uneasy look flickering across her face while she processed his words. "I don't eat. I am—"

Suddenly a wave of sharp pins rippled through her belly. Confused, the girl involuntarily doubled over as she cramped up.

What just happened?

"I feel—what is—the pain…" She looked around, bewildered. Had she poisoned herself? The only thing on the table was the mug in front of her. "But I only had these few cups of coffee," she said, confused.

Randy smiled a sympathetic grin, commiserating and knowing full well what she'd unintentionally fallen victim to. It had taken him quite a while to develop his tolerance to the coffee in this joint, and as tired and worn-out as this girl looked, it was no wonder she experienced a strong reaction to it, especially having overindulged as she had.

"Yeah, the coffee's pretty strong here," he said. "Takes some getting used to. The ladies' room is right down that hall if you need it." He pointed toward the restrooms.

She looked at him, her watering eyes briefly holding his gaze for a moment. She was finally beginning to see him clearly as she processed what he told her, when another cramp hit. Her guts twisted painfully inside her, and she felt a strange and urgent sensation.

She lurched to her feet and bolted for the bathroom, instinct taking control and guiding her flight. The girl moved as quickly as she could, given her situation, but to her eyes, the formerly short hallway now seemed to stretch on forever, her acute discomfort and sense of increasing urgency making every step agony.

From behind the counter Angela observed her friend's brief exchange, along with the girl's rapid retreat to the restrooms. She looked at Randy and raised a curious eyebrow as she strolled over to the booth he now occupied alone.

"Made a new friend, I see."

He sniffed his armpits exaggeratedly. "I even showered this week. Too bad, pretty girl."

He shrugged, letting it go. He was actually rather bummed at the way things had turned out. For some reason he couldn't put his finger on, he felt a visceral draw to the odd young woman. He hadn't felt that since, well, ever really.

Must be pheromones, that's all, he thought to himself, then dug in his pocket and glanced at the time on his antique blue enamel pocket watch.

"Okay, I guess I might as well head home," Randy said as he rose to his feet. He pulled out his wallet and paid his check, then thought about it for a moment and handed another few bills to Angela.

"Hey, when she comes back, get her whatever she wants on me, okay?"

"You got it, hon. You sure you don't want to stick around?"

"Nah, that went pretty sideways on me. Anyway, I'll see ya tomorrow, Ange."

He leaned over and gave his friend a quick hug and headed for the door, pausing for just a moment to look back toward the women's room before stepping out into the chilly night air.

Meanwhile, in the restroom, the young woman's surprising sense of urgency was greeted with an overwhelming feeling of relief as the girl who thought she was Death instinctively dropped her pants and flopped down on the seat, letting loose what felt like a fire hose stream as she emptied her bladder.

The discomfort was great, but the relief was even greater, so much so that she didn't even notice the assorted jokes, phone numbers, and dirty drawings gracing the walls around her, as focused as she was on her bodily functions.

As the pain slowly yet steadily faded from her belly, her initial expression of shock and disgust at what her body had just done slowly changed to a smile as the terrible cramping finally subsided.

That was horrible. Horrible, but I feel so much better now. She sighed. *I hope this isn't a regular thing.*

Gathering herself, she cleaned up and unsteadily headed back to her booth, a few liters lighter, but a whole lot more comfortable.

The old couple had finished their meal and departed just after Randy, so with no customers left in the diner, Angela sat in the booth, resting her feet, when the girl returned. Angie noticed that while she looked a bit pale and shaky, she seemed otherwise all right.

"You okay, hon?"

"The pain was… well… That was pain? Huh. Pain."

Ignoring the slightly odd response, Angela looked at her apologetically.

"Yeah, our coffee is pretty strong. Sorry about that. I refill on autopilot. I really should have warned you better."

"It was disgusting. Disgusting yet so relieving. But the pain, it's gone now."

"Well, listen, hon, Randy's buying you dinner, so whatever you want, it's covered."

"Dinner?" she asked, a bit unsure what to do.

"Yeah, that sweet guy you left sitting here all confused? Dinner's on him. I know you've gotta be hungry. What are you in the mood for?"

"I don't know."

"If you want, I can make some suggestions."

Thoroughly sated, the girl who thought she was Death sat in her booth and picked at the mélange of scraps remaining on the plates scattered in front of her. Not sure which of Angela's suggestions to try, she had sampled an assortment of different things. Sweet and savory, fried, broiled, steamed, and grilled, all of which she had tucked into with the enthusiasm one would expect of someone eating either her very first, or her very last meal.

Angela surveyed the aftermath spread across the table with amazement as the girl looked up at her, quite full and with gratitude in her bright gray eyes.

"Incredible," she said, suppressing a belch. "Thank you."

"Wow, I guess you really were hungry after all." Angela picked up several dishes and headed back to the kitchen, amused at just how much that girl managed to pack into her slender frame.

"Ah, youth." She laughed to herself as she pushed through the kitchen doors.

The girl sat there in her booth for a moment, mellow in the carb-and-fat-fueled glow of a satisfying food coma. She was content, amazed at all the goodness she just experienced, when she felt an unexpected rumble in her belly. A distressed, queasy look flashed across her face.

Oh no, not again! she thought, but then noticed this sensation was something different than before. *This is—I feel—oh, now what?*

Sensing that something was definitely not right, she bolted down the hall once more, making a beeline to the ladies' room.

Several minutes later, looking quite drained and wobbly, she made her way back to the booth. Her eyes were a little bloodshot and watery, and her nose was running a bit as well. The girl actually looked paler, if that was possible, as she lowered herself into her seat.

She grabbed a handful of napkins from the chrome dispenser on the table and unceremoniously wiped her nose, which triggered a bit of a coughing fit, strong enough that it caught Angela's attention. The girl coughed a few more times, then slowly drank a mouthful of the ice water sitting on her table, the condensation ring staring back from where the glass had sat.

That was horrible. I feel like I've just lost half my insides, the girl thought and grimaced to herself.

"You know, it's not worth it," Angela said, eyeballing her.

She had put down her side work and quietly returned to check on her wayward stray. She hovered at the table, looking the girl over with a concerned gaze. Something flashed behind her eyes as she studied the slender girl. A glimmer of a pain long forgotten.

Back in her teen years, Angela's best friend had suffered from an eating problem. It wasn't a pleasant thing to see someone go through, especially at that age, and despite intervention, she eventually lost her friend to the disorder.

That, and several other hurdles she was forced to deal with in her formative years, had made her mature quickly. Growing up fast had given her both a healthy dose of street smarts, and, fortunately for the girl in black, a lot of empathy.

Now, when it came to lost kittens or random Goth girls, Angie really wasn't an over-the-top, bleeding-heart type in the habit of taking in every stray she came across, but for some reason, that night in the alley, she felt a strange need to protect this one. She couldn't put her finger on the how or why of it, just that it needed to be done.

Wiping her mouth with a napkin, the girl looked up at her.

"What do you mean 'not worth it'?" she asked.

"Just to be skinny? You'll rot your teeth out and burn your throat. Trust me when I tell you, that's not a road you want to go down."

Ah, she thinks I'm bulimic. Lovely.

"No, I just felt unwell is all."

Angie looked at her, an internal debate raging within her. She shouldn't get any more involved should she? No, that's crazy, no more taking in strays. Yet still…

She finally ignored her better judgment and decided on a course of action.

"Well, listen, you seem like a sweet enough kid. You got somewhere to sleep tonight?"

"I don't sleep."

"Uh-huh." She flashed her an incredulous look. "Well, if you change your mind, I've got a couch you can crash on. I'm off in a half hour, so you can let me know then."

Not long after, the girl who thought she was Death was soundly asleep on a well-worn and remarkably comfortable couch. She may have argued that she was Death and didn't sleep, but Angela had convinced her to 'lay down, just for a minute or two,' and relax a bit while she cleaned up.

The girl was out cold almost as soon as her head touched the pillow.

The old couch been around and had seen its fair share of wild times, as well as quiet nights. Perhaps it was a psychic residue of the many very mellow and very stoned evenings the couch's assorted owners had spent on it. Or then again, perhaps it was just a comfy place for an exhausted girl to lay her head after a long and trying day. Whatever it was, she drifted into a deep sleep as Angela quietly turned off the lights and headed off to her bedroom.

CHAPTER 4

The girl who thought she was Death felt a warm flush as her senses sharpened. With the greatest of ease, she opened her eye, finding herself floating through the skies, soaring high above the tiny specks of people below from a seat on a flying carpet.

For some reason, this seemed perfectly normal to her.

With the fragrant, maple-scented wind steadily blowing in her hair, she calmly gazed down on the city below, surveying the sprawling expanse of land from her vantage point. The tiny people looked like ants from this height, barely distinguishable as they hurried to and fro.

What is that? she wondered as a whiff of something rich and savory drifted to her nose. She inhaled deeply, noting the smoky aroma mixing with the sweet breeze on which she rode.

That's odd, she thought, looking around for the source.

She shifted her focus from the ground far below to the carpet she was riding on, and was only slightly surprised to find that her carpet wasn't a carpet at all, but actually a giant, wavy strip of bacon. Well-done and crispy around the edges.

Oh, this won't do, she thought. *I'll get grease all over my pants.*

With a sudden lurch, the bacon-carpet spiraled into a dive, hurtling toward the ground. As the bustling specks below quickly grew from unrecognizable dots to actual people, she was startled to recognize the face of the girl toward whom she was rapidly plummeting.

Walking the street without a care in the world, the girl who thought she was Death paused mid-step as if she sensed something, but didn't know what.

She looked up to the sky, and saw, of all things, a giant slice of bacon streaking right toward her.

To her surprise, just before impact, she noted that the slender, black-clad woman riding astride it looked quite familiar.

The girl came to her senses with a start. Forcing herself to calm down, she took in her surroundings, realizing she was still in Angela's apartment, sprawled out ungracefully on her couch.

Well, it beats waking up on a nasty hotel floor. She rubbed the gritty sleep from her eyes as the aroma of a sizzling breakfast wafted to her from the kitchen. *What's that amazing smell?*

She propped herself up to a seated position and took a moment to look at Angela's home in proper daylight as she slipped her feet back into her black leather boots.

The apartment was clean and cozy, a simple one-bedroom, but with decent square footage, good light, and a fairly large living/dining room area. A pair of sturdy wooden bookshelves sagged under the weight of a wide assortment of well-read books from a variety of genres. A slender stack of select DVDs and a few boxes of classic vinyl sat tucked neatly next to a vintage solid-state stereo system and direct-drive turntable.

On the wall, a French poster for *Attack of the 50-Foot Woman*, gazed down at her, the ginormous woman straddling a highway, a sedan held high in her hand as cars piled up at her feet.

A pair of glasses filled with fresh orange juice were already on the dining table, and sounds of pots and pans being jostled emanated from behind the kitchen door.

Angela was in the zone that morning, happily cooking, humming cheerfully to herself. Wearing a black wife-beater rather than her work uniform, several well-aged tattoos were now visible on her shoulders and arms. Also peeking out from under the fabric were traces of old scars. Long healed, lingering reminders of her wild past.

Angie whizzed around her workspace with ease. The aroma of hot toast wafted through the apartment, making her houseguest's mouth water as the toaster worked its magic on some locally made multi-grain bread.

One of the benefits of living in a gentrifying neighborhood was artisan foods, including fresh bread from the local store owner, who gave up his hedge fund job to pursue his passion as a baker rather than banker. He joked that he had wanted to open a juice bar next door, but the neighborhood council wouldn't let him. After all, he laughed, bakers can't be juicers.

In her well-seasoned cast iron skillet, Angie had a few slices of bacon merrily crackling away, along with a few eggs, over-easy. The morning sun illuminated the smoke as it gently wafted up from the stove, looking for just a moment like the spirit of good eating was visiting the room, possessing it with thoughts of delicious meals.

The smells brought an involuntary smile to the girl's lips as she stepped through the doorway, watching as her host worked her culinary magic. She paused, noticing a steaming pot of coffee resting in the machine on the counter.

I won't make that mistake again, she thought with a faint shudder.

Sensing a presence behind her, Angela turned and looked over her shoulder, not missing a beat as she worked her magic on the stove.

"Hey, she lives! Ya know, for someone who doesn't sleep, you sure do a convincing act of it." She smiled at her guest, then turned back to cooking.

"Thank you for your kindness," the girl replied. "You had no reason to help me."

"Well, you seem like a good kid underneath all that black leather. Anyway, call it building good Karma. This way I can really mess something up later and still break even."

Yeah, it doesn't quite work that way, the girl mused.

"Hope you're hungry," Angela quipped as she plated two dishes to the limit with eggs, bacon, and toast and carried them to the dining room table. "You mind grabbing the coffee?" She saw the look on the girl's face. "Don't worry, at home I only make the good stuff. Promise."

The girl obliged, carrying the pot to the table and filling the two mismatched mugs, while Angela placed the larger of the two plates in front of her guest.

"Here ya go," she said, fixing her gaze on the young woman she'd taken in. "Now I want you to keep this down, okay? You don't have to stick a finger down your throat to be beautiful."

"A finger?"

Angela looked at her for a moment, then decided not to get into it. "Just eat," she said and sat down across from her.

The two dug into their breakfast, the quality of a home-cooked meal hitting the spot. A few minutes of happy chewing elapsed before either of them spoke.

"So, where are you from?" Angie asked.

"From?" the girl wasn't expecting that question, but it reminded her of her plight. "I've got to get back. I really can't be here."

"Well, listen, if you'll wait until I get back from work, I'll see what I can do. Maybe I can help you get a bus ticket or something. Maybe even find you a ride if it's not too far. Sound good?"

She didn't wish to appear ungrateful to the kind woman who had helped her, nor did she think it wise to get into a lengthy discussion of the difficulties of crossing to the realm of the dead, so instead, the girl just politely said, "All right," and continued with her breakfast.

Angela was savoring the last of her coffee when a glance at her watch told her time had flown by faster than she had realized.

"Oh, crap, I'm going to be late! Hey, would you mind doing the dishes while I'm gone? I'll be back later, but if you feel like stopping by the diner, come on in." She grabbed her keys and headed out the door, calling back over her shoulder, "We'll see about getting you a ride home when I get back," then closed the door behind her.

The girl who thought she was Death found herself suddenly sitting alone at the table, thinking.

She's sweet, but there's nothing she can do to help me get back. But perhaps there's something I can do.

Rising from the table, she walked across the apartment.

Angela's bathroom was much like the rest of her apartment:

clean with a bit of a classic look. It sported tasteful old tile and a refinished claw-foot tub next to the spotless toilet. The pedestal sink had to be from the 1950s, but with good care, it still looked relatively new. All of these were secondary to the girl's main objective, however.

She made a beeline for the medicine cabinet above the sink, pulled it open, and started rifling through it.

Toothpaste, eye drops, hair clips, an assortment of Band-Aids, along with all the random things people tend to accumulate, thinking they may find it useful someday.

She picked up a razor, but it wasn't the shiny, straight kind people see in movies, but rather a crappy disposable plastic one.

Nope, that won't work, she thought.

After much digging, she finally found what she was looking for behind a few bottles of nail polish remover. She brushed the fine layer of dust from the lids, then opened the two old bottles of pills and studied them for a moment, wondering if they would suffice.

Is this enough? This will work. It has to work.

Without another thought or hesitation, she started popping handfuls of pills into her mouth, swallowing them en masse as best she could until both bottles were completely empty. She then took a seat on the toilet lid to wait for her impending demise.

Shouldn't be long, she thought. *I'll be back where I'm supposed to be any time now.*

Fifteen minutes later, as her digestive tract dissolved the pills, she was pretty sure she felt the drugs finally kicking in. Twenty minutes later she knew it was working. Despite having just awoken, she was becoming sleepier and sleepier. Oddly enough, it was at this moment that something unusual fluttered through her head.

A foreign feeling.

Uncertainty?

Fear?

That makes no sense. Why would Death be afraid of dying? she pondered.

Of course. It must be this meat-sack body. Fear has been hard-wired into them for thousands of years, so why should this one be any different? She found it harder and harder to think as her mind began to shut down and drift into unconsciousness. *Doesn't matter,* she thought. *It will be done soon.*

Shortly thereafter, the chemical cocktail churning in her belly took full effect, and she finally passed out.

As she slumped over, sliding off the toilet lid she'd been seated on, she happened to fall forward, the edge of the bathtub slamming across her ribs, right in the diaphragm.

The hard, porcelain-glazed iron hit her much the same as a hard punch to the stomach, and likewise, just as if she'd been hit by a boxer, her abdominal muscles jerked and twitched as her body vomited up both her breakfast and the dissolving pills into the bathtub. When the convulsions ceased, she slid away from the tub, slumping to the floor, unconscious, with vomit drying in her hair.

"And, of course, it was caked in my hair." Randy laughed as he sipped his mug of piping-hot coffee. "That was the last time I ever let an artist do a live painting session during a crowded opening. Oh my God, it was a disaster!"

Angela topped off his cup. "Well, how does that old saying go? 'May you live in interesting times'?"

"Actually, I think that was supposed to be a backhanded curse."

"Eye of the beholder, though, isn't it?" She plopped down next to him at the counter. "Speaking of which, I'm glad you came by early today. I wanted to tell you something."

"Oh?"

"Remember the girl you were chatting up last night? Well, after she ate, and thank you for that by the way, I decided to let her crash on my couch. She's back at my place right now, cleaning up. She keeps talking about getting back home, but if she sticks around for a bit, maybe you might still have a chance."

"Such the matchmaker, Angie. You sure you didn't miss your true calling?"

"Just trying to help my friend finally get a date. Tell ya what, I'll swing home at lunch and drag her back here if you'll stick around."

"I appreciate it, I really do, but you know my situation."

"It's been four years, Randy. It's time to get on with living."

He squirmed in his seat. "Yeah, maybe, but I've got responsibilities. Samantha lost her mom. I can't just go picking up random women if I'm going to have her move back in, and—"

Angela cut him off.

"Randy, she's staying with her grandparents until the end of the school year no matter what, so what's your real excuse? You're a young guy. You should date again; it'd do you good."

"I don't know..."

"Tell ya what, hang out for a while, and we'll see if you're up for it when I take my break, deal?"

"Okay, I guess... but no promises."

"All right, Romeo." Angie quipped as she moved off to check on her other tables.

Randy stared into his coffee, a bit nervous at the thought of a second chance with the unusual girl from the night before.

"Maybe she's right," he mused. "What's the worst that could happen?"

A few hours later Angie broke for lunch, and with a tiny bit of arm-twisting, Randy had tentatively agreed to hang around just a little bit longer while the happy matchmaker scurried home to collect her young houseguest.

Angela walked into an apartment with the smell of breakfast still hanging in the air, and a dining room table full of dirty dishes sitting where she'd left them that morning.

"What the hell? Hey, are you here? I thought I'd swing back by and pick you up on my lunch hour. Helloooo?"

Either her houseguest was ruder than she thought, or something was wrong. The uneasy feeling washing over her made her suspect the latter.

She made a quick check of the house, starting in the kitchen. Nope, not there. Then she moved on to her bedroom. Likewise empty.

"Well, nothing's missing," she muttered as she walked to the bathroom.

Angela pushed the door open and nearly jumped out of her skin at the sight of the motionless girl sprawled on the floor, empty pill bottles strewn nearby. Pushing down her panic, she quickly grabbed her phone and called 9-1-1.

"I need an ambulance!" she began, then rushed back to the bathroom and checked on the girl, while the operator took her information and told her help was on the way.

She watched her unconscious guest's chest rise and fall slowly.

"Yes, she's still breathing, thank God," she told the emergency operator.

Angie realized what had happened, weighed her options for a moment, then reluctantly pocketed the pill bottles before rinsing the dozens of half-digested pills that had been vomited into the bathtub down the drain.

The paramedics arrived minutes later, sirens blaring down the street as they sped to her home. With quick efficiency, they loaded the unconscious girl into their ambulance and took off, Code Three. As slow as her pulse and respiration were, the man taking her vitals commented that it was surprising she was still breathing at all.

The girl who thought she was Death might have found that comment amusing, but in her current state, she wasn't aware of a single thing.

What...? Where am I? Did it work? No, wait, what's that noise?

It took her a moment, but when she finally managed to open her eyes, she saw Angela standing nearby.

She did not look amused.

Is this a hospital? That can't be right. I should have crossed back over. I don't understand. Why didn't it work?

The girl who thought she was Death glanced around and realized she was sharing a hospital room reeking of disinfectant with several other patients.

The one-size-fits-all bed was fine for her slight frame, but the obese man hooked up to a ventilator two beds down, she noted, was nearly spilling out of his inadequately small accommodations and onto the floor. The woefully inadequate side rails were only the only thing managing to keep him in, and just barely at that.

Gluttony—he's done quite well in America, she thought. *Certainly keeps me busy, that's for sure.*

The sterilized floors and walls cast a slightly greenish glow from the fluorescent lights above, making the whole scene feel a bit surreal to her as she tried to further gather her wits.

She slowly turned her head, still fighting the fuzziness wrapping her senses, watching quietly as Angela talked to a man in a white coat. Her doctor, apparently. The haze was lifting, and she found that if she focused, she could just make out what they were saying.

"She woke for a moment, but was totally disoriented," the doctor said. "Then she passed out again."

"She's okay, Doctor. I'm sure she just misread the label is all. I should have clarified when I told her she could have a couple for her back pain."

"Well, she's lucky she threw them up. Only a few too many and she could have been a goner."

"Oh, believe me, I know. It was a foolish accident, totally my fault. I'm so sorry I washed them down the drain. I didn't realize you'd want to see them. I mean, it was only a couple of pills. The bottle was almost empty anyway... but don't worry, I'll keep an eye on her. It won't happen again."

The doctor looked at Angela, trying to decide if he believed her. She didn't seem like the compulsive liar type, nor a junkie. Acting on his gut, he decided to cut her a bit of slack.

"All right, I'll release her to your care, but I have to warn you, if she comes back like this again, we'll have to place an involuntary hold on her for an evaluation. Clear?"

"Crystal. Thank you, Doctor."

The doctor stepped out into the hallway to continue his rounds, leaving Angie to fret over her overdosed couch surfer.

"And you. What the hell kind of crap was that?" she fumed, spinning to stare hard at the girl in the hospital bed. The drowsy girl just weakly met her gaze with exhausted and bloodshot eyes. Pissed as she was, Angie felt a pang of sympathy well up in her chest, and found her anger quickly fading. She had taken in a stray but left her alone without really getting to know her, and look what happened.

Studying the girl as she lay there, Angie thought back to her own somewhat troubled youth and came to a crossroads. *This one gets a second chance,* she decided, something she herself could have used on more than one occasion. *And besides, it's building good Karma, right?* she thought as she approached the bed.

"Oh, come on then," she grumbled to her new ward. "Get up."

Still a little unsteady on her feet, the weakened young woman relied on Angie's support to make it through the door of the apartment. Angie guided her back to the comfort of the couch.

Sinking into its cushioned embrace, the worn-out girl really did start to feel a little better.

Angie let her settle in for a moment before fixing her with an upset, yet understanding gaze.

"Look, I'm trying to help you out here. I covered for you, but you've got to promise me there'll be no more stupid stunts like that, okay? I want to help, but if you pull that crap again it'll come back on me, and that shit will not fly. So, can you manage that, or is it back on the street?"

The girl felt her cheeks get warm.

"I'm sorry I got you in trouble. I just wanted to get back where I belong."

"I told you I'd help if I could."

But you can't.

Angela might have been fed up, but her anger was rapidly fading, along with her energy. Helping people can be tiring, and this girl had just made her spend hours in a hospital, and had cost her half a shift to boot.

"It's been a long day. Let's get some sleep, we can continue this in the morning." And with that she headed to her room, falling into a deep slumber the moment she lay down, letting the stress of the day flush from her mind and body and become a thing of the past.

Tomorrow would be a fresh start.

"Rise and shine! Who wants a waffle?" Angela called out as she emerged from her bedroom.

Morning light warmed the living room, but as Angie scanned her abode, she discovered her couch empty, a pile of folded sheets and a blanket neatly off to one side. She checked the rest of the apartment, just in case, but the strange young girl was gone.

CHAPTER 5

The morning air was brisk, and the girl who thought she was Death walked with purpose in her stride. The clop-clop of her boots as she moved along at a rapid pace echoed off the buildings and alleys as the sounds and smells of the morning swirled around her.

She paid them no heed.

Though she could see her breath in the chilly air, it wasn't really all that cold, and on top of that, the walk had warmed her considerably. She had briefly considered stopping and having a cup of coffee, having decided she was fond of the hot and bitter drink, but she then realized that she had no money with which to buy said coffee. More importantly, she would have no need of coffee where she was going.

Just get home, she thought.

Pushing her pace as she continued on down the street, she steered out of the more residential area and toward a mixed-use business district. One with a great deal of new construction going up.

Occasional slivers of sunlight shone through gaps between buildings as she strode among the increasingly tall structures. At last she caught sight of what she'd been looking for. Just down the road was a construction site with an unlocked and unattended gate. She increased her pace as she headed toward it with purpose.

That should do just fine.

She barely took the time to look to see if anyone was watching as she ducked through the chain-link. Even if someone had been, she really didn't much care, but by a twist of good fortune, her entrance had gone unnoticed. She had the run of the area to herself, at least for the moment.

Leaning up against a half-finished wall was a twelve-step

ladder, and nearby lay a discarded coil of old rope.

Yes, that'll be perfect.

She gathered the items and started dragging them toward the exposed beams overhead.

It only took her a few moments to position herself and set things in place. In no time at all she was gingerly perched atop the wobbling ladder, a blatant violation of OSHA safety guidelines. Balancing precariously, but nevertheless fearless and determined, she worked her hands quickly, then swung the length of rope over the beam. The rope flew true, the looped end dangling right in front of her as she'd planned, leaving the hastily tied noose hanging at roughly neck-height.

Content with her calculations, she climbed down the ladder and secured the tail end to an exposed beam. That accomplished, she surveyed the apparatus. Finding it adequate, the girl began climbing back up. She made quick time on the shaky a-frame, and upon reaching the top, the girl who thought she was Death quickly grabbed the noose with her outstretched hand.

With no hesitation or fear, she slipped the rope over her head, slid the loop tight, and immediately jumped off the ladder, which tumbled off to the side with a crash.

This is it. I'm coming back! she thought as she fell.

The rope, which had seemed sound enough moments before, snapped the moment it went taut, barely scuffing her neck as gravity sent the girl straight to the ground with a thud. A small puff of dust rose from her body's impact. The wind had been knocked out of her from the unexpected landing, but she was otherwise unscathed.

Struggling for breath, it took her a moment to get to her knees, but she eventually managed to do so. The girl examined the split rope with frustration. Anger tinged her voice as she looked up to the sky.

"Why are you doing this to me?" she lamented.

She received no reply.

The clatter of the falling ladder, along with a woman's

distraught voice, had brought several construction workers running. They were rather surprised to see a beautiful young woman dusting herself off, throwing what looked like a noose into the nearby trash bin.

"Hey, are you all right?" one of the men asked.

I am far from all right, she thought as she silently shouldered past him and back out onto the sidewalk.

She had been walking for a bit, and the sun had gradually risen higher in the sky, which, even in her disgruntled and distraught state, she couldn't help but notice was an impressive shade of blue. As people joined together in their daily commutes, traffic had increased noticeably. People rushed to and fro in their own little bubbles of urgency, oblivious to the lovely morning as they worried about their day-to-day.

The girl who thought she was Death at first walked aimlessly around the neighborhood after her failed hanging, mulling things over, trying to make sense of her situation. Finally, she stopped for a rest in a quaint little park, bordered by a somewhat busy stretch of road.

Sitting alone in a sunny spot, quietly pondering her troubles and quite lost in thought, she didn't even notice the homeless man who had sat down next to her on the bench. In fact, only after he had started feeding the pigeons crumbs from the half loaf of bread tucked in his grimy jacket did she even take note of his presence. To her surprise, she found that it felt kind of nice having someone to share space with, even if it was a total stranger.

He was fairly clean, for a hobo, she noted. A scraggly beard clung stubbornly to his cheeks, and he could have been forty just as easily as he could have been sixty, depending on how long he'd been out on the streets. He had that look that so many vagrants possessed, the sunburned cheeks and wind-blown hair, which would have fit in just fine with the well-off snowboarding crowd if he were in different environs.

The man had an air of regal confidence that belied his lowly station, and held himself like he was king of the park, overseeing his domain, entitled to sit wheresoever he pleased.

She didn't mind. He could sit next to her if he wanted. Of course the fact that he didn't smell like he had just crawled out of a sewer filled with burning garbage also helped make his presence acceptable.

It wasn't long before the two struck up a conversation, and with just a little prying, he managed to learn the details of her unusual plight.

"That is quite a story," he mused. "So after all she did, you just up and left, without even saying goodbye?"

"There was no reason to," she replied. "The important thing is to return where I belong. I just don't understand why I can't."

"Well, it's too nice a morning to be sad about it," he said with a cheerful grin. "I mean, sure, you're stuck here, but it ain't all that bad, right?"

"I just have to get back," she replied. "You get it, right? I simply need to cross over. It should not be such an ordeal. It should be easy."

"Well, nothing's ever easy in my experience. And besides, even if you really are Death, why would you want to leave? I mean, look at how gorgeous it is today. Plus, this city is great. I mean, look at all the nice people, the clean air. Hell, look at this beautiful park, free for everyone to use. It's just so nice here." He reached into one of the pockets of his oversize coat and produced a small silver flask. He took a long swig, belched a high-octane cloud of booze, then offered her a taste.

She turned it down.

"Being hot, cold, hungry, sad—who wants to exist like this?" she griped.

"Not to be presumptuous, but have you ever considered that maybe those are parts of what makes life worth living?" the man said, sliding the flask back in his pocket.

"Well, aren't you the insightful one?" she replied, with an unintentionally snarky tone. She realized she was unnecessarily harsh with the man, even for her mood.

"Hey, I'm just trying to help. Seemed like you were a little lost, is all."

She pondered what he said in spite of herself.

Maybe he has a point.

The thought quickly left her head as she again turned to the important task of getting back to the other side.

"Nice thought for mortals maybe, but not for me. No, I've got to get back." She rose, agitated, and saw a bus round the corner, heading down the street.

Oh yeah. Now THAT should do it.

She took off running, scattering the pigeons before her and nearly bowling over a man walking his teacup Chihuahua.

"Hey, watch it!"

On a mission, and moving at a full run, she ignored him. Her pace increased even more, and she soon found herself in a flat-out sprint.

The bum watched her speed off, a sad but slightly amused look on his face as his gaze followed her dash toward the street. Still over a block away, but approaching fast, he saw what had caught her attention.

The silver-and-blue bus surged forward in the heavy morning traffic, swerving between cars like a powerful fish knifing through a river's flow as it forced its way ahead.

Packed with a shuffling throng of morning commuters, the air, as is often the case in small spaces packed with fast food-eating office drones, was rapidly becoming quite stale, the unappealing reek of hastily eaten breakfasts and strong coffee forming a noxious stench wafting from peoples' mouths with every breath.

As a super-duper extra bonus, riders were also occasionally treated to an equally offensive emission from another orifice entirely.

Bad as that was, just as unpleasant was the musky odor of human sweat from those who had skipped deodorant that morning.

Unfortunately, there was really no way to avoid the smell, as it was down to standing room only on board.

The driver grumbled to himself in frustration, his displeasure evident in the form of a lead-foot liberally applied to the gas pedal as he accelerated a bit too quickly, rapidly bringing the several-ton vehicle above normal cruising speed. There had been an "issue" with an aggressive and rather pungent vagrant several stops back, and after a delay of several minutes spent removing the man from his bus, the driver found himself forced to try to make up time from the delay.

Sunday drivers clogged the road, though it wasn't even Sunday, and it looked as though he likely wouldn't be able to get back on schedule, despite his best efforts.

"Come on, merge, you idiots," he muttered as an indecisive driver timidly changed lanes a few car-lengths ahead. "Oh, come on, turn signals are there for a reason, dumb-ass," he hissed, then violently stepped on the gas as he swerved around the slow-moving car, making several passengers lose their balance, the unexpected burst of acceleration taking them by surprise.

If you asked the bystanders on the street that morning if any of them had anything of note to say about the young woman dressed in black as she sprinted past them, they'd say they hadn't noticed anything in particular. At least nothing that stood out. She just looked like anyone else running to catch a bus, a not-uncommon occurrence at that time of day as people rushed to work.

That was the observation most people shared as she ran past them, her long, black coattails flapping behind her.

The young woman had a far different motive, however. One made quite clear when she reached the curb at full stride just moments before the bus arrived.

Rather than stopping and flagging it down, she took one final, powerful, step, and leapt high in the air, flinging herself in front of the speeding vehicle.

Naturally, this elicited a chorus of screams, which accompanied the squealing brakes, and the high-pitched tinkling of breaking glass as the young woman impacted the windshield.

"Shit!" was the only thing the startled bus driver managed to blurt out as he stomped on the brakes with all his might, hoping the extra force applied by his foot would somehow make the vehicle stop faster.

It didn't.

As the girl in black flew, tumbling through the air, a smile formed on her face.

This time it'll work, she thought. *I'm going home.*

She felt her body become light, and before she even hit the pavement, an all-encompassing darkness closed in, slowly engulfing her in its embrace as her rag-doll body rapidly approached the unforgiving ground. While the impact from the bus had started the process, it was her impact with the pavement that abruptly turned out the lights for real.

CHAPTER 6

The girl who thought she was Death felt something tickling the edges of her awareness. Consciousness wavered in and out as the most basic of her senses returned. Slowly, she found herself becoming alert, though surrounded by an encompassing darkness.

Sounds registered, but everything was strangely muffled, as if she were listening to the world through great big balls of cotton. She was vaguely aware of her body, but connecting the dots from her brain to her limbs was not quite working, much like when she first woke in that strange little hotel room. But also not.

What was different this time, was that her body was being jarred, and every once in a while, a bright flash of red or white light or a burst of a shrill noise would thrust its way into sharp focus, but only for a moment.

Floating in the dark like that, she didn't have the awareness to really contemplate and analyze those sensations fully.

That changed in an instant when, without warning, she was violently yanked back to full consciousness, wide awake, and much to her consternation, in excruciating pain.

Her eyes slammed into focus, her gaze laser-sighting on a man in blue gloves as he pulled a now-empty syringe from her arm.

The flood of agony that washed over her was intense.

Words failed as her primal brain kicked in. Without knowing what she was doing, the girl let loose a piercing scream. Coherent speech was simply not an option. All she could do was cry out, her mind and body so overwhelmed by the horrible sensations that hit her, like pummeling waves of hammers and nails cascading and piercing every inch of her body, leaving her unable to articulate a single word. All she could do was scream until she ran out of breath.

It was too much for her senses. The agony engulfing her body, the antiseptic smell of the ambulance, which she somehow had the presence of mind to realize she was in as it bumped its way to the nearest trauma center.

Lights and sirens. The realization sank in.

She gasped, coughing out the metallic-tasting fluid pooling in her mouth. Her nose sensed the chemical odor of industrial disinfectant, but also a tinge of old blood and vomit that stubbornly clung to the air.

In that brief moment of clarity, she thought, *So this is what real pain feels like.* The thought quickly passed as her body was jostled by a bump, sending sharp pain surging through her, erasing her thoughts as she was overcome by agony once more.

The medic was laboring feverishly on the bloody woman as the ambulance bumped and raced down the road. With practiced skill, he quickly worked her up, attaching heart monitor leads and taping down the tubing directing the fluids now rushing into her veins.

Seeing the shot he'd given her had the desired effect, he quickly reached for another syringe, which he injected into her new IV line taped into place.

"Hold on, you're going to be all right. Just hang in there," he promised.

The drugs quickly found their way through the twists of plastic tubing and into her veins.

The last thing she remembered as the pain melted and consciousness began to fade, was the blurring lights flashing outside the windows as the ambulance whisked her down the street, the sound of the blaring sirens dimming as she slipped once more into the void.

The horrible, bumping ride, and the shrill blare of sirens both abruptly stopped. Though heavily sedated, the girl opened her eyes and managed to somehow force them to focus, at least a little. All she managed to see were the blurry lights of the waiting emergency room as her gurney was jolted to the ground, its wheels juddering on the pavement, softly vibrating her body as she was quickly rolled into the hospital.

The ambulance had called in the details of the patient as they drove, and the emergency room staff was prepped and standing by for her arrival. In fact, a full trauma team was on hand as the gurney came crashing through the double doors.

Hit by a bus? The ER had pulled out all the stops.

Her head would have rolled from side to side as she tried to take in her surroundings, but she noticed it seemed to be strapped firmly into place, and a stiff collar was locked around her neck. Unable to turn, she weakly resigned herself to looking straight forward, watching the light fixtures flash by overhead as they rolled her down the hallway.

One of the nurses rapidly checked her vitals, flashing a light in her eyes and jotting notes on a chart, ignoring the fact that her patient could quite possibly hear her as she talked to the orderly pushing the gurney.

"I don't know how, but she seems to be stabilizing, but whether she'll ever recover full brain function after a trauma like this I don't know. You sure a bus ran her over? I would have expected it to be far worse."

"Still a lot of blood, though," the orderly replied.

The girl wanted to speak out, to tell her that she most certainly had brain function, thank you very much, but she felt herself growing dizzy and nauseous, either from the multitude of drugs and chemicals added to her bloodstream or from the fluorescent bulbs flitting past in a blur in front of her face. She coughed and gagged back a flush of acidic bile.

"Prep the ET kit. We're going to need to intubate," was the last thing she heard before slipping under yet again.

Time had passed. That much the girl knew, but the question was how much? For that matter, where exactly was she? Running through her senses was still difficult, but the process slowly became more manageable as the fog enveloping her cleared.

A faint beeping filtered in, rhythmically keeping pace with her heart. She took a deep breath, the distinct disinfectant tinge to the air filling her nose.

Wait, am I in a hospital again? It was a bus. Seriously, how could that have not worked?

Willing her eyes to open, she struggled to focus for a few moments, then finally having achieved at least some degree of clarity, looked around and surveyed her surroundings as best she could.

From what she could see, it appeared she was in a bed in the Intensive Care Unit. At least she was pretty sure that's where she was. She struggled to move her head until she was finally able to shift position and glimpse down. She evaluated herself as best she could and was startled by what she saw.

An impressive mix of bandages, splints, tubes, and wires swarmed her body as they electronically monitored every breath she took.

Breathing. Now that is really uncomfortable. I've got to do something about that.

She raised her bandaged hand to her face to clear whatever was obstructing her airflow. The girl who thought she was Death recoiled in shock as her fingers brushed against the smooth plastic of the breathing tube that had been inserted into her airway. It was warm to the touch, heated by the humid air pumping into and out of her lungs.

Panic started to build, and ignoring her pain, she somehow mustered the strength to lift her arm farther and weakly try to pull it out.

The sensation was agonizing.

One of the nurses on duty saw the movement coming from the bed of the girl who'd been run over by a bus and hurried over, calling to the attending physician as she moved.

"Doctor, she's coming to."

The stubble-faced doctor stepped into the room with no real sense of urgency. He looked as tired as he obviously felt, namely like he'd spent a few years too many doing overnight shifts and covering back-to-backs, taking care of battered wives and car crash victims alike.

The job was taking its toll on him, that was for sure, but despite the exhaustion, he still managed to maintain that air of extreme competence that comes with the ease of expertise. Despite her panic, or perhaps because of it, the girl found his presence calming, to a degree, and stopped pulling at the endotracheal tube as he approached her bed.

"You need to lie still. Can you do that for me?" he asked in a soothing tone.

She nodded yes.

"Good. You're in the hospital. You were in a very bad accident. Can you understand me?" the doctor asked, taking a penlight from his coat pocket, dancing the beam across her eyes as he spoke, noting her pupillary response to the light.

She managed to nod a very slight yes.

"Good," he said, then turned to the nurse. "Pupils equal and reactive." He pocketed the light and spoke to her as he examined her dressings. "Do you have any loved ones we can contact? You had no identification on you when you were brought in."

She shook her head again. This time a no.

"I see."

"What's your name, honey?" asked the nurse.

She must be new here, thought the girl. *She just asked a woman with a tube down her throat what her name is.*

In fact, that wasn't too far off. Before nursing school, the young nurse had worked as a waitress, and during her time in that career, had always excelled at asking diners if they wanted anything else just after they'd taken a bite. Nevertheless, the girl who thought she was Death stubbornly ignored the pain and answered her as best she could.

"Drrtthh," she said, the plastic tube in her throat not doing her any favors.

"Dorth?" said the overly chipper nurse. "Oh, wait, Dorothy? I get it. Okay Dorothy, you hang in there. We'll take good care of you."

"Nnnnnuuu, Drrrrthh!"

Dorothy struggled to speak, to tell them that she was in fact Death, and that she really couldn't be here, you see. Death can't be hospitalized. The very thought is ludicrous, but her battered body lost that fight, and she slipped once more into unconsciousness.

CHAPTER 7

The days following the bus accident had been good to Dorothy. Much to the surprise of the hospital staff, she was healing at a rate far exceeding the expectations of the doctors and nurses. Bones thought broken soon appeared merely bruised, and the black and blue that had initially covered much of her body, was fading rapidly to far less disturbing shades.

She had improved so much, in fact, that she had been moved out of the busy ICU and into a regular hospital room.

Doctor Phelps was among the doctors on rotation who counted the odd girl as one of his patients, and, after she regained consciousness and could speak coherently, he had begun engaging in discussions with her during her physical evaluations.

At first he was amused by her declaration that she was, in fact, Death, but that quickly shifted to concern when he realized she was serious. A most troubling frame of mind, especially in light of her recent bus-jumping actions.

Standing at the nurses' station outside Dorothy's room, Doctor Phelps watched her through the open doorway, then reluctantly picked up the phone. Unfortunately, the girl was mentally troubled, so he really didn't have much choice.

"All right, thanks, Doctor Vaughan. I appreciate it. See you shortly."

He hung up the phone, picked up her chart, and walked in to see what new twists his troubling patient would throw at him today.

The first thing he noticed was her ongoing OCD obsession, as next to her picked-at tray of food were several meals' worth of utensils, organized by size. Sometimes he really wondered what drove his patients to their strange compulsions.

Dorothy turned her gaze to him as he entered the room.

"Hello, Doctor, I would like to leave now," she informed him. "Where are my clothes?"

"I see you're still not taking this seriously," he replied. "Maybe you don't realize just how close to dying you really came, Dorothy."

"I told you, I am not called Dorothy. I am Death, and dying was my intent."

"Yes, so you said. But you told the nurse the other day that your name was Dorothy. Do you remember that? Now, Doctor Simms tells me you were in just one day earlier following an apparent overdose." He sized her up with a piercing stare. "Is there something you want to tell me, Dorothy?"

"Just that I want to get out of here. You have no right to keep me here."

"Well, actually, we do. You see, while your recovery these past few days has indeed been quite amazing, if you are a threat to yourself, we have a legal obligation to protect you from harm. Including harm from yourself."

This guy still just doesn't get it.

"Look, I am Death, and I need to die to get back where I belong, only I can't seem to manage it. I took pills, I hung myself, I even threw myself in front of a bus, but I'm still stuck here. I'm being punished, for some reason, forced to live like this. I just don't know why."

"I see." His brow furrowed ever so slightly. "So I should release you because you are Death and apparently you cannot die."

"Now you're getting it." *Come on,* she thought. *It's obvious. I'm not some nutjob, I am Death!*

"And you truly believe this? Can't you see how outrageous this sounds?"

As if to make her point, two nurses walked by the open door, talking about Dorothy.

"—in front of a bus! I've never seen anything like it. She should be dead."

"It's one in a million. She got lucky."

"A miracle, is more like it."

Dorothy turned her gaze back to Doctor Phelps and raised an eyebrow.

Told ya so, her eyes mocked him.

He leveled his gaze at her. "I want you to talk to another doctor. A specialist. I've made a call, and he said he can come by later this afternoon. If you'll do that for me, I'll see if I can get you out of this room, all right?"

He sounded almost relieved at the thought of getting his troubled patient out of his hair. If he was lucky, his week might start to slide back into the realm of normal. Hopefully very soon.

She thought about it for a second. *What can it hurt?*

"All right, I'll talk to him."

"Fantastic. Until later, then," the doctor said, then hastily exited the room.

Dorothy thought things were finally looking up. That she'd be out on the street in no time. That things were finally starting to go her way.

She couldn't have been more wrong.

Doctor Francis Xavier Vaughan walked down the halls of the hospital with a steady staccato of highly polished shoes, radiating an air of somewhat arrogant and confident superiority, his cologne leaving a faint trail of spice in his wake.

He was in his mid-fifties, hair thinning slightly on top, with a dark, perfectly trimmed beard, styled much as one would expect to find on a showman or magician. He didn't wear a white lab coat, but rather, preferred tailored suits, cut to fit his slightly stocky frame.

As he approached Dorothy's room, counting door numbers as he closed in on his target, his face morphed from that of a powerful and stern man used to getting his way, into a sympathetic and gentle 'friendly doctor' visage. His eyes were still intense, but somehow he managed to appear kind and wise.

The gentle smile he had practiced for many years had the effect of putting people at ease, though truly observant patients could catch the briefest glimpse of something darker lurking behind it.

His chosen persona locked firmly in place, Doctor Vaughan reached his destination and gave a quick shave-and-a-haircut knock before letting himself in.

Dorothy had been expecting another stiff in a lab coat.

Huh, not what I thought he'd be.

The doctor paused for the slightest of instants as he entered the room.

My God, he marveled, *she looks like Katie when we first met.* The sensation was ever-so-slightly unnerving. He quickly forced the jolt of unexpected anguish in his heart aside as he refocused his energies on the patient who was most certainly not his wife.

"Hello, I'm Doctor Vaughan. Doctor Phelps asked me to come speak with you. Is this a good time?"

She nodded her head.

"Sure."

"Excellent. So, Dorothy—"

"I told them, my name is not Dorothy."

"Yes, so you said. Well, Dorothy, you certainly aren't in Kansas anymore," he said with a friendly chuckle.

She stared at him, puzzled by where this odd conversation was going.

What's this guy's deal? she wondered.

"Kansas? What are you on about?" she asked, the annoyance clear in her voice.

"I see that obviously bothers you," replied Doctor Vaughan. "I'm sorry, please accept my apologies. If we may, let's start over. You know what, let me show you a little something," he said with a cheerful grin. "My patients really get a kick out of it."

He reached into his coat pocket, revealing an old silver coin, which he started smoothly palming from hand to hand, twirling it across his fingers back and forth as he worked the conversation toward his amateur magician's patter. For an amateur, he was actually quite skilled at sleight of hand, and the coin seemed to almost float across his knuckles. The fluidity of his motions would easily mesmerize most people.

But then, Dorothy was not most people.

He launched into his routine.

"There once was a young girl who wanted to buy a candy bar," he began. "Her mother was poor, but she loved her daughter, so she saved her money until she was able to give her a single coin so she could walk to town and buy a treat," he said, holding the coin with his thumb and index finger.

"'Don't lose it!' her mother said. 'And don't talk to strangers.' Well, wouldn't you know, but as the girl walked down the road, a thin man appeared from out of nowhere and asked if she could spare something to eat."

As he said this, Doctor Vaughan moved his palm, as if to protect his valuable coin from a stranger's gaze. His misdirection was good enough that it would have fooled the majority of people in an audience.

He's actually got decent hand-work, she thought, reluctantly admiring his skill, even as his patter annoyed her.

"The girl saw how thin the man was, and faced a dilemma. She wanted a treat, but also felt sorry for the him. 'I was going to buy a candy bar with this,' said the girl." He moved his hands in sync, briefly flashing the coin. "'But you need it more than I do.' And with that, she placed the coin in the man's hand. He looked at her and smiled. No one else had offered to help him. When he opened his hand—"

"It's in your shirt pocket," Dorothy interrupted.

Doctor Vaughan was taken aback. "Wh-what?" he stammered.

"You put the coin in your shirt pocket."

His carefully composed façade faltered for just a split second, the faintest hint of his displeasure leaking out through his gaze before he regained his composure.

This one is going to be difficult, he thought. *She really is like Katie.*

"Ah, yes, right you are," he said with a smile as he took the coin out of his shirt pocket, right where she said it would be. A frustrated little sigh escaped his lips, and the corners of his eyes hardened just a touch.

"Well then, enough chit-chat. Based on my evaluation, I am prepared to, um, release you from this ward, but you'll have to sign these documents first." He removed several neatly folded pages from his coat pocket.

"What are they?"

"Standard release forms. It's all boilerplate," he said.

"The Devil is in the details," Dorothy quipped, fixing him with a hard stare.

He was taken aback by the girl, surprised at finding himself a little uncomfortable with her for some reason, shocked by her lack of any intimidation at all. Doctor Vaughan was also most irritated that a patient would dare speak to him in that manner, but once again, he managed to hide his displeasure, firmly affixing his false smile to his face.

"Yes, well, I assure you, these forms are standard in cases such as yours. Just sign here." He indicated several highlighted areas.

She paused for a moment, unsure if she should sign, or what she should sign, for that matter.

They're all calling me Dorothy anyway. I guess, what could it hurt? Whatever it takes to get the hell out of here, I suppose.

Doctor Vaughan could see she was on the fence.

"You do want out of this ward, don't you? Just a few signatures and we'll have you out of here in no time," he said, flashing a used-car-salesman smile.

She studied him again for a moment.

Do I want out of here? What kind of question is that? Of course I want to get out of here.

She took the pen and quickly scribbled an illegible signature, starting with a flowing "D" and ending with a quartet of letters that rather resembled "eath." As she replaced the cap, pushing it home with a click, the clip snapped in her hand, jabbing her finger with a shard of plastic.

"Ow!" she exclaimed as a drop of blood fell, spattering the page next to her signature.

"Excellent," Doctor Vaughan cooed. "I'll have an orderly come help you shortly. Goodbye, Dorothy. See you soon."

Highly unlikely. I'm staying as far away from this place as I can.

Her clothing had been washed and returned to her room, and she wasted no time quickly dressing and lacing up her boots. She then gathered her things and stared at the door, waiting for the orderly to come discharge her.

Dorothy's boot tapped on the shiny linoleum floor impatiently as she waited. *Tap-tap-tap-tap*, an impatient rhythm hammered out on the scuffed linoleum tiles.

She had been waiting for nearly a half hour. Her discharge was taking a bit longer than she had anticipated, but upon reflection, and another glance at the clock on the wall as it slowly marked the passage of time, she realized she really hadn't been waiting for that long at all.

It was the being ready and then forced to wait that was driving her batty. Long before the orderly finally came to get her, she was fully dressed and ready to go.

When the man finally opened the door to her room, she looked mostly like her old self, save for the tears in her clothes from her run-in with the bus. As it was, only a few remaining bandages poked through her clothing, visible only if you were looking for them. Aside from those little reminders of her recent accident, she looked otherwise healthy, and something about wearing her own clothes again put her a bit more at ease.

At least my jacket looks to be in pretty good shape for being run over by a bus, she mused with a little smile.

The orderly held the door for her, as a gentleman should, and escorted her through the maze of look-alike, sterile, white hallways.

"This way, miss."

As they passed a nurses' station, a second orderly finished up his conversation and joined them on their walk, falling in and matching her pace.

They must really want me out of here to give me two guides to make sure I leave. The thought amused her as they approached the hospital lobby.

The smaller of the two orderlies gently took her by the elbow and steered her away from the lobby and down another hallway.

"But that was the lobby," she said, looking back over her shoulder.

"The discharge exit is this way, miss," the man replied.

Finally, after several more twists and turns down featureless hallways, they arrived at a set of double doors. The sign above read, *Loading Dock.*

"Hey, are you sure this is the right way to the discharge exit?"

"Yes, it's right through here, miss."

The orderlies helped her through the exit, each taking hold of an elbow as they approached the automatic doors. Stepping outside, Dorothy realized something was terribly wrong and stiffened in their grasp.

"Hang on a minute!" she blurted, but the realization came too late. She tried to pull her arms free but found herself held firmly in vise-like grips, wholly at the mercy of the large men.

The orderlies nearly lifted her off her feet as they swept across the loading dock, then roughly tossed her in the back of a waiting transport truck. The reinforced-steel doors swung shut and locked behind her with a metallic click the moment she was inside. The lone bench seat and thick walls were thinly padded, and a small opaque plexiglass divider separated the driver's compartment from the back.

Scanning the interior further, she realized there were no handles, locks, or latches whatsoever on the inside of the passenger compartment.

She was locked in.

"Hey, let me out of here!" she yelled, thumping her hand on the plexiglass window. But it was no use. The orderlies were obviously complicit in her abduction, and there had been no one else on the loading dock to hear her cries.

She was still futilely pounding on the doors as the truck fired up its engine and pulled away.

CHAPTER 8

The drive was relatively short, as their destination was well within the city limits, just outside the newly gentrified part of town. So far as Dorothy could tell, they had likely driven no more than five or ten miles from where she'd been swept away by the padded truck. Not that the knowledge would do her any good once she saw where she was being taken.

The truck rounded a corner and approached an old building, three stories tall and somewhat squat in appearance. Despite its seemingly diminutive size, it nevertheless took up half a small city block, an alleyway separating it from its more traditional neighbors. The facility's well-lit sign appeared to be the newest part of the place, and even that was fading with age.

As she watched the thick stones of the wall surrounding the building's courtyard entry gate grow closer, the illuminated words came into view.

Oh, you've got to be kidding me.

Once a proper medical facility, Camview Psychiatric Hospital had first opened back in the late 1940s when masses of World War II vets came home from the war. The regular facilities already in the area found they couldn't handle the overload of mental trauma cases, and thus Camview was born.

From there, the hospital grew in fits and starts as more space was needed. Being situated in an already-developed city, the architects found themselves quite constrained by the lack of available land on which to expand. They had their half of a city block to work with, and nothing more.

Wings were modernized piecemeal. Large picture windows had been replaced with bars and security screens in the lockdown wings, and large ventilation grates for the growing facility were installed sporadically along the ground-level façade, allowing for modern air-conditioning and heating for the ever swelling numbers of patients.

The result of all the little additions was something of a 'Frankenbuilding' that lacked anything an architect would consider style, but despite its somewhat unsightly appearance, the massive beast served its purpose perfectly.

The rumbling truck pulled through the large electric gate to the rear courtyard. A few other vehicles were parked in the small lot, but it was otherwise empty.

Dorothy peered out the thick windows as the truck backed into the loading area and noted that several orderlies even larger than the ones she'd just encountered—if that was possible—and with much more intimidating looks on their faces, were standing in a semicircle, waiting for the vehicle to park.

She would have wondered at the turnout, but it was pretty obvious why they were all there.

Intake.

The doors were opened, and she hesitantly exited the truck, taking in her surroundings.

"You. Let's go," the man with the most keys on his key ring growled.

Dejectedly, she trudged toward the orderlies.

"That's right. You don't give us any trouble, we won't give you any."

Not likely, she thought as she gauged the men's nasty leers.

As they reached out to escort her inside, she pivoted from their grip and bolted for the gate. She was quick and actually evaded them all, moving faster than they'd expected as she shimmied from their grasp. She ran across the loading dock and jumped nimbly to the driveway, making a beeline for the only exit in sight.

She hadn't counted on the driver of the truck, who had just exited the cab.

His massive paw reached out as she ran past and somehow managed to grab her coat as she flew by, yanking it hard, sending her flying backwards off her feet.

Before she could make a second break for it, she felt the

crushing grip of the less-than-amused orderlies haul her up in the air.

"You can't do this! Let me go!"

Their stony faces showed no reaction whatsoever as they dragged her, struggling, into the building. Dorothy stopped struggling once the large doors slammed shut behind them, locking with a heavy click. She realized fighting wouldn't help, at least not now.

Like it or not, she was trapped inside a nuthouse.

Calm down, pay attention. There's got to be a way out.

There wasn't.

She was roughly ushered into an empty concrete shower room and left to wait. The walls were painted an uninviting industrial green, streaks of rust leaving great tears of iron running down them where some of the older pipes had corroded. It looked kind of like jail, but not quite. If she was a moviegoer, she'd likely have found that it was rather reminiscent of those places you see in films where inmates get a fistful of delousing powder thrown on them, then are given a fire-hose shower. But she wasn't a cinema buff, and fortunately, delousing wasn't on the menu.

A key rattled in the lock and the door squeaked open, the hinges worn from years of moisture despite regular oiling. Stepping into the damp room, a rather burly female orderly, in a uniform that fit her meaty mass a little too snugly, entered carrying a small pile of folded hospital clothes in her arms.

"Strip down and put these on," she said, her square, Germanic jaw flexing as she paused to give her newest charge an unimpressed once-over. "Place your effects in this bag. No personal items are allowed inside the facility. Your items will be held for you in secured storage until such time as you are released from care at Camview. Do you have any questions?"

Dorothy looked at the grim clothes with distaste.

"I will do no such thing."

The large orderly crossed her arms, her jaw flexing rhythmically as she decided what to do with her troublesome newcomer. She was clearly not impressed.

"One way or another, you're putting those on," the woman said, completely confident in her statement. A nasty smile began to form on her face, and as Dorothy sized her up, she decided now was probably not the time for another smart-ass remark.

Dressed in her unflattering new psych ward attire, Dorothy found herself ushered rapidly down the maze-like halls of the old building. Passing by nurses' stations and locked doors between wings, her circuitous path bypassed the off-limits isolation wards until she finally arrived at what appeared to be a reception area. A secretary sat at the lone desk, both gatekeeper and sentry posted in front of a single office.

The middle-aged woman looked up from her magazine, took note of Dorothy, and nodded at her escort, who pushed the confused girl through the thick wooden door. It closed loudly behind her.

She surveyed the new environment and realized she was standing in someone's office.

Unlike the rest of the run-down facility, this room had a richness to it. The walls were covered in deep mahogany paneling, the tall bookshelves were crammed with an impressive range of thick books, many appearing to be early editions of noted classics.

A collection of animal heads stared down from their mounts on the wall, sightless marble eyes gazing, yet never blinking.

Resting to the side of the large oak desk, she noticed a deck of cards and a handkerchief. Something about that struck her as a bit out of place in an obvious power-tripper's office such as this, yet it also struck her as very familiar, but why?

Hang on a second, she thought.

A second was all she got. She heard a flush, then moments later the door to the office's private bathroom swung open. Doctor Vaughan eyed her as he strode into the room.

He looked different on his home turf.

Bigger.

Tougher.

Colder.

Gone were any traces of empathy or kindness as he sized her up with an icy stare. He leisurely walked to his desk and picked up his deck of cards, shuffling them absentmindedly as he stared her down.

"Sit," he said, hovering over her.

She looked at the chair nearby, but decided she'd rather stand.

Doctor Vaughan was not amused, not one bit.

"I said sit!" Gone was the calm professional she'd met earlier. His tone was that of a man not even remotely messing around, and she thought it would be wise, at least for the moment, to not rock this particular boat. Slowly, she took a seat.

"Better." He walked around his desk, staring at Dorothy with fire in his eyes.

This one really gets off on this power trip thing.

He stared for a moment longer, then chuckled at something, amused by a secret joke known only to him. He stopped his rhythmic shuffling, replacing the cards in his hand with a slender file. The doctor opened it with a contented sigh as he lowered himself into his plush leather chair.

"So, the great and mighty reaper graces us with her presence."

"If you know who I am, why did you bring me here?"

"Oh, please," he snapped at her, "we've had nearly a dozen grim reapers in my facility since I've been chief of staff. You could at least try to be original."

"But I'm telling the truth. I really am Death."

"That's what they all said."

He slowly flipped through the pages in the open file, then stopped at a particular spot that caught his attention, a malevolent little smile tugging at the corners of his mouth as he pulled out a grainy scan printout for Dorothy to see. The image was an older one, and was rather poor quality, but it appeared to be a slender young woman in dark makeup.

A girl who looked a lot like Dorothy.

"Dorothy Maitland," he read aloud. "Escaped from low-security psychiatric custody in Portland, Oregon, eight weeks ago." He lowered the page and stared at her. "Long way from home, aren't you, Dorothy?" he said, looking at her the way a cat would observe a bug as it decided whether to eat it or just crush it for fun.

"That isn't me."

"And yet there's quite a resemblance. Same name, even."

"It isn't me."

"Fine, play it your way for now. I really don't care one way or another, but if I catch you trying to run off like you did up in Oregon, you'll be very sorry you did. I run a drama-free facility, Ms. Maitland, and troublemakers are dealt with quickly and efficiently."

Something in his eyes told her he almost wanted her to call his bluff.

This man is dangerous, she knew in her gut. *I need to get out of this place.*

"You can't keep me here. You have no right."

"Oh, you'd be surprised what I can do," he said, a calm sense of power conveyed in his gaze. "I've spoken with Doctor Atkins up in Portland," he continued. "It seems you caused him a lot of trouble up there. Quite a lot. So much, in fact, that after he and I chatted for a bit, he gladly agreed to transfer your state-mandated care to me. Seems you're just not worth the headache to him. Congratulations, Dorothy, you're now an official resident of Camview, courtesy of the taxpayers of the state of Oregon."

He pushed the red intercom button on his desk.

"Yes, Doctor Vaughan?" a voice answered.

He gave Dorothy one final appraising glance, then answered, "We're done here. Take her."

The heavy door swung open and a pair of orderlies stepped in, roughly pulling Dorothy to her feet and out the door.

There's got to be a way for me to get out of this place, she thought with increasing worry as she was led down the halls. *How can I cross back over from in here?*

They walked quickly, but Dorothy took care to try and note all that she could about her new environment. Of course, the fast pace at which she was being led made it a little tricky as her linebacker-sized escorts hustled her along.

Most of the rooms she passed were empty, doors ajar, as their residents were either in the dining hall or the recreation room. She also noted that a few of the doors were locked tight, sounds of screaming, ranting, and sobbing leaking past the imperfect soundproofing.

They continued to march her along, then paused at a set of large propped- open industrial double doors.

"Pay attention, newbie. This is where you'll spend most of your time."

Inside, she saw what was obviously the rec room, unless they played ping pong in the dining hall. Drug-addled patients stared into space, while others, less medicated, played ping pong or board games.

One particular group of patients sat at a nearby table playing a very old Candy Land board game, rings from beverages and unidentifiable stains spattering its playing surface. As Dorothy was marched past them, the group turned to observe her passing, ogling the new girl in the nut house. While they briefly noted Dorothy's entrance, they were rather engrossed in their game and didn't really pay more than cursory attention.

Except for one of them.

Curtis, a forty-something strawberry blond with a somewhat disheveled bedhead mop of hair, and a seemingly permanent gleam of amusement in his eyes, was different.

Dorothy fascinated him from the moment he looked up and took notice of their new guest as she was led past. Their eyes met briefly as she walked by. He saw her see him see her, and gave her a conspiratorial little smile and a wink, then returned to his game as Dorothy continued on her way, led by her oversize babysitters.

"She's pretty," Warren, the large man-child with a penchant for knock-knock jokes noted.

"Not really my cup of tea," Curtis replied. "But you know

what? I think she and I are going to be the best of friends."

After what seemed like ages, the long march down the halls finally ended in front of an open door.

The room inside was painted an institutional "soothing" beige, the space bare but for a steel toilet bolted to the wall, a small sink, and a low, tubular steel prison bed sporting crisp white sheets and an industrial-grade blanket.

The bed was made so tight you could probably bounce a quarter off it and put a chip in the ceiling.

They probably had one of the OCD patients make it, she mused.

"This is your room," said the smaller of the two orderlies. Larry was his name. With his buzz cut and demeanor, Dorothy guessed he was likely either former military or just a wannabe when she first saw him. He also had a creepy vibe, the kind that any sober woman would pick up on and run the other way.

"You will be expected to keep it clean," he continued. "And you will have your bed made every morning before breakfast."

She looked around the room. There was a single tiny window high on the wall. Even if it wasn't covered by a steel grate, she'd be hard-pressed to fit through it.

"You will be visited by the floor charge nurse in the morning to get you acclimated and give you the new resident tour." The orderlies smiled at one another, sharing an inside joke. "Welcome to your new home. If you need anything, just ring the bell."

She scanned the stark space.

"I don't see a bell."

"There isn't one," he scoffed.

Very funny, asshole.

The two men laughed as they stepped out, Larry pausing a moment to look Dorothy up and down once again, like he was assessing his new toy. She most certainly didn't like the way he was leering at her, and felt a slight shudder run up her spine.

In an act that might seem harmless from most people, the creepy man winked and blew her a little kiss as the door swung shut with a solid thud. She didn't hear any keys turning in the cylinder, and though she expected the attempt would be futile, she still tried the door, just in case.

It was unlocked.

She pushed it open and peered out into the hall. Camview, it seemed, was an open-doors facility. At least this wing was.

Interesting, she noted.

Dorothy shut the door and stepped to the middle of her room, slowly turning in a small circle, taking in the confined space that was her new home as the nature of her situation truly sank in.

Being trapped in a small space made her feel claustrophobic for the first time in her existence. She felt her chest start to grow tight as the stress of the day finally caught up with her. A small quiver tugged at her lips.

Emotionally drained, she lay down on top of her perfectly made bed, curled up in a ball, and did something that Death does not do.

She started to cry.

Doctor Vaughan sat at his desk in the lush privacy of his office, his phone pressed to his ear as he forced himself to listen quietly to the man on the other end of the line. His face showed the stress he kept veiled so well when among the staff and patients. His furrowed brow and the slight sweaty sheen that glistened on his forehead betrayed just how much he didn't want to be on this particular phone call.

"I understand, sir," he said, managing to get a rare word in edgewise. "But I've made adjustments and we—no sir, I'm personally overseeing—" He sighed.

His boss, the chief executive of the hedge fund that owned the hospital, *his* hospital, never even bothered to come see how well he ran things with his own eyes. Rather, he relied on spreadsheets and patient logs, oblivious to just how much work it was to keep the facility in top shape. "Management without understanding," Vaughan had called it. He had long said, if it were a surgical facility rather than a mental one, would a bean-counting fund manager without a lick of medical training dare stick his nose where it didn't belong?

Not likely.

"Yes, sir." Doctor Vaughan sighed, snapped back to the dreary reality of his phone call. "I understand what you want, and I know you expect retention rates to increase. You can rest assured I'm doing all I can, but—Yes, sir, what I was trying to say was that one example is how I've just taken in a new patient, one whose care is state mandated with full, undiscounted payment rates—But, sir, it's —Yes, sir, I'll make sure there are no disruptions." A look of worry briefly appeared on Doctor Vaughn's face. "No, no, I assure you, sir, there is no need for a visit from the board of directors. Everything is under cont—yes, I understand, I—"

A shocked look flashed across his eyes as he held the phone away from his ear and stared at it in disbelief.

He had been hung up on.

As calmly as he could, though with knuckles so white the force of his grip could have likely turned a lump of coal into a diamond, he placed the phone back in its cradle on his desk, took a deep breath, and turned back to his stack of paperwork.

CHAPTER 9

Breakfast hour in the nuthouse was always an interesting time.

Some of the patients docilely marched wherever they were directed, happy to be out of their rooms, and looking forward to receiving a bowl of oatmeal and a muffin. That clique cheerfully enjoyed their repast as if they were guests in a fancy bed-and-breakfast. Maybe their scattered minds actually believed they were.

The less medicated patients, on the other hand, had an uneasy, institutionalized look to them, hunched over their trays, guarding their food from invisible thieves like paranoid inmates in a bad prison movie.

Then there were the select few who started the morning combative, kicking and screaming all the way to the dining hall. That habit was quickly noted by the staff and broken up post-haste.

Patients learned very quickly that violent or disruptive behavior was not a wise choice in Doctor Vaughan's facility.

It was a bit of a balancing act, staying off of everyone's radar, but Curtis and his loose-knit group had managed to find a comfortable groove, making things easy for the staff, which, in turn, meant they were pretty much left to their own devices.

Dorothy sat alone at a table, a glazed-over look on her face as she absentmindedly picked at the food in front of her. All the utensils nearby were lined up by size, satisfying her sense of order, even if she was drugged to the gills and unaware she was even doing it.

Curtis caught sight of her sitting there all by herself. Just as importantly, he noticed her untouched muffin, so he finished loading up his tray and headed over toward her table with a jaunty hop in his step.

Stein, a wiry man plagued by germaphobia so bad that he ceased being able to function in the outside world, tagged along, attracted to Dorothy's table, not for free muffins, but rather, because it was empty. Empty meant less people spreading their germs if he sat there. For him, the antiseptic tinge to the air of Camview was actually calming, though he still took care to not touch anything the other patients had laid hands on whenever possible. He even went so far as to have his own sterilized dice stashed away for game time, so he wouldn't have to share cooties with the others when his turn came up.

"Heya, new girl, welcome to the loooooony bin!" Curtis greeted her as he flopped into a seat. "Hey, you gonna eat that?"

Not waiting for a reply, he deftly swiped the muffin from her plate, peeling the paper back from one side and biting into the treat.

"Blueberry. Man, I love blueberry."

"That's not sanitary, you know," Stein piped up. "You could catch hepatitis like that, or maybe necrotizing fasciitis."

"Don't mind Stein, he's a bit of a hypochondriac." Curtis laughed. He held out his hand to Dorothy. "I'm Curtis, and you are?"

She blinked her glazed-over eyes, struggling to focus, then slowly turned her doped-up gaze to the man beside her.

"Ah. Obviously drugged out of your mind. Looks like somebody got a visit from the morning nurse and hasn't learned to palm her meds yet. Don't you worry, new girl, Uncle Curtis will look after you. Just think of me as your guardian angel."

His words didn't really register with Dorothy, at least not much, anyway, though there was a slight flicker of understanding behind her glassy eyes.

"Oooh, if you're not going to finish that," he said, and without missing a beat, reached over and started eating off her plate.

Stein winced. "I'm sure it's possible for humans to transmit rabies. Salivary transmission by food is not unheard of, you know."

"Come on, Stein, live a little. Am I right, new girl?" he said with a smile. Dorothy had just the slightest of reactions in her brain as something told her that the crazy guy stealing her food was a good egg. Then she went back to focusing what little awareness she did still possess on not drooling all over herself.

After breakfast all the patients were herded into the rec room, where they could play games, watch the few TV channels allowed, or just nap on a couch, as many chose to do.

The lighting was warm and calming, the sounds largely muted, partly because of the padding installed here and there, partly because of the overall calm of the mostly drugged patients. As long as they didn't raise a fuss, the staff didn't much care what they did.

Curtis spotted Dorothy sitting on a small sofa near a barred window. She was quietly enjoying feeling the sun warming a spot on her legs as she tried to clear her head. She was much less dazed as the drugs metabolized, but she was still pretty out of it.

A nurse began making rounds, handing out small paper cups with pills in them, watching each patient as they swallowed their drugs.

Curtis strolled over and casually squatted down in front of her. He looked over his shoulder to make sure no one was watching, then, satisfied he was unobserved, held up one hand. In it was a paper cup like the nurse was handing out. He opened his other hand, revealing several Tic Tacs. He made sure Dorothy was watching as he dropped the mints into the cup, which he tilted back to his mouth, making 'yummy yummy' sounds, then opened his mouth to show 'all gone.'

Dorothy wondered what on Earth this crazy person was doing. Smiling at her, Curtis dramatically looked both ways, then spit the Tic Tacs out into his hand, tucking them into his pocket.

"Got it?" he asked.

Ah, I see, she managed to realize through the fog clouding her brain.

Dorothy nodded.

"You'll be okay," he said, giving her a wink.

Jumping to his feet, Curtis firmly reattached his crazy face and made a beeline for the ping pong table, beating his chest like an ape as he strode across the rec room.

"Who dares challenge King Pong? Any takers? Come on, I welcome all who would try to unseat the king!"

To Dorothy's slowed senses, a white-haired man appeared to her left, seemingly out of nowhere. Had she been more lucid she would have seen him enter from the opposite door. One thing was certain, he was extremely animated and quite worked up about something.

"Eureka, I say! I've solved the world's energy problem!" he yelled.

"That's great, Professor. How did you do that?" a nearby social worker humored him.

"Why, cold fusion, of course. It was the only logical way."

"So how'd you do it?"

The professor looked puzzled by the question, then upset. "Well it's surprisingly simple, you just... no wait, first you... Damn!" He stormed off, muttering to himself about fusion.

The staff looked on, amused, and let him go on his way.

His name was William Ford, but everyone just called him Professor. He'd been a big-wig scientist before being committed when he had developed some mental "issues" later in his career. Nowadays, he would invent amazing devices in his head, or solve some daunting equation, but try as he might, he just couldn't hold on to his results. Worse, he would forget how he did it, sometimes just moments after his revelations.

Doctors said it definitely wasn't early onset Alzheimer's that was causing it. In fact, nobody could figure out what exactly he suffered from.

Fortunately for the professor, he'd forget he was upset just as quickly as everything else, and would refocus his attentions to solving another of the world's problems.

The room settled back into a quiet buzz after his departure, leaving Dorothy time to sit and think. At least as much as she could until her head finally cleared.

Evening fell, and Dorothy found herself seated alone once

more, though with the drugs finally out of her system, she found her appetite had returned with a vengeance. As she hungrily dug into her meal, Curtis, Stein, and the odd white-haired man from earlier strolled over and joined her at the table.

"Hey, new girl has her appetite back!" Curtis beamed like a proud parent watching his kid take her first steps.

"Thank you for your help. What were they giving me?"

"Depressants. They like to keep folks calm around here. I'm actually kinda surprised they don't just start prescribing Bluetooth earpieces to everyone while they're at it. I mean, at least then it wouldn't look like everyone was just walking around talking to themselves."

She couldn't help but smile.

"I'm Curtis. I know technically I already introduced myself, but you were a little out of it. This is the Professor, and that's Stein."

"Hello," she replied, feeling the last remnants of the drug-induced haze from earlier clearing by the minute.

"And you are?" Curtis raised an eyebrow, waiting for a reply. Dorothy, however, didn't answer. She simply sat there, somewhat overwhelmed by her situation.

"Everyone around me is a total stranger," she muttered.

Curtis smiled and broke into song. *"Everyone avoids me like a psyched Lone Ranger, everyone."*

Dorothy looked at him, confused.

"The Vapors? Turning Japanese? No? Okay, not a music fan, I see. Well, let's try this again. Hi I'm Curtis, and you are?"

She left him hanging once more.

"I don't want to get into it."

"Don't want to get into your name?"

"We already know it's Dorothy. We were just making conversation. Jeez," Stein grumbled.

"My name isn't Dorothy."

"And you sure aren't in Kansas anymore." Curtis laughed.

"Why do people keep saying that to me? I am not named Dorothy. I am Death, Reaper of Souls!"

Curtis paused for a moment, stopped in his tracks by that one. He seemed about to say something, then thought better of it. Instead, he slowly pushed his chair back from the table, stood, and picked up his tray.

"Okay, then, well... um, everyone have a lovely evening. I'll just be sitting over, um... Hey, Molly, that seat taken?" he called across the room to a madwoman in her twenties muttering to her dinner as he hopped to his feet and left the group.

Professor had been deep in thought throughout the whole conversation, focused on something entirely different. His face lit up as he broke from his meditative state.

"I just devised a way to transcend the bonds of this space-time and pass our corporeal matter *through* other matter. We could walk right out the door. Well, through the door, technically," he jabbered excitedly.

Stein had heard it all before. "Yeah, Professor, and how do we do that?"

"It's easy, you just... Oh, wait. I mean..."

Stein chuckled, but not in a mean-spirited way. "Ya see, Professor is always inventing things, but he never writes them down. He's kinda like Tesla's mentally ill kid brother."

Dorothy watched the older man mumble to himself, trying to recall the calculations he'd just had in his head moments ago. Stein swung his attention back to the girl who thought she was Death, not really seeming to mind having the Grim Reaper seated across from him.

"It's funny, people think labs are sterile, but they're full of germs," he blurted. "He used to be a big-shot science professor, you know. Before he lost it. Accidentally killed his kid, I hear."

"People die every day, why does it matter?" Dorothy replied indifferently.

"Wow, that's seriously cold. It was his kid."

Warren chose that moment to lumber into the room, scanning the tables as he decided who to visit with. He'd made a bit of a mess loading his plate for dinner, part of his meal gracing his shirt with an abstract made of protein and carbs, but that was of little concern to him. He just wanted to share his hilarious jokes with his friends.

Stein shrank in his chair like a kid in a classroom who desperately doesn't want to be called on.

"Oh no, it's Warren," he hissed. "Whatever you do, don't say 'Who's there?'"

Of course, what always happens to the kid who doesn't want to be called on? Warren beelined toward the poorly hidden man.

"Knock-knock."

"Not now, Warren," Stein sighed.

"Knock-knock," he repeated. Wanting to continue the joke, he grabbed Stein's arm, hoping to get his attention.

"Oh God, don't touch me, you're all sticky!" he cried out. "Oh, that's disgusting! I need to wash my hands. You could be carrying smallpox!" Stein jumped to his feet in a flash and quickly ran across the room to pump handfuls of sanitizer from a wall-mounted dispenser, leaving the simpleton to turn his attentions to the new girl.

"Hello!" He grinned at her. "Knock-knock."

CHAPTER 10

Evening washed over Camview, and with its arrival, the patients were ushered back into the rec room for some post-dinner activities and games. Certain residents were led to a secure wing of the building, away from the general population for a bit. It was the time of day when the staff actually had to pay a bit more attention to the residents. Like clockwork, a handful of patients would experience "sundowning," a phenomenon where mentally impaired become increasingly disoriented and agitated when the daylight changes as evening sets in. This unpredictable twist in their otherwise predictable day tended to irritate the staff, as the unplanned outbursts just led to more work for them.

Dorothy had no such problems as she sat quietly in a chair. Beckman, a former IRS auditor with a pretty serious obsessive-compulsive disorder, occupied the seat just to her left. She had been observing Larry, the creepy, buzz cut orderly, as he berated a timid patient on the other side of the room.

This guy has got to go, she thought. Looking up, she pleaded to the skies, "At least let me do this one thing."

She raised her hand, reaching out, trying to use her powers to kill the man and take his soul. She furrowed her brow and concentrated her force, but unfortunately, despite all her efforts, it had no effect.

Shit.

As she lowered her hand, Curtis flopped down in the empty chair next to her.

"I like the hand-wavey thing," he said with a chuckle. "Very intimidating."

Dorothy paid him no heed. Ignoring her, or just simply oblivious to her obvious mood, he jumped right back in.

"So, you're Death, huh? Well, now there is something I did not know."

She cast a sharp glance his way.

"I once heard someone say that ignorance is bliss. You must be the happiest man alive," she shot back.

"Oh, ouch! That hurts. No, really." He laughed, brushing it off. "So listen, I was wondering, if you really are Death, why exactly is it you're in here with all us loonies?"

"I don't know. For some reason I'm trapped in this realm. I'm stuck."

Beckman stopped counting to himself and chimed in.

"Why don't you just click your heels together three times and say 'there's no place like home, there's no place like home, there's no place like home'? And you know, travel can be deducted if, uh, if it is for legitimate business purposes."

"That was good, Beckman. You almost didn't talk about accounting this time," Curtis complimented.

"Is everyone in here insane?" Dorothy sighed, exasperated.

Curtis just raised one eyebrow and gave her a look, one mental patient to another.

"Point taken," she conceded.

"Oh come on," Curtis said. "You mean growing up with the name Dorothy, you never got *Wizard of Oz* jokes?"

"What's a Wizard of Oz?"

Gasps of shock could be heard.

Sacrilege! The unified thought of a dozen mental patients buzzed in the air.

Heads turned, conversations stopped, and if there had been a record player spinning vinyl in the rec room at that moment, the needle would most certainly have skipped across the disc and screeched to a halt.

"You've never seen *The Wizard of Oz*?" Curtis blurted, amazed. "Now *that*, my friend, *is* crazy. Lucky for you, they play it twice a month on movie night, so this unacceptable deficiency of yours will soon be rectified."

"Movie night?"

"Yeah, it's basically this place's version of putting the kids in front of the TV so the staff can go screw around while all the nutters just stare at the screen, drooling on themselves. Pretty much like parenting these days, actually. You know, turn on the TV, push play, and walk away. They don't give us iPads, though. Even three-year-olds have iPads. I may need to file a complaint about that."

Looking over her shoulder to make sure no staff was nearby, she leaned in and whispered to him, "I have to get out of here."

"Everyone says that," he whispered back. "Wait, why am I whispering?"

"You don't understand, I *must* get out," she said, louder. "They're not crossing over, at least a lot of them aren't, though I don't know how it is that some still are."

"Wait, who aren't doing what?"

"The dead. The dead aren't going where they need to. If I don't get back, there's no telling how bad things might get."

"Bad?"

"If I don't return, then yes, very bad. For everyone."

"How bad are we talking here?" Curtis asked.

"Streets overrun with the horribly injured but somehow alive. Population growth exploding as people don't die. Eventual planetary collapse as resources simply cannot keep up with the sheer numbers of inhabitants."

"Okay, you made your point, but you said some were still crossing over. If you're really Death, and you're not doing your job at all since you're here with us, how's that even possible?"

"I don't know, but I hope to cross back over and set things right long before I would need to find out."

Curtis looked at her, contemplating what to do with his new friend, when she mentioned one more thing. Something that most certainly caught his attention.

"And Curtis," she gazed directly into his eyes, "Doctor Vaughan would never die."

With that his mind was made up.

"All right, so I have a plan," he chimed in.

"Already?"

"Yep. Desperate times, and all that. Plus I may have wanted to try this for a while, but the opportunity never presented itself."

"How so?"

"Well, it hinges on what I call the clipboard effect. If you act like you belong somewhere, no one questions you, ya know? Carry a clipboard and look official and you can go almost anywhere. Add to that the fact that there's pretty high burnout rate here among the staff and you've got a prime opportunity. Lots of turnover means lots of new faces, after all. The problem with any of us trying is they know all of us. The thing you've got going for you is you're so new that you've only met a few of the staff. Honestly, you might be the first person who could actually pull it off."

"Pull what off?"

Dorothy didn't look like a patient that night as she navigated the halls of Camview. Her hair was different, for one, pulled back into a very business-like ponytail. More importantly, she was also wearing a long white lab coat Curtis had managed to pilfer for her.

She strode quickly down the hall, stolen clipboard in hand.

He was right, it's amazing what you can do with a clipboard and some confidence, she marveled. Her pajama pants were carefully rolled up and hidden under the long coat, a "liberated" pair of ill-fitting white nurses' shoes, courtesy of Curtis once again, shifted loosely on her feet with every step.

His words played over and over in her head as she made her way down the hall.

"Try to look tired and stressed out. You know, like you just pulled a twelve-hour shift and want nothing more than to go home. They all know that feeling, and it gives you a good reason to not talk to anyone. Just don't walk *too* fast. You're so new that almost no one knows your face yet. You could just be another new hire, for all they know, so if you do it right and stay calm, it might actually work."

As she strode down the hallway, she did her best to play the part Curtis had laid out for her, looking at the clipboard as if studying some work-related drudgery when she passed an orderly.

Dressed as she was, and walking with confidence, she didn't even warrant a second glance.

Rounding the corner, she saw it, just as Curtis had described. A locked door at the far end of the long hallway, right at a T-intersection.

"Time your arrival at the doors so you get there right behind someone with a key," he had told her. "Just don't make it obvious."

She had to force herself to slow her pace. She was alone in the hallway and approaching the door far too fast.

Slow down. You're getting ahead of yourself.

She knew if she reached the door and had to turn back it would draw attention to her, and her escape attempt would likely be all over. No way they'd miss that kind of suspicious behavior from an unfamiliar face, even if she did look like she belonged.

Step by step she closed the distance.

Fifty feet away, then forty. Thirty.

What do I do if I get hung up at the door? Can I stop and tie my shoe maybe? No, that's too obvious…

She was still getting there too fast. Dorothy tried to slow her pace even further without looking obvious about it, but another few seconds and she'd be in a serious bind.

They're looking this way. What now? She continued walking, trying her best to look calm, though she knew they'd realize something was wrong any second.

The echo of footsteps rapidly approaching made the hairs on her neck to stand up.

Don't panic. Act normal.

She knew it. Her goose was cooked. Somehow they had figured it out. An orderly was rushing down the hall right toward her.

She felt her pulse quicken, but rather than grabbing her, he brushed right past, reaching to his belt, cursing as he fumbled with his keys, then finally yanked open the door in a hurry.

"Hey, hold the door!" she called out.

He turned, saw the coat and clipboard, and held the door as she hurried through.

"Thanks," she said, but he was already rushing to his destination, not giving her a second thought.

It actually worked. I guess Curtis was right.

"If you act like you belong, no one will question you," he'd quipped.

So far, so good.

Once past the locked doors, Dorothy found it a bit easier to navigate the corridors. Finally, she looked up and saw the sign she was searching for. *Staff Lockers.*

Okay, here we go.

She knew this had the potential to be the most tricky part, though to be fair, Curtis's whole plan was pretty much based on nothing more than bluffing and luck.

"The really sketchy bit is going to be exiting through the staff locker room," he had told her. "If you make it that far, that is. You'll have to get there before anyone else, but then you can't leave the premises until the shift change. If you try to go before then, the guards will take notice."

She tried the locker room door.

Unlocked.

Quietly, Dorothy slipped in and surveyed the area. Three parallel rows of industrial gray lockers with simple hardwood and steel benches bolted to the floor between them stood at one side of the room, an L-shaped wall blocking view to the open-plan showers. Just past those were the restrooms, again laid out in an open format, but the stalls at least had doors.

She made her way to a middle stall, shutting the doors of the others as she passed to help divert attention from what would otherwise be her lone closed door, then she lowered the lid, locked the door, and took a seat, waiting for her chance.

If anyone happened to check, all they'd see were the white shoes of a hospital worker and hopefully think nothing of it.

An hour later, Curtis's voice ran through her head as she heard the first few employees filter into the locker room.

"You'll need to hide out until the shift ends, but then you'll need to get out of there quick, before anyone gets a good look at you."

She eased off the toilet, flushed for appearances sake, and opened the stall. Only a few people had arrived, and most were currently in the shower, which she took as a good omen as she headed out the exit door.

"Now remember, there are cameras," Curtis had warned her. "Security expects employees to exit at shift changes, so just be sure you're out before the others. You don't want to be answering questions about why they don't recognize the new employee."

Making a beeline for the doors to the outside, Dorothy could almost smell the free air. She pushed, yet the door remained stubbornly shut.

Shit!

Again she pushed, this time harder, leaning her shoulder into it, and with a sticky hinge finally releasing, the door swung open with a pop.

Remembering Curtis's words, at the last moment she turned her face, hiding it from view while acting as if she was simply looking at something in her hands as she walked past the wall-mounted camera.

"Manage all that, and you should be home free. Of course, this is all totally hypothetical, so don't hold me to it," he'd said with an impish grin.

She quietly thanked her odd new friend, while wondering, could he be considered a friend when they'd only just met? Whatever the case, she was grateful for his help as she quickly walked away from Camview Psychiatric Hospital and into the frigid night air.

CHAPTER 11

Quite some time, and many cold miles later, Dorothy's aching legs were pistoning in a steady rhythm, propelling her along on autopilot as her frozen feet carried her past the bare metal skeleton of a rusty, and thoroughly stripped, old sedan. Bracing herself against the chill as best she could in her insufficient attire, she wrapped her arms around herself as she fought against the frigid night air and pressed on.

The temperature had dropped quickly, and she found herself faced with the familiar and quite uncomfortable sensation of being cold.

Really cold.

She trudged ahead, marching down the deserted street, watching her shadow grow tall and then shrink as she passed under each dim streetlight. Her eyes scanned farther up the way, where a flickering light from under a traffic bridge caught her attention.

That looks like a fire, she thought, relishing the idea of someplace to warm her chilled bones. *Finally, things might be looking up.*

She adjusted course and headed straight for the source of potential heat, knowing full-well that anyone could be lurking in the dark surrounding the bridge. Of course that could mean going home, and in any case, as cold as she was, she simply did not care.

The aromatic waft of smoke from burning pallets greeted her as she drew closer, and could see that the flickering light was indeed fire-borne.

Something else was there. Something that tickled the back of her neck. An uneasy vibe of sorts. Her senses sharpened to a razor's edge as she approached, but as she listened to the crackling fire, she realized that there were no voices to be heard. She likewise noted that there were no flashing lights or sirens.

I guess it's as safe as it's going to get, and what's the worst that could happen?

Cautiously, and desperately in need of warmth, she walked toward the corner of the underpass, preparing herself for whatever lay on the other side, just out of view.

She was but a few steps from rounding the corner when her ill-fitting shoes crunched loudly on the broken glass that littered the area.

Shit.

The murky blotches the firelight reflected on the underpass morphed and changed as a dark form rose to its feet near the fire. The blurry figure was slowly given shape by the flickering light, the shifting of the shadows on the wall startling her as she realized what she'd awakened.

A massive, three-headed dog's silhouette solidified against the wall, growing as it lurched from its resting spot close to the blaze and slowly started moving in her direction. A low chorus of growls emitted from around the edge of the bridge's thick stone base.

At least it's from my realm. I guess that's something. I wonder, if a beast from the other side kills me, will I finally cross back over?

With that thought hanging in the air before her, she pressed on, undeterred by the threatening rumbling from the beast's throats.

Dorothy was prepared to meet her possible demise, but when she turned the corner, she found herself actually disappointed.

It was not one enormous, supernatural beast, but rather three large, and well-fed, dogs, their shadows blending together on the far wall to create a much larger silhouette in the semblance of a mythological beast.

"It's okay, it's okay. Come on now, you three, calm down." A scruffy, old vagrant spoke to the canines from his spot next to the fire, where he sat on an overturned crate. "Stop acting up and get back over here."

The dogs calmed at his voice but were still unsure of the intruder. After a long pause, they looked at Dorothy one last time, then back to the old man, finally deciding in unison to obey the hand that feeds them.

"You look outta place, young lady," the old-timer said as he warmed his hands by the fire. "You lost or somethin'?"

"In a way," she replied.

"Well, don't be shy. I don't bite, and neither will they," the old man said with a chuckle. "You look half-frozen. Come on, warm yourself by the fire. It's a cold one tonight."

She didn't need to be told twice and gladly accepted the invitation. As she stepped closer to the restorative heat, toasty-warm pleasure flowed toward her in waves as she rubbed her icy hands near the flames.

The man raised an eyebrow as he skeptically took in her attire.

"You aren't really dressed for this weather."

"I... well, I hadn't thought that far ahead."

For some reason her comment seemed to give the man pause as he once again looked her up and down with concern in his eyes.

"You know, it's really not safe for a pretty thing like you out here," he finally said. "Once you've thawed out a bit, you might want to try the bus depot over on Sixth. It's not the Ritz, but it's warm, well-lit, and a lot safer than out here in the sticks."

Styx. I should be so lucky.

She hadn't seen another soul when she'd wandered under the bridge to the old-timer's den and wondered what could be so unsafe about the area, but decided it wise to take the man at his word. He lived there, after all, and likely knew the real flavor of the neighborhood far better than a tourist in a borrowed lab coat and flimsy pajama pants. She'd go to the bus depot as he suggested, but first she would enjoy the hospitality of his fire just a little bit longer.

The bus depot on Sixth hadn't been that bad of a walk, all things considered, especially after she'd heated up for a spell by the fire. Of course, that was a double-edged sword, as once she'd savored the heat, it made the cold she faced as she walked away sting twice as sharp.

The cavernous, echoing depot was indeed as the shaggy old man had described. Warmth flowed over Dorothy as she passed through its doors, effectively soothing the bite of the night air from her chilled flesh the moment she stepped inside. He had been correct about the other aspects of the locale as well.

Well-lit, at least for a bus station well past midnight, it was populated by many others seeking refuge from the night's cold. There was safety in numbers as well, always a concern among vagrant communities.

She scanned the benches and noted that there were all sorts present. Women, men, some teenage runaways, all without a home to call their own, and all glad for a safe place to spend the night.

The Ritz it was not, indeed, but it would do just fine.

Interspersed with the homeless who called this place home, were backpackers, both domestic and international, as well as exhausted budget travelers, dozing on benches, lying on the floor using their luggage as a pillow, or crashed out up against a wall as they tried to catch a bit of shut-eye before their early morning departures.

Most of those who had tickets seemed to congregate together, almost as though some invisible rope cordoned off the travelers from the homeless, though no such physical barrier was present. It didn't seem a conscious decision on their part, but more a natural tendency of people to gather with those similar to themselves. In any case, the more permanent residents didn't seem to mind one bit.

Dorothy spotted an inviting bench nearby and plopped her exhausted body down on an open seat by two rather grungy teenagers. They were engrossed with a show on one of the TV sets spaced throughout the terminal to keep waiting travelers entertained 24/7.

The picture wasn't too great, the color and pixels long ago damaged from non-stop use, but it was entertainment. The volume wasn't set at what one would call an obnoxiously high level, but the fact that the TV had no accessible controls to turn it down if one desired made that fact a small comfort, especially as the current program was a cheesy martial arts movie from the seventies. The teens seemed to be enjoying it, though, their bodies tensing and swaying as if they were participants in the on-screen combat.

The protagonist—at least she thought he was, judging by his heroic stance—unleashed a flurry of blows against a group of on-screen attackers, the boys poorly mimicking the moves from their seats.

After disarming a slew of bad guys, one of the assailants unwisely charged the hero and was rewarded with a snap-kick to the groin, immediately falling over in a heap. Both boys instinctively covered their groins and groaned in sympathy.

"Oh man, right in the nuts!" said what appeared to be the elder of the pair with a pained laugh.

Again? she thought at the sight of the familiar cinematic defense technique. She allowed herself a smile as she observed the lads. *They really do all react the same way no matter where they are. Must be something in their Y chromosome,* she mused with a small chuckle, then turned her back to the flickering light to try to catch a bit of rest, despite the constant drone from the television.

Eventually she found a relatively comfortable position, and after the night's exertion, her body seemed to know exactly what it needed as she fell quickly into a deep sleep.

Morning came quickly, the bright light shining through the high windows, providing a cozy illumination to replace the artificial lights that had burned through the night.

Daybreak brought with it the buzzing hustle and bustle of arriving and departing travelers, their voices and the clatter of luggage layering and amplifying, adding to the constant drone of the televisions running at all times.

The sheer volume of the barrage of language, slang, insults, and banter was almost overwhelming to Dorothy, and she found it difficult to filter the chorus to just one or two voices at a time as she tried to acclimate to so many unusual means of communication.

To her ears, the discourse of the youths seemed the most unconventional, their blurting expletive-laden nonsense and hip linguistic shorthand that apparently held a deeper meaning that anyone over the age of fifteen could not possibly fathom.

When she finally rose from the bench, her body stiff from the night's exertion, as well as sleeping in an odd position, she leaned slowly to one side then the other, letting out a contented sigh as she felt her muscles stretch and relax, blood flowing once more to her cramped appendages.

Oh yes, that feels wonderful, she thought, just as her stomach started to rumble, reminding her how long it had been since her last meal. That discomfort, despite her regained freedom, took the shine off an otherwise pleasant moment.

It was early, and thus still quite cold in the city. The morning breeze outside the bus depot was crisp, but the rising sun had begun to take the edge off the otherwise chilly air. Dorothy pulled her coat tight and stepped out into a new day.

Reaching her arms up to the sky, she filled her lungs deeply with the brisk air, relishing the feeling of the rising sun before a slight gust of wind made her hug herself with a shudder.

Twenty feet away, there was a bit of commotion at the curb. A traveler's suitcase had mistakenly been left behind in someone's rush, marking it as fair game for the first transients who happened upon it. It was splashed with red with white polka dots, a red piece of yarn tied around the handle. The cheery little case had seen far better days, though, as its lid was torn wide open.

A pair of hefty older men and an obese middle-aged woman had pried the lock open faster than a TSA worker stealing an iPad and were busy tossing contents aside, looking for anything of value, when Dorothy approached.

"Get away, it's ours!" growled the large woman.

"Yeah, back off!" concurred her equally large male companion.

Dorothy stepped back a few paces. The clothes were being tossed aside, obviously too small for the treasure-seeking trio. Dorothy quickly gathered up what she could before the large woman turned on her and yelled for her to, "Move off, bitch!" Her tone that made it quite clear that the next warning wouldn't be a verbal one.

Dorothy hurried back inside to the bus depot restroom, where she finally had a moment to take inventory of what she'd managed to grab before being driven off.

She was happy to see it wasn't a total loss. Her haul included some tan pants that looked like they'd fit, a fairly ugly, bright-colored sweater, and, much to her pleasure, a long-sleeved black shirt, which although a bit stretched in the chest area, its previous owner having been far more "gifted" than she, was far more her style.

Beats a lab coat and pajamas, she thought as she stripped out of her mental ward attire and dressed herself in her new wardrobe.

A little bit on the loose side, but not bad, she thought as she looked herself over in the heavily scratched bathroom mirror. *Okay, this is better. Now I've just got to find out how this happened. Why I'm here. How to get back. Hell, for that matter, if I can get back.* She assessed herself in the mirror one more time, and was not pleased by what she saw.

I really am human. Shit. This is not good.

Dorothy stashed her hospital garb under a bench, and headed out into the day, hoping to find some answers now that she was free. Her mind may have been elsewhere, but come morning, the staff of Camview were most certainly thinking about her.

Picture a museum, if you will. A very, very clean museum. Perhaps a spotless and dust-free showroom of some sort.

That's how many might have described Doctor Vaughan's immaculate home at first glance. His almost obsessive drive to keep things in order showed in his personal space just as much as it did in his work environment. Everything was in its place, clean and proper. Nothing out of sorts.

If you stopped to look at the big picture, it would be noticeable that the whole of his abode had the look of a homemaker keeping everything in perfect shape. Of course, she was gone now, but Doctor Vaughan still kept up his deceased wife's routines.

He'd once been lax, letting her fret over the housekeeping alone while he dealt with his work. After all, he rationalized, he had bigger things to think about. Now he lived alone, and the only sign of his former married life was a small, framed photograph of his wife on the counter near his glistening-clean coffeemaker.

It was still early in the morning, the perfect time to slowly get up to speed for what was sure to be a busy day herding cats at Camview. Yet, despite the craziness looming over his day, Doctor Vaughan was relaxed. This was one of the rare mornings he was allowing himself to come in to work a bit later, and there was something ever so soothing about the calm morning ritual of his coffee and newspaper that made him look forward to these days.

He knew that newspapers were rapidly going the way of the dodo, but the feel of the paper in his hand, and the simple act of filling the crossword puzzle in, with pen, of course, just felt right.

As for brewing his own coffee, he was also fully aware that he could just as easily pick up a fresh cup of small-batch organic micro-brew artisanal coffee from one of the hip coffee shops on the way to work. He actually did just that most days when he was unable to justify a late start and indulge his home brewing ritual, but the simple act of making a pot at home always just felt *right*. Like it reconnected him with a time in his life when things seemed to make sense. Like when he was more in control.

Sometimes, on quiet mornings like these, he really missed his wife.

He was just reflecting on his past, lost in thought while taking his first glorious sip of a Tanzanian single origin peaberry, when his phone rang. He reluctantly lowered his cup from his lips and gazed at the device with distaste.

"Yes?" he answered with a sigh.

The buzzing voice on the other end was the panicked harbinger of a downright shit day.

As he listened to them speak, his knuckles whitened around the handle of his cup as his hand reflexively squeezed. Deep red flushed in his cheeks, and his brow rapidly transitioned from smooth and relaxed to tense with anger. His temple pulsed as a throbbing vein thundered beneath his skin.

His day had gone right to hell, all right, without even bothering to pass Go or collect $200.

"How did you imbeciles let her just WALK OUT!" he raged into the handset, enunciating the last words with such venom his employees were thanking their lucky stars they weren't physically in front of him.

"No, I don't care about overtime! You get them out there, now! Yes, *all* of them! I don't care if you have to put recreation on hold. Damn the other patients, this is your only priority! Get them out there NOW! She couldn't have gotten far." He was now pacing the kitchen, his precious coffee sloshing out of his mug, cascading onto his slippers.

In his rage, he didn't even notice.

"They what? Well tell them they'll be lucky if they still have a job!" he yelled. Vaughan took a deep breath, trying desperately to lower his heart rate and blood pressure before he had a stroke or blew out some other vital organ.

"Oh, and do me a favor. Try to not let the rest of the patients escape before I get there," he hissed, then slammed his phone down and hurried to get dressed.

It was going to be one of those days, and goddamn it, heads were going to roll.

CHAPTER 12

The Cadillac rolled down the road, the two male occupants sitting quietly as they listened to the end of Pink Floyd's "Dark Side of the Moon." In the plush interior, the road noise was reduced to near-nothing by the extensive soundproofing of the luxury sedan.

Randy's father turned the stereo off as the final song ended.

"Still such a good album," he said with a cheerful smile on his face.

"Yeah, one of the best," Randy agreed. "I'll never forget when you first played it for me when I was a kid. Blew my mind."

"You can imagine my joy at finding my boy had good taste in music. I can't fathom what it would have been like if you'd grown up in the house listening to disco, or bad rap."

"Not all rap is bad, Dad."

"Are you saying it gets a bad rap?"

Randy groaned. "Oh, God, again with the dad jokes!"

"Sam's getting older. You need to work on yours, you know. It's a fatherly rite of passage. I can jot a few down for you, if you want."

"I am so *not* going to be that dad."

"I said the same thing," his father chuckled.

They drove quietly for a bit, comfortable in the temporary silence, not needing to fill every second with chatter. It hadn't been until he was a teenager, spending time at his friends' houses, that Randy realized his was an unusual childhood. Where other households had drama and conflict, his family all really got along, for the most part, and genuinely liked one another.

Apparently, this was not the norm.

When his wife died, it hadn't even been a question whether his family would step in to help any way they could. It's just what family does.

After the accident, Randy had relocated with his daughter to be closer to his parents. With their support, and mailing address, Samantha settled in at a good school. Eventually she started to heal after the trauma of losing her mother, the way young children do. For Randy, the process took a bit longer, and more than a few dark patches were navigated in that first year.

"So are you really going to be ready to move her back this summer?" his father asked.

"I think it's time," he said. "I'm stable, the job is going great, and I've got a few guest curating gigs stacking up on top of what I've got going on at Gary's space. Yeah, it's the right time. Plus, I can't ask you to keep looking after her now that I'm so far away."

"She's our granddaughter. You know we love having her with us. Plus— and pardon my French here, Son—your mom and me won't let her go until we're damn sure you've got your shit together."

"Yeah, I know. I swear, that's all behind me now. I've been focusing on making a good home for her. It's my number one priority. And Pop, I've gotta tell you, I really do appreciate everything you and Mom have done for us these last couple of years, but now that I'm back on my feet, I really need to step up and be a good dad."

"You *are* a good dad. You've just had to deal with things. Hitting a rough patch is perfectly normal with what you went through. We know you'll be okay eventually, but Sam's just a kid, and she needs stability and a safe-feeling home environment. We're family, Randy, and we're glad she's with us, for as long as that may be. It's not a burden at all."

"You just say that because she's an easier kid than I was."

"Oh, just wait until her teen years. I bet it's going to get a lot more interesting. I don't envy you having a teenage daughter in this day and age!" He laughed at his poor son. "So, are you going to get behind the wheel again anytime soon? Don't get me wrong, I don't mind these drives. It's like when you were a boy and we'd take those long trips to go skiing, but if you had a car again, you could come visit whenever you wanted."

"I don't know. It still feels a bit soon."

"Okay, I'm not pushing or anything, it was just a thought. I'm sure she'd like to see you more often, though it is a pretty long haul for just a day or two."

"Skype, Dad. That's what video chat is for."

"Call me old-fashioned, but I still prefer face-to-face."

"Don't we all? But until she moves into the new place after school's done, video is a good compromise."

The car slowed as they pulled up in front of Randy's building.

"You sure I can't drop you somewhere? Maybe grab an early lunch?"

"Nah, I need a shower, and I've got a bit of work to get done before I head out to meet Gary. We've got a new artist we're thinking of representing, and we're going to check out his latest body of work over at his studio. Besides, you've still got a long drive back home. If I keep you any longer, Mom's going to worry."

"All right then. Love you Son."

"Love you too, Pop."

The men embraced, then Randy stepped out of the car, took his suitcase from the trunk, and watched his father drive away. Pulling his keys from his pocket, he headed into his building.

Several hours later, far across town, and rather near the depot on Sixth, Randy rode uncomfortably in a jam-packed bus, rethinking his decision to turn down that ride from his father. He was grateful when the bus finally pulled up to the corner and popped its doors open, spewing its human cargo onto the sidewalk.

He spotted a familiar face waiting for him. "Hey, Gary!" he called as he jostled out of the vehicle along with the surging throng of afternoon travelers.

"Hey, man, glad you were able to come. Thanks for meeting me all the way out here in the sticks. I know the bus kinda sucks."

"No worries, I'm used to it. Artists always seem to gravitate toward these outskirt areas. At least until the trust-fund babies and techie brogrammers buy out their neighborhood and fill it with overpriced gastro pubs and niche cafes selling six-dollar coffee and twelve-dollar juice."

"Glad to see you're not bitter or anything."

"Not at all. I *love* watching the cool neighborhoods turn into the homogenized spawning grounds of hipsters and trust fund babies," Randy groused sarcastically.

Working for a friend could be awkward for some, but when your friend also happens to run one of the hottest art galleries in the city and you get to pursue great new artists for a living, it really isn't a bad gig at all. As for Gary, giving his buddy a job to help him get back on his feet was really a no-brainer when he came back to town. And Randy was no slouch in the art scene. Helping his friend was also helping his sales, so it was most certainly a two-way street.

"Come on, let's see what he's got for us. I'm hoping to get him to commit to a three-man show later this year."

Randy pulled out his old blue enamel pocket watch to check the time. He flipped the case shut with a snap and slid it back into his pocket's fabric nest.

"Seriously, why do you still carry that thing?" Gary wondered.

"Conversation piece."

"Well, at least you chose that over a monocle," his friend said with a laugh.

A very drunk vagrant sitting by the door had watched the sarcastic exchange, his bleary, red eyes somehow managing to focus on the pretty blue watch as it caught the sun's rays as the two art dealers stepped past him and opened the door.

"Pretty watch," the bum muttered as they passed. "Shiny."

"Why, thank you," Randy replied. He turned to Gary. "See? Conversation piece. Told ya so," he said with a chuckle as they stepped through the doorway.

Mere moments later, a ragtag young woman in stolen clothes rounded the corner, focused on her search for some answer as to how and why she was stuck in human form. She paused near the homeless drunk, deciding her course, when she overheard him muttering to himself, seemingly oblivious there was anyone nearby.

"Pretty blue pocket watch. So shhhhhiiiny…" he slurred.

Dorothy froze, then spun toward the man.

It can't be a coincidence. That's the last thing I saw before…

"Hey, what did you say about a blue watch?" she grilled the inebriated man.

"You're a pretty girl," he said, eyeing her up and down with his bloodshot peepers.

She ignored the comment. "The watch?"

"What? Oh, the watch… blue, so blue. And shiny! That's the key, ain't it, though? All about time. Time marches. Marches on. Hmm… marching bands, wedding bands! Band-Aids!" He paused his incoherent rambling, not for breath, but to take a big swig from his brown-bagged bottle of high-octane rot-gut.

"What do you know about a blue pocket watch? Have you seen one?"

He took another swig.

"Huh? Oh yeah, I seen it! Important, that is! Or… I dunno. Where'd it all start anyway? Two by two, watches of blue." He seemed amused with that bit and laughed so hard he tipped over, wheezing from the exertion, then promptly passing out when his body finally reached a lateral position.

"Wait, what did you mean important?" Dorothy persisted, but it was no use. The man was quite unconscious, and likely to stay that way for some time.

He said something about where it all started. I wonder… he couldn't possibly mean the street where… A look of revelation flashed in Dorothy's eye. *Could he actually be a seer? An oracle?*

She wondered if it could be possible that maybe, just maybe, this was a sign, some kind of hint or direction guiding her where she needed to go.

Where it all started.

At random, she grabbed a passing man, startling the hell out of him with the abrupt contact and surprisingly strong grip.

"There's a park near an old flophouse hotel somewhere not too far from here. Older part of town. Do you know where that is?"

"Uh…"

"A park. Small slope, bus stop. Do you know it?"

He did a double take as the adrenaline surge that had flooded his system subsided as he realized she wasn't a mugger, or even a filthy vagrant for that matter, but just a young woman dressed in mismatched clothing. His pulse slowed as he regained his composure.

"What, you mean Lafayette Park? It's just a few miles that way," he said, pointing down the road.

"And Donny's Happy Hour?"

"Yeah, it's maybe half a mile from there, but I'm not sure you want to go to that place. I mean, it's not really the safest of spots for women."

"I'll manage," she huffed in reply, then spun on her heel as she let go of his sleeve. She had a destination in sight, and with it, a possible answer to the how and why of her situation. With purpose driving her feet on their way, she set off at a quick walk.

"Hey, you're welcome," the man called after her, but she was already long gone.

She arrived at the dive bar, having made surprisingly good time on her walk, though that could easily be attributed to her extreme motivation to figure out what was really behind her present situation.

Okay, that's the place, she thought, *and I was standing right over there.* She shifted on her feet, scanning the area as she stood across the street from where she'd first failed to take that poor drunk's life. *Andy was his name,* she recalled, before she stepped out into traffic.

She made a beeline right for the spot she'd been all those days ago, only this time her passage was a different story. Cars shrilled their horns, and tires screeched as thousands of pounds of metal and rubber resorted to evasive maneuvers to avoid hitting the strange young woman crossing the middle of the road.

Even though she had been trying to kill herself and still had no fear of death, having recently survived the horribly painful experience of being hit by a bus, and recalling the agony that followed, Dorothy found herself unconsciously flinching from the near misses in spite of herself.

"Watch where the hell you're walking, asshole!" shouted a woman from a black SUV before returning to texting and speeding while drinking her iced soy chai latte.

Dorothy's ill-fitting shoes crunched to a halt at the curb, just as her slick black boots had so many days before.

Am I supposed to feel something? Because I don't feel anything here.

Everything looked the same, down to the vomit stains on the sidewalk and food wrappers and cigarette butts littering the gutter, but she felt nothing.

Come on, this is where it started, she thought. *Wait, this is where it started on the other side. What if I'm doing this wrong? What if I need to go where it all began on this side?*

Finding the run-down hotel required a bit more searching than she'd anticipated after having so little trouble ferreting out the bar she'd been looking for.

It took far too long for her liking before she finally stumbled upon the ancient (by American standards) building. She scanned the skies with a concerned look, troubled that the light was already shifting. It was getting late in the day, and if this didn't pan out, the long walk back to the bus depot would be a cold one.

In addition to her unease with her investigative prowess, she also noted that her stomach now growled with a renewed intensity as she surveyed the exterior of the old hotel. Focusing on her quest, Dorothy pushed her hunger aside and placed her hand on the worn, brass doorhandle.

She still didn't feel anything from the location, no spark or intuition, but she hoped her luck would change once she stepped inside.

She took a deep breath, then pulled.

Walking the dimly lit labyrinth of the filthy hotel's corridors, Dorothy realized she didn't remember which exact room she'd woken up in. Of course, she hadn't exactly been paying the most attention to room numbers as she fled the building that morning, but she did think the current hallway she was walking, the one with the ancient carpet, smoke-stained walls, and flickering lights, held some promise.

Then again, for all she knew, every hallway might be in a similar state of disrepair.

With her arms slightly raised from her sides, Dorothy paused, stood silently in the hallway, and focused, closing her eyes and reaching out with her senses, trying to connect with a trace of the fateful day gone by.

What is that? I think... I think I feel something... maybe? No... There's nothing here.

She stood there a long moment, her eyes still closed as she desperately tried to connect with anything that could put her on the right path. The only thing she felt was her spirits fall even further. All that walking, all that searching and effort, for nothing.

"I'm going to fucking kill you!" a man down the hall shouted.

"Oh, yeah? Well, who's got the knife, Eddie? Who's got the fucking knife?" a shrill woman yelled back.

Further sounds of a violent altercation escaped from behind the thin door, and thinner walls, echoes of breaking glass and furniture crashing that abruptly pulled Dorothy from her attempts to reconnect with any shred of hope. She opened her eyes just as the hotel desk manager rounded the corner, accompanied by a pair of uniformed police officers.

Dorothy felt her heart race at the sight of them, but she wasn't their quarry, and they passed her by with only a cursory glance.

"I'm telling you, they've been at it all afternoon, Officers. They're tearing the place up! Ya gotta do something," the manager pleaded.

As the police pounded on the door, Dorothy made a hasty, but calm, escape down the hall. Once out of their line of sight, she increased her stride and sped out of the building, disappearing into the bustling crowd outside.

CHAPTER 13

It took Dorothy hours to make her way back to the warm shelter of the bus depot. A few wrong turns, stemming largely from exhaustion and low blood sugar, had led her on a rambling, circuitous path. It was well past dark when she finally slid her hungry and aching frame down onto a bench, her dogs barking in weariness, her body aching in tandem.

She sensed someone looking at her.

"You're new," said the middle-aged woman staring at her from the other end of the bench.

She was dressed in a hodgepodge assortment of clothes, similar to Dorothy's attire, but quite a bit more worn. All of her worldly possessions appeared ready to burst from their home in a pair of over-stuffed suitcases she had propped next to a shopping cart full of bottles and cans. Still, Dorothy noted, the woman's eyes lacked that dangerous look she had come to recognize, and avoid, with increasing regularity since hitting the streets.

"Yes, I am. I just got here last night," she cautiously replied.

The woman looked her up and down. "You eat today?"

Dorothy shook her head.

She glanced at the motley bunch camped out in the terminal and saw that now, come sundown, most were dining on whatever they'd managed to scavenge, beg, or steal over the course of the day.

The woman leaned over and dug down in a paper bag at her side, then pulled out a bagel. Breaking it in half as she slid down the bench closer to Dorothy, she reached out and offered her the piece of high-gluten heaven.

"Here," the woman said, handing Dorothy the bagel. "We look out for one another. I'm Beth."

"Thank you," was all Dorothy managed to say before her

hunger took hold and she sank her teeth into the chewy delight. Her salivary glands trilled with joy, shouting "eat it all!" while her rational mind tried to convince her to go slow and make it last as long as she could. She forced herself to savor each bite, until her hunger finally lessened and she felt her body relax noticeably onto the hard wood bench.

At ease, at least somewhat, she reflected that, despite a few rough spots, the day could have been much worse.

That evening was destined to be far less pleasant for another group of men and women, standing at attention, the focus of stern scrutiny as they lined up in a quiet, antiseptic-tinged hallway far across town.

Doctor Vaughan paced in front of his assembled staff, the anger almost visibly bleeding off him, like a smoky shadow beast lurking behind its master, waiting to snatch up and bite the head off of anyone who dared utter a word, or even blink in a manner he disapproved of.

He paused his pacing for a moment near one of the closed doors to an adjoining wing.

Doctor Vaughan had chosen his location with a purpose. He was not a man who did things without a plan, and he had a point to make. While the staff stood silently at attention, he reached out his hand and rattled the door.

It remained locked.

He turned and walked back to the waiting employees and stopped in front of them, fixing them with a silent gaze long and hard enough to make them shift in their shoes.

"All doors into or out of each wing are to remain locked at all times."

He spoke in a calm and deliberate manner, but there was no doubt about the anger lurking beneath the surface, ready to claim any one of them as a victim of his wrath.

"Additionally, all doors to any exterior area are to remain locked at all times," he added. "There are no exceptions. Are we all absolutely clear?" he asked, fixing the group with a look of bare contempt.

The group answered in unison, or at least what passed for unison from a non-military crew.

"Yes, sir!" they cried out as if their very jobs depended on it. And on this evening, they very well may have.

He nodded, allowing himself the slightest hope that this lesson had penetrated their thick skulls. He supposed it was the best he could hope for from his staff of double-digit IQs.

"Good. Now get back to work," he growled.

The staff scurried off, avoiding Doctor Vaughan's scorching gaze as they passed. He dug his cell phone out of his pocket and punched a number on speed-dial as he walked down the hall.

"Any sign of her yet?" he grilled the man on the other end of the line.

The frown on his face would have telegraphed his displeasure at the answer had anyone been foolish enough to stick around after his speech to witness it.

"Well, it's cold out, so go look anywhere warm. Do I have to hold your hand through this? No? Then step it up! Must I do everything?"

He ended the call with an aggravated jab, then pocketed the phone, a palmed coin from his pocket replacing it. He began to roll it back and forth across his knuckles absentmindedly as he anxiously paced his fiefdom of the mentally unsound.

The following morning had been a busy one by the time Doctor Vaughan finally closed the door to his office behind him after making his rounds. The man in charge needed to be seen, after all, and he couldn't afford any more disruptions from his patients.

He let his shoulders relax ever so slightly as he slid into the deep, leather chair behind his desk. He sat there, unmoving, for many minutes as he stared at the printed letter in his hand.

The board of directors must be serious if they took the time to send him a certified mail copy of the notice of pending review. Sure, there had been some issues in the past, but after a reprimand or two and some state-mandated training overhauls for staff, things seemed to be moving much more smoothly.

At least they had been, until a certain disruptive resident breezed into, and just as quickly out of, his facility. Now his entire kingdom could be at risk, and all because of one pesky girl.

While not exactly two strikes into the count, he knew that he was already under the ever-increasing scrutiny of the board of directors as they endeavored to keep the profits rolling in to their shareholders, while minimizing potential disturbances in cash-flow.

Bumps in the road do not happy investors make, he had been warned. This bump needed to be smoothed over, and fast. Well before the board caught even a whiff of any trouble.

Of course, run-of-the-mill lawsuits and insurance claims would continue to be a major inconvenience, if and when they should they arise, and thus, Doctor Vaughan had found himself forced to work within their new system, shunning some of his past techniques for those more suitable for management with weak stomachs.

It frustrated him, but he'd finally managed to reach an equilibrium with the men and women of the board that seemed to suffice.

A particularly heavy hand knocked on his door. It could only be one person.

"Come in, Stan."

The enormous, bald orderly ducked his head as he entered the room, then took a seat across from his boss.

He was in street clothes, an unusual sight for the few residents who had seen him breeze down the hallway on the way to his off-the-record meeting with Vaughan.

"As you well know, we have a problem."

"I've got everyone I could dig up out there looking for her, sir. Even the guys on disciplinary leave, though those ones are still off the books."

"You know, Stan, of everyone here, you're the one person I can actually count on."

The large man smiled at the compliment, but also knew it was not just empty flattery. He had come through for Doctor Vaughan many times, and had become his go-to, right-hand man when it came to getting things taken care of. It was a position Stan was determined to maintain.

Vaughan sized up his lackey for a moment.

Yes, this one is loyal to the end, he thought.

"Stan, we are facing another review from the board."

The big man winced at the news. Last time there had been a cleaning of house, and it had taken much of Doctor Vaughan's persuasion to keep Stan from being fired along with them.

"I need you to do something for me. Off-hours. Off-book. Can you do that?"

"Yes, Doctor Vaughan." His loyalty was unshakable as ever.

"Good. I knew I could count on you. This current incident must not appear anywhere in our case logs or incident reports. Any record of Dorothy Maitland's escape must be purged. She did not escape. She was simply transferred elsewhere for evaluation or treatment. Can you make that happen?"

"No problem."

"Good. If you do this for me, we may get through this review intact."

"I'll get right on it."

"Fantastic. And Stan, keep me apprised on the search. The sooner that little nuisance is back, the sooner we can all breathe a bit easier."

Pushing open the door with his foot and deftly snagging his keys out of the lock as he lurched into his home, Randy hefted several bags of groceries into his kitchen. Gary, likewise loaded with bags, followed in tow.

The walls of Randy's place looked like you'd expect from a gallery director; excellent art hanging in just the right places, a decent selection of books on the shelves—books actually read and savored, not just placed there for aesthetic appeal, or bragging rights. The place still had more than a bit of that messy bachelor feel to it, though, and Randy knew he'd have to keep chipping away until it was ready for his daughter to move in.

On the mantle of the antique fireplace sat a few framed pictures of her, from the time she was an infant up to her present, smiling eight-year-old face. Her room, while mostly bare, was painted and ready for her return.

Randy heaved a bag of produce onto the counter before heading over to his answering machine. Its red light was steadily blinking a bright ruby-red notice of a waiting message.

"I swear, Randy, you're the only person under sixty in this city who still uses one of those things," Gary chided.

"Hey, cut a guy some slack. I'm lucky if can even get one bar of service in this building, and that's on a good day. Would you rather you didn't have any way to reach me when I'm at home?"

"Yeah, yeah, whatever, grandpa. This is why I'm your only friend. Maybe I'll show you how to program the DVR later. Anyway, I'm gonna go swing by the gallery to finish up the last of those edits for the showcards. You got anything you need me to drop off there while I'm going?"

"Nah, all good. Hey, and thanks for the ride. Grocery shopping without a car can be a bitch if I'm getting more than top ramen and toilet paper."

"My pleasure, though one day you're gonna have to get back on that horse."

"Not so long as I've got you to be my chauffeur."

"You just love pushing your luck, don't you, Miss Daisy?" Gary laughed as he flipped a little one-fingered salute to his friend and headed out.

Randy pushed the play button on the answering machine, a smile blossoming on his face when he heard his daughter's voice.

"Hi, Daddy. What? Oh, Grandma says hi..."

Even just a few days living on the streets can sometimes lead to interesting and unexpected friendships being forged between people of vastly different worlds. Case in point, the girl who thought she was Death and the woman who once owned twenty cats sat together on a bench and divvied up the food they'd scavenged during the day.

Dorothy had done well and pulled a shiny, green Granny Smith apple from her pocket, along with a packet of jerky and a small bag of day-old muffins procured from a friendly local baker as he closed shop.

"Getting the hang of things," Beth noted approvingly as she produced a small knife from the folds of her garments and began cutting the apple, pausing to break off a tiny piece of a muffin to feed to her small, curly-whiskered pet rat as he poked his head out of her pocket. "A miniature long-tailed dog," she had described her loyal pet, and the more Dorothy observed the two interact, the more she thought the comparison fit.

With as happy a look as a rat could muster, (which, let's be honest, is pretty happy,) the tiny critter took the offering in his tiny hands and merrily chewed, crumbs dropping between his little fingers.

"So, any luck today?" Beth queried.

"Five days and still nothing," Dorothy replied sullenly.

"Well, you'll get there, girl, I just know it. Egon thinks so too." She scratched the little rat's head as he happily gnawed on his treat.

"But it's taking so long, and I'm no closer than when I started," Dorothy lamented.

"Yeah, but the thing you have to consider is, it just might be a different road than the one you're on is all."

She considered her new friend's take on the situation. Beth could be right, for all she knew. After all, her current path seemed to have run her into a dead end.

If only I had an idea which road might be the right one.

She was just starting to think that maybe she'd need to take the advice and try a different approach, when, out of nowhere, a pair of large hands grabbed her by the upper arms from behind and roughly dragged her backwards, over the bench, and up onto her feet.

"Hey, get off of me!"

Heads whipped around at Dorothy's cry, but then quickly returned to their previous business.

The pair of orderlies were accompanied by a transit cop, and the mere threat implied by his presence made the otherwise outspoken and often rowdy throng a bit restrained. Even the fighters in the bunch decided this wasn't something they wanted to get mixed up in.

Beth, on the other hand, jumped to her feet, still holding the small knife in her hand.

"Let her go! You've got no right!"

"Lady, put that thing down before someone gets hurt," growled the orderly. From the tone of his voice, he knew damn well he wasn't going to be the one injured.

The transit cop had his hand on his gun but hadn't drawn it. Unlike so many of his trigger-happy compatriots, he wanted to deescalate the situation if he could before resorting to lethal force.

"I understand you're trying to protect your friend, but you have to understand that she's an escaped mental patient. She needs care, and I know you don't want to spend the night in jail. Just stand back and let these men do their job."

Beth looked at him with pleading eyes, but he slowly shook his head no. He didn't want to be forced to act, but he would if pushed too far.

She had to make a decision. Reluctantly, she put her knife away and sat back down with the others, while one of the orderlies hauled Dorothy out the doors to their waiting van.

"Call Doctor Vaughan," he shouted over his shoulder. "Tell him we've got her and are on our way in."

CHAPTER 14

Doctor Vaughan's face looked as if he wore a mask. No emotions betrayed, his visage showing nothing but calm. It remained that way a good long while as he reclined in his chair and observed the girl who thought she was Death. He coolly studied her as she sat just across the large desk from him.

He hadn't spoken a single word since she'd been ushered in. He just looked at her.

What's his game? she couldn't help but wonder.

A red light on his phone had been flashing for over a minute, yet with his tranquil façade of cool and calm, he acted as if he didn't even notice.

"Pure folly, Dorothy," he finally said, opening a folder on his desk and casually glancing at its pages. "Bringing you back was hardly an effort at all. We'd have gotten around to you much sooner, were you not such a low priority on our list. But at last, you are now back where you belong. This is your home, and if you shape up and get with the program, things will go smoothly for you. If, however, you insist on being disruptive..."

His mask of tranquility slipped, and the glare that peeked out spoke volumes about just how unpleasant he could make her stay if he so wished.

"Behave," he said ominously. "Or else. Clear? Now get out." He didn't even wait for a response as he turned his attention to the papers on his desk, acting as if she wasn't even there and he hadn't a care in the world.

The flashing light on his phone still didn't warrant even a glance.

That's it? She wondered if it was a trick, but when, after several moments Doctor Vaughan continued to pay her no heed, Dorothy rose and exited, quietly closing the door behind her.

As soon as she was gone a slight shudder passed over Doctor Vaughan's body and his posture deflated just a bit. He looked at the phone, his shoulders slouching even more as his calm expression slowly cracked, until his true distress shone through.

With obvious dread, he reluctantly reached for his phone and held it to his ear. He paused for a moment, his finger hovering over the flashing light, then finally took the call off hold.

"I'm so sorry for the delay, I had to take care of a little—No, sir, I assure you there's been no disruption here. We—No, they must be mistaken. Of course, sir, I'll have the logs sent right over. I can assure you, there has been no—Yes, of course. I can bring them personally. Would sometime next week work? Oh, I see—"

Again he had been hung up on, though he wasn't sure which emotion was stronger in him at that moment. Anger at his boss's actions, or gratitude that he was finally off the uncomfortable phone call.

"Susan," he called over the intercom, "I'm going to be visiting our board this evening. Would you please pull together our incident logs for the past two weeks? And bring me a few blank pages, if you'd be so kind."

It was more cover-your-ass time, something he had become quite familiar with during his tenure as chief of staff. Unfortunately, he sensed this new girl was going to be far more trouble than he'd originally bargained for. He just hoped the additional revenue from her state-funded care would make the trade-off worthwhile.

He wished he didn't have to wait until the following quarter for the board to next review the financials. Incidents could be swept under the rug if the numbers looked good. Cold, hard cash was all that really mattered to the board and the shareholders they answered to. He had to formulate a plan, and quickly.

Wrapped in a light robe, Dorothy sat quietly, sipping a mug of steaming tea in one of the over-stuffed chairs in the hospital recreation area, lost deep in thought. From the corner of her eye, she registered someone approaching.

Curtis plopped down next to her, a bit over-dramatically, with a pair of pudding cups in hand.

"Hey, she's back!" he said, offering her one of his sugar-laden treats. "Pudding?"

She shot him a sour look. *After all I've gone through, this guy wants to feed me pudding?*

"No? Okay, your loss. More for me." He chuckled, then dug in to his treat with obvious relish.

What's with this guy and his ridiculous sweet tooth, anyway? I mean, okay, despite his oddness, he did actually help me, and he doesn't seem to be a bad person. Of course, the escape was a wash. Now I have to find another way out of here. Some way to get back. I wonder if—

The lights flickered as she heard a guttural bellow echo down the sterile hallways.

"Did you see that?" she asked, staring at the lights.

"See what?" Curtis replied, as he licked his spoon clean.

The sounds of a fierce struggle reverberated off the walls, getting louder. Closer. The source of the ruckus became visible as the yelling man passed the doorway, while several large orderlies, wearing gloves and goggles, struggled to lead the exceptionally combative fellow to his room.

As the fracas drew near, the reason for the protective gear became clear.

The man was a mess, covered in weeping boils, though they seemed to be healing, and layers of sloughing scabs, which had apparently taken the place of oozing sores on much of his body. The man looked far from healthy.

His energy seemed to finally be fading, his struggling lessening, when his gaze panned across the room. As soon as he caught sight of Dorothy, his eyes widened.

With a burst of unexpected energy, he broke free and ran straight for her.

"It's YOU! You can't be here—what if the apocalypse comes? The horsemen can't ride without YOU!"

The rabble in the rec room abruptly went totally silent, and as a result the television became audible, the news anchor's voice clear over the suddenly still room as everyone stared at the wild man.

"Though the car slid all the way down the ravine, no fatalities were reported. In other news..." the anchor reported.

"You see! You're not doing your job! The others can only do so much to cover for you, but some people are slipping through the cracks. The system wasn't intended for others to do it. It was designed for you! Those people were supposed to die! It's only going to get worse. The rest of us can't pick up your slack forever!"

He was about to continue his rant when two pairs of very large gloved hands yanked him back on his heels, dragging him toward the door. Thrashing and twisting in the men's grasp, the ill fellow somehow managed to once more break free, though only for a second, but it was long enough for him to run up to Stein and give him a bear hug before being torn away and hauled off, kicking and screaming, but also laughing.

Molly, who had always been one of the more off-kilter residents, watched with twisted amusement as she saw the imminent germ-induced freak-out building steam.

"Oh man, this'll be good," she laughed. And indeed it would.

Poor Stein. The germaphobe had just been hugged by his worst nightmare.

"Oh. My. God."

He looked shell-shocked. Horrified. Disgusted to levels he would have never thought possible. Then he started shaking from head to toe.

"Ohmygod-ohmygod-ohmygod!" he yelled, running towards the restrooms. "Get it off me! Get it off! Oh my God, I need a shower! Get out of my way!" His cries of panic and disgust echoed off the linoleum floors and industrial-painted walls as he frantically raced for a disinfectant soap and scalding hot water salvation, shedding clothes in the hallway as he ran, not caring that he was about to be naked for all to see.

The ill-looking madman laughed maliciously as he watched the scene unfold as he was escorted from the room, the duty nurse scolding him as he was unceremoniously hauled away.

"Now you know if you don't take your medicine we'll never get the rest of that rash cleared up. You have to listen to Doctor Vaughan and do what he says." Her tirade was cut short as the doors closed behind them, only muffled chastising audible, and rapidly growing fainter.

Curtis turned to a rather surprised Dorothy.

"Oh yeah, should have told you. We've got one of the Horsemen of the Apocalypse now. Came in while you were away. Thinks he's Pestilence. I guess that's kind of obvious."

"More like just a pest, if you ask me," Molly chimed in. "That guy's a total dick. And he smells."

Dorothy just sat there, stunned, for several moments with an astonished look on her face as the muffled yells of the supposed Horseman of the Apocalypse faded to silence in the halls.

Fortunately for Dorothy, she had learned the ropes from Curtis quickly and had mastered the art of pretending to take her pills as the nurse made her morning rounds. Clear-headed and with her wits fully about her, she was worried things might be spiraling out of control.

What could the appearance of a Horseman of the Apocalypse in the same realm, and same mental hospital as her, possibly signify? And if the others were helping reap souls while she was away, just how much time did she have before things got really bad?

Is he some sort of sign? Maybe a possible way out? she pondered. *I should get Curtis's take on this.*

Though Dorothy had only been there a short time, much to her surprise, she and Curtis had developed an easy sort of friendship, locked away behind the walls at Camview. She felt he was trustworthy, and once that had been established, found herself appreciating his unusual, but often accurate, take on things.

Afternoon came, and Dorothy had once more taken up a comfy spot in the rec room, her legs curled under her as she sat on the old couch, discussing her situation with her insane friend while he downed his fourth pudding cup. At least she wasn't worried whether he thought she was crazy.

This is a mental hospital, she thought. *Crazy fits right in.*

"So," Curtis said, "about your new best buddy."

"If that really is Pestilence, well, he shouldn't look like that. I mean from what I understand, he should be all boils and pus from head to toe."

"Charming."

"I mean it. Something isn't right."

"Well, they did put him on some pretty serious antibiotics, from what I hear. Maybe that's why he looks like he does," Curtis hypothesized. "Still, he really doesn't seem much like a supernatural being. That, and Molly's right. The guy *is* kind of a dick."

"But what if that really is him? I can't risk passing up the opportunity to learn what he knows. I've got to see him, to find out why he is here. He may even know how I can get back."

Dorothy clearly wanted to find a way out of her dilemma, and badly at that, but for the immediate future he knew that simply wouldn't be an option.

"Look," he said, "they've got him locked up in isolation for the time being, so I'm afraid that if you really want to talk to him, you're going to have to be patient and wait."

"I don't like waiting."

"Who does?" Curtis looked around, making sure no one could overhear them. "Listen, I get it that you feel you have to stick around for this guy, but in the meantime, why not have a little fun? Life's short, after all. So what do you think? You wanna go out tonight?"

She looked at him like he was nuts. Then she remembered.

Oh yeah, he is nuts.

"Out?" she asked. "I have a feeling they've tightened security quite a bit since I've been gone," she said with a grim laugh.

"Oh, yeah, the exits are all locked down tight these days, but I have a little backup option no one knows about. It's super-secret, so you have to double-special-pinkie-swear-promise me you won't tell anyone."

She looked at him with a doubting stare.

"I'm serious. Promise."

"Fine, I promise."

"Pinkie swear?" He extended his little finger.

"Pinkie what?"

"Just do it."

She held out her pinkie, which Curtis promptly locked with his in a conspiratorial shake.

"Excellent! Okay, so here's the thing: If Big Stan is on duty you can forget it. That guy's a serious pain and damn near impossible to get past, but it's Friday, and he never works Fridays. The others really aren't so hard to get around."

"But you just said the exits are all locked down."

"Yeah, well, the thing is, yes, they're paranoid about the exits, but they never lock the doors to the rooms at night."

"That doesn't make sense."

"Word is, the people who own this place are cracking down on Vaughan to boost revenues, so even though he's reducing people's hours to save a few bucks, the doors still have to stay unlocked in case of fire or emergency, since they're understaffed. Anyway, all of that doesn't matter. What does is that if you come with me, I know a way out."

She looked at him dubiously. "Then why are you still here?"

"Hey, out there I have to find an apartment, pay bills, get a job. I mean have you tried finding one lately? At least in here I get three square meals, a warm bed, and free movies three nights a week. Sure, it's the same movies over and over, but still."

Gears were turning behind her eyes, but Curtis found he couldn't read the expression on her face as she studied him.

Can I really trust this guy? she thought. *So far, he's been the one person to look out for me in here…*

"So whaddya say?" he chided. "Let's hit the town. Besides, if you really are Death, then maybe it'd do you some good to live a little."

She snickered at his attempt at humor but still seemed hesitant.

"Oh, come on, that guy will still be locked up when we get back, and you can't talk to him until they let him out of isolation, anyway. What else have you got to do? Have some pressing game of Candy Land or Monopoly you'd rather get back to?"

Well, I guess he does have a point.

"Hey, you know what? You may even find a different way back to wherever you need to go while we're out. Then you wouldn't even need to talk to that nutter. You think of that?"

What can it hurt?

Convinced, but only just, Dorothy nodded her head as she quietly agreed.

"All right," she said. "But I can't go out like this." She motioned to her pajama-like hospital outfit.

"Don't worry," Curtis replied. "I'll take care of everything. I'm sure I can find you something that will fit."

Doctor Vaughan had been waiting in the reception area for nearly half an hour when the pretty brunette receptionist informed him, again, that it would be just a little bit longer before the board would be ready for him.

"Are you sure I can't get you anything while you wait? A coffee maybe, or some water?"

"Thank you, but I'm fine," he replied with a warm smile, his calm demeanor hiding the turmoil raging inside. What she didn't know was his stomach was doing somersaults in anticipation of another grilling from the board. He was certain he'd covered his bases. Stan had been thorough in helping him paper over the incident with his troublesome patient, but no matter how thorough he may have been, Doctor Vaughan was nonetheless ill at ease as he was forced to wait.

The board consisted mainly of old money; people who held seats largely as vanity positions due to family connections rather than actual business acumen. The chairman, however, was a different nut to crack.

With a background of running several successful medical facilities, as well as having founded two diagnostics technology companies, which he had sold for a pretty penny, he was a very shrewd, and equally cutthroat, business mogul. The others, Vaughan was confident he could handle, but the chair would require great tact and care if he expected to emerge from this review with his job intact.

Nearly twenty minutes of waiting later, Doctor Vaughan was finally ushered into the conference room. As was expected, the board sat at the long table, the lone empty chair waiting for Vaughan ominously.

"Francis, thank you for joining us. Please, take a seat. We have a lot we wish to discuss with you."

"Thank you. I can assure you, things have been running quite smoothly at Camview. In fact—"

"So what's this we hear about a patient escaping?" the chairman interrupted. "We find that report most distressing, especially as you were just beginning to improve the facility's financials."

Vaughan stumbled, but only for a millisecond, then he fell smoothly into his practiced speech.

"Rumors and conjecture, nothing more. Some disgruntled staff have been spreading these lies, but I assure you, there are no such problems under my leadership. If you'll look in the logs I sent over, you'll see it is quite clear that the patient in question was merely transferred temporarily for a second evaluation. This is quite normal, and the cost was paid for by the State of Oregon, just as her full care at Camview is being paid for. Having top-dollar paid by a government entity without any reduction in fees, as we are forced to accept from insurers, is a windfall for us. In fact, if you look at the financial sheet I've included—"

"We're not here to discuss financials, Francis. You know that's not something we're covering until the next quarterly meeting."

"Yes, I know, but I thought the board would be interested to see how this one patient alone has helped our books tremendously. Profits are up, and I thought the good news would be welcome since we were already having this meeting."

The board murmured amongst themselves. The thought of higher profits had piqued their interest, and Vaughan knew he had them. All he needed was to steer the conversation to money and he would get through this, and it looked like he had succeeded.

"Very well, let's see what you've got, then," the chair capitulated. And with that, Doctor Vaughan allowed himself the tiniest of smiles, knowing he was in the clear.

Late that night, long after Doctor Vaughan had managed to survive his review and return to his home, Camview's bustling had finally slowed as the night shift took over.

The patients had been gathered up and herded to their rooms when the facility wound down for the night. As a cost-cutting measure, in the late hours of the night, the hospital wings were only monitored by a skeleton staff, just as Curtis said. A managerial decision that made his plan that much easier.

Dorothy heard a slight click as her door quietly swung open. Curtis, ever the showman, leaned inside and bowed with a flourish.

"Are you ready to depart, madame?" he whispered.

She nodded and stepped out of her room.

Flattened against the walls as best they could, Dorothy and Curtis cautiously inched their way down the hallway. As they maneuvered past the lone manned nurses' station in their path, Curtis, with an impish gleam in his eye, held up a finger to his lips in a "shhh" gesture.

I don't need you to remind me to be quiet, Curtis. We're breaking out of a mental hospital here.

As if she had somehow picked up on Dorothy's thoughts, the duty nurse looked up from the reality show flashing on her tiny television set and turned the volume down. She cocked her head as she listened for any out-of-the-ordinary sounds coming from the halls. The duo stood frozen in their tracks, just out of her line of vision, barely breathing.

Seconds ticked by, stretching on for what seemed like forever.

Just stay in your chair, she thought. *No need to come out into the hallway.*

A few moments later, convinced she hadn't heard anything, the nurse relaxed her posture and returned her full attention to her television show. Dorothy and Curtis breathed a sigh of relief and continued on their way.

They arrived at a door that looked pretty much like all the others in the hallway, when Curtis bent over and removed his slip-on shoe. No laces after all—can't have patients hanging themselves, now can we? After a moment of fishing around under the insole, he produced a lone key.

"No one notices a missing key if it's to a door they never use," Curtis said in a hushed voice as he opened the door, then hid the key back in his shoe. "Come on," he whispered, and together they passed through the open door.

They stepped into an industrial-looking space and onto a small landing leading down a few short and dusty stairs to what appeared to be the boiler room. The steps let out a faint metallic sound with every step, but with the heavy door closed behind them, there was no way anyone in the halls above would possibly hear them.

They had only traveled a short way into the pipe tunnels when Curtis held up his hand.

"Hold on a sec."

He scooted toward a set of machines and reached between some pipes, retrieving an old gym bag of men's clothes. He had just started to remove his hospital garb when he paused, remembering his manners. Digging farther between the pipes, he produced a crudely wrapped package and handed it to Dorothy.

"Here ya go. Happy Birthday. Or happy Wednesday. Happy something anyway. Whatever works for ya."

She looked at him like he was a madman. *Well, it is a nuthouse.*

"What I meant to say is, these are for you, m'lady," he said with a wink.

She took the package from his hands and peered inside.

"Don't worry," he said. "I won't peek. Besides, you're not my type."

CHAPTER 15

The alleyway on the south side of Camview Psychiatric Hospital was accessible from two directions, yet for some reason, this side of the facility hardly ever saw foot traffic. Perhaps the dark nature of the alleyway was a natural deterrent for random pedestrians, or maybe it simply wasn't a shortcut of any usefulness. Whatever the reason, the lack of prying eyes was a fortunate turn of events, as it was in that particular alley that one of the half-dozen large metal ventilation grates swung open.

Curtis appeared first, poking his head out of the opening and scanning both ways, making sure the coast was clear before navigating the three-foot drop to the ground.

He was wearing a horrible 1970s paisley shirt, which did not go at all with his slightly too-short skinny jeans. He looked like he'd stolen half of his wardrobe from his grandfather and the other half from his little brother, but it was better than pajamas, so it would do. That, and he seemed to actually like the outfit.

Content that the alleyway was clear, he reached up behind him to help Dorothy out of the vent, shutting it quietly when she was safely at ground level.

Unlike the other vents, this one was not welded shut, though to any curious eyes, it appeared to be. The ancient hinges, however, had been lubricated regularly, and the broken welds looked whole to the naked eye. Curtis's escape route may not have looked like much, as was key with any functional camouflage, but he made sure it worked smoothly whenever he needed it.

Unlike Curtis, Dorothy was not wearing bad seventies reject clothing, but despite that small blessing, she didn't look too thrilled with the attire he'd wrangled for her.

Sure, the black jeans were fine, as were the black Chuck Taylors (where did he find all this stuff, anyway?), but the Black Sabbath T-shirt with a grim reaper on it seemed a bit much.

Curtis saw her glance disappointedly at her wardrobe yet again as they started down the alleyway toward the main street.

"Look," he said, "I knew you liked black, and it was all I could find on short notice. I didn't mean for it to be ironic. Really."

Dorothy shot him a glare, looked at the shirt again, then fired off another glare for good measure, though this time, it was accompanied with the tiniest hint of an amused smile.

Sighing with resignation, all she could say was, "Seriously?"

Fortunately, Curtis had plans for the evening's fun, which he was more than sure would make up for any wardrobe issues.

"C'mon, the bus should be here in fifteen minutes. This is going to be fun!"

The bright lights, myriad sounds, and mélange of tantalizing smells of the small carnival Curtis had navigated them to were a multi-faceted assault on Dorothy's senses, but rather than shy away, she reveled in the experience. She also noticed that in this environment, Curtis's odd attire actually worked quite well, though at least one kid had mistakenly thought he was a poorly dressed clown.

As they strolled the grounds, taking everything in, one thing in particular stood out to Dorothy. The carnival was a safe place. A fantasy world. One where, unlike the 'real world,' everyone seemed to be having a great time, their troubles forgotten, at least for a little while.

Games were played, prizes won, rides ridden by screaming, laughing kids. She may have *seen* plenty of interesting things in her day, but in all her years, she had never really *experienced* anything like a full-fledged carnival, and she found herself smiling at the novel experience in spite of herself.

Curtis stopped at a kettle corn vendor and acquired a fresh bag of the sweet concoction.

"Here, you've got to try this."

"What is it?"

"Kettle corn. Second-greatest food on Earth."

She popped a few pieces into her mouth, which immediately started watering at the salty-sweet goodness.

Oh wow, this is really good. Maybe his sweet tooth isn't so crazy.

Curtis watched her reaction like a proud parent. "See, I knew you'd like it!" he chirped with glee.

"Mmmhmm," was all she could reply as she chewed the sticky-sweet mouthful.

They walked farther into the fairground, where each turn revealed some new sight. As they rounded the corner of a tent proclaiming it contained the "Eighth Wonder of the World!" a large inflatable ball rolled right into Dorothy's feet. She stooped and picked it up.

"Where'd that come from?" she asked with a confused look.

No sooner had she posed the question, than an eight-year-old girl came running toward her at full speed chasing after it. Her eyes were so focused on the ball, she nearly ran smack dab into Dorothy's legs, stopping only at the last moment.

"Give me my ball!" the child said rudely, as is so often the case with filter-less kids.

"Say please." Something about Dorothy's gaze made the child behave herself and ask politely.

"Please."

"Okay, here you go," she said as she handed the ball back to the little girl.

Curtis bent down and offered the girl some of his kettle corn. "You want some?"

"Sure!" Apparently, she had never heard the adage about taking candy from strangers. Either that or she didn't care when kettle corn was involved.

"What's your name?" asked Curtis.

"Tessa," the girl replied. "What's yours?"

"I'm Curtis," he said, dropping into an exaggerated bow, complete with arm flourish. "A pleasure to make your acquaintance, Miss Tessa."

The little girl giggled, then looked at Dorothy.

"What about you?" she asked the odd woman in black.

"I am Death," she replied.

The girl's eyes grew wide. After the briefest of pauses, she shrieked at the creepy lady and turned on her heel and quickly ran away.

"You really have to stop telling people you're Death. Is Dorothy really such a bad name?"

The corners of her mouth actually turned upward for a moment, the rarity of seeing a smile on her face totally disarming Curtis and making his annoyance a thing of the past.

"Oh, all right. C'mon," he said, letting her off the hook. "Let's go on some rides."

"But we don't have any tickets."

He dug in his pocket and produced a wad of ride tickets clutched in his fist.

"Don't worry about it. Five-finger discount. Come on!"

"Five-finger what?"

He ignored the question and took her by the hand, dragging her into the undulating sea of cheerful revelers.

They spent what seemed like hours hopping from ride to ride, periodically stopping to play the rigged carnival games before jumping back to the rides again.

Curtis wasn't picky. He was like a twelve-year-old in a grown man's body, enjoying every single ride that came his way no matter how cheesy it might be. Dorothy, on the other hand, was a bit more discerning, deciding that her favorite of all was the one Curtis found the least exciting. Still, it was her turn to choose a ride, and she made her selection without hesitation.

Reluctantly, he joined her for a ride to the top.

"What's wrong with the Ferris wheel?" she asked her disappointed companion.

"Nothing's wrong with it, per se. It's just such a boring ride when there's all this other cool stuff to do!"

"I like the view up here, being able to see over the city and all the people at once." *The way my view is supposed to be.*

"Well, I still think it's boring."

"Then we'll have to agree to disagree."

"Fine. But I get to choose our next stop... which will be the greatest food experience on Earth," he said, beaming ear to ear. "You've had the second best, but now for the cream of the crop. Come on, spin faster, stupid wheel!"

They eventually reached ground-level and left the Ferris wheel behind, which pleased Curtis immensely. He took Dorothy's hand, and like a sweet-seeking missile, he guided his friend on a weaving, but precise, path to his culinary target with the uncanny accuracy of a cotton candy radar.

Minutes later, Dorothy and her paisley-clad friend, cotton candy in hand, sat side by side on a bench in one of the food areas that dotted the carnival. "Food courts," some would say, or as Curtis liked to call them, "monuments to gluttony."

Curtis was happily tearing off pieces of his enormous blue ball of saccharine fluff, shoving the enormous wads in his mouth, occasionally tossing and catching them out of the air. He was having an all-around great time with his treat.

Dorothy, on the other hand, looked a bit confused as she tried to figure out exactly how you're supposed to eat it without winding up covered in sticky, spun sugar.

"No, you just eat it with your face. It's supposed to be messy."

She paused, considering the prospect.

"Oh, all right," she finally said, taking a big bite, wispy remnants sticking to her chin. "Oh my, this feels so strange. It's like, I don't know, like sweet spiderwebs I guess."

"I know, right? Nothing quite like eating things that would never occur in nature. I LOVE cotton candy. L-O-V-E. it. Like, want to marry it love. It's totally my favorite food in the world."

"But it's so messy."

"Don't care. In fact, I've always wanted to stick my head in the machine and go to town. I'd be like a giant, sugary Q-Tip. Man, that would be awesome!"

Their G-rated snack time was rudely interrupted by a pair of thirty-something men in college sports jerseys floating to an adjacent table on what must have been somewhere between their tenth and twentieth beer apiece.

In the short time Dorothy and Curtis had sat eating their treat, the drunken pair's pontifications on college sports had grown louder with each pint imbibed, their ramblings finally approaching a fever pitch.

"No, Dickerson sucks!"

"Does not! He'll kick Myer's ass any day of the week!"

"No way, that whole team is pathetic. They should still be playing high school ball. In fact, I think that entire place is like the thirteenth grade."

"Oh yeah? They've been one of the top-ten collegiate teams the last five years."

"Yeah, yeah, a bunch of sissies playing on mommy and daddy's dime."

And on and on it went.

Curtis glanced at Dorothy, and the two shared a look of eavesdropping exhaustion.

"You wanna go... *anywhere* else?"

"Yeah, this is getting ridiculous."

"Seriously. Kidding, you are not."

They rose to their feet and headed out toward the game tents area, Curtis leading the way.

"You know, the funny thing is, for all their fervor about those teams, I'll bet neither of them even graduated college."

They chuckled and left the two overgrown wannabe frat boys behind as they strolled into the maze of flashing lights, bells, and sirens that made up the game area.

"Shouldn't we be getting back?" Dorothy asked after several rounds of games.

"Soon, but let's go on one last ride," Curtis replied.

"Okay. Your choice, since this whole outing was your idea."

"Excellent. Teacups it is!" he whooped enthusiastically.

They headed off through the crowd, weaving their way around the numerous bodies on the way to the spinning ride. Dorothy was trying not to spill her soda, while Curtis kept bumping into people with the three-foot tall stuffed Cat in the Hat he had won at the ring-toss game.

When they arrived at the ride, a young girl of maybe six years old looked up with wonder at the enormous stuffed animal, like it was the coolest thing in the world. Naturally, Curtis did what any other self-respecting escaped mental patient hiding out in a carnival would do. He flashed his brightest smile and gave it to her.

The girl was unsure at first, looking back at her mother questioningly to see if it was okay. After all, why would a stranger give her such an amazing thing? Curtis simply smiled at her and gave a cheerful wink at her mother.

"Go ahead, he's yours," he said, handing it to her. "He told me he wanted to go home with you instead. You two have fun now!"

With his arms now free of the hindrance of an enormous stuffed animal, he stepped through the turnstile with his fellow escapee in tow. Dorothy stared at him with a confused look on her face as he took his seat.

"Didn't you just spend twenty minutes trying to win that thing?"

"What? It's not like we can take it back with us. Might as well make a kid happy, right?"

"Curtis?"

"Yeah?"

"You didn't *really* hear the stuffed animal talking to you, did you?"

He smiled and gave her a wicked little wink and pulled her to the nearest teacup.

This guy is full of surprises, she thought, just as the ride jolted with a start and her world began to spin. Naturally, the faster it spun, the harder Curtis laughed.

When the whirling teacup ride eventually came to a stop and

spilled them out into the thinning crowd, they finally decided it was time that they left. Dorothy weaved a bit as she walked, a residual dizziness tweaking her gait. What she found unusual was that she was totally all right with it. Her first outing with Curtis, doing ridiculous things no less, and she was having a blast.

She could also tell he had no romantic intentions toward her whatsoever, which was convenient. He had instead latched on to her as a protector, seeing her much as his kid sister he needed to look out for. The way things had gone up to that point, she was glad for it.

Of course, he still gave her grief from time to time, though one could argue that's exactly the sort of thing a big brother would do.

"Come on, I want to hear you say it again," he prodded her as they walked.

"Fine. 'Hello, my name is Dorothy,'" she said. "There, you happy?"

"If that keeps little kids from crying, and their parents from calling the cops on the crazy Death-lady, then yes, I'm quite happy, thank you very much." He hip-bumped her affectionately as they walked, letting her know he wasn't really mad.

"You can't keep introducing yourself as Death. Freaks people out. Now me, I don't mind. Then again, I'm an escaped mental patient, so I guess that doesn't say much, does it?"

"Not so much, no," she replied with an amused chuckle.

They had just turned down a dimly lit street on their long trek back to Camview when Dorothy felt an unexpected wave of gratitude wash over her as she reflected on her wonderful night out.

"I think I get what fun is all about," she said after a moment. "Why people value it so much."

"Well, carnivals are kind of required by law to be fun. I think there are even fines and stuff if they aren't."

"I just want to say thank you, Curtis. That was wonderful. I never would have guessed. Experiencing is so much different than observing."

"Aw, don't get all sappy on me. It was my pleasure. See, I told you there were good things in life."

As if to provide a counterpoint to the statement, a rather large and heavy-bearded man stepped out of the shadows, his denim-clad mass blocking their path. With a creepy leer, he looked Dorothy over appreciatively.

"Hey there, pretty thing, how about you and me go have a little fun?"

Curtis took a half-step in front of her.

"You know, I don't really have a type, but you're definitely not it, big boy."

"Oh, a funny guy."

He roughly shoved Curtis to the side as if he were just a scrawny child, to which Dorothy instinctively, and without fear, raised her hand to use her powers to kill the man.

Of course nothing happened.

Oh come on. Seriously?

"What, you tryin' to use 'The Force' on me?" the man said with a malicious chuckle. A hungry look flashed in his eye and he made a move to grab her outstretched hand, but she was ready.

Dorothy quickly dropped her hand out of his reach and then swiftly delivered an Earth-shaking (or in this case ball-shattering) kick to the crotch, dropping him in his tracks.

Curtis stood there staring in awe, his jaw dropped wide open at what she had just done.

"Hooooly shit!" was all he could manage to say, a huge grin spreading across his face.

Dorothy realized the man would only stay fetal for so long, so she grabbed Curtis by the arm and pulled him down the street toward an area with more people, and more light.

Once they were safe on a well-lit stretch several blocks away, Curtis finally gathered his wits enough to say something coherent.

"That was awesome!" His grin was immense. "Where did you learn to do that? Some secret, grim reaper martial arts academy?"

"Saw it on TV."

He stopped in his tracks and stared at her. She was dead

serious, the realization of which made him burst out laughing even harder.

"And they say nothing good is ever on," he laughed, tears of mirth trickling from his eyes.

He couldn't stop his fits of laughter until a block later, when they paused at a sports bar with several TVs in the window. One television showed a newscast describing a narrowly averted tragedy with unexpectedly minor casualties. This time the scene was that of a tour bus carrying a load of senior citizens back to Arizona from a casino trip to Las Vegas.

It had been sideswiped by a car and had rolled off the road, but despite the advanced age of the passengers, miraculously, nearly everyone survived, though there were a few serious injuries.

"They should have died," Dorothy said with a sigh, her mood suddenly sullen.

"Jeez, maybe you really are Death on hiatus."

The news report had snapped her back to her dilemma, the fun of the night suddenly seeming far away.

"He was right. People are slipping through the cracks. It's not nearly as bad as I feared, but I don't know how bad it can become. Something is stemming the tide, so it could be years, even, but I must find a way back to set this right."

"How do you plan on doing that? I thought you said you didn't know how to get back."

"Retracing my steps didn't work, and I can't seem to die. I hate to say it but Pestilence might be my best bet."

"But that guy? Really? I mean, I don't mean to be super rude, but he's kind of an asshole."

"Well, he *is* a Horseman of the Apocalypse."

"Doesn't mean he has to be a complete tool."

"Maybe not, but whatever his personality quirks, it's imperative I figure out how to get back. You see what's happening, Curtis. Eventually it'll be more than just a few people here and there who survive when they shouldn't. This will continue to build." *And if that happens, then things will start to get bad. Really bad.*

"Okay. But one big question. Have you even figured out *why* you're here in the first place? Maybe that's a good place to start."

Gee, you think I haven't been wondering that?

"Thanks, that's a good point, Curtis," she replied, managing to say it without the razor-sharp sarcastic edge she had running through her mind.

Curtis stopped, a serious expression on his face for a change.

"Look, as much as I enjoy your company, you really don't have to go back with me, ya know. You've made it back outside. You're free."

"No, I must speak with him."

"But he's still in isolation."

"Even so, I have to find a way. He may be my best chance at getting back."

A realization flashed across Curtis's face. "Oh, shit," he said. "Look at the time! I wasn't paying attention. It's late! If you're coming back with me, we've gotta hustle!"

Daylight crept into the sky, and the sound of heavy footsteps echoed down the halls of Camview as the morning shift fanned out to begin their day, herding the easier patients to breakfast as chore number one.

It had become a two-tier feeding system, not by some grand design, but rather, out of necessity. There were only so many hands on deck to run the lines and watch their charges, and but a handful of difficult cases could easily throw the whole thing out of whack if there weren't enough staff nearby to keep them in check. Just one more side effect of Doctor Vaughan's cost-cutting maneuvers.

The patients confined to wheelchairs tended to be a bit challenging at times, but not a huge problem. Of course, having to use the hydraulic lifts to transfer them from their beds to their chairs and back could be time-consuming, pulling multiple nurses and orderlies from their other duties.

Really, though, it was the combative ones that made things difficult.

Staff had to sit with each one of them to not only make sure they ate their food, but also ensure it went in their mouth and wasn't flung at other patients or employees in a sudden outburst. They would have liked to just drug them up, but they had quickly found that the food-throwing instinct seemed to find a way to manifest regardless of how clouded a patient's mental state was.

Dorothy had found she was one of the people lumped in with the earlier group, as they had classified her as a fairly easy patient to handle, despite her earlier escape, and subsequent recapture. With exterior doors and connecting wings locked down, the staff felt secure in their new routine, and she wasn't perceived as a real problem.

Sure, she thought she was Death, but at least she wasn't *actually* killing off the patients and staff, and aside from her superior attitude, she was easy enough to deal with. Unfortunately for her, however, she had managed to make things difficult for Doctor Vaughan, and no matter what she did moving forward, she had already lodged herself quite firmly on his bad side.

The resonating footsteps moved closer to Dorothy's room, the sound of doors opening and shutting as they spilled their residents out in the hallway, one after another, until they stopped in front of her room. With only a quick knock's warning, her door swung open, and the morning nurse leaned in, glancing at the bed as she called out. "Wake up! Breakfast!"

There was no movement from under the sheets.

Slightly annoyed, the nurse stepped into the room and crossed to the bed, leaning over to reach down and shake the lump under the covers.

"I said breakfast."

Dorothy's head popped into view as she sleepily looked at the woman.

"Thank you, I'll be right there."

Satisfied, the nurse left the room, letting the door swing shut behind her as she continued down the hall.

Dorothy threw the blanket off, still wearing her outfit from the night before, having only just barely made it back into the ward before the lights came on and the morning shift began their routine.

That was too close, she thought as she pulled her psych ward clothes grabbed in their mad dash from the tunnels out from under her pillow, ten slipped out of her Black Sabbath T-shirt, and began dressing in her mental hospital attire.

Curtis had been a resident at the facility for quite some time, and his comings and goings were damn near an art form. He could improvise, if needed, but most importantly, he knew the ebbs and flows of the hospital and how to ride them as needed.

When the morning staff came to tell him it was breakfast time, they found him already standing in his room, bent in a strange pose twisting with one hand resting on his bed.

"Curtis, breakfast," the nurse said.

"Thanks, Myra."

"What on Earth are you doing?"

"Morning yoga. It's good for the circulation. You should join me sometime," he offered.

"Me? Yoga? Not likely. Now get cleaned up and join the others, all right? We'll see you in the chow hall."

"Okay, be there in a minute."

Myra closed the door behind her and continued on her rounds, leaving Curtis to what was apparently his latest habit.

If she only knew.

He untwisted his body, the motion letting his hospital clothes slide into place, then tucked his outside clothes under the mattress a bit more discreetly, flattening the lumps as best he could. Ideally, he'd have stashed his clothes in their usual place in the boiler network, but he and Dorothy were so late in returning that there really hadn't been any time.

Still, it hadn't gone that bad. He'd nearly been caught and had only barely broken a sweat. Of course, sweating while doing yoga was perfectly natural, so suspicion about his activities had been zero.

"Damn, I'm good," he chuckled to himself as he made his bed, smoothing it over one last time.

He stepped out of his room and began the slow stroll to breakfast, a rising commotion easily heard coming from one of the adjacent hallways. From what he could make of it, it sounded like one of the early riser group had chosen today to make a fuss, and a pretty sizable one at that. It seemed that someone was about to be put on the naughty list, and he seriously doubted they'd even get so much as a lump of coal in their stocking come holiday time.

All hands on deck quickly reacted to the disruption. Myra and two orderlies dropped what they were doing and answered the call for assistance, taking off down the hallway at a fast trot.

It was then that Curtis noticed the door left adjacent in their haste.

It was simply too tempting to pass up.

Curtis ambled over to the unattended supply room nonchalantly, then, trying to look as casual as possible, he took the knob in his hand and gave a gentle push. The door swung open.

He was both thrilled and amazed they'd forgotten to lock the door in the commotion, and who was he to pass up such a prime opportunity?

"Bingo!" he whispered to himself excitedly as he slipped into the room, careful to be quiet as he closed the door behind him.

He scanned the shelves, eyes lit up like a kid in a candy shop. The med cart with paper cups of pills sat unattended, and the normally locked cabinets were still open. The first one he looked in was full of gauze, tape, Band-Aids, and other basic first-aid gear.

"Lame," he muttered to himself as he dug through it. "Boring."

He opened another cabinet.

"Hmm, and what do we have here?" he mused. "Risperdal, Prozac, Xanax," he read the labels as he pocketed several small bottles, taken from the back so hopefully no one would notice their absence for a long, long time.

"Namenda, Ativan... ooh, what's this?" he said, holding up a forgotten and dusty bottle. "Chloroform." With a little smile, he briefly added it to the collection in his pocket, but the huge bulge it created gave him second thoughts about it.

Sure, it was neat to have, but Curtis knew that unlike movies and TV shows, it actually requires several minutes of breathing concentrated chloroform to knock someone out. Not terribly efficient, and not nearly as cool as films made it out to be.

With a reluctant sigh, he slid the bottle from his pocket and returned it to the cabinet, nevertheless happy with his other newfound treasures.

Peering out the door, he carefully made sure he left the room as he'd found it, then slipped back into the hallway, off to stash his new treasure in his room before heading to breakfast.

CHAPTER 16

Petty dictators always seem to enjoy giving rousing speeches to crowds of adoring followers. A personality trait of megalomaniacs in need of ego inflation and validation. Doctor Vaughan certainly fit the bill.

Lacking traditional means to bolster his own self-worth, at least so far as dictatorial stage performances go, Doctor Vaughan would, on occasion, stake out a section of his facility to perform amateur magic tricks for the patients under his care.

While, at face value, it may have seemed a good deed, done for the betterment of the morale of the Camview residents, the unsavory reality was Doctor Francis Xavier Vaughan wasn't a performer who enjoyed providing entertainment for his audience with his tricks and sleight of hand. No, his performance was influenced, and some might have even said purely driven by, a rather thinly veiled mean streak. Where those with good motives might take pleasure in the smiles and reactions of an audience's joyous amazement at his skills, he reveled in the feeling of superiority that tricking mental patients gave him.

Yes. Tricking mental patients.

Decidedly not cool.

Now, make no mistake, there certainly exist plenty of other men and women with nasty streaks in his profession, but more often than not, they had once dedicated their lives to helping others less fortunate until one day, it finally burned them out, leaving them bitter and resentful.

Doctor Vaughan was not one of these people.

He had *always* possessed a bit of a mean streak, along with a substantial ego problem, and his quirks and cruel habits had only strengthened with age. In fact, some employees mused (out of Vaughan's earshot, of course) that if he weren't the chief of staff of

Camview Psychiatric Hospital, with all his quirks and personality issues, he might very well have been a patient there.

As he performed a series of sleight-of-hand illusions for his small but captive audience, he felt his pride swell with every 'oooh' and 'aah' from his mostly sedated and easily impressed audience. The flashiness of his performance seemed to increase in tandem with his ego, growing as it was stroked.

While some people were addicted to drugs, Doctor Vaughan had a less chemical, yet equally addictive, proclivity.

He was ramping up his performance when the large door to the meeting room just down the hall swung open, releasing a quietly murmuring throng of patients, some of whom sported tear-reddened eyes.

Dorothy followed them out with a more-than-slightly annoyed expression plastered firmly on her face.

As was required of the more coherent patients, she had been forced to attend yet another mandated group therapy session, and was most certainly not amused. Instead of being enlightened and unburdened, she found herself in a foul mood after more than an hour of obnoxious rah-rah, feel-good therapy.

"No wonder these people are insane," she grumbled as she filed out of the room with the others. "These meetings are enough to drive anyone over the edge."

"Dorothy," a voice called after her.

It was Pam, the rotund, middle-aged woman in an ill-fitting cardigan tasked with running the group sessions.

"I really hope you'll share with the group next time," she cooed, resting her moist hand on Dorothy's shoulder.

Yeah, like that's going to happen, Dorothy thought, finally breaking free from Pam's clammy grip and seizing her chance to make an escape down the hall.

The sight of Doctor Vaughan performing his illusions as she walked toward the rec room refocused her attention. In a flash, she felt her annoyance zero in on a new target.

He was nearing the climax of his routine, twisting and turning his hands, flourishing a red handkerchief with delight. As Dorothy crossed his line of sight, his eyes flicked to her for a nanosecond, a brief expression of extreme annoyance flashing across his face, immediately replaced with a showman's grin, of course.

It was fast, but Dorothy saw.

Saw, and was not amused.

He moved his arms in small circles, then, with a quick flick of his wrist, the red handkerchief disappeared. His audience of lunatics was amazed and looked as if they were about to burst into applause, and Doctor Vaughan reveled in that moment.

"It's in his sleeve," Dorothy said, loud enough for all to hear.

Snapped rudely from his moment of glory, Doctor Vaughan shot her an openly angry look.

Dorothy just walked on by, not even slowing her stride.

He tried to regain his composure and continue, but already, the patients had started murmuring amongst themselves.

"What did she say about his sleeves?" asked one man.

"She said he put it up one."

"Really?"

Discomfited, Doctor Vaughan did his best to ignore them and continue with his routine, moving on quickly to another illusion, but one of the glassy-eyed patients curiously tugged on his sleeve.

"Where's the hanky?" the lunatic muttered.

"Get off of me, you idiot!" Doctor Vaughan growled as he shoved the man back into his seat, then continued with his show, eyes shooting daggers at Dorothy as she walked away.

For her part, Dorothy really didn't care about him or his impromptu magic show. She just didn't like his malicious nature and welcomed the opportunity to toss a monkey wrench in things. Still, she knew speaking out had been impulsive, and likely not the brightest thing she could have done. It would be wise to distance herself from him for the time being, and thus, she plopped down in a chair far away from Doctor Vaughan, well across the rec room.

I always get a really bad vibe from that guy, she thought as she tucked her legs up under her and settled deep into thought.

So, I'm trapped. Not only that, but aside from being stuck in human form, now it would seem my best bet to cross back is a Horseman of the Apocalypse, but he's also trapped in the nut house. She sighed. "Small comfort knowing that at least I'm not crazy," she muttered under her breath.

No sooner had the word "crazy" passed her lips, than a patient she didn't recognize came buzzing through the ward a red cape flapping behind him as he ran, his one good arm raised over his head. He didn't raise the other arm, she noted, as it sported a fresh cast. She also spotted a fair number of bruises on his face.

Are they beating this guy? she thought, her anger rising.

She soon had her answer, though, as he rounded a couch, speeding up to a full run, then crashed right into the edge of the ping pong table, tumbling to the floor beneath it, making Curtis miss his shot.

"Aww come on, Clark. Again?" he griped as the little white ball bounced merrily across the linoleum floor.

Clark hopped to his feet, banging his head on the table as he did, then took off again, gathering steam, his good arm over his head just like a superhero.

He's trying to fly, she realized. *But that still doesn't explain all the bruises.*

"Oh," she said, moments later.

He had bent his knees mid-stride and leapt into the air, but his attempt at flight, needless to say, was far less than a success.

Oh sure, Clark stayed aloft… for a millisecond that is, before he hit the floor hard, knocking the wind out of himself upon impact with the polished linoleum, then sliding headfirst into the wall.

He was dazed, winded, and writhing in obvious discomfort.

Well, that answers that question.

The pair of orderlies who had been watching his antics took their time walking over to him, apparently quite familiar with his shenanigans, finally dragging him to his feet and helping him limp out of the room to the nurse's station to get cleaned up.

Again.

Dorothy felt a tingle in the hairs on her neck. The feeling of eyes firmly upon her.

Shifting her gaze from the commotion and scanning the room, she noticed Doctor Vaughan staring at her, a particularly evil look beaming from his eyes as he wrapped up his magic show.

Dorothy was just thinking of some snarky observation to amuse herself when she was interrupted by Larry, the creepy orderly who had harassed her when she first arrived. Apparently, he had decided that this would be the perfect moment to hover near her.

Really near.

It was quite uncomfortable.

Oblivious to the effect his presence caused, or possibly very well aware of it and enjoying her discomfort, he stood there, right next to her chair, his crotch at face level, hips slightly thrust forward in her direction.

Whether it was done consciously or not, it was a seriously creepy move.

"Hey, beautiful," he finally leered, after hovering far too long. His hot-shot schtick struck her as a socially inept man acting in what he must have thought was a casual bad-boy way.

Oh you've got to be kidding me.

She, did her best to ignore him, hoping he'd catch the vibe and just go away, but, unfortunately, guys like him never seem to take the hint.

"How'd you like to come join me for a drink in the staff lounge?" he propositioned.

She quietly ignored him.

No, I wouldn't, you idiot. Take a hint and just go away!

But men like Larry always seemed to have a problem with subtlety. Like, they missed it entirely.

"You know, if you're real nice to me, I could even show you the new linen closet up on the third floor. It's really cozy. And really private."

She just couldn't take it anymore and fixed him with an icy-cold look.

"Hitting on a mental patient? Really?" Her gaze burned, and she noted his cheeks visibly flushed.

"Oh, you think you're so special?" he stammered. "Think I'm some kind of loser, don't you?" He was getting worked up, which was drawing attention to his plight. This wasn't going as he had planned. Not at all.

"I didn't say that, but now that you mention it, if the shoe fits..." she fired back. "Now go run along and play with the other creeps. Go on, shoo."

A few patients within earshot chuckled.

"I'll remember that," he said, face red, and glaring at her as he stormed off in a huff.

I'm just making friends left and right in this place.

A gravelly voice spoke in her ear.

"From what I hear, back in the old days, you would have just killed him with a glance."

Pestilence had quietly slid into the chair beside her while she was focused on her altercation.

Sloppy. I should have sensed him.

"I thought you were locked up," she said, for some reason only mildly surprised to see him out of confinement. "You know, I've been trying to find you."

"Yeah, I traded my antibiotics with one of the staff to let me out. His kid is sick, and drugs are really expensive, what with the crappy health plan they offer here. Of course, I made sure to cough on them first." A gurgling chuckle rumbled from his chest. "To thy nature be true, right?" he said with a crooked smile, then noticed something across the room. Something that made even him seem uncomfortable.

He twisted where he sat, shrinking in his chair, trying to blend in with the aged upholstery.

Dorothy looked over and realized Doctor Vaughan's angry gaze was now firmly fixed on Pestilence, eliciting the scab-covered man's worried reaction.

"All these new drugs," he said in a hushed tone. "It's getting harder and harder to do my job. I mean, look at me, I almost look healthy! Of course, Famine is doing quite well over in Africa, and War, well, I'm sure you've seen his handiwork in the Middle East all over the news. Man, that guy's got it good. I heard he was even a presidential advisor. Of course, he had his fingers in the election too, so that doesn't really surprise me—"

"Look," she interrupted him, staring intently into his bloodshot eyes, "my power is gone, and I need your help. I need to find out why I'm here, and how I can get back."

His shoulders relaxed ever so slightly as he reclined in his seat, a massively amused grin spreading across his features as he sized up the girl sitting across from him.

Then he laughed.

It started as a throaty chuckle and slowly grew into full-fledged howling, phlegm-rattled laughter, ramping up, getting louder and louder. Pestilence was not just laughing, he was crazy-guy laughing, and even in the nuthouse, people had started to take notice.

Curtis saw what was happening and dropped his ping pong paddle.

Pestilence was raving.

"You haven't figured that out yet?" he cried. "You, the great and mighty reaper! Ha, that's priceless! I could get back any time I want. Hell, I could even tell you how to do it too, if I wanted. But you know what? I'm not going to give Him the satisfaction! No, sir, I'm not going to bow down to the man anymore!"

Dorothy felt herself yanked from the chair, her feet slipping on the linoleum floor as she tried to gain her footing while being quickly hustled away from Pestilence as his raving grew worse.

She turned as best she could in her attacker's grip, ready for a fight, but it was Curtis dragging her away, a worried and determined look on his face.

"What the hell are you doing? I need to talk to him!"

"Shut up, and don't move if you want to ever get out of here," he hissed in an urgent whisper.

No sooner had he spoken than she became aware of the rapidly approaching sound of rattling keys bouncing against a *very* large leg.

A huge orderly she had never seen before came barreling through the open rec room door. He was enormous, close to seven feet tall, with a nasty sunburn making his bald head shed little bits of skin.

As he grew near, she could see the name on his muscle-stretched shirt said *Stan,* and for just a moment the light caught his eyes in a way that made them glow ever-so-slightly red. She flashed a questioning look at Curtis, but he hadn't seemed to notice the man's unusual peepers.

Huh, she thought. *So that's the infamous Big Stan. This is odd, and there's a little too much space between the S and the TAN on that shirt, almost like there should be another letter there.*

Unlike the other staff, Stan ignored the lunatic's scabby nastiness and grabbed the man calling himself Pestilence with his bare hands, yanking him unceremoniously to his feet.

"Well, if it isn't crazy Jerry," he growled. "It's been a while. I haven't seen you since what? Was it over at Riverwood Psychiatric?"

Pestilence/Jerry squirmed in his rock-solid grip, but wasn't going anywhere. Not on Stan's watch.

"So who are we this time, then? You still think you're a cowboy?"

"I'm not a cowboy. I'm a Horseman of the Apocalypse, you mendicant!" he spat venomously. "You may think you can keep me down, but you can't keep me out!"

The huge man started moving toward the door. The poor fellow in his crushing grip had no choice but to move with him.

"Oh, so that's how it is? Well, how'd you like a case of the crabs? Or maybe the Black Plague!"

Stan was clearly unimpressed as he shouldered past a group of doped-up wanderers gathered near the door and pulled Pestilence into the hallway.

"Enough of your ridiculous babble. You're going into isolation, little man."

When the screaming, flailing patient had finally been hauled out of the room, Curtis relaxed his grip on Dorothy's arm, a relieved look passing over his face.

"Trust me, you want to stay clear of Big Stan."

"How can he treat people like that?" she asked, still shaken from her encounter with the man claiming to be Pestilence.

"Stan just thinks he's doing his job, which includes roughing up your pal if need be. Some folks compartmentalize like that, know what I mean?" He looked in her eyes with both curiosity as well as concern and saw she was more upset than he'd first thought.

"Hey, you okay?" he asked.

"He said he knows how I can get back."

"Do you believe him?"

"I don't know. Yes, I suppose. I mean, I have no choice, right? Nothing so far has worked, and believe me, I've tried. Do you think I'd still be in here otherwise? If there is a chance he really knows how I can get back, I have to find out. Eventually, the un-deaths will add up. There's a balance to be maintained, and even with the others picking up the slack, the big question is, how long will it take?"

Curtis studied his troubled new friend's face for a moment. She was throttling back, but still rattled by the encounter.

Dorothy slowly forced herself to calm down as the seconds ticked by.

"Well, it looks like it really is going to be a while before you get a chance to talk to him again," Curtis said. "I don't think he'll be bribing his way out this time. Isolation lockdown is pretty serious, especially since Vaughan saw the whole thing."

"Wait, how did you know he bribe—"

"Word gets around," he replied with a wink. "C'mon, let's do something to cheer you up. What say you to a nice late dinner out tonight? Stan's obviously on day shift today, so we should be able to swing it."

After that little ordeal, getting out for a few hours sounds wonderful.

"All right, you're on. I'll even wear my best Black Sabbath T-shirt."

"Great, meet me after bed check. Tonight will be something special, I promise," he said with a gleam in his eye. "Oh, and I found you something nice to wear."

CHAPTER 17

The restaurant Curtis selected for their much-needed outing was one of the trendy new places that had recently opened as the area's shift from urban blight to hip arts district had accelerated.

A multitude of interesting establishments had sprung up, like those hearty wildflowers that somehow take root in a rocky terrain. What they offered was an adventurous and staggering variety of cuisine, ranging from traditional, to fusion, all the way to obscure molecular gastronomy cuisine.

Moving in lock-step with the changing neighborhood, older go-tos had begun recreating themselves into more trend-friendly establishments. It was a sound business tactic, though not always popular with the locals, who watched their favorite eateries and bars transform from comfy neighborhood joints into flavor-of-the-week gastro-pubs and hipster-overrun dive bars. Dive bars that now served fifteen-dollar drinks, and weren't really dive bars at all any more.

The invasion of hipsters had brought with it a freedom of dress, and Curtis's early eighties outfit, which would have been out of place just a few years prior, now fit right in.

He had also managed to score something nice for Dorothy to wear, and the knee-length black dress she sported was not only tasteful, but also quite stylish. Even without makeup, her defined cheekbones and contrasting pale skin and dark hair made her stand out in the crowd of hipsters in overpriced vintage clothes mixed with Botoxed bleached blondes with heavy-handed makeup.

Curtis, always a gentleman, held the antique patina door open for his friend, then approached the hostess, flashing his brightest smile.

"Good evening, sir. How many in your party?"

"Yes," he replied.

The hostess looked confused. "Um, that isn't a yes or no question, sir."

Dorothy rolled her eyes and elbowed him in the ribs.

"Two, please," she said.

"Right this way," replied the hostess, giving Curtis a curious sideways glance as she showed them to their seats.

As they slid into the tastefully styled booth, Dorothy couldn't help but notice the subtle but unmistakable smell of new vinyl. The table top was a mélange of dried flowers and foreign coins, sealed in a thick layer of resin. Small candles in colored glass holders flickered softly, giving the whole place a rather cozy ambiance.

"Okay, you did good. This place is really nice," she had to admit.

"I had a feeling you'd like it," he replied, before being distracted by an overly made-up woman staring at her phone as she texted, carrying a teacup dog in her handbag.

"Lady, the dog has four legs and you only have two. It should be carrying you, not the other way around!"

Dorothy shot him a quieting look, but it merely bounced off him, like water off a duck's back, as his attention shifted focus to the man the dog's owner had come in with. A sugar daddy, most likely, he was many years older and sporting a broad-collared shirt that was open a few buttons too many, showing off his rain-forest-dense thatch of chest hair.

"Will ya look at that guy. Damn, he needs Head, Shoulders, Neck, Back, and probably Ass shampoo! What is he, a Yeti?"

"Shut up, Curtis, you're not in Camview. Don't make a scene," Dorothy whispered.

"Don't worry, I know," he calmly replied.

Dorothy wasn't so sure.

They had just received a basket of bread, which Curtis was happily munching on while he and Dorothy scanned the menu, when his attention was caught by a man coming back from the Indian-Thai fusion buffet that sat in hot chafing dishes near the bar. He stared in amazement at the enormous mountain of food piled on the man's plate as he made his way back to his table.

"Hey, buddy," Curtis said, a bit too loud, "when a buffet says 'all you can eat' it's just an offer, not a challenge!"

"Are you trying to get us kicked out before we even eat?" Dorothy hissed, kicking him under the table as she shot him an icy glare.

"Come on," he replied with a mischievous grin. "Am I that guy?"

Yes, he was that guy.

They walked down the street, still hungry, booted unceremoniously from the eatery, having only managed to nibble on bread.

They hadn't even ordered.

"Okay, I'm sorry I ruined dinner, but—"

"The sign said 'Employees Only,' Curtis," she shot back.

"Yeah, well, I'm employed."

She raised an eyebrow.

"Okay, I *was* employed. Come on, it looked interesting. Besides…" He proudly held out a fistful of crumpled bills.

"Where did you get that?"

"Five-finger discount. Took it from the apron of that goon who threw us out. I tell ya, men in aprons. Sheesh."

She shook her head in disappointment. "Bad Karma, Curtis."

He chuckled lightheartedly.

"What? Are you going to come get me?" he joked.

She fixed him with a serious stare, only the slightest hint of amusement peeking through the corners of her eyes.

"Someday, Curtis. Someday," she deadpanned.

He stopped laughing. "Hey, not cool, man."

Dorothy let a tiny grin peek through and, after a pause, decided to finally let him off the hook.

"So how much do you have?"

"About eighty bucks, give or take." He paused and sized up his friend. "You know, I've been meaning to mention it, you've changed a lot since you came back to Camview. You talk different. Less stilted and stiff. More slang. You seem to have found yourself a sense of humor too."

"Well, I was stuck watching reality TV every night for days on end. I guess it must've rubbed off a bit."

"Eww, not exactly the culture you want to absorb. But seriously, I don't get it. How can a super-powered, millennia-old entity be so out of touch?"

"Told ya, observing is different than experiencing," she replied. "But I'm working on it. I've been making an effort to pick up cultural references. Slang. Stuff to help me fit in. If I'm stuck here any length of time, blending in will be to my benefit."

He studied her for a moment as they walked down the street. She had most certainly changed, and to his mind, it was definitely for the better.

"You said you have eighty dollars?" she asked. "Well, we might as well make the most of your wicked ways. I owe someone who helped me out when I first became trapped in this realm and would like to repay her kindness. This neighborhood looks familiar, and her place isn't too far, I think. If we can find her building, I can slip it under her door."

"But I'm hunnnngry," whined Curtis.

Well, she does work in a diner. I suppose it wouldn't hurt to drop by. Besides, it would probably be the right thing to do to let her know I'm all right.

"Fine," she said after a moment's thought. "If I have my bearings right, she works in a diner just down the road a ways, I believe. We can grab a bus and stop there for some food. That way you can eat, and I can repay her favor. Win-win."

"Works for me!" he said. Just knowing he'd soon be filling his belly, Curtis's attitude took an immediate turn for the better. In fact, he seemed downright chipper.

Dorothy and Curtis hopped off the bus and walked the half-block to the next intersection. Dorothy's sense of direction was on-target as the storefronts looked familiar to her.

"We go right up ahead," she guided.

They rounded the corner and began walking the remaining blocks to the diner where Angela worked. It was pretty late, and the streets were quiet with just light traffic passing by. It was quiet enough, in fact, that Dorothy managed to unintentionally catch snippets of the conversation a pair of Goth girls across the street were having.

What she heard made her stop in her tracks.

"—and then, when we'd finished the diagram, Corvus lit the final candle and we said the incantation," said the slight girl with dyed-black hair, who called herself Raven.

"Wait, you mean Daniel, right?" asked her friend, Strange Emily.

"Corvus. You've got to call him by his warlock name."

The teen rolled her eyes.

"Fine. *Corvus.* So? Did it work?"

Raven smiled.

"The dark powers were with us. Corvus and I closed the circle and banished the spirit from our realm, straight to the Underworld." Raven was gloating, looking downright pleased with herself, and not even her thick black makeup could conceal her happy grin.

"Whoa, that's so cool!" chirped Emily. "So that old book you picked up from Dante's Books was the real deal? Awesome!"

Dorothy's ears had picked up the key points of the duo's conversation, and it had most certainly captured her attention.

They know a way!

Her focus intensified on the pair as she darted across the street, ignoring traffic, oblivious to the cars narrowly missing her. Fortunately for her, traffic was light.

Still, it was all Curtis could do to keep up.

"Whoa, cars!" he chimed out in warning. "Hello? Hey, wait up!" he called as he scampered after her.

"I heard what you said!" Dorothy abruptly halted in front of the teenagers, blocking their path. The intensity of her gaze was more than a little unsettling.

"You have the power. I need you to use it on me."

The teens stared, confused.

"You must kill me!" Dorothy continued. "Cross me to the other side at once!"

Curtis stepped in front of her, breaking her laser-focused gaze, which provided a small window for the two girls to sidestep the crazy woman in black and scurry away.

"Where are you going?" she blurted, surprised by their flight. "Wait! I need you to cross me back!"

"Don't mind her!" Curtis called after them. "She's just pulling your leg. Ha, what a joker, right?" He pulled his friend by the arm, dragging her away from the fleeing girls.

"Come on, you're scaring the spooky kids, and I'm still hungry."

She watched the black-garbed figures shrink in the distance.

"But they said—"

"Just kids talking out their ass."

"But—"

"Oy, focus! Me. Belly. Food!" he said, turning her attention to the neon sign now visible a block ahead.

As she stepped into the diner, well rested, and entering via the front door this time, Dorothy felt an unusual sensation of warmth and relief flow over her.

Comfort.

Safety.

That's strange, she mused. *Why do I feel so at home here?*

The restaurant was fairly empty, as it had grown late since Curtis had managed to get them thrown out of their original destination. He bounced from foot to foot, doing the pee-pee dance as he tugged on Dorothy's sleeve while she scanned the mostly empty establishment.

"What?" she finally said, annoyed at his constant tugging.

"Sixteenth letter!" he replied.

"What? What are you talking about, Curtis?"

He stared at her a moment, waiting before finally giving up.

"Where's the can?" he inquired.

"The what?"

"The bathroom. I gotta go!"

Ah yes, she was well-acquainted with that particular room in this establishment.

Note to self: no coffee this time.

"It's down that hall past the register."

"Thanks!"

Curtis headed off toward the restrooms just as Angela emerged from the kitchen. He took her lightly by the arm, drawing her aside for a moment.

Angela listened to him, then looked over and saw Dorothy, a smile lighting up her face as she recognized the former stray she'd taken in off the street. Curtis said something else to her, then continued down the hall as Angela hurried over to greet the girl who thought she was Death.

"I'm so glad you're okay," she said. "I was worried what could have happened to you."

"I had some trouble," Dorothy replied. "But it seems to be sorting itself out. Somewhat, anyway." She reached into her pocket and removed a wad of bills. "Here," she said, holding them out to Angela. "You took me in. You fed me. I owe you a debt for your kindness."

"Oh, hell, I only made you some eggs, girl, and I should have thrown those pills out ages ago. Damn hazard they were."

I shouldn't have used them in her bathroom. That was an inconsiderate mistake on my part. One that could have caused her a lot of trouble.

"In any case, you helped me. Please take it, if not for putting me up, then at least for feeding me."

Angela smiled, but didn't take the money.

"You want to pay someone back? How about Randy over there?" She gestured to the man sitting alone in a far booth, picking at his food, engrossed a dog-eared paperback. "You were kind of rude to him that night, but he still bought you dinner."

"That was him?"

"Uh-huh," Angela said as she looked at him, a hint of sadness in her eyes. "He's a good egg, that one. One of the few regulars I'd call a friend."

"He seemed nice enough."

Angie got a gleam in her eye and leaned toward Dorothy conspiratorially, looking over her shoulder to make sure Randy wasn't watching.

"I probably shouldn't say anything," she began, "but you were the first woman he's shown any interest in since he lost his wife. It's been tough for the guy. Maybe go talk to him for a bit. He seemed to take a shine to you."

"Um, I didn't really talk with him much the other night," Dorothy blurted.

"Well, I think you should go keep him company anyway."

He was interested in me, looking like a raggedy popsicle, fresh off the street? Strange taste.

"Well, I would, but I'm here with a friend. He just went to the bathroom and should be back any time now."

"Oh, that nice man? I almost forgot, he said to tell you, he said he had an emergency come up and would be back as soon as he could."

"Wait, he left?"

"Headed right out the back door."

Shit! Why is Curtis ditching me? Oh I am going to kick his ass when he gets back! she thought. *If he gets back,* she added with a tinge of worry.

The girl who thought she was Death came to the sudden realization that she may very well be on her own again.

"Look, you don't have to talk to Randy. I didn't mean to pressure you. I guess sometimes maybe I stick my nose in other people's business a bit too much. Sit anywhere you like, hon, up to you. I've gotta finish up my side work, but I'll come check on ya in a few. It's really great to see that you're all right."

Angela stepped back behind the counter to pour a warm-up for the lone older woman, who was slowly chewing her way through a grilled cheese with a cup of tomato soup as she sat alone, the whole counter to herself.

Dorothy stood there a moment, scanning the establishment, pondering her next move.

Oh, hell, why not? she finally decided, and started walking across the restaurant.

"Hey, mind if I join you?" she asked over Randy's shoulder as she approached his booth.

He stopped reading and looked up from his book. Now that she was in a better frame of mind than that first evening, Dorothy was able to give him a proper once-over.

She hadn't paid much attention to him on their first encounter, but now that she had a moment to give him a proper look, she noted that he was a rather handsome man in his early thirties. He had a bit of scruff to his cheeks, which she found appealing for some reason, and was casually dressed but well groomed. The faded flannel he wore fit his broad shoulders well, the specks of paint that didn't quite wash out only visible if you looked closely enough.

Strangely, she felt a momentary flash of an unfamiliar warm-tightness flush across her lower belly.

That was odd, she mused.

He put a two-dollar bill in the book to mark his place as he put it down, his face warming with a broad smile when recognition clicked and he realized who was talking to him.

Like a true gentleman, he rose and offered her a seat.

"Oh, it's you! Please, sit, I'd be delighted for the company."

"Thanks," she said, slipping into the vinyl booth. *Was this the booth I sat in before?* she found herself wondering.

"Hey," he said as he slid back to his seat, "I just have to ask.

Um, you're not having coffee again, are you?"

Dorothy chuckled. Ice officially broken.

"Yeah, sorry about that. It was my first cup. Kinda ran right through me."

"Your first cup? What, you mean ever?"

She nodded her head.

"Hang on, are you some kind of Mormon or something? Wait, I know. Never talk about religion or politics on a first date."

"Oh, is that what this is?"

"Let a boy have his fantasy, okay?"

She smiled at the man sitting across from her, and, strangely enough, found him rather charming. In the short time she'd known Curtis, he had always been the playful big brother to her, hitting her on the arm, giving her good-natured grief, and poking fun. This, however, felt different.

A good kind of different.

Flirting with a cute boy was a new thing for her, and much to her surprise, she found she quite liked it.

Hours had passed, but it felt like it had just been minutes, as Randy regaled her with stories of his ridiculous adventures. The pair had quickly become comfortable with each other, and the conversation flowed without any effort. For the most part, Randy had done the majority of the talking, as Dorothy was careful to heed Curtis's advice.

Don't introduce yourself as Death to everyone. Don't freak people out. She repeated it to herself like a mantra, and so far, the man sitting across from her at the table seemed quite happy with her being there.

"So I woke up to the sound of sheep and this clanging bell," he said. "I jumped out of my sleeping bag and go running out of my tent, buck-naked, and next thing you know, I find myself standing in the middle of a herd of sheep in nothing but my birthday suit, face-to-face with an eighty-year-old shepherd and her great-granddaughter."

"Sounds like you gave them a good show," Dorothy said with a laugh.

"I don't know about that, but I sure hope that poor girl didn't need too much therapy."

"You must've had a wonderful time there," she mused, staring into his eyes. Dorothy admired the passion with which he spoke.

"Yeah, that was a great trip," he said. "But, there are so many places I still want to go. Galapagos, Vietnam, Easter Island, maybe Thailand. You ever been there?"

"Oh, yes. December 2004 stands out."

"The killer tsunami? You were there for that? That's crazy! What was it like?"

Oops.

"Later," she said, quickly changing the topic. "First tell me more about Greece."

"Greece. Right. Well, after the sheep fiasco, I met up with some Aussie backpackers, and we decided to hitchhike to Athens."

Dodged that bullet, she thought.

"Well, you know how Aussies are, so there we were, standing on the side of the road…"

Randy continued with his stories, and as he did, Dorothy let her guard down further. She found herself, much to her surprise, simply relaxing on a nice evening out. Angela dropped by from time to time, and the three of them laughed at his ridiculous stories as the late hours passed.

Meanwhile, across the street in a shadowy doorway, Curtis watched his friend as she let her hair down a bit and enjoyed herself. He was tempted to head back in, but seeing her in such good spirits, he decided to hang back a while longer, smiling cheerfully, and quite pleased with himself.

It was well past midnight, though not yet approaching the time when it transitions from very late at night to very early in the morning.

Dorothy and Randy exited the diner, waving good night to

Angela as they stepped out into the night, both feeling better than they had in a long time. As they paused outside the diner's doors, they found themselves standing a little closer than new acquaintances normally would.

It was an unexpected situation for the boy with the broken heart and the girl who thought she was Death.

"So, uh, can I walk you home?" he asked.

"Um, that's okay. I'll be fine," Dorothy answered, then followed quickly with, "Actually, I'm waiting for a friend."

"A friend is meeting you at this hour?"

"Well, more like my roommate, and I'm kind of locked out of our place otherwise, so…"

"Oh, gotcha."

They stood there silently for a moment, uncomfortable for the first time that evening as the seconds suddenly began to feel like minutes.

"So, am I going to see you again?" Randy suddenly blurted out. "Wait," he said, "that sounded pathetic. What I meant to say was, when will I see you again? Can I take you to dinner sometime? A proper dinner, not like last time."

Dorothy felt a little flutter in her chest and a flush in her cheeks. *It's just the cold.*

"I don't really get out much…"

"Come one, live a little."

She considered the offer a moment. *He's nice, but I need to stay focused. The only thing that matters is crossing back. I'll just be polite and tell him I can't.*

The thought had just run through her mind when Randy rummaged in his coat pocket and pulled out his blue enamel pocket watch. He flicked the lid open and held it to the light, checking the time.

Dorothy's eyes widened at the sight of the unusual timepiece. She couldn't help but recognize it immediately.

It can't just be a coincidence.

"Okay," she blurted. "You're on."

Randy misread her excitement, taking it as interest in him, rather than Dorothy's sudden realization that this man with the unique pocket watch might be more important in the scheme of things than she'd originally realized.

"Great!" he said, reaching for his cell phone. "Let me get your number."

Number? Shit, what am I supposed to say, "Just call Camview Psychiatric Hospital and ask for Death?"

"Hey, let's just meet here next time. That's easiest," she improvised.

"What, with your coffee experience you still have good memories of this place?"

"I do now," she said, smiling at him.

She noted the sudden hint of red in his cheeks and wondered if he was blushing, or was it just the chilly night air? Either way, Randy was glad for the follow-up date.

"Okay, here it shall be," he said. "Let's say Tuesday at eight?"

"I don't think I can get out before Friday. And let's make it ten. I'm kinda locked into something before then."

"Friday at ten it is. I'll see you then."

He paused a moment, his body language awkward as his mind tried to process what had just happened.

A date with a girl. How long had it been?

He studied her for a moment, unsure if he should give her a hug, or try for a kiss. Maybe just a handshake.

God, I'm so out of practice with this stuff, he lamented. With a shrug, he opted for the easiest choice rather than make a fool of himself.

"All right, see ya Tuesday!" Randy said, then turned and walked down the street, looking back and smiling at her before rounding the corner.

"Wow, a new boyfriend already. No wonder you wanted to come here," Curtis laughed as he popped out of the shadows.

Dorothy smacked him, startled.

"Don't do that!"

He leaned on her playfully as the duo started walking back toward the late bus that would take them home to Camview.

"Come on, we need to get back."

"Where did you go, Curtis? You ditched me."

He was about to answer, when they came upon a middle-aged bag lady. She was there alone, wrapped in blankets, her legs sprawled across the sidewalk as she mumbled to herself while sitting in a doorway.

Curtis, unlike the residents of the neighborhood, stopped in his tracks and looked at the woman. Dorothy could see his permanently jovial mood shift as a flash of pity and concern filled his eyes. That out-of-character, un-Curtis look only lasted a moment, though, and quick as a flash his goofy self was back, grinning happily as he dug through his pockets.

"Right. Now, let's see, where is it?" he said as he dug deeper. "Ah, here we go! Risperdal." He held a small pill bottle up to the streetlight to better read the label. "Now I want you to take this once in the morning and once at night, all right? Better take it with some food too," he said, handing her some crumpled bills from his pocket. "There, that'll get you started."

For whatever reason, the woman stopped her mumbling and took the offering from him, her eyes seeming to clear from her demented haze, if only just for a moment.

"Yes, Doctor, thank you."

"My pleasure. Now remember, twice a day, and get some food. I'll see you in three weeks."

With that, they continued on their way. Dorothy looked at him, confused and not understanding what had just happened.

"What? Just doing my good deed for the day. Not like Camview's going to miss them."

They walked in silence for a moment.

"So, you didn't answer me," she said a bit more pointedly. "Where did you run off to?"

He held up a fistful of cash in one hand, while the other appeared from the depths of his coat pocket holding a watch, an iPhone and a cheap gold plated money clip with a rhinestone dollar sign on it.

"I had some stuff to take care of," he replied. "You know, a little three-card Monty, some back alley dice..."

"And what exactly did you say to Angela? You ditched me, Curtis!"

"Oh, I just told her I was your doctor, and getting you out and about was part of your therapy. Your treatment is coming along quite nicely, I must say. I must be pretty good."

She fixed him with a cold stare.

"What?" he said with a laugh. "I didn't ditch you, I had things to do. Besides, you seemed to be in good hands. Good, strong, manly hands."

Dorothy felt her face growing flushed and warm.

"Aah, learning her way around a strange new world, meeting exciting new people. Our little Dorothy's not in Kansas anymore!"

"Why do people keep saying that?" she asked, exasperated.

"Movie night tomorrow," he said with a wink. "You'll see."

CHAPTER 18

There was a buzz in the air as movie night wrapped up. Even the more sedated of the group seemed energized by the entertainment, though in their case that often meant they just drooled with more enthusiasm. Regardless, the crowd, as a whole, seemed to be in a particularly cheerful mindset as the credits scrolled.

Beckman had stopped talking about tax codes for once, and even Stein, the germaphobe, seemed to not mind being in close proximity to so many potential Patient Zeroes.

As they filed out of the room, Nurse Myra took the plain, silver DVD out of the player and placed it back in its case.

"Thanks, Myra!" Curtis called out to her from across the room. "Great film, as always!"

The tired and overworked woman just nodded to him and shuffled back to her nurse's station.

A bit of tension crackled through the front of the line as the crowd bottlenecked on the way out. As if the universe could sense that little bit of stress as it worked its way back into an otherwise Zen evening, Stein found himself stuck in the exit line, the unfortunate target of a good-natured, but nevertheless annoying bombardment.

"Knock-knock."

"Oh, come on, not now, Warren," Stein sighed. "No knock knock jokes tonight, okay?" He really should have learned by now.

"Who's there?" Warren replied, his enthusiasm growing.

"No, I didn't—Oh, shut up, it's time for bed."

"Shut up it's time for bed who?"

"Seriously?" lamented Stein. "Can't someone please medicate him? Just for a day? Please?"

Fortunately for him, the crowd surged, and he was pushed

across the threshold, out into the freedom of the nice, wide hallway, where he could make his escape.

Dorothy and Curtis were in no rush, and took their time, leaving at the tail end of the pack. She didn't seem amused, per se, but she did appear a bit more enlightened, at least about the constant references to her name.

"Okay, Curtis. I get it now."

"See?"

"Yeah. But flying monkeys? Really?"

Curtis was still riding the high of the film he adored. "Yeah, right?" he said with glee. "I told you it was awesome!"

The line thinned, and they finally made it to the hallway. Curtis turned to the left to head back to his room, but Dorothy turned the other direction, heading straight toward the isolation area.

"Hey, this way."

"I'll catch up," she said. "I've got something I need to do."

He threw her a concerned look but thought better of trying to talk her out of it.

"Okay, just be careful."

"Yes, Dad," she replied with a smirk.

Walking the facility end-to-end down the dimly lit corridors, Big Stan rattled each and every door securing the path between wings. He made a point to give an extra tug on any and all doors leading to the outside, just to be sure.

They may have been checked by the security staff and hooked to alarms to boot, but Doctor Vaughan had made his wishes clear, and Stan sure as hell wasn't going to have any patients going MIA on his watch.

"East hall three, secure," he said into his walkie-talkie. "West, how are we looking?"

"Finishing up now," was the reply.

"Copy that. Movie over?"

"Copy, it's done and they're heading back to their rooms."

"Copy, out."

Stan pulled the keys from his hip and opened the door to the next wing, slamming it shut behind him with a bang, yanking it hard to ensure it was firmly locked before continuing his rounds.

Dorothy moved quietly down the hallway, tip-toeing silently in her slippered feet, sticking to the walls and ducking under the windows of the break room and nurse's station as she passed by.

With great caution, she quietly made her way down the hall, scanning the locked doors as she passed, finally stopping near the end of the hall.

I think this is the one.

"Hey," she whispered to the thick metal door. "Can you hear me? Are you there?"

The silence stretched on.

Could they have moved him? What if he's in a different wing?

From behind the thick door she heard a phlegmy cough, followed by a familiar rumbling voice asking a question with an obvious answer.

"So, you're still here? Now, why is that? Thought you'd be long gone by now."

"I need to speak with you about getting back... but also about something else," she said, hesitating, unsure what her course of action should be. "You seem to know what's going on here. Could a human somehow be connected with me being trapped in this realm? Maybe if they possessed a relic of some sort? A timepiece, maybe?"

A throaty chuckle found its way to her ears from behind the door.

"I thought you would have figured this all out by now. They always made you out to be so smart."

"Look, jackass, I just need you to tell me this one thing," she shot back. She was quickly getting pissed at the uncooperative man inconveniently locked out of reach. "That, and how I can cross back."

"Oh, well, the second part is simple," he replied, but she heard no more as a calloused hand closed on her shoulder and yanked her to her feet.

"Just what do you think you're doing?"

She didn't recognize the orderly.

He must only work this wing. He doesn't know who I am.

"Um, I got turned around. Merry go round, round and round. Where's my... I can't find my room."

Man, that was a horrible crazy person impersonation.

"See your nutjob friends down there?" He gestured to the open door down the hall. "Go follow them and don't wander off. This is an isolation area. You aren't supposed to be here."

He actually bought it? Maybe I'm better at this than I thought. Curtis must be rubbing off on me. I wonder if that's a good thing.

"Thank you, yes, thank you... walking, walking... down the hall," she muttered as she made her way to rejoin the others while the orderly just watched her go, a potential bullet dodged.

Dorothy may have pulled one over on the night orderly, but any feeling of relief she may have had evaporated the following afternoon when she was summoned to Doctor Vaughan's office.

Sitting on the uncomfortable bench outside his door, she was forced to wait. There was nowhere for her to go, no chance of escape, but he had decided to make a statement. So it was she found herself flanked by two of his more intimidating minions as she sat outside his closed door.

Inside his office, Doctor Vaughan was unusually relaxed as he chatted on the phone, fiddling with his magic hanky absentmindedly, not a care in the world, at least not for the moment, as he ignored the flashing intercom light on his desk.

"Of course, it was my pleasure. I'm glad you like it," he cooed into the phone. His voice was calmer than likely anyone on staff had ever heard directed their way. "Yes," he said soothingly, "I'll be happy to show you how to use it when I see you this weekend. No, it's no bother, I don't mind at all. It just plugs in to the USB port— No, not that one, it's the one on the side—"

A knock on his door interrupted him, then his secretary poked her head inside.

"I'm sorry to disturb you Doctor Vaughan. The patient you asked to see—"

He held up a single finger and fixed her with his gaze.

One. Moment.

Wisely, the secretary didn't utter another syllable as she waited for him to finish.

"Okay, I have to go. Yes, I know. Yes, but I really do have to go now. All right, see you this weekend. I love you too, Mom."

He hung up the phone, and as he glanced at his aide, the familiar hardness slid across his visage.

"Send her in."

The two burly men roughly ushered Dorothy through his door, closing it behind her with an ominous click.

Taking more detailed notice of his office this time, she realized it was designed not so much as a workspace than as a way for him to impress and intimidate.

The books were arranged so visitors could see the multitude of heavy titles in difficult subjects, the animal heads were carefully mounted, a slight downward tilt to them, their gaze aimed at the space in front of his desk. Even his degrees and awards were hung with an audience in mind.

Of course, what most didn't know was that only the certificates closest to the door, and thus within reading range, were real. The half dozen impressive-looking certificates and awards mounted behind his desk were nothing more than Latin gibberish with large foil-embossed stamps.

Her eyesight was better than most, as was her grasp of Latin, and Dorothy wondered if any of his visitors ever called him out on his fraudulent papers, or if she was the only one to notice.

Judging by the look in his eye, she decided today wouldn't be a good day to ask.

Doctor Vaughan eyeballed her disdainfully from behind his immaculately polished desk, the dark wood's deep luster nearly glowing from the many hours it had been polished over the years. He silently, and deliberately, tucked his magic hanky into his coat pocket, staring her down as he did so.

Ah, so he's still upset about that, she thought.

She had realized, as she observed him in his personal environment within the hospital, that his magic tricks were just a tactic used to demonstrate his superior skills and knowledge. To show he was more clever. That he was the boss. A reinforcement of his power that allowed him to keep control of the facility, both patients and staff.

He was all about being one move ahead of everyone else, and she'd rocked that boat.

More than once.

Doctor Vaughan's gaze shifted briefly to the old picture of his wife on his desk. *Uncanny,* he thought as he looked at the troublesome young woman standing before him.

"Please, sit," he finally said. The 'please' sounded more like a statement of habit than an invitation born of politeness.

Pulling out one of the chairs facing his desk, Dorothy slowly sat down, unsure what he had in store for her. For several moments he just stared at her. Obviously this was meant to make her uncomfortable, but as the good doctor was already learning, his manipulative tricks didn't seem to work on this one.

Hey, she thought as she looked up at him, *why up? These chairs are much lower than his,* she realized with silent amusement. *It figures. This guy just loves playing intimidation games.*

Seeing her sitting comfortably, and not at all intimidated by his routine, he finally broke the silence.

"So, Dorothy. My nurses tell me that you persist in this fantasy that you are a supernatural being. That you are in fact Death."

"I'm telling the truth."

A hint of deep annoyance flashed briefly across his face. "And have you ever noticed that it's always the sane people who say they're crazy, while the crazy ones keep insisting they are perfectly sane? So, would you care to try again?"

"I am Death. I can't help being what I was created as," she replied without hesitation.

He was not amused.

"I get it," he sneered. "'I'm not bad, I'm just drawn that way,' is that it?" She looked at him, confused but not intimidated.

To him, it was inconceivable she wouldn't react at all to his machinations. He realized, to his consternation, that he simply didn't know how to handle this difficult patient, and she had already very nearly cost him his job. His kingdom. The frustration as that settled in was finally too much to contain, and his displeasure began boiling to the surface.

In an instant, Doctor Vaughan's anger jumped from a three to a nine, threatening to go all the way to eleven.

"You listen to me, you will stop this charade at once!" he fumed. "You are a disruptive presence in my facility, and I will not have you upsetting the other patients with your nonsense."

"I'm not doing anything to your patients."

"You are an instigator! Your actions cost this facility money and resources we cannot afford to spend. My job is hard enough without you bringing me under even more scrutiny." He paused, catching himself. He was giving away too much information in his anger.

Doctor Vaughan forced himself to take a deep breath, after which his tone calmed somewhat, though the message was just as fierce.

"Either you shape up and get with the program here, or I swear you won't see the outside of these walls again until you're so old that the death you always talk about will be the one thing you pray for. Do I make my self clear?"

She nodded affirmatively and wisely kept her mouth shut.

"Good. Now get out!"

The patients who had been lingering in the hallway nearby couldn't help but overhear his outburst, despite the soundproofing of his door. When Dorothy exited his office, they quickly looked away.

Even the heavily medicated ones knew something was very

wrong at Doctor Vaughan's office, and like prey animals sensing a hungry predator, they all scurried off en masse lest they become his next meal.

A funk had settled over Dorothy after the meeting. Doctor Vaughan had never liked her, she knew that, but this was excessive, even for him. She realized that there was a distinct possibility that things might actually get worse before they got better. For now, however, she would carry on, and hopefully cross back over before any further problems arose.

She sat at a small table, deep in thought, managing to force down her lunch, despite not being hungry. Beckman sat across from her, but he was engrossed in his plate and hadn't even noticed that she had once more arranged the plastic utensils by size and type.

As she digested her food, the sustenance fueled her speeding mind, and Dorothy soon felt the dark mood left by Doctor Vaughan's rant slowly begin to lift. It was Friday, after all, and she had something to look forward to at ten o'clock.

I wonder if he'll remember to come.

"Hello? Earth to Dorothy." Curtis waved his hand in front of her face as he pulled up a seat next to her. "Daydreaming isn't like you."

"Just thinking," she said, her focus shifting to her friend.

Beckman meanwhile was quietly counting kernels of corn on his plate. "Forty-three, forty-four, forty-five, forty-six..."

Dorothy noticed the overly amused expression on Curtis's face as he watched the pair.

"What?" she queried.

He chuckled. "I guess I should have figured you two would be hanging out together," he said, barely suppressing a laugh.

Both Dorothy and Beckman looked at him with puzzled expressions.

"Oh, come on, really?" he said. "You're, well, you. And he used to work for the IRS."

No reaction.

"Seriously? Anyone?"

"She got chewed out by Doctor Vaughan again," Beckman explained.

A look of concern flashed across Curtis's face. "Hey, I told you, you need to be careful with that guy. He really seems to have it in for you."

"I still don't understand why. I did him no wrong."

"It's worse than that. You aren't afraid of him. He feels it weakens him in the eyes of the others, and that's a dangerous thing."

"Well, he's a fraud."

"I don't care what he is, you just be careful, okay?"

"Mmmhmm." She nodded. *It's kind of nice having someone looking out for me, even if I don't really need it.* "Hey, I forgot to ask you. I need some decent clothes, think you can get me some?"

Beckman, at the mention of an acquisition of any kind, slipped into his Rain Man-esque recitation of tax codes.

"Clothing can be a write-off if used in a business endeavor. Fifty percent deductible while sleeping in your own domicile, but one hundred percent deductible if purchased while away from your place of residence."

"Thanks, Beckman," Curtis said as he shifted his gaze to Dorothy and raised an eyebrow. "Decent clothes? I think I can manage something."

She stared at him, and he knew exactly what that look meant. He sighed.

Man, she is so predictable.

"Yes," he relented. "They'll be black."

An upbeat electro-swing mix was pumping from the speakers as Randy buzzed about his apartment, a jumble of nerves, though he knew he really didn't have reason to be jittery. Still, he just couldn't help it.

A pile of selected, and then discarded, shirts and pants lay strewn on his bed. He realized he was more than just a little bit nervous about his first actual date in more years than he cared to count. Making himself stop for a second, Randy noticed the growing pile and consciously tried to slow his roll as he dressed.

"Come on, it's just a date. It's no big deal," he muttered to himself as he slipped into an acceptable pair of pants and pulled on his shoes.

It had taken far longer than he'd planned, but he was finally clothed, coiffed, and ready to head out. He turned off his stereo, pocketed his keys and wallet, killed the lights, and headed for the door.

Something caught his eye, though, and he stopped in his tracks.

His gaze had fallen on a small, silver-framed picture of his deceased wife.

He stood there for what felt like forever, though it was really just a minute, hesitant and suddenly a bit unsure as he was about to actually go on his first date since his wife had died.

"No, this is okay, Randy. This is good. You can do this," he said to himself.

He then took a deep breath and walked out the door.

CHAPTER 19

Friday night finally arrived, and Curtis and Dorothy silently slipped out of the ventilation grate, dropping down into the alley, unnoticed. Curtis was sporting his usual tussled mop of bedhead, which, lucky for him, was fashionable at the moment, and was, much to Dorothy's surprise, wearing a relatively normal outfit of jeans, T-shirt, and jacket.

Unsurprisingly, Dorothy was clad entirely in black, sporting a pair of sleek, form-fitting slacks, along with a slightly opalescent black top that was snug in just the right places.

Curtis did a good job, she had noted as she dressed. *I wonder where in the world he manages to get all this stuff.*

"How do I look?"

It wasn't Dorothy who had asked.

The question was posed by the Y-chromosome sporting member of the duo as they weaved down side streets, avoiding the routes frequented by Camview staff.

"You look quite dapper, Curtis," she complimented.

"No, seriously, be honest. I can take it."

"Seriously, you look fine." She couldn't help but be amused at his sudden attention to his appearance.

"You're not just saying that?"

"Curtis, you look great. Give it a rest."

"All right, I'll take your word for it. Come on, we've gotta hustle. The bus should be here soon."

They walked several more blocks, getting good and clear of Camview's looming shadow, then hopped their ride across town. On another occasion, they might not have minded strolling much of the several miles on foot; after all, it was nice to be out in the fresh air. Tonight, however, they were on a timetable.

A few streets from the diner, they exited the bus and cautiously darted through what was surprisingly heavy traffic for that time of night, to get to the correct side of the thoroughfare. As they neared the diner, Curtis stopped and looked questioningly at Dorothy.

"Are you *sure* it's okay if I come along?" he asked.

"Of course. Why wouldn't it be?"

"Well," he began, "bringing a friend on a date *is* kinda weird."

"A date?"

He smiled. She really was clueless when it came to men.

"Trust me," he said. "Even if it isn't technically a date, he'd like it to be."

They started walking again, Curtis with a little spring in his step, while the girl trying her best not to call herself Death, at least not to strangers, kept pace, pondering what he had just said.

Angela happened to be wiping down the counter nearest the door when they entered, a broad smile forming when she saw who had just walked in.

"Hey, Dorothy! Glad you're back," she said. Then, recognizing Curtis, more by his hair than his new attire, "And nice to see you again doctor."

"Please, just call me Curtis."

"Okay, Curtis it is," she said, blushing a little from the penetrating warmth of his friendly smile. Looking at Dorothy, she gestured to the booth in the back. "Randy's over there, hon."

"Thanks."

Dorothy strolled toward him, noticing that Randy had dressed a bit nicer than his usual torn jeans and worn flannel for the night out.

Does he really think this is a date?

Curtis followed close behind, almost as excited as Dorothy was pretending not to be.

Seeing them approach, Randy rose to greet them, looking her over (in a non-creepy way) as she crossed the floor, appreciating just how well she cleaned up.

"Wow, you look amazing," he gushed.

Dorothy couldn't help but blush slightly from the attention.

"Aww, thank you," Curtis chimed in, gesturing to his new clothes. "I just threw this outfit together."

His quip drew a laugh, and in that unspoken guy code amongst men, Randy somehow instinctively recognized Curtis as Dorothy's platonic friend, not romantic competition. The escaped mental patient extended his hand in greeting.

"I'm Curtis, Dorothy's flatmate. My date got tied up tonight, a real nutcase that one. I hope you don't mind my tagging along."

"No, of course not," Randy replied.

"Great, thanks. Ya know, it's really nice to finally meet you. She's been talking about you all week."

What? I did no such thing.

Dorothy shot him a glare, but immediately wiped it from her face as Randy turned to look at her, smiling, an eyebrow raised in a silent query.

She hadn't noticed until now just how perfect his teeth were, she realized.

"Come on, you two, pull up a seat," he invited, and the three of them

settled down onto the inviting cushioned vinyl.

As during her prior outing with Randy, Dorothy found the conversation flowed effortlessly, only this time there was the periodic comic interjection of her "roommate" adding to the mix. Fortunately, the boys seemed to really hit it off and had bonded over a shared love of post-modern surrealist artists and cheesy comedy movies.

"…and so he says, 'Okay, I'll try the soup. Where's the spoon?' 'Aha!'"

Curtis and Randy laughed heartily at the shared joke, and Dorothy chuckled as well, though she had no idea what they were talking about. She found herself realizing Randy's laugh had the most wonderfully pure sound to her ears.

She felt a slight flutter in her stomach.

Really? This again? she grumbled to herself.

"Excuse me, fellas. I think even half a cup of that coffee might have been too much," she said as she rose to her feet and excused herself to head to the restroom.

"Hurry back now!" Curtis called after her as he stole a spoonful of her sundae with an exaggerated scoop.

"Promise we won't eat all your dessert while you're gone," Randy added with a chuckle, reaching dramatically for his own spoon.

She looked back at them over her shoulder, an amused little smile on her face as she made her way down the hall.

The two men laughed, but in a display of true chivalry, refrained from stealing any more of her ice cream. The three of them had been cracking each other up almost non-stop, and it was good.

After far too long spending his days and nights as a hermit, Randy realized just how good it felt to interact with people again.

"So, Randy," Curtis's face took on a slightly serious look, "you like Dorothy, right?"

Ah, so here comes the protective friend talk, he thought.

"What sane man wouldn't?" he replied.

"Listen, you're a good dude, and she's obviously into you, and I'm glad. But you've gotta understand something." He looked toward the restrooms, making sure she hadn't come out yet. "Look, don't tell her I told you this, but she's recently gone through some, uh, pretty serious emotional stuff. I probably shouldn't even be telling you this, but you seem like a cool guy, and I wouldn't want it to get between you two if things progress."

"What happened?" Randy asked, truly concerned. Curtis could read the sincerity in his face. A good sign, in his book, so he continued on.

"Like I said, it's not really my place to get into it. I just wanted to give you a heads-up that since that stuff happened, well, once in a while, if things get tough, she can get overwhelmed and—well, she can get a little, uh, wonky."

"Define wonky."

He paused, then decided it was best to simply tell him.

"Well, one of the manifestations is she sometimes thinks she is Death in human form."

"Whoa, seriously?" Randy had expected maybe eating binges, or perhaps even talking to cats or something, but this was a bit unexpected. "Is she schizophrenic or something? My kid's moving back in with me this summer. I can't get involved in anything that jeopardizes her staying with me."

"Nah, it's nothing dangerous. It's just how her psyche copes," Curtis replied. "Defense mechanism. Look, we all just humor her. I mean it doesn't hurt anyone, it's just her quirk. She doesn't really talk about it much—all I'm saying is, if she brings it up, try to be understanding and cut her a little slack, okay? That's all I'm asking. Life's been kinda tough for her lately, but she's a really good person."

Though he didn't know why, he was really starting to like the lovely girl he'd only just met, so with but a moment's hesitation, Randy agreed.

"That's really out there, but she seems to be a really cool girl. I'll try my best. You've got my word on it."

Right answer, thought Curtis with a smile.

"You know, you're one awesome dude, Randy."

"I've been told as much," he chuckled.

Dorothy returned to the table shortly thereafter to find the men hamming it up, but with a faint hint of something heavier in the air that she couldn't quite place.

"Ahh, much better," she sighed as she slid back into her seat. "So what've you boys been talking about while I was away?"

Almost as one, they replied.

"Nothing."

She cocked an eyebrow. *Nothing my ass. What're you up to, Curtis?*

As if he had heard her thought, Curtis shifted his gaze to her and flashed his brightest smile and gave her a mischievous wink.

"Hey, you guys wanna get out of here?" he asked.

The trio walked down the street like the Three Amigos, albeit minus the six-shooters, *fabulous* outfits, and plethora of piñatas, still riding the high of their uproarious evening.

I'm having a really great time, Randy thought, surprised at the evening's turn of events. *And we haven't even been drinking. Most excellent.*

Curtis fished in his pocket, pulling out a few crumpled bills as they neared a middle-aged homeless woman quietly reading a dog-eared book by the light of a shop's doorway. She seemed calm, at ease, and quite content to sit where she was, reading as if she hadn't a care in the world.

Dorothy recognized her as they approached.

The woman who looked up at them had clear eyes, a bit more flesh on her face, and a gaze that seemed more than a little bit coherent. A smile blossomed as she saw Curtis approach. He leaned down and pressed the money into her hand, then gave her an affectionate pat on the shoulder as they continued down the way.

Just when I think he can't surprise me any further, Dorothy thought as they continued down the street.

Several blocks later they found themselves in a hip section of the neighborhood, populated by pop-up boutiques and quirky little local stores.

"Hey, you guys cool with stopping in the record shop?" Randy asked.

"Sure, but are they still open this late?" Curtis asked.

"Should be. It's Friday night," he replied, pulling out his watch as they neared the illuminated storefront. He flipped it open, the light reflected across the face of the vintage timepiece briefly dancing in front of Dorothy's eyes.

Okay, there definitely has to be something about this guy. About that watch.

"That's a beautiful watch, Randy, really unusual. Is it a family heirloom?" she queried.

"Oh, this old thing?" Randy replied. "Nah, thrift store find. Total score, right?"

He handed it to her for a closer look. The girl who thought she was Death examined it closely, studying every detail, looking for some special meaning. Fine lines of copper graced the case with a delicate design interwoven in the blue enamel, she noted, but otherwise, nothing seemed otherworldly.

"Thought it'd be a cool conversation piece," he said. "Thanks for proving me right, by the way," he grinned at her.

Curtis had popped into the shop while they were looking at Randy's timepiece, and he quickly emerged excited by what he'd seen.

"Hey guys, they've got a used DVD section too! Some really cool stuff, even out-of-print special editions! You've gotta check this out!"

"Okay, we're coming," Dorothy called to him, handing Randy his watch.

Her fingers brushed his palm, just briefly, but she felt a strange tingle in her belly when they did. If he had felt it too, he showed no outward signs.

Inside the shop, the comforting warmth and faint smell of slightly dusty records seemed to put Randy in an even better mood.

"I love this place. It's one of the last great neighborhood record shops. Others may try to recreate the feel, but this place is the real deal. It's been here for decades."

"So I take it you're a vinyl fan?" Dorothy asked.

"I have something of a collection, you could say."

"Such a Renaissance man," she joked at him.

The inside of the store was actually pretty impressive. She could see why Randy liked it, and why Curtis was so enthused. It really was a treasure trove of unusual goodies that seemed right up his alley.

The vinyl bins were full of plastic-sleeved LPs, all organized by genre, with a few bins set aside for bargains. The truly collectible bits and a smattering of colored vinyl and picture discs rested prominently on the shelves behind the cash register.

A motley assortment of posters covered the walls, and even the ceiling, but rather than making the establishment feel claustrophobic, they only served to increase the sense of intimacy. This was a place for people who loved their music.

The video section, though smaller, was equally well stocked with quality films.

Curtis bounded over excitedly with a find in his hand.

"*One Flew Over the Cuckoo's Nest* Criterion Edition!" He popped the case open, revealing a plain DVD with a green band circling the center. He held it up to the light and scanned the disc for any scratches. It was immaculate.

"Oh, man, this is such a great movie!" he gushed. Dorothy looked at him skeptically.

"Oh?"

"That's some classic Nicholson," Randy interjected. "Though the whole mental institution aspect was a bit of a downer. Good thing there aren't awful facilities like that anymore."

"Yeah," Curtis quickly chimed in. "I hear those places are much more cheerful nowadays, and run by really kind-hearted people to boot. Isn't that right, Dorothy?" He gave her a look, and to his relief, she got the hint.

"Oh, um, yeah. What he said." Curtis nearly cringed at her lack of enthusiasm. It was not an Oscar-worthy performance, but it would have to suffice.

"Hey, guys," Randy said, "I don't want you to think you have to leave on my account, but I've got an early meeting with my gallery owner tomorrow, so I've got to get home for the night. Sorry to cut out on ya."

"It's all good," said Curtis. "We're coming."

He jammed his hands in his pockets and strolled toward the door, waving a cheerful goodnight to the cashier on the way out. Dorothy and Randy didn't notice the DVD-shaped bulge in his coat pocket, and fortunately for him, neither did the clerk.

"That was an excellent suggestion, Randy," he said as they

stepped out into the night. "Truly excellent."

He nudged Dorothy and raised an eyebrow as a thought illuminated his brain.

"Stan's working days next week," he whispered to her conspiratorially.

Okay? she thought. *And I care about that why, exactly?*

"Hey Randy," he blurted, "Dorothy was wondering if you're free next Wednesday night for another outing. Whaddya say?"

Wait, I what? She flashed a perplexed look at Curtis, who promptly ignored it.

"Wednesday? I'll still be out of town visiting my daughter. Can we do Thursday?"

"Yeah, we can do Thursday," Curtis replied.

"In that case, yeah. That'd be great," Randy replied, pleased by the promise of another evening out with the girl he'd taken a shine to, even if it meant her goofy roommate would likely be tagging along again as well.

"Cool, we'll come meet ya. Same place at ten." Curtis had it all planned out. "See ya then!" he called out, taking Dorothy by the arm as they went their separate ways.

"Okay, see you then," Randy replied. "Looking forward to it!"

"Yeah, me too. See you later," was all Dorothy managed as she was pulled off down the street. She noticed he was really picking up the pace.

"What's the hurry, Curtis?"

"I forgot, Nurse Myra called in sick today, and I don't know who they got to cover for her. We should be okay, Stan almost never works doubles, but I don't want to press our luck."

Back in Camview's dimmed halls, a lone orderly walked the hallway on his periodic sweep of the patient wings.

Curtis and Dorothy had quickly changed into their patient attire in the boiler room, waiting until they heard his footsteps fade before they emerged from their secret escape. They crept silently down the hall toward their rooms. When they arrived at Dorothy's closed door, she gave it a gentle tug, opening it with barely a sound.

"Okay, I'll see you in the morning," she whispered. "And hey, I didn't say it before, but thanks for coming along. That really went well, and I'm glad you were there. We'll talk more about it in the morning. I don't know why, but I think somehow Randy and his watch may be tied up in why I'm stuck here. It's good to have another set of eyes on things, and I want your take on it."

"My pleasure. And besides, it was really fun. He seems like a good guy."

"You think?"

"Yeah, I do. Anyway, get some sleep. We've got plenty of time to talk tomorrow."

Dorothy slipped quietly into her room and eased the door shut behind her.

Curtis turned and stealthed—yes, it was a verb in Curtis's own personal lexicon—down the hall toward his room.

As he rounded the corner, his face ran smack into a very large chest.

"What do you think you're doing?" an intimidating voice rumbled.

Big Stan.

Apparently, this was one of those rare occasions where he *did* pick up the overtime shift.

"Oh, hi, Stan. I'm just out for a stroll. You know, good for the circulation."

"You know the rules," the large man growled as he took Curtis by the arm, dragging him toward his room. "No wandering allowed after lights-out."

Stan pulled his door open and unceremoniously dumped Curtis on his bed.

"Stay put," he said, then shut the door.

"Will do. Thank you, Stanley," Curtis called through the door. "And a lovely evening to you too!" he added for good measure.

The weeks that followed were relatively uneventful, at least compared to prior ones. Dorothy made several attempts to gain access to the alleged Horseman of the Apocalypse, but she found herself thwarted at every turn as she tried to reach the man claiming to be Pestilence. The one man who claimed he could get her back where she belonged.

Finally, her luck seemed to change for the better when he was moved from the isolation lockdown wing back to his old room. His door was still locked at all times, but at least she could talk to him. For some reason, however, he had gone silent, and no matter what she said, her pleas for information went unanswered.

In lieu of grilling him for details on how to return to her own realm, Dorothy resolved to fully commit herself to investigating the odd blue watch, and the man who owned it. At least for the time being.

It had all begun immediately after being distracted by the shiny timepiece that fateful day. It was her hope that pursuing that lead would get her home. It might even provide a far better way back than whatever option Pestilence might have.

Curtis and Dorothy were fortunate, for a stretch. Big Stan had taken to working the day shifts with some regularity, leaving them free, or at least with a better likelihood to sneak out come the late-shift. They had kept their outings relatively simple, namely meeting up with Randy on Fridays. They also occasionally managed to sneak out on other nights, adventures during which they simply explored the city, keeping an eye out for possible clues to help speed Dorothy's return.

Dorothy didn't mind the excursions, even if they were unfruitful. It was fascinating to her, seeing all these different and new things.

Another constant was that whatever they were up to on the outside, every night when they returned, Dorothy would stop and seek answers at Pestilence's door, just in case.

And every night, he would not reply.

CHAPTER 20

The television anchors had a "serious" look for delivering disturbing news. It was a look Dorothy was hoping to see with more regularity.

Some things were still fatal, she was thrilled to learn. Decapitation. Being crushed by several tons of debris, or blown into little pieces. Of course there were other equally horrific ways of dying that seemed to be inescapable despite her absence, but the drama-hungry mainstream media didn't seem to follow those stories.

Nevertheless, knowing the slack was being picked up, at least for the most egregious deaths, put Dorothy's mind a tiny bit more at ease. If only she knew exactly who was helping, and just how much they were doing in her absence. Working from hypotheticals frustrated her to no end.

As she lay in her bed in the darkest hours of the night, she would often find herself painfully awake, staring at the ceiling as her mind kept churning away. While some people would perhaps relax every muscle, from their toes to their ears, or count fluffy, white sheep until they drifted off, Dorothy passed the time with math. It was a somewhat morbid calculation she had fixated on, but if it helped pass the time, why not?

One hundred years, give or take.

That was how long she figured humanity had until the un-deaths reached critical mass. She couldn't be sure, though, as she was basing her estimates from the very rough numbers extrapolated from assorted news reports. Also not figured into her calculations was what would happen when the existing medical system was simply overwhelmed by the massive increase in patients sucking up resources in the days to come.

One hundred years? That was a best-case scenario. Realistically, things would most likely get a whole lot worse, a whole lot faster.

For all her worrying, however, none of her fears were developing in a manner visible to the rest of the world. She had only been gone a few months, and the ripple effect hadn't even begun to spread. To anyone she spoke to, her talk about the dead overflowing the world seemed like pure crazy-talk.

Just wait until the bodies really start piling up, she consoled herself. *But if I can just figure out how to set this right, they'll never even know.*

For just a second, she found herself wishing things actually would fall apart, just to prove she wasn't crazy.

No. The world is managing for the moment, and vindicating as that might be, I have a job to do. If that damned Horseman won't help, then my best hope lies with Randy and that weird talisman watch.

Despite the seriousness of the matter, a slight smile found its way to her lips at the thought of their next outing.

As the clock ticked closer to midnight, Dorothy, Randy, and Curtis found themselves gallivanting once more, a merry trio running amok in one of the older parts of town, where quirk hadn't yet been priced out by chic.

More than a month had passed since their first meeting, and several enjoyable nights of banter were firmly tucked under their belts. It was a short time, at least in the grand scheme of things, but as happens when like-minded individuals meet, the three had become thick as thieves in no time at all.

They wandered the streets, exploring. The majority of the shops had closed much, much earlier, leaving but a few stragglers cruising the sidewalks with them at that late hour.

As the trio made their way down the quiet road, Dorothy and Randy seemed to subconsciously gravitate closer to one another. Curtis had noticed Randy's frequent glances, and, being the friend that he was, he continuously, yet nonchalantly, nudged them closer together when opportunity arose as they strolled.

Dorothy paused, the chipped and faded gilt lettering in the window of a used book store catching her eye in the dim light.

Dante's Books, it read.

Why is that name so familiar? She furrowed her brow in thought before it came rushing back to her.

That first night heading to the diner with Curtis.

The two Goth girls.

A way to cross back.

"Okay, I guess we're going in here," Curtis noted as Dorothy barreled right past him and Randy, moving full steam ahead toward the front door. The bell mounted to the doorframe sounded a faint jingle as she breezed across the threshold.

The boys followed her in, and found themselves browsing around the unusual little shop, seeing what interesting treasures they might uncover. Dorothy, however, had a sense of purpose, if only she could zero in on what she was looking for.

With no real target in mind, but knowing it had to be there somewhere, she scanned the store again and again until finally something caught her eye.

There we go, she thought as she strode to a small section of shelves with a small sign that read *Occult* marking its contents.

It was a collection of mostly new editions, but the shelves were home to a few older, cloth and leather-bound tomes as well. She gazed at the rows of titles, her eyes dancing across the spines of the books as she searched for something that might provide a few answers, or better yet, might even help her get back where she belonged.

The pale, goateed shopkeeper noticed the slender girl in black staring particularly intently at the shelves in *that* section.

He sat quietly, observing her for a few moments from his perch across the room, then slowly rose to his feet, carefully placing a worn, paper marker in his book before casually gliding over to the section of somewhat obscure books where his unusual young customer stood.

"Looking for anything in particular?" he asked the girl who thought she was Death.

"I... I don't know," she replied. *What exactly am I looking for, anyway?*

Studying her with a knowing look, the old shopkeeper asked, "Well, then, what sort of thing did you have in mind?"

She paused, not knowing how to phrase it in any coherent, non-crazy-sounding manner. She looked into the eyes of the kindly man and decided to just be frank.

"Okay," she began, "say, for example, what if a supernatural entity was somehow trapped in a human body against their will? How would they free themselves?"

"A ghost, or something more... powerful?"

"Not a ghost."

The shopkeeper looked at her with a gaze not of skepticism, but rather with an engaged and intrigued look on his face. He thought for a moment, then mounted a small ladder, climbing near to a very high section of the shelf.

"Ah, I see," he said, scanning the covers. "That's a tough one. What did this being do wrong, if you don't mind my asking?"

"I don't know."

"Hmmm, interesting. One would normally assume it was punishment of some sort, but could it possibly be something else? A quest, perhaps?"

I swear, old man, if I knew I'd tell you.

"Like I said, I don't know," she replied.

A bemused look flashed across his face. "I see. Well, that is a pickle indeed."

"Tell me about it," Dorothy groused.

The man's fingers slowed as he scanned the spines of a few older editions until they rested on one particularly aged and worn book.

"Ah, yes. There it is," he said, pulling it free from the shelf. "It's an older edition, but this may be of some use. I think you'll find chapter eleven particularly interesting."

"How much?"

"It's not in the best of condition, so for you, let's say seven dollars, tax included."

She pulled a few crumpled bills from her pocket and handed them to the man as he slid the book into a paper bag for her.

"You know," he posited, "in a situation such as you described, one would usually expect some sort of otherworldly assistance. It's almost expected, in fact. Maybe an oracle, or a talisman, or perhaps a guide of some sort."

A thought flashed. *A guide, indeed. Like someone who knows how to get me home for instance. And an oracle...* Her mind replayed the words of the drunken man on the street. The man who knew so much about an antique blue pocketwatch. *The keeper of the blue watch, perhaps? Is he the key? Is the watch? But then what about Pestilence? Could he be a guide? As a Horseman, it would make sense. He's still the most likely way back.*

The shopkeeper watched her standing there, furrowing her brow with interest. Dorothy quickly realized she was making a bit of a scene, albeit a silent one.

"Well... great. Thank you so much for your help!" she chirped and headed for the door. Curtis noticed and tugged Randy's sleeve.

"Hey dude, I think this means we're going. Dorothy, wait for us!"

"Man, she's moving. I wonder what's up," Randy blurted, a bit surprised at her sudden departure. Curtis, for once, was equally out of the loop.

"Don't know, but she's heading toward home. I guess we're calling it a night. We'll catch ya next week, okay?"

"Sounds good."

"Cool, see ya then!" Curtis said, then spun to catch up to his fast-walking friend. "Hey, wait up!"

"You *will* tell me."

Silence.

Dorothy was crouched by Pestilence's door, looking far more intense than usual, and for a girl who thought she was Death, that really was saying something.

I'd bust this door down if I could, you uncooperative little— She took a breath and forced herself to calm down. When she spoke again she sounded in control and sure of herself.

"You have no choice in this. You will tell me what I ask of you, Horseman."

She heard a slight rustling behind the closed door. Then, after so many days of silence, he finally spoke to her.

"Oh, will I now?" he chuckled, amused rather than intimidated by her tone.

"Yes," she answered, angry and confident.

"You sure about that?" He continued to chuckle. She was about to answer when she caught sight of an orderly making rounds at the far end of the hall. Again, her plans were interrupted by fate.

It will have to wait.

"When you get out," she muttered, an unsettling, cold certainty in her voice, "you and I are going to have a little chat."

A rumbling, phlegmy laugh began to rise from his room. With attention drawn her way, she stood and did the one thing she could.

She played crazy and walked right toward the orderly.

"Back to your room," the man said. "You can't be out wandering at night."

"No wandering, no wandering, yes, yes, to the room," she babbled, then scampered down the hall, pausing for just a moment at one of the chalkboards covered with patients' scribbles and designs, deftly snagging a piece of chalk and tucking it in her waistband as she continued on her way.

Back in the familiar confines of her room, Dorothy wrapped her pale hands around the tubular metal frame of her bed and quietly pulled it from the wall, creating a blank canvas of floor space, easily hidden by sliding the bed back in place. Fortunately the legs weren't long. They didn't want patients who fell from bed to hurt themselves, so unless someone was on all fours, they'd never see clearly under the bed.

Dorothy sat on the floor and crossed her legs, easing into a comfortable position as she opened her new book to a dog-eared page. She skimmed for a while, ascertaining which sections might be of the most use to her.

One chapter had multiple incantations and runes that seemed appropriate, and after carefully studying the symbols for a bit, she cautiously, and ever-so-slowly, began drawing them on the floor.

No, that's not right.

Dissatisfied with her first attempt, she erased the chalk lines with the palm of her hand.

It has to be perfect, she thought as she focused on the nuances of the symbols and tried again.

The next morning, despite waking up within the walls of Camview, Dorothy rolled out of bed feeling like a million bucks. Action was far better than spinning her wheels, and she now had a new possibility of getting back. Something within her control. Something to constructively direct her energies toward. Something that didn't rely on an irritating Horseman of the Apocalypse.

Sure, it would take time to see if it panned out, but it was so much better than her previous state of seemingly endless standby.

Another thing had begun bothering her less as well.

Being locked up.

She knew that, for the time being, she was stuck spending her days in Camview, waiting for the man claiming to be Pestilence to be released back into the ward, but at least a night or two per week were her own. When not working on her runes, studying the old text, she found herself looking forward to her next outing with Curtis and her charming new watch-owning friend.

She stretched languidly as she rose, then stepped out of her room, walking to the dining hall well before most of the other patients had even risen. With a little quiet time to herself, she poured a cup of herbal tea—no caffeine in the mental hospital, thank you very much—and curled up on one of the vacant lounge chairs near the windows.

The sunlight felt excellent as it warmed her feet while she sipped from the steaming mug.

Not a bad day, she mused, surprisingly content, even in her current confines. *Let's see what tonight brings.*

"I said they're pretty good!" Curtis yelled over the music booming from the sizable speakers.

Mad Hatter's was a relatively small club that had been around for ages, and despite the newer venues popping up, the place had serious street-cred, and still managed to book some of the best local talent. This night was no exception.

Curtis had found out about it from a fellow music lover while watching a street performer busking for change months before he had even met Dorothy. Now seemed like a perfect time to finally check it out. Seeing the smiles on his friends' faces, he was not disappointed with the decision.

The set ended, and the trio stepped outside into the fresh air, smiling as the good vibe moved right along with them.

"Great band!" Randy said with a grin. "I can't believe I hadn't heard of this place."

"Been wanting to check it out for months now, so this all worked out perfectly," Curtis replied.

"Yeah, good call, man. So do you guys want to get some munchies? There's a Szechuan place that's open late off the number three Line on the way back."

"How spicy is it?" Dorothy asked. "I don't want to destroy my innards, after all."

"Come on, spice is nice!" Curtis chided.

Randy took her side. "You saw what a simple cup of coffee could do, so I understand the concern." He turned to Dorothy. "Don't worry, you can order mild, no problem."

"In that case, let's do it."

"Sweet. I'll grab our coats. Be right back." Randy winnowed his way through the crowd toward the coat check.

Curtis grabbed Dorothy's arm and quickly guided her away from the front of the club.

"Hey, what are you doing?" she asked, annoyed at the

manhandling.

He pointed to the smokers who had congregated at the front door.

"Sorry. It's just we can't go back smelling like smoke. We'd be busted the second they caught a whiff of us."

"I don't know how I didn't even think of that," she said, mildly annoyed with herself.

"Not something you'd usually have to think about," he comforted her. "I'm just looking out for you. It's my job, after all."

Randy wove his way through the crowd back to his friends, coats flopped over his arm.

"Thanks, Randy!" Curtis said as he lifted his off the pile.

"For you, m'lady." Randy held up Dorothy's coat for her as she slid into its warmth.

"How chivalrous of you."

"I try."

"At least she isn't making you drop your cape across a puddle for her," Curtis said with a laugh.

"Just wait until it rains," she joked.

"Come on, you two, let's get a move-on. I am hon-gray!"

Over the course of the next several weeks, Randy would continuously steer them toward festive activities they could enjoy as a group. The one constant, regardless of where they went and what they did, was the vibe. The trio never ceased to have a good time, and laughter was their common language.

Another constant, though one that took more time to present itself, was that Dorothy and Randy seemed to continually gravitate closer to one another as they roamed the streets on their adventures. That and the interesting fact that Dorothy in general was starting to look less like the girl who thought she was Death, and more like a happy young woman.

Randy, likewise, was undergoing an attitude shift. For the first time in years, he finally looked less like a depressed widower and more like a contented man. One rapidly becoming enamored of the lovely young woman he found in his company once a week. He really would have liked to see her more often, and, to his fortune, a rather nasty flu making the rounds of Camview would shortly grant his wish.

With schedules shuffled and shifted to cover sick employees, Dorothy and Curtis found themselves left to their own devices as the nasty flu spread through the staff. Pestilence had gone silent once more, and Dorothy found her frequent visits to his locked door filled more with frustration than hope.

A whole different set of emotions churned in Dorothy as the days passed as well. While she was certainly looking forward to seeing Randy again, she also found herself deeply engaged in her mystic studies. She was finally beginning to understand the subtleties of the rune structures hidden in the pages of her old book, but she was also beginning to feel a little torn between her possible paths home. With no other option for the time being, she focused on what was accessible to her.

Many hours, and several more stolen pieces of chalk later, she felt she was actually getting somewhere. Though not nearly ready, the runes were taking shape into something that felt right.

Dorothy wound up so caught up with her mystical studies, that time passed without her noticing. Before she knew it, the weekend had arrived.

Short-handed, Camview came to a grinding halt come nighttime, and with the hallways empty and the staff spread even thinner than usual, Dorothy and Curtis's escape was actually relatively easy to swing. They even managed to sneak out a bit early, as the overworked staff had put the patients to bed earlier than usual after an exhausting evening covering multiple sick people's jobs.

With the crazies in their rooms, the staff finally took a much-needed break from an overwhelming shift, and Dorothy and Curtis easily snuck down the halls of Camview.

And so it was that they made their trek early, merrily strolling to the diner where Randy sat waiting for them in their usual booth, reclining comfortably as he savored a cup of hot chocolate.

He spotted them and waved happily, and whether it was the warmth of the diner, or just seeing Randy again, Dorothy felt a slight flush rise to her face. In fact, aside from her rosy cheeks, her overall appearance had been decidedly less cold in recent days, a bit of life finally showing through her skin despite the cool seasonal temperatures.

As they approached their friend, Dorothy could smell the alluring aroma of his beverage, sensing not his usual cup of molten lava coffee, but a mug of thick, dark cocoa, the tiny marshmallow boats floating in the chocolaty sea, sinking as they slowly dissolved into pools of saccharine tastiness.

"Hey, there you are," he said, the smile growing larger on his face as Dorothy walked closer. "I was wondering if you were going to stand me up."

"I'd never stand you up, big boy," Curtis chimed in with a chuckle.

Randy snorted a bemused laugh and rose from his seat, greeting Curtis with a friendly fist bump (with an explosion flourish).

After his wife had passed, it had been tough making new friends as an adult, especially during his hiatus from the art scene. Though he was back in the gallery world again, he had remained rather folded-in, only seeing the same few people for the most part, not really connecting with anyone new. Of course, he realized why his social circle had shrunk.

In the real world, you're no longer surrounded by thousands of people taking classes with you, and if you don't happen to wind up working in a large group environment, you typically just don't meet that many new people in your daily activities. On top of that, most of the people riding the bus with him, who weren't raving vagrants that is, were walled off behind their ramparts of earbuds and cell phones.

Coming from that history, it was particularly satisfying that

Randy and Curtis had really taken to one another, quickly becoming buddies even though they had only recently made each other's acquaintance.

Randy turned to Dorothy, someone else he had grown quite fond of, though in a very different way.

As he moved toward her, his body language betrayed a tad of uncertainty as he internally debated how exactly to greet her. He finally settled on a hug, though one they both held a bit longer and a bit tighter than either expected. Stepping back, Dorothy broke the tension, pointing to his beverage.

"Reverting to your childhood, I see," she quipped, dipping her finger in his melting marshmallows to steal a taste.

"Nah, just wanted to get in the festive spirit, is all."

"Oh?" she said, one arched eyebrow raised with curiosity.

Curtis flopped down into the booth lengthwise, leaving Dorothy and Randy no choice but to sit next to one another as they took a seat and joined him in his repose. Appearing from nowhere, Angela dropped off two more mugs of cocoa.

"We didn't—" Curtis began.

"Saw you two come in. Randy told me what you were doing tonight, and I thought you'd want to warm up with a cup first to get in the spirit."

"Spirit of what?" he asked, tossing a curious glance at Randy as he reclined comfortably in his red vinyl cozy-spot. "I want to do something fun tonight, and judging by that grin, shall I assume you have something up your sleeve?"

Randy couldn't contain his smile any longer. "Oh, I've got something fun lined up alright."

"Fun?" Dorothy queried.

"Yeah, you know, that thing that's the opposite of 'not fun,'" Curtis teased as he reached across the table and drew his mug of hot cocoa close.

"Yeah, definitely the opposite of 'not fun,'" Randy joked as he watched Curtis wipe marshmallow foam from his lips. "Come on, you two, drink up and get warm. We've got a bit of a trek to make," he said, a gleam in his eye. "But trust me, you're gonna love this."

CHAPTER 21

It had taken a little while navigating a few late-night buses before Dorothy and her companions at last arrived at their destination. Curtis's eyes lit up at the sight.

"Oh hell, yes!" he yelped with glee.

Several hours later, the cheerful trio lined up at the final hole on a classic miniature golf course Randy had steered them to.

Curtis kept raving about how amazed he was one even still existed within the city, having assumed they'd all long ago gone the way of the video game arcade. But this one somehow survived, and seemed to be thriving, surprisingly crowded with exuberant youth.

The ridiculous buildings fit the expectations of a mini-golf course, with the usual assortment of obstacles and whimsical structures strewn across the premises, each one unique in its theme and difficulty.

As was common on so many courses, when the trio had finally played their way through and arrived at the end of the game, a giant windmill stood before them, tilted askew, lacking only a faux Don Quixote as its blades slowly transcribed a lazy arc as they blocked the cup with each rotation.

Randy was in last place, so he had the honor of being the first to step up to the tee for his final putt. He leaned over and set his Day-Glo yellow ball on the ground before lining up his shot. Then, with a little butt shimmy, he took an untraditional stance and wound up for his swing.

"No way you make this."

"Shut up, Curtis. Let him take his shot," Dorothy laughed. *Though I think you're probably right on this one,* she thought as she watched him take a practice swing.

"Both of you give it a rest. I've got this," Randy chuckled. He may have had the worst score of the three, but he was having a delightful time engaging in adolescent games with his friends. Of course, mini golf is all about the fun, and not so much about the score, and by that metric, he was clearly a winner.

Finally, Randy swung his club, the face tapping the ball firmly, sending it rolling toward the tunnel that would deposit it right into the cup.

"I've got it! Yes!" he exclaimed. It looked like he'd finally made a perfect putt, but at the last moment, the slowly rotating arm of the windmill barely tagged the ball, sending it careening off course as it snatched success from his grasp.

"Gah, stupid windmill!" he griped.

"Step aside, Tiger, it's my turn," Dorothy said playfully as she plopped her orange ball in place. She took just one glance at the spinning arms of the windmill, and without hesitation, knocked the ball toward the hole.

"Comeon-comeon-comeon…"

Denied. Her ball was also knocked to the side.

"So close!" she jokingly lamented.

"Uh-huh? No. Not even. Now watch Uncle Curtis closely, kids. Class is in session."

Curtis stepped up to the tee with a cocky air and dropped his ball to the turf. He barely hesitated long enough for it to sit still, then putted it straightaway. Dorothy and Randy watched in amazement as the ball rolled.

Naturally, as is often the case with cocky bastards, his putt cruised past the swinging arms of the windmill, rolled through the funnel, and right into the hole.

"Yeah now! That's how you do it!" Curtis goaded. "Man, you guys suck."

Randy gave him a playful kick in the ass. "Hey, I haven't played since I was a kid."

"And I've never played at all," Dorothy chimed in. "It's a fun game though. Thank you, Randy. This was an excellent idea." She smiled warmly at him, and he reciprocated, holding her gaze a bit longer than usual.

"Yeah dude, this was a good call," Curtis agreed, noticing their shared moment. "Hey, why don't you two give me your clubs. I'll go return them for us. Go-karts next?"

"Sounds good."

They handed their shiny chrome implements of golfing failure over to Curtis just as something caught his eye across the park.

"Ooh, do you see that?" he asked excitedly, his eyes wide with joy. "We have just lucked out! Cotton candy! You guys want one? Wait, what am I saying? Of course you want one."

"No, thanks," said Dorothy.

"Seriously? How about you, Randy?"

"I'm good, thanks, though."

"Wow. Okay, your loss. Food of the Gods I tell ya!" he said as he started walking toward the club rental kiosk. "I'll meet you guys at the karts."

Randy and Dorothy turned and started casually strolling toward their next adventure. Walking side by side, Randy glanced at Dorothy with a little smile.

"So, are you any better at go-karting than at mini golf?"

"I've never driven one," she replied. "Actually, I've never driven anything."

"You know, I'm starting to think you really did come from Amish country," he said as he playfully bumped her with his hip.

Randy was amused and in great spirits, but a small cloud of doubt seemed to cling to Dorothy as they walked.

He's such a good man, she thought. *I can't lead him on. He deserves to know the truth.*

"Hey, Randy," she said with a hitch in her voice. "Listen, I have to be honest with you about something, although so far that seems to bring me nothing but problems."

"What's up?"

"Well, you're a great guy, and, well, I think I need to be up front with you."

"Um, okay," he replied. "But you're not actually a forty-year-old man in disguise, are you?" he asked with a wink.

She paused for a moment, not sure if she should let him in. Despite her gut telling her he'd be understanding, she also knew this could very well end their friendship.

It's the right thing, regardless. He should know.

"Okay, look," she began. "My name's not really Dorothy." She paused, looking at his face for a reaction. So far he seemed curious but not off-put. "I'm not Dorothy because I am actually Death. I know it's not what you expected to hear, but I am Death, and I'm trapped in human form. I don't know how or why it happened, but here I am, all flesh and blood for whatever reason. Okay, I said it. There. Go ahead and freak out now."

She felt her pulse racing as she waited for his inevitable crazy girl comment before turning and running away, but it never came.

"Wow, that's heavy," he said after a moment. "So you mean you've never driven a go-kart because you've been a trans-dimensional non-corporeal soul-reaping entity?"

"More or less."

"And you were too busy offing people around the globe to learn to drive, but now you're human?"

Oh, great, here it comes.

"Hmm, I don't know, it doesn't sound so bad. In fact, I think it sounds like an amazing opportunity. I mean, even the simplest things are new experiences for you, right?"

"You're making fun."

"No, I'm serious. Why look at your situation as a curse? Think of all the cool things you get to do for the first time."

"So you're not freaked out by this?" she asked.

He gave her a smile.

"Look, it's not normal, if that's what you mean, but you're really cool, and Death or not, I'm having a wonderful time with you."

She felt a flush warm her cheeks as she involuntarily broke into a broad smile.

Oh, what's up with my stomach? Not now, I don't want to be sick again! Not now!

Randy noticed the flutter of uncertainty flash briefly across her face. Even so, the moment felt right, and he started to lean toward her.

A massive crash echoed loudly from across the courtyard, the metallic bang of a cart overturning snapping them out of their moment.

They both turned, scanning the crowd, to see what the ruckus was all about. A few moments later it became abundantly clear as they saw Curtis walking toward them. Very, very out of sorts.

His face, and much of his head, was covered in cotton candy.

Oh no, please tell me he didn't actually…

But before she could finish the thought, Dorothy caught sight of the overturned cotton candy cart.

He actually did, she thought, shaking her head in amused disbelief.

Curtis greeted his friends with a pained grin, looking none too thrilled.

"This is not nearly as awesome as I'd imagined," he grumbled.

An exasperated, "Curtis, seriously!" was all Dorothy could muster.

"Oh, dude," Randy chimed in. "You did not actually just do that." He couldn't help himself, the laughter finally seeping out. Curtis, for his part, didn't seem to mind much.

"Hey, it's all right guys. Yuk it up, really, it's okay. Don't worry about your poor friend Curtis. I'm sure I'll be fine."

Their laughter continued, though they did rein it in just a little.

"Har-har. Laugh it up while you can, 'cause I'll have my revenge on the track! I'll meet you guys over at the go-karts. I've gotta make a quick pit-stop in the men's room."

And with that, as quickly as he had rejoined his friends, Curtis was off in search of the bathroom, picking bits of cotton candy from his hair, popping them in his mouth as he walked.

Though his fit of laughter was dying down, Randy was still unable to stop chuckling.

"That is one crazy guy."

"You have no idea."

He smiled and reached out, taking Dorothy by the hand. She felt her pulse quicken again at his touch.

"Well, come on," he said. "It shouldn't take him too long to clean up. Let's go teach you how to drive."

She looked at her hand in his for a moment, and a small grin crept onto her face as the pair started off along the path, hand in hand.

Pausing outside the bathroom, Curtis pulled a sticky ribbon of cotton candy from his hair and popped it in his mouth as he watched them from the shadows, smiling to himself as Dorothy and Randy strolled away. Satisfied things were going well, he stepped through the doorway to clean himself up.

Ten minutes later a race was underway.

It turned out that while Randy did not own a car, which in its own way had been fortuitous, as it helped Dorothy and Curtis avoid any awkward offers of a ride home, he was a rather skilled driver, at least as far as go-karts were concerned.

Dorothy had taken to it quickly, and wasn't half-bad either, especially given it was her first time driving. Then again, she drove with no fear of death because if she crashed horribly, who'd come and take her? The thought had morbidly amused her when it flashed through her mind.

Of course, it would be hard to do any real damage anyway, since the karts had speed limiters on them.

Curtis, on the other hand, was a terrible driver, though he didn't appear to mind one bit, and seemed to be enjoying himself immensely, even as he was lapped by other drivers. It fit his character, of course, and he simply reveled in the fun of the moment, not concerned with ranking or place.

All in all, it was a good suggestion on Randy's part, and by the time they pulled into the pit stop area and climbed out of the karts, the three of them seemed to have bonded even further over the evening's festivities.

The friends leisurely walked back toward the bus stop, leaving the colored lights and sounds of laughing youth behind them. Dorothy couldn't seem to stop smiling.

"That was amazing. The wind, the speed—I feel... I feel... tingles. I feel electric."

Curtis couldn't help but notice her glowing from the experience.

"Adrenaline," he said. "Told ya you'd like it."

"Yeah," Randy chipped in. "You're a natural. You almost beat me a few laps there."

"But, dude," Curtis cut in. "You are a madman. Seriously, you're really, really good. Why don't you have a car?"

No, don't go there, Curtis!

The thought passed through her mind, but she couldn't even flash him a warning look. It was already too late.

Randy's demeanor sobered a bit as a memory pulled him from the festivities. After a moment of reflection, he looked at his friends.

"There was an accident," he began uneasily. "Um, it's kinda hard to get into..."

"His wife was killed in a car crash four years ago," Dorothy said quietly.

"How... how did you know...?" Randy stuttered.

Curtis jumped in.

"That Angela, man ,she's sweet but sometimes she shares a bit too much. Look, man, I'm sorry I brought it up."

"It's all right. I just never really talk about it is all."

"I can imagine. Well, like I said, I'm sorry I mentioned it. Forget I ever brought it up."

Randy, however, felt it a bit of relief, as if now that the cork had been loosed, he was free to let out the ghosts that had been haunting him all those years. His gaze turned to Dorothy.

"You know, it's kind of sappy, but I had always believed in The One but then... oh, man, I was young, we had a fling, and the next thing you know..." He paused, misting up a little. "Well, I flipped my shit at first, and it got kinda ugly between us. Not what I'd planned in the slightest, you know how it is. But then we talked it out, and I did the honorable thing and proposed."

"Oh, man, that's a tough one," Curtis commiserated.

"We weren't soul mates," Randy continued. "But I did eventually grow to love her, in her own way. Then, when our daughter was three, her mother was..." He paused, reliving the tragedy. "The first few years after were hard on her. Hard on us both, really. After the accident, well, I kinda went on a bender. My folks stepped in to help, and eventually we moved away to stay with them and get a fresh start."

"That's tough, losing your mom like that."

"Yeah, but you know kids, they heal fast. She's eight now, and I figured it was time for us to come back home. She's still staying with her grandparents for the time being to finish out the school year with her friends, but I've been working hard to make us a home again. She's going to finally come join me when the school year is done." He shook himself a bit, clearing the gloom from his head like an inconvenient cobweb he'd inadvertently walked into. "Anyway, enough dreary stuff. It's been too fun an evening for me to get all morose and bring us down, am I right?"

"Amen, my brotha!" Curtis hooted, grasping the chance to lighten the mood with both hands. "Hey, did I ever tell you about the time I got locked out of the beach showers with nothing but a wash cloth?"

The bus rolled up a few minutes later, and much to the chagrin of the elderly woman riding with them, Curtis regaled them with ribald tales of his many shenanigans for the duration of the trip.

While it may have been a bit off-color, his antics also lightened the mood so well that by the time they arrived at their destination, all traces of gloom had been well eradicated, and they exited the bus with light hearts and bellies full of laughter.

It had been a fantastic evening, but it was finally time to go their separate ways, as they always did at the end of an outing, but after giving Curtis a hug, Randy paused before saying goodnight to

Dorothy.

"Randy, a pleasure as always. Great idea, it was a hoot," Curtis said with a grin.

"Me too, I had a blast," he replied, then turned to the girl who thought she was Death. "Listen, Dorothy, um, could I talk to you for a minute?" he asked, shifting slightly on his feet, uncharacteristically nervous.

Curtis took the hint. "Hey, I'm gonna start walking. I'll catch ya at the bus stop. See ya, Randy."

"Later, Curtis."

He walked off, leaving Dorothy and Randy alone, two figures illuminated by the lone streetlight on the dimly lit avenue.

"So," Randy began, "I had a really great time tonight"

"As did I," she replied. "I never knew that fun could be, well, so much fun."

"Like I said, maybe this being human isn't such a bad thing." He shifted from foot to foot, seemingly uncomfortable in his own skin. "Look, um, I was wondering, um, do you think you and I could maybe go out sometime without Curtis?"

"But you two seem to get along so well."

"Yeah, he's a great guy. I just thought it would be nice to get to spend some time on our own is all. Maybe grab some dinner, play some chess over a glass of wine."

"Chess? I've never played."

"Really?" he said, surprised. "Well, we can remedy that. What do you say, just you and me, next Tuesday night?" He pulled out his old blue watch and popped it open, glancing at the time before sliding it back into his pocket.

Dorothy thought about his offer for a moment and found herself not only wanting to follow up on the unusual timepiece, but also warmed by the idea of spending an evening with her friend.

"All right," she agreed. "I think I can make it. Tuesday night. Ten o'clock."

"Excellent!" Randy beamed.

Dorothy turned to catch up to Curtis when Randy put his hand on her arm, stopping her and drawing her closer. Nervously, he lightly cupped her face in his hand and leaned in, giving her a kiss on the lips.

It was quick, but it was also certainly more than just a peck.

What the hell was that? she thought as her insides flushed with a startling heat.

Randy stepped back, a happy smile in his eyes as he looked her over.

"Okay then, see ya Tuesday," he said, then walked off toward home, stealing a glance at her over his shoulder before rounding the corner.

"Uh… see ya," was all she could muster.

Only a few moments passed, but it felt much longer to Dorothy as she stood still, fixed to the ground, until, finally, she forced her legs to move and headed off down the street. She found her fingers lightly touching her lips as she pondered what had just happened.

Curtis popped out of the shadows, easily falling in step beside her. She didn't even flinch.

"So?" he queried, features animated with obvious curiosity.

"So, what?" she replied.

"So what happened?" he clarified, growing impatient. If Curtis were a cat, his curiosity would have already likely cost him the bulk of his nine lives.

"The strangest thing," she began. "He kissed me. Why would he do that?"

Curtis beamed like a proud parent.

"Boy meets Queen of Darkness, boy likes Queen of Darkness, boy kisses Queen of Darkness. Quite normal, really." He chuckled. Dorothy threw him a look. "Ya know," he continued, "I like him. He's a really good guy. Has a good energy."

He glanced over at his friend and noticed she looked a bit unwell, her hand on her stomach, though she didn't quite look like she was going to be sick.

"Hey, you feeling okay?" he queried, genuinely concerned.

"I don't know how to describe it. My stomach, it's churning…

but I don't think I want to vomit... It's..." She was at a loss for words. In a flash her friend went from concerned to amused.

"It's called butterflies." Curtis smiled a Cheshire grin. "You, my dear, have a crush."

What is he talking about? I am Death! I do not get crushes.

"No, Curtis, it must be the coffee or something, that's all."

He just gazed at her knowingly with a cheerful gleam in his eye.

"Hon, we didn't even drink coffee tonight," he said, amused by the whole thing. "Wow, Death in love, who'da thunk it? Kinda gives 'the kiss of death' a whole new meaning, eh?"

Dorothy slugged his arm, but couldn't help but be amused by his contagious mood. Nevertheless, she was disconcerted at the effect Randy had on her.

It could just be a side effect of his relic. That's got to be it. The watch must have affected me, that's all. Just part of whatever this cosmic plan is.

"Something good is on the horizon," Curtis mused. "Funny, you're getting more action than I've had in years, and you only just got here."

"What are you talking about?"

"You've got a hot date to look forward to."

If I'm still here, she thought as they made their way back to Camview for the night.

I've got some reading to catch up on.

Dorothy split with Curtis when they entered Camview's empty hallways and stealthily made her way to her room. She quietly closed the door behind her, a grim look on her face despite the night's previously light mood.

The watch isn't panning out quickly enough. What am I missing? I'm running out of options.

Carefully, she pulled her bed from the wall, revealing the increasingly complex series of chalk runes and symbols hidden beneath it. In the weeks she'd been working on it, the language of symbols had begun making sense more and more, and the resulting glyphs were almost perfect in their design.

Digging under her mattress, she pulled out her book and piece of chalk, then sat down and began to carefully add to the already complex chalk circle.

For a brief moment she stopped, her fingers touching her lips, remembering the kiss and the warmth that accompanied it.

Despite the stress she was under, Dorothy found a slight smile forming on her lips at the memory.

Shaking it off, she forced herself to focus again on her work, laying out runes with ever-increasing precision.

It's getting there, she thought, *but will it actually work?*

Working in the dim light, she was so focused that she kept at it until exhaustion claimed her. Just before sunup, she finally curled up in her bed and succumbed to sleep.

CHAPTER 22

The hip art gallery Randy directed was situated in an up-and-coming part of the city, as cutting-edge venues so often are. Gary had been able to pick up the building for a steal years prior, seeing the potential in its high ceilings, open spaces, and exposed beams and infrastructure, even if the neighborhood was still a bit sketchy.

Perfect for a trendy art spot.

When his long-time friend had finally recovered from the upheaval of his life and returned home, Gary didn't think twice about bringing Randy in to curate a few shows. Hell, he'd wanted to headhunt him from his former gallery gig well before the accident, so it was quite serendipitous the way things worked out, timing-wise that is.

In no time at all, his feet back under him once more, Randy had shown that he still had what it takes, spotting great new artists and securing showings from well-established ones, and racking up solid sales even during a bit of an economic downturn in the art collecting world.

He had been nose-to-the-grindstone for the most part, focused on work seven days a week. Unfortunately, he was also ever-so-slow to come out of his self-imposed fun exile, which was why his appearance that morning took Gary by surprise.

"Hey, dude," Randy chirped as he happily strolled into the building.

"Everything lined up?" Gary asked as he gave his friend the once-over, pouring him his daily ritual cup of coffee from a fresh pot.

"Yep, we'll be good for the opening," he replied. "The band confirmed, both food trucks said they'll set up out front, the email blast went out, and we got almost all of the online preview images up. There's already a lot of interest in quite a few of the pieces. Ya know, I think we'll have some solid pre-sales this month."

Gary handed him the piping-hot cup of coffee, eyebrow raised quizzically.

"Okay, man, what's up? You look like a giddy schoolgirl."

"Nothing," he replied, a slight blush rising in his cheeks.

"Uh-huh." Gary didn't buy it for a second. "Seriously. C'mon, spill. Is Sam moving back early or something?"

Randy hesitated for just a moment, then the excitement started to crack his cool façade.

"I... well I kinda have a date," he finally admitted.

"Holy shit, dude, at last! I mean, no disrespect, but it's about time. Tell me about her!"

The slow burn of a growing smile ignited on Randy's face.

"I'm still getting to know her. I mean it hasn't been that long, but so far she's kind of amazing."

"Tinder?"

"What? No! I met her at the diner, and things just sort of happened. I don't know how to explain it, but it just feels right, you know? It's like how when you're trying to hang a show, and it doesn't quite work, but then an unexpected piece arrives and as soon as you unwrap it the whole wall suddenly comes together and makes perfect sense," he gushed.

"Wow, she really made an impression. So when do I get to meet this new girl?"

"Soon, I hope."

"Awesome. Come on, tell me all about her while we unpack these pieces," Gary said, glad to see someone was finally drawing his friend out of his reclusive funk and back to his old self.

Maybe even better than his old self.

Across town, lunchtime arrived in the nuthouse, and surprisingly the bulk of the residents were behaving themselves, at least for the most part.

Naturally, there were the occasional fits and tantrums. There were also those who just drooled on themselves because they were drugged to the gills, a direct result of their prior fits and tantrums. For the most part, however, it was a calm day.

That is until Dorothy, more pale than usual, suddenly doubled over in pain, nearly falling out of her chair.

Molly put her arm around her, showing a rare moment of concern.

"You all right?" she asked, then turned to Curtis. "Hey, she don't look too good."

At that moment, Dorothy folded even tighter into a ball, her fingers turning white from the pressure they exerted on the table as she grabbed it for all she was worth, fighting whatever was ailing her.

"Get the nurse!" Curtis called out, a little panicked, eyes darting around the room as he looked for help. For once he skipped his usual levity and banter and focused solely on his ailing friend as she writhed in pain.

"Take my hand, it's going to be okay."

He quickly regretted that offer.

"Holy shit, you've got a grip! Whoa, ease up, ease up!"

With an effort, she let his hand go, slapping hers back onto the table just as the nurse made her way to them. She gestured to the nearest orderly to come help her.

"Give me a hand. We're taking her to the medical station."

Carefully, they gathered Dorothy up to her feet, then lowered her into a wheelchair and rolled her off down the hall. Curtis tried to tag along, but his attempt to follow his friend was nipped in the bud.

"Nope, no way. Back to your seat, Curtis," the orderly said, blocking his path.

Reluctantly, Curtis went back to his chair to worry about his friend over a cup of pudding. Fortunately for him, pudding seemed to make everything right in the world, at least for a moment or two.

"At your age, you should be prepared for these things," the nurse said to Dorothy as she lay on the cold, paper-covered examining table. "Cramps happen to all of us. Making such a big deal of it won't win you any new friends, you know."

Dorothy had been looking over one of the old, detailed posters of female anatomy desperately clinging to the aged wall by even more ancient tape that seemed ready to peel off at the slightest breeze. What she saw fascinated her.

"I've never had them before," she said, turning her attention back to the nurse.

"Uh-huh," the woman replied with an incredulous look. "All right," she said, "I'll let you rest here for a bit. The Midol should kick in soon, but I don't want any more of this foolishness from you, are we clear? You're making more paperwork for me, and I do not enjoy that one bit. More importantly, Doctor Vaughan *really* doesn't like it, and you do not want to piss him off any more than you already have."

"I didn't mean to cause you any trouble."

"Well, intentions and results aren't exactly always the same thing, now are they? I'll be back in fifteen minutes. You have until then to rest here."

The nurse walked out of the room, leaving Dorothy to recover on her own. A look of disgust grew on her face as she read the instructions on the small packet of pads left for her.

You've got to be kidding me. No way I'm walking around with one of those things… She paused to think about the alternative.

This is going to suck.

"So, I think that scabby freak gets put back in with the rest of us loons in five days. Think you can wait that long to grill him for details?" Curtis asked Dorothy with a mischievous grin. "I know how anxious you are to torture the information out of the poor guy with a dull spork."

"Is there any other kind of spork?" Molly asked from her seat across the table as she finished her pudding. "I mean it seems kinda redundant, is all."

"Yes, thank you, Molly, very astute of you. The point I was

trying to make is that perhaps there are better ways to get what you want. Maybe even a little bribery, because who here doesn't love pudding cups?"

Dorothy couldn't help but crack a faint smile at her friend. The cramps had finally gone, and she managed to get a fair amount of the sandwich Curtis had put aside for her into her belly without incident.

"Okay," she playfully agreed. "Maybe not a spork."

"Ah, listening to reason at last!" Curtis laughed, but his smile faltered as he noticed a shadow at the door.

Doctor Vaughn was in a fit of pique as he stormed into the room, scanning his psych ward fiefdom for the poor individual who had raised his ire.

"Shit, looks like Vaughan's on a rampage again," he said, hunching lower in his seat.

No sooner had the words left his mouth than Doctor Vaughan's eyes locked on Dorothy from across the room. Red in the face, he made his way toward her, frightened patients parting like the Red Sea for Moses as Big Stan followed in the doctor's wake.

"What the hell is this I hear about you faking cramps to get drugs?" he tore into her. "These behaviors reflect poorly on us in board reviews. We do not allow this sort of behavior at Camview. I thought we were clear about you not making waves, Dorothy."

"I didn't fake anything," she replied calmly. The lack of any fear in her voice once again touched a nerve, and Doctor Vaughan was not so blind as to miss the other patients taking notice of her standing up to him, if only in tone of voice.

Time to take it up a notch.

He raised his voice, getting into character for a good show of force to establish for everyone in the room just who exactly was boss in this place.

"Don't you mouth off to me," he said, building steam to what he felt would be an impressive browbeating that would surely keep the others from daring to follow her lead. "You are powerless here, and you will not mouth off!" he said, volume increasing even further. "In my hospital, what I say is the law, you get me? Scofflaws and disruptions will not be tolerated!"

He was really starting to get into his spiel when Dorothy unexpectedly threw him for a loop.

With the calmest of expressions on her face, she uttered the one thing that could actually push him over the edge for real.

"Oh, stop already," she said. "Just because you're insecure about your life, your career choice, and your manhood doesn't mean you have to go and yell in front of everyone." She paused for effect, then continued.

"Really, Doctor Vaughan. *Francis*. The way you treat people, it's no wonder your wife killed herself."

He froze. Coming from the girl who had reminded him of his dead wife, the knife dug especially deep. For one painful, conflicted moment, all he could do was stare at her, blinking in wide-eyed disbelief.

Then he lost his shit.

Doctor Vaughan's face flushed crimson-red, his body shaking with rage. All acting and showmanship was gone, and what remained was pure, unbridled fury.

"How did you—" he started. "You couldn't possibly—" The vein on the side of his temple was throbbing a staccato beat, and his eyes seemed ready to pop from his head.

"I've had enough of your constant attitude and badgering, Katie!" he growled.

Katie? Wow, he really has lost it.

The staff looked at one another as a wave of discomfort passed over his worried minions. Even Stan, his most loyal lackey, seemed uneasy. Nevertheless, every last one of them knew better than to ask why he called his most vexing patient by his dead wife's name.

Doctor Vaughan surveyed the room, noting the concerned looks of his staff. He forced himself to take a deep breath as he pulled himself together, compressing his anger inward into a rumbling ball held tight in his belly.

"Stan," he finally said with frightening calm in his voice, "take her to room forty-two."

Big deal, a few days of isolation is nothing, and besides, Pestilence should be back when I get out, she mused with a little grin.

Then she noticed the shocked looks on the faces of even the most hardened of his staff.

What's that all about?

The duty nurse timidly approached Doctor Vaughan as Stan grabbed Dorothy by the arm.

"But Doctor Vaughan, the board decommissioned—" she began. Vaughan spun on her, face red, and damn near foaming at the mouth, which was all the scarier because of the dead-cold tone in which he replied to her.

"Do I have to repeat myself?" he questioned. Something in his eyes told her, and everyone else in the room, that it'd be best to keep very, very quiet.

Everyone but Curtis.

"Doc, you don't need to do that. I'll keep her in line," he offered.

Vaughan turned to Curtis, fixing him with an icy gaze as he sized him up.

"I don't know what you've been telling your little friend about my personal life, Curtis, but you'd better watch your step *very* carefully, or you'll join her."

Confused by Curtis's concern, Dorothy gave her friend a little smile as she was dragged from the room.

Don't worry, it's no big deal, she thought. *Oh shit, but Randy...*

An hour later, her throat was raw from screaming, her hair plastered to her head with sweat, neck veins distended from effort. Dorothy tried to focus her blurry, watering eyes, but found she didn't have the energy even for that.

"Again," said Doctor Vaughan, his eyes as cold and emotionless as a shark's.

Stan turned the dial to the right, once more sending thousands of volts of electricity through her body as her back arched in pain and spasm, her mouth frothing as she bit down on the airway bite plate lashed firmly between her teeth.

Dorothy was strapped firmly to an older medical table. It looked like it had once been used for exams, or perhaps childbirth, but now it was used solely for restraint. Her arms, legs, and torso were held down by thick, padded leather straps. Though the room and its equipment may have been decommissioned by the board many years prior, Doctor Vaughan had always demanded it necessary to keep things in place and in working order.

Today was the day he felt his foresight had paid off.

Stan turned the dial down to zero, and Dorothy flopped, limp, back to the table, her breath coming in gasps as tears flowed from her bloodshot eyes.

"Again?" he asked.

Doctor Vaughan approached his helpless patient and firmly took her face in his hand, roughly twisting her head to one side then the next as if examining a piece of meat or animal for the slaughter.

"No," he replied. "I think that's enough." He got close to her face, her eyes trying to focus on him as best she could. "For now," he sneered, then let her head loll to the side.

"Take her back to her room. No dinner tonight, not that she'd have the energy to eat it."

Vaughan seemed markedly more relaxed as he strolled from the room. He hadn't realized just how much he'd missed these sessions. Feeling the rush once more had reminded him of just what the board had taken from him when they shut the program down.

No matter, he'd keep it off the books, and they'd never be the wiser. Best of all, no one would dare question him now.

Down the sterile corridors, Stan opened Dorothy's room and unceremoniously dumped her barely conscious form onto her bed. She landed askew but didn't even have the energy to adjust herself. She just lay there with her clothing sticking to her in a sweaty pile until sweet unconsciousness wrapped her in its soothing embrace.

Late that night, in his apartment across town, Randy headed for the door, an old chessboard tucked under his arm. He paused in front of the small, silver-framed picture of his deceased wife and gave it a long look.

After several moments of thought, he finally made a decision. He took a deep breath, then picked it up from its resting place and carefully tucked it into a drawer. He then headed out for his first real date in years, a spring in his step, totally unaware the object of his affection would be standing him up.

CHAPTER 23

Randy sat in their usual booth, trying to get comfortable, but found himself fidgety and nervous no matter what he did. He felt like a schoolboy on his first date, he realized, amused at himself, which did at least seem to take the edge off a tiny bit.

The door swung open, and he looked up expectantly, happily anticipating his date's arrival.

It was Curtis.

They gave each other a familiar nod as Curtis headed straight to the booth. Randy did his best to hide both his confusion and his disappointment.

"Hey, man, how've ya been?" Curtis queried.

"Good, good," Randy replied. "Didn't know you'd be joining us this evening," he continued. "Where's Dorothy?"

"Yeah, about that. Well, the thing is, Dorothy isn't feeling well. I came to tell you. She's really sorry, but she won't be able to make it tonight."

"Oh, okay," he said. "No big deal." Randy did his best to hide his emotions, but Curtis still saw him deflate at the news, crestfallen.

"She likes you man, she really does. Just be patient with her. She's got some issues at home bringing her down," Curtis said, resting his hand on his friend's arm.

"But you're her roommate, Curtis. What's going on?"

Curtis faltered momentarily, then caught his footing. "Um, yeah. You see, our, um, landlord, the two of them don't really get along and, well, he went kinda nuts on her earlier. Really went to town on her." He gauged Randy's reactions, then continued. "She was shocked. I mean, it really took the wind out of her sails."

"Yeah, I guess I can see how that sort of thing could catch you by surprise."

"Exactly. Look, just be patient with her. She's a good kid."

"I'll do my best." Randy sighed.

The two sat quietly for a moment, then Curtis noticed the old chessboard sitting beside Randy on the seat.

"Since it's just you and me, you up for a game?" Curtis asked.

"You know, she said she's never played."

"Are you serious?" Curtis raised an eyebrow in surprise. "Oh, the irony." He shook his head in disbelief.

"I know, right? Apparently not a Bergman fan."

"Well, we might as well make the best of the evening."

With the mood lightened, Randy flagged down Angela and ordered two thick slices of apple pie and resolved himself to enjoy a different evening than he'd planned, as the pair started setting up pieces on the old board.

The following morning Dorothy exited her room looking understandably haggard, with dark bags under her eyes, and a particular slowness to her step as she made her way to breakfast.

Once there, she found she could barely manage to carry her tray of food. Fortunately Curtis spied her from across the room, and flagged her down to come join him at the table he was sharing with Warren, taking the tray from her shaky hands before she dropped it as she slid into her seat.

Warren didn't register any of this, but was thrilled, in his simpleminded way, to see the pretty new girl again.

"Knock-knock!" he chirped.

Curtis could see Dorothy flinch and almost visibly wilt even further, if that was actually possible.

Today was not the day for this.

"Hey, Warren," he said, "you know, Stein told me he wanted to tell you a new knock-knock joke. Why don't you go find him?"

With a silly grin, Warren popped to his feet and scampered off to find the poor hypochondriac. It may have been a mean thing to do, but Stein was far better equipped on this day to handle the incessant chatter than Dorothy.

With the coast now clear of sweet but annoying giants, Curtis was able to turn his attention fully to his friend.

"So, you okay?" he asked as he sized her up, his concern evident in his tone.

"I've had better days," she managed. "Is this what being human is like? 'Cause if so, this really sucks."

"Nah, only what it's like for people on Doctor Vaughan's shit list. And, oh man, you *really* pissed him off. Like, we're talking epic pissage. For a minute there, I thought he was gonna blow a gasket. I'm almost surprised he didn't have an aneurysm."

He handed her a container of orange juice, but she pushed it away. Ignoring her, he slid the container right back toward her.

"You need to get your blood sugar up. Drink it."

Relenting, she picked it up, slowly sipping at the sweet and tangy liquid. After a few moments, when the sugars began to absorb into her system, she actually did start to feel a little better.

"Why are you so good to me, Curtis?"

"I told ya, I'm your guardian angel. Someone has to look out for you. Besides, I figure being on Death's good side can't hurt, right?"

She flashed a weak smile as she absentmindedly arranged the utensils near her by size and type.

"Wait, what day is today? Shit!"

She abruptly stopped fidgeting with silverware, a flush quickly rose to her cheeks and slight panic tightened her voice.

"Oh no! Randy... I—"

"Don't worry, I met up with him and told him you were under the weather and would see him on Friday instead," Curtis told her, soothing her panic.

"You really do look out for me." She gazed warmly at him, taking his hands in hers and looking deep in his eyes. "You're the only friend I've ever had, Curtis. Thank you."

Though a bit uncomfortable with the mushy stuff, he squeezed her hands and flashed his brightest smile.

"Glad to help. Now, as your most-bestest and only friend, it is my official duty to make sure your tapioca isn't poisoned." With a wicked little grin, he swiped a spoonful of her dessert.

Dorothy, somehow, actually managed a weak chuckle and a smile.

Later that day, the yellow afternoon light filtered through the small window high on the wall of Dorothy's room, adding a degree of warmth to the bare fluorescent light. It couldn't open to let in a breeze, of course, or even admit just a few molecules of fresh air, but the light still brought her a calming feeling as she sat on the floor.

Her bed was pulled away from the wall, exposing her chalk-lined handiwork. The rune circle was now filled with a great deal more symbols, both large and small, in what appeared to be increasingly intricate patterns, interconnecting with one another in ways only one versed in the arts would recognize.

All right, she thought as she looked over her handiwork, *I think that may actually be it. No time like the present to give it a try.*

She skimmed the book in her hand. The chapter heading read "Cross-Realm Transference," and the pages bore a number of verses associated with specific glyphs and runes, depending on the reader's wishes.

Yeah, this looks right. I don't think I missed anything. Time to get back where I belong and set things straight.

She closed her eyes and took a deep breath, ignoring the antiseptic smell of her four-walled confinement as she concentrated. She then tried to focus on filling her lungs with air and the natural power that flowed through all things.

Okay, here goes nothing.

Chi, chakras, call it what you will, Dorothy felt her body build with energy, secretly hoping that it wasn't all just in her head.

Parting her lips, she quietly intoned a verse, slowly at first, then picking up speed as she focused on the diagram in front of her.

"Eeanay Sudominey Vorghalisi Nictu," she said, wrapping her mouth around the odd words with what she hoped was the correct pronunciation.

A fine sheen of sweat began to form on her brow as she focused her will on the runes before her. The light flickered, once, but she kept focus, intoning the words over and over.

With a flash, the lights flickered again and then went out entirely.

Well, that's something, she thought. *But not what it was supposed to do.*

Meanwhile, down the now-darkened hall, the nurse on duty picked up the walkie-talkie on her desk with an exasperated sigh.

"Get maintenance up here. That stupid fuse just blew again."

One of the orderlies poked his head into her station.

"Again?" he asked.

"Yup."

"Awesome. I sooo love working in the dark," he muttered, sarcasm dripping from his lips.

They shared a look of commiseration, then continued on with their work in the dim light of the emergency battery system. Back in her room Dorothy scanned her book intently, trying to figure out what could have gone wrong.

The door to the pawn shop opened with a creak, the bell affixed to a spring bouncing a greeting chime as Randy strode in. The slightly dusty smell that permeated the cluttered space filled his nose, but not in an unpleasant way.

The heavy-bearded pawn shop owner glanced up from his magazine as he sized up Randy for a moment, then rose to his feet to greet his client.

"I remember you," he said. "Blue watch fella, right?"

"Good memory," Randy replied, pulling the watch from his pocket in a little salute.

"So," said the older man, "was it as good a conversation piece as I told you it'd be?"

"Better than you'd believe, actually," he replied with a grin.

"Glad it worked out for you. So, what brings you in today?" The man pushed up his sleeves in anticipation of another sale.

"Well, I've got a special occasion and was hoping you might

have…" His gaze fell upon the exact thing he'd been searching for, conveniently on the counter just past the pawn shop owner's chair. A beautiful chess set, one that made his beater board look even more run-down than it was.

The man smiled. "Want to take a closer look?" he asked, knowing the answer full well judging by his young customer's face.

In the cozy warmth of the diner later that night, Dorothy sat alone in their usual booth. She was a bit quiet, but that would be expected of someone who'd been through electro-shock therapy a few days prior. Otherwise, she seemed no worse for wear.

She was wearing her usual black attire, but Angela noticed as she walked over, that her top was ever so slightly patterned with a deep red.

Just a touch of color, but for a girl who only wore black, it was a start.

"You feeling better, hon?" she asked, setting a cup of tea in front of Dorothy.

"Yeah, thanks, Angie. I truly do appreciate your concern."

"You got it, kid. I'm just glad to see you feeling better. And happy, for that matter. You look like you finally got a little life in you. Suits you nicely." She gave her young friend an affectionate squeeze on her shoulder as she meandered back to her other tables, flashing a smile and a little wave to Randy as he strolled in.

"Hey, pretty lady, buy you a drink?" he said, sliding into the booth next to Dorothy. She felt her cheeks flush for an instant at the contact.

"Hey, yourself," she replied, smiling wide as she found herself savoring the warmth in his eyes. "Look, I'm really sorry I couldn't make it the other night. Things were… um… complicated."

"No worries. Curtis told me all about it. Sorry you had to deal with such an ass of a landlord. Doesn't matter, though, you're here now. I'm just glad you could make it tonight."

She squeezed his arm affectionately. "Wouldn't miss it."

"So, you up for a late movie?" he asked.

"What did you have in mind?"

The old revival theater had recently begun playing a series of late-night screenings on weekends, and this particular Friday provided Randy with a perfect date for the girl he liked.

The girl who thought she was Death.

The pair strolled out of the theater well past midnight, walking by the marquee that read, "Bergman Festival," and below it, "Midnight Movie: *The Seventh Seal*."

Their fellow theatergoers filtered out, chattering about what a classic it was and how handsome and dashing Max Von Sydow was when he was young.

"Oh, you always had a thing for Swedes," they overheard one woman say to her gushing friend as they exited the theater.

"But he was *gorgeous*," her friend replied.

Randy reached out and took Dorothy's hand in his as they strolled down the sidewalk.

"So?" he queried, pretty sure she liked it judging by the smile on her face. "What did you think?"

She leaned closer to him affectionately.

"It was wonderful, Randy. Thank you."

He smiled. Yes, this was going very well indeed.

"You know," he said, "I think the bald and brooding look could work for you, though the black robes might not be terribly flattering."

Dorothy laughed and smacked him playfully as she quoted one of Death's many lines from the movie.

"Det är ditt drag, Antonius Block!" she said in Swedish.

He looked at her, surprised.

"It's your move, Antonius Block," she clarified. "From the film."

He continued to look at her incredulously. She spoke Swedish?

Dorothy just smiled innocently. "What?" she deadpanned as they continued to the bus stop.

They arrived at Randy's apartment shortly thereafter.

Randy found himself all thumbs, momentarily awkward as he

was about to invite a woman into his home for the first time in years. He clumsily dug his keys from his pocket and opened the door, stepping inside and holding it open for his guest.

"Please, come in," he said. "No, wait, it's only vampires you have to invite in, right?"

She shook her head with a chuckle and stepped into his home.

Laid out on the coffee table by his couch was an unlit candle, two crystal glasses, an unopened bottle of wine, and, much to her surprise, a beautiful chess set.

"Oh, Randy, that's gorgeous," she gushed, appreciating the board now that she'd finally seen the Bergman flick. The whole concept of Death playing a game of chess with a knight for his immortal soul was a beautiful story to her, and she appreciated the effort he was making to connect, but not make fun of her in so doing.

"Well, I thought you might want to try your hand at a game."

"All right," she replied. "You've inspired me."

"Oh, have I now?" he murmured, a warm look in his eye.

"More than you realize," she answered, returning the look. A tingle and flush had begun to warm her belly, as if a small blaze had started to kindle there. A small blaze that was starting to grow.

He studied her for a moment longer, not attempting to hide the affection in his eyes, but rather, letting her see his unguarded intent.

She blushed and felt the fire in her belly flare even more.

"Where's your restroom?"

"Right down there."

"Thank you. I'll be back in a minute," she said as she stepped out of the room.

He popped the cork from the bottle of wine and poured two glasses to let them breathe a bit. That task done, he stepped into his kitchen, pausing at the sink to splash some cold water on his face, his pulse racing and cheeks aglow.

Just across the apartment, Dorothy stood quietly in the bathroom, leaning forward on the cool porcelain sink, bracing herself against its soothing chill as she studied herself in the mirror.

What is going on with me?

She lightly ran her fingers across her face, gently touching her lips. Her cheeks had an uncharacteristic flush of color in them, and even though she was simply looking at herself, she couldn't help but notice how her eyes flashed and sparked, alive in the moment.

Okay, get a grip. Take a breath.

She splashed cool water on her face, paused to recompose herself, then stepped back out to the man she had finally, much to her surprise, realized she very well might be falling for.

Hours had flown by, and the bottle of wine was long gone. Whether it was very late, or very early, was a matter of opinion at that hour.

Dorothy and Randy sat close, curled up on the couch as they both studied the chessboard in front of them. It was vacant many of its pieces, and Dorothy was poised for victory. A quick learner, that one. She gave him a mischievous glance, eyebrow raised in a dare, then moved her bishop.

"Checkmate."

He studied the board for a moment and smiled in amazement at her prowess. "Indeed it is." The flush in her cheeks and flash in her eye made his heart skip a beat, and he knew it was time.

Randy leaned over and kissed her tenderly.

Dorothy felt her heart race at his touch, her whole body flush with adrenaline and warmth. He caressed her cheek and held her gaze, then slid back to his seat, reaching over and knocking his king over, conceding the game.

"Congratulations, that's three straight. You killed me again. You win."

No sooner had the words left his mouth than they snapped her out of what had been such a perfect moment as if she'd been struck by a terrible blow.

Dorothy felt tears well in her eyes as emotions ran rampant through her slender frame.

"I... I can't—" she sputtered. "I'll kill you... I—"

"Dorothy, look, I didn't meant to—"

She cut him off and rushed for the door.

"No!" she sobbed. "I'm not meant to—I just can't."

"Wait!" he cried after her. "I didn't mean—I'm sorry!" But it was too late. She'd dashed out the door and was already gone.

"Shit, what have I done?" Randy wondered as he closed the door. "Fuck!" He turned and stormed into his kitchen, hoping to find another bottle of wine to dull his emotions.

CHAPTER 24

Dorothy jumped off the bus near Camview Psychiatric Hospital and took off running down the street. The sky was rapidly getting lighter by the minute, and she was painfully aware just how late she was getting back.

Too late.

Shit, what was I thinking? Stupid, stupid!

Dorothy was so distracted that she didn't even notice Doctor Vaughan as he exited the artisan coffee and donut shop across the street.

He normally wouldn't have been anywhere near his hospital at this hour, let alone on a weekend, but the board wanted to review several files the following week, so he had headed in very early this particular Saturday to get on top of his financial reports before the board found anything else to bitch about.

He took his first sip of his scalding-hot coffee of the morning. *Impressive, though not as good as my home brew. Well, it will have to suffice.* His attention shifted to a young woman rushing down the opposite sidewalk. *What the hell?* He was shocked by an unexpected and unmistakable sight. There, plain as day, was Dorothy Maitland, hurrying by across the street.

She was outside of Camview's walls. Again.

Vaughan froze in his steps for a moment, then took off at a brisk walk in pursuit, pausing briefly to curse as he spilled hot coffee on himself, which only served to anger him more, while giving his mental ward troublemaker a greater lead.

Doctor Vaughan weaved through the few pedestrians on the street, keeping an eye on her as she fled. A half a block ahead, she rounded the corner into an alley. He quickly hustled across the street after her, but when he finally turned the corner, drawing a deep breath of the fetid air as he primed his lungs to yell for her to stop, he was quite surprised to find no one there.

The Camview early risers were quietly eating breakfast, unaware of the drama unfolding just outside their walls. The frenetic energy of the nuthouse was dialed down several levels as the normally gregarious bunch wiped sleep from their eyes and sat down for their morning oatmeal and anti-psychotics (with a nice tranquilizer for good measure for the more troublesome ones).

Curtis had a place saved for Dorothy, but her seat remained empty. He knew she had gone out to see Randy the night before without him, but had felt secure that she'd be just fine without him there just this once. Now that she wasn't safely seated across from him, he wasn't so sure.

He craned his neck and scanned the room anxiously.

"Maybe I'd better go wake Miss Sleepyhead up. Wouldn't want her to miss out on such a particularly lovely batch of oatmeal."

For some reason, this particular morning was not a good one for former delivery driver-turned-paranoid-delusional Donald T. Elliot, and his anger control issues were coming back in force.

"That's bullshit!" he spewed, a red flush quickly rising to his oily face. "Why does she get to sleep in whenever she wants? Is she better than us? Is that it? That's bullshit!" He was starting to rev up into full-swing angry mode.

Curtis tried to calm him as best he could. "Hey, Don, it's no big deal. Just chill out man. It's all good."

"All good?" He spun on Curtis. "Chill out? How the hell can I chill out when she gets special treatment?" he railed on, drops of spittle flying as his temper rose.

"Oh my God!" Stein shrieked, horrified as he scooted to the far end of the table. "You spit when you yell. That's how Ebola spreads!"

"He doesn't have Ebola, Stein," Curtis quickly tried to calm the panicked germaphobe, before he had *two* raving lunatics to deal with instead of just one.

"Screw this. I'm telling Doctor Vaughan!"

Donald tried to rise but Curtis locked a hand around his arm and pulled him back into his seat, quietly but very firmly. Don tugged futilely, and was about to lay into Curtis, but he saw an unfamiliar look in the perpetually cheerful man's eye.

One that unsettled him ever so slightly.

That uncertain pause was all Curtis needed to seal the deal.

Like a parent bribing a child, he took his beloved pudding cup and offered it up as a sacrifice in the name of peace and quiet.

"Look," he began "there's no need for you to get all riled up. Here, you can have my pudding, okay? I know you like pudding, and I'm going to give you mine, but you have to promise to chill out, and shut up, all right?"

He waved the sweet treat in front of Donald's face. Indecision flashed across the angry man's face, options weighed, a choice being made. Finally he snatched the pudding cup and sat back down with a grumble.

"Thank you, Donald. Wise choice. Now you just sit *quietly* and enjoy that." Curtis rose and headed for the hallway.

"Back in a minute, Beckman. You mind keeping an eye on my food?" He called back over his shoulder. The OCD accountant nodded and went back to counting the vowels on a magazine page as he shoveled cereal into his mouth.

Curtis tried his best to look perfectly calm, which was certainly not his usual state of being, pretending he wasn't up to anything, which likewise, was also not his usual state of being. With a quick stride, he made his way quickly down the hall to Dorothy's room. Looking both ways to be sure he wasn't being observed, he cracked open her door and poked his head inside.

No one home.

"Oh no," he said to himself quietly. "This is not good."

He spun on his heel and hurried back to the cafeteria, hoping to see his friend's face there when he arrived back.

No such luck.

Sitting anxiously in his seat, his leg bounced an anxious staccato while he played with his food, unable to eat, his nervous eyes glancing back to the doorway every few seconds.

"Come on, Dorothy, where are you?"

The majority of the breakfast crowd had filtered in, but still, she was not there.

The door at the far end flung open, and Doctor Vaughan, a dark coffee stain across his pants, his face red from his rush to Camview, strode into the room and gazed across the motley group with laser intensity. Curtis watched with dread as Vaughan waved Stan over. The vein on the side of his head was visibly throbbing, Curtis noted, pounding so hard he could see it even from across the room as he barked commands to his lackey.

"Oh, now this *really* isn't good," Curtis muttered, desperately worried about his friend.

Beckman had been droning on, though Curtis had tuned him out, but the incessant mumbling had finally driven Stein a bit mad. More so than usual. The man wouldn't shut up.

"...but the deduction parameters are somewhat vague, what with the cost of the balloon being in question, but still, the Wizard could clearly deduct—"

"Oh, shut up!" Stein blurted. "I don't care about fantasy tax deductions! None of us care! *The Wizard of Oz* is just a stupid movie, you socially inept git. It's not real!"

Beckman looked horribly offended, and in a rare outburst of carbohydrate sacrifice, he threw his half-eaten muffin at Stein, bouncing it off his face. A few crumbs lingered, stuck to the germaphobe's otherwise immaculately clean skin.

"Oh my God, that's not sanitary!" he shrieked, trying not to gag. "Is that a cold sore?" Stein snatched up a napkin and viciously scrubbed at his skin. Quite unintentionally, he gave Curtis an idea.

Across the room, Stan nodded at his boss's orders, then flagged down another two orderlies before turning toward the hall leading to patient rooms.

Out of nowhere, food started to fly, a direct hit landing on Stan's bald head.

He turned to see who the culprit was, but the other patients immediately took the cue, and an all-out food fight quickly ensued. The orderlies scrambled and ducked flying oatmeal and muffins, having to momentarily forego their task to help stop the high-calorie mayhem.

Several minutes later, Doctor Vaughan, Stan, and his two underlings, all splattered with food and looking none too thrilled about it, yanked open the door and stormed into Dorothy's room.

Dorothy rolled over under her blanket, face a bit red and sweaty as she calmly gazed at Doctor Vaughan.

"You!" he growled, his voice cracking in his anger.

"I'm sorry, Doctor Vaughan," Dorothy said. "I wasn't feeling well this morning, so I thought I'd skip breakfast and just stay in bed. I'll just eat at lunchtime. Thank you for your concern, though." She rolled back over, hoping he'd just leave.

No such luck.

Doctor Vaughan lunged forward, and ripped the blanket off her bed, flinging it across the room as he did. Dorothy was still wearing her outside clothes, having not had so much as a spare second to change when she had sprinted back to her room.

"Take her!" he cried.

The burly men grabbed her, easily yanking her from her bed and out her door. Dorothy struggled futilely as they dragged her down the hall. Curtis poked his head around the corner and watched, horrified but powerless.

Vaughan called over the nearest nurse. "I want every room locked down. All of them!"

"But, sir, we don't have the extra staff. We—"

"Just do it!" he shouted in her face, his rage clear in his eyes. It was abundantly clear she'd be wise not to say anything other than, "Yes, sir," if she wanted to keep her job.

"Good," was all he said in reply before he turned on his heel and stormed down the hall to room forty-two.

They hadn't even bothered to remove Dorothy's street clothes before strapping her to the table, and had only just tightened the last restraint when Doctor Vaughan burst into the room.

"Hook her up! Now!" he yelled. No one said a word, but just quickly did as he commanded, attaching electrodes to her head and strapping a bite plate into her mouth.

"Doctor Vaughan," the nurse on hand began, "should I set the —" He pushed past her and flipped the power switch on, then without hesitation cranked the dial far to the right. Dorothy screamed as electric current flowed through her body.

Patients flinched as her cries echoed down the hallways.

A week later Doctor Vaughan seemed quite relaxed as he walked down the hall carrying a few files under his arm to review in the peace and quiet of his office. He paused at the rec area to give his patients a once-over.

There was a buzz among the residents, a sense of nervous calm, as he strolled through his hospital with the air of a king walking amongst his frightened serfs. Word of what happened had quickly spread, and everyone with a pair of ears knew what he'd done. Even the normally combative patients toned their antics down a notch, not wanting to meet the same fate as the girl who had pushed Doctor Vaughan too far.

Curtis looked up from his jigsaw puzzle as he strode by. "Hey, Doc, come on, it's been a week all ready. She didn't mean anything by it. She's a good kid."

"A good kid?" he rebutted, his anger quickly returning. "Let me show you something about this 'good kid' of yours." Doctor Vaughan flipped through the files he was carrying, stopping on the newest one.

Dorothy Maitland, the tab read.

He opened it, showing the contents to Curtis.

"Hey, isn't that covered by HIPAA confidenti—"

Doctor Vaughan glared at him, and Curtis, wisely, clammed up. "Um, never mind."

"As I was saying," Vaughan continued. "Dorothy Maitland." He pointed to her grainy police scan. "Kicked out of the linguistics program at Oregon State for intoxication and assault. Attempted suicide three times while under care in Portland. Prior history of drug abuse stretching back to her teen years." He paused for effect, looking at Curtis like a snake would a mouse. "Let's see, what else? Oh yes, prone to violent outbursts, and this one's great. It says she even stabbed an orderly with a pen." He shut the file, utterly satisfied with himself. "So this is what you call a good kid?"

"That's not her," he quietly replied.

"Oh, come on, Curtis, has she got you believing that too? The charts don't lie. It's all right here, plain as day, and neither her delusions nor yours make the facts any less real. Your little friend is a very sick girl, and I'm going to make her better," he leered. "My way."

The way he said those last two words left no doubt what he meant by them.

Drenched in sweat, exhausted from yet another round of shock-therapy, Dorothy was unceremoniously dumped on her bed, the door locked shut behind her. She tried to rise, but the effort was too great.

What time is it? How long has it been?

The light filtering through the window had changed, she noted.

Okay, it must've been a few hours at least, she thought as her eyelids slipped closed.

A jingling of keys outside her door a few hours later brought her to her senses, though her energy was still hovering near empty. The knob turned and a tray of food slid in, the door slamming shut immediately, the bolt locking in place once more.

She was running on fumes and knew what she had to do.

I have to eat, she thought. *I don't think I'll be able to take much more of this if my energy gets any lower. Come on, legs, move!* She struggled to sit, finally resolving to just slide to the floor and pull the tray closer.

She was so drained that she didn't even bother with the plastic utensils, but rather picked the food up with her bare fingers, barely managing to get it into her mouth. She chewed slowly at first, but when the first bite found its way to her stomach, her body went on autopilot. From that point, she wolfed down the rest of her meal like a feral animal, unsure it would ever see another bite.

Sated and exhausted, she slumped back against her bed frame and drifted off into a restless and uncomfortable sleep.

At the same time, across the city, Randy, too, was eating a meal, though with far less urgency. Food had lost much of its taste of late, he found.

Since Dorothy had fled that night, he hadn't heard a single word from her, and even Curtis had stopped showing up to the diner.

Randy had tried a few of their favorite places, but no one had seen either of them in weeks. He thought back to that night and wondered to himself just how badly he had messed things up with her while he picked at his french fries, absentmindedly painting an abstract in ketchup as his mind wandered back to the girl who thought she was Death.

She always heard the jingle of keys long before they reached her door.

Dorothy had learned the pattern of her abuse, and was sure to be ready when they came, seated placidly on her bed as they man-handled her to her feet and down the hall.

For some reason, on this particular day, they came early. She sat on the floor, working another fine rune into her chalk circle, when they arrived. There was no warning jingle before she heard keys pulled from a pocket right outside her door.

Panicked, she quickly shoved her bed back into place, jamming her treasured book under her mattress and sitting atop it just as the door swung open. The orderlies pulled her to her feet and dragged her out into the hall.

She allowed herself the slightest sigh of relief as they led her away. She'd managed to stash her book. Everything would be all right.

But it wouldn't.

In the rush, Dorothy had failed to notice her piece of chalk had fallen to the floor and was sitting in plain sight.

Doctor Vaughan made a point to free himself from whatever he was doing to personally supervise Dorothy's "treatment" every single time, taking a sadistic joy in breaking the will of his most troublesome patient. Any other person and he really wouldn't have cared. Hell, he would have never even dreamed of recommissioning room forty-two, for that matter, but then this one came along, and her antics jeopardized the order of Camview. Worse than that, she had jeopardized his very job.

That simply would not do.

Times such as these called for drastic measures, or so he managed to convince himself. Meanwhile, Dorothy received her daily session, writhing and screaming as the power arced through her body, while Doctor Vaughan calmly looked on.

Dorothy was unceremoniously tossed back on her bed, sweaty and exhausted. She lay still for a moment, soaking in the blissful peace of not being subjected to electroshock, but somehow, despite her exhaustion, her senses tingled. She opened her eyes and looked around.

Something felt off.

Wait, I didn't leave my bed askew like this.

In a panic, she mustered energy she didn't know she possessed and managed to rise to her feet and reach under her mattress.

The book was still there.

That was close, she sighed, relieved. Since the book was already in her hand and her adrenaline had given her a much-needed energy surge, she decided to move her bed frame and continue working on her intricate chalk project. As the bed slid aside, she was greeted by a blank surface. Her weeks and weeks of hard work had been erased, and nothing but a tiny trace of a chalk smear remained on the smooth floor.

No! How could they have known?

With what was left of her energy, she searched her room high and low, but her chalk was nowhere to be found. She couldn't even start from scratch again if she wanted, at least not until she managed to steal another piece to draw with.

Hot tears welled in her eyes. All that effort, all that study, and now her most promising chance to get back home was gone in an instant. It was looking as if Pestilence had once again become her best bet, but now she was the one locked in isolation.

Exhausted, she couldn't take any more and finally gave up, at least for the day. Caving to her body's wishes, she flopped down on her bed, passing out almost immediately into a sleep so deep, she didn't hear Curtis talking through her door.

"Dorothy," he whispered, "can you hear me?"

Nothing.

"We're all locked down at night, and I haven't been able to get out to tell Randy what's going on. I need to know if you know his phone number. I want to try and sneak out a call from the nurses' office. Are you there?"

But at that moment the girl who thought she was Death was sound asleep, and quite dead to the world.

CHAPTER 25

Standing on a street corner, Dorothy felt a sense of calm familiarity wash over her as she watched the drunk stagger to his car. Everything in the world was as it should be.

The man reached his destination, fumbling in his pocket for his keys as she raised her hand, slowly plucking his soul from his body. The man's eyes widened in shock as his legs got wobbly.

His life force was slowly pulling free of his chest, when, for no visible reason, it stopped.

Stuck.

Then it started to pull back.

Dorothy strained, both arms now outstretched as she tried with all her might to pull his soul free.

Stubbornly, it simply wouldn't come out.

Then, in one quick motion, it snapped back into his body, slamming her to the ground as it did.

Dorothy lurched awake in her bed, sweat beading on her brow, her breaths coming hard and fast as her heart raced from the nightmare. She looked around, realizing, gradually, where she was. Still locked in her room in Camview. Still powerless, but in a different way, and if she didn't get back soon, the world would be in big trouble.

The crowd was thick in the gallery that night, the scores of art patrons mingling shoulder-to-shoulder as the local food trucks fed the hungry among them out front, while those seeking adult libations sidled up to the bar conveniently set up inside.

The high-ceilinged gallery was dimly lit for the most part, creating a mood of intimacy, while the artwork was illuminated by bright beams shining from meticulously aimed track lighting hanging from the exposed rafters high above.

The show cards said eight p.m. to eleven p.m., but by the looks of things, it was going to be another late one, which was quite all right with Gary, so long as art was sold and connections were made.

"Randy!" he called out as he approached his friend, a drink in one hand and a young man with an SLR camera in tow. "This is Todd McClure from Low Saccharine magazine."

"Nice to meet you. I love the mag, it's one of the few that has really committed to getting exposure for new artists these days."

"Thanks man, we try, but it's mostly up to you guys to find them in the first place. You going to be around later? I was hoping to discuss the show when it calms down a little."

"Yeah, I'm here until the lights go out," Randy said with a little chuckle.

"Excellent. I'm going to get some candid shots of the crowd. Let's catch up in a bit."

"I look forward to it," he replied as the young man waded off through the crowd to capture the essence of the evening through his lens.

Gary grabbed Randy by the shoulders, a happy smile plastered to his face.

"You've outdone yourself this time. Really, this is the best turnout yet. You went balls to the wall for this one."

"Yeah, I wanted it to be special."

Gary would have to be blind and dumb to miss the shift in mood.

"Ah yes, the new girl you've been talking so much about. Where is she? You've got to introduce me."

"She wasn't able to make it tonight." Randy kept it together as best he could.

"Aw, shit man, I'm sorry to hear that. I was looking forward to meeting her finally. She sounds like a real keeper."

"Yeah…" Randy's mood fell further.

"Everything all right?"

"Yeah, she just… something came up. No worries. Sorry to be a bummer."

"Then don't look so down." Gary shook his friend playfully. "There will be plenty of other openings you can bring her to. Don't sweat it so much. Now wipe that frown off your face and get out there and schmooze! I want to see lots of little red 'sold' dots next to those paintings!" He gave a friendly slug to Randy's shoulder and wandered off into the crowd.

Randy reflected for a moment, sighed, then took a deep breath and forced a cheerful salesman's grin back onto his face before heading once more into the fray, immediately spotting one of his long-time collectors.

"John, great to see you. So glad you could make it!" he chimed. For a moment, the big smile on his face looked almost real.

Much later that night, after the opening finally wrapped up, Randy found himself sitting alone at the familiar linoleum counter, nursing his woes with a slice of pie and a cup of Angie's finest coffee. Lucky for him, he'd built up something of an immunity to it.

Angela had given him some space at first, reading his body language with a single glance, like the good ones in the waiting game always do. Then, when it looked like he was finally getting over his initial funk and settling down, she strolled over and topped off his coffee, casually checking in on her friend.

"You okay, hon?" she asked, a hint of concern peeking through her casual expression.

He paused, not sure if he really wanted to talk about it.

"It's been three weeks, Angie," he finally said. "I'm afraid I scared her off." The dark cloud returned, but Angela pressed on.

"Hey, don't beat yourself up. She likes you, and I mean a lot. Anyone could see that. I doubt she's gone for good. Maybe she just needed some time to think."

"But it's been nearly a month, Ange. Maybe I'm just a fuck-up."

"Or maybe she's busy with other things. You know better than most people how time sometimes has a way of catching you off guard and flying by."

"I guess," was all he could manage, so instead of making small talk, he slid another bite of pie into his mouth and chewed slowly, thinking about the girl he'd grown so fond of. The one he feared he had driven away.

In the dim light of Camview, Curtis rose from his bed, quietly padded to his door, and pushed.

Still locked.

It had been hours since Big Stan walked the hallway calling out, "Lights out, lock 'em down!" and, unfortunately, no one had unlocked them since. He'd have to wait, yet again, for an opportunity to present itself if he wanted to check on his friend.

Lady Luck smiled on him the following morning.

When an older patient took a little tumble, drawing the attention of the nurse and staff, he managed to slip away, using the opportunity to scurry down the hall as the staff was occupied giving medical aid.

Sitting in her isolated room, Dorothy was awake, but unlike Curtis, she had no energy to even try the locked door. Since they slid trays of food to her daily, she had become accustomed to only seeing the four walls of her room.

Those, and the walls of room forty-two.

She sat, her back against the wall, arms wrapped around her knees to keep upright. Her tray of food held no appeal as she quietly sobbed to herself.

Outside her room, Curtis slid up to her door and heard her quiet anguish.

It broke his heart.

"Hey, can you hear me?" he said in a hushed voice. "You've got to hang in there. Don't let them break you. Don't give the bastard the satisfaction. You're stronger than he is. Never forget that."

Curtis sensed something behind him, the hairs on his neck tingling.

Stan had walked up to him unnoticed, surprisingly quiet for such a large man, and gave him a shove.

"Move along, little man," he threatened.

Curtis rose to his feet and paused, flashing an angry look.

"What?" Stan challenged. "You wanna try something?"

Curtis glared at him, but turned and moved off down the hallway, shooting daggers from his eyes as he headed to join the others.

"Yeah, that's what I thought," Stan called after him, ever the bully.

Curtis passed Doctor Vaughan as he made his way back to the rec room. The doctor was once more performing his hanky trick with a flourish, reveling in the rapt attention of his captive audience now that Dorothy wasn't there to ruin his illusions.

With a flash, the hanky disappeared, replaced by an old silver coin, prompting applause from his small audience of drugged patients. He smiled broadly, ego expanding even further as he basked in the spotlight. He was about to launch into another illusion when he saw Curtis and paused, looking theatrically at the clock on the wall.

"Oh my," he said loudly, his eyes fixed on Curtis as he passed. "Look at the time. I mustn't be late for this morning's appointment with our favorite guest."

The patients grumbled.

"Don't worry," he continued, "I'll be back just as soon as I've given her my extra-special attention." He gave Curtis a wink as he walked off to room forty-two.

It had been nearly a month, and Dorothy was worn out. She barely managed a scream at all as Doctor Vaughan dosed her with electricity. Her bloodshot eyes teared up, and her body convulsed from the charge, but she didn't resist. All she could do was flop like a rag doll.

He smiled. It looked as though her will had finally broken.

Uncharacteristically, Doctor Vaughan stopped the treatment he'd only just begun and studied her carefully as she lay strapped to the table. He looked her over a moment longer, then headed to the door.

"Clean her up and bring her to my office."

Patients turned their heads to stare, then quickly averted their gaze as Dorothy was led down the hall to Doctor Vaughan's office. She was haggard and tired, but at least she'd been spared a full round of shock therapy, and her appearance showed it.

They'd actually taken the time to bathe her, providing clean garments for her to wear to her rendezvous with the doctor. She walked slowly, head down, watching the tiles pass as she drifted down the hall guided by two orderlies. Dorothy readied herself for whatever would come next.

When Doctor Vaughan's door swung open, she knew what she'd find. Her bearded nemesis was seated on his throne, everything in place to convey a sense of power and control. To be honest, given what he'd put her through for the past month, it wasn't that much of a stretch. So long as she was on his bad side, he had the ability to make her life a living hell, if he so desired.

And for nearly a month, he most certainly had.

The door closed loudly behind her, causing her to flinch.

Doctor Vaughan smiled at her reaction and gestured to the nearest chair. Dorothy gingerly slid into it, trying to find a comfortable position, her hands unable to stay still as she squirmed under his intense gaze.

"Stop that fidgeting," he commanded. She stopped abruptly.

"I'm sorry," she said timidly.

"What was that?" he asked, an edge to his voice.

"I'm sorry, Doctor Vaughan," she replied, emphasizing his name and title. His brow relaxed ever so slightly as he relished the feeling of having brought his most troublesome guest under control.

"I still don't know how you managed it, but that's behind us now. What is important to me, what is important to your continued well-being, is that I don't want to see you outside of these walls again. Clear?" He fixed her with a piercing gaze. Somehow she'd managed to keep Curtis's secret despite her daily torment.

"Yes, sir," she peeped.

"Any more unrest, any more disturbances from you, and

there'll be hell to pay. I think by now you know just how serious I am. Do you understand?"

"Yes, sir."

"Yes, sir...?"

"Yes, sir, Doctor Vaughan."

"Good." He stared at her until she bent under his gaze, looking away in discomfort. "Now, what is your name?"

Without a trace of guile or trickery, she answered.

"Dorothy."

"Are you quite certain about that?"

"Yes, sir, Doctor Vaughan," she quietly replied. "My name is Dorothy."

"How do I know you're telling the truth? How do I know you're not just lying to me? Do I need to question you more intensely?" He let the threat hang in the air. She was broken, that he could see, but he couldn't afford any more disruptions. Not if he wanted to keep the board from firing him.

"I wouldn't lie to you sir—Doctor Vaughan." She started to quietly sob. "I was very sick before. I was so confused... I was so sad. I wanted to die so badly, I-I thought I became Death." She looked at him through tear-filled eyes. "I understand now that I'm not well. I need help. Please, Doctor Vaughan, my name is Dorothy and I want to live."

Doctor Vaughan slowly reclined in his butter-soft brown leather chair, smugly admiring his handiwork, smiling to himself as he watched her sob.

"We're done here," he said into his intercom. "Take her back to her room. This phase of her treatment is complete."

Shortly after Dorothy was returned to her room, her door unlocked with a noticeable click. She looked around, unsure. The light filtering through her small window had shifted to an uneasy, dim hue as a rainstorm started to roll in. With a sense of unease and uncertainty, she tried the door.

It swung open.

Cautiously, she stepped out into the hallway. The orderlies and nurses took note, but didn't move to restrain her. They actually seemed relieved that the whole lockdown ordeal was finally over. While the overtime shifts were a welcome source of extra income at first, as the weeks had drawn on, they had grown weary of constantly working without proper rest. Her cooperation with Doctor Vaughan had been a good thing for the entire staff, and most of them gave her a slight smile as she walked slowly to the rec room.

Dorothy found a comfy lounge chair away from the others and curled up in it like a cat who'd finally found a ray of warm sunshine on an otherwise cloudy day, and the day was indeed cloudy. Rain had started spattering gently on the windows, but the increasing wind signaled something far bigger was in store.

She was absentmindedly staring at a ping pong game, near catatonic in her trance as she watched the little white ball bounce back and forth, when Curtis strode into the room. He spotted her almost immediately, a happy smile erupting from ear to ear.

"Hey, you," he said, gently placing his hand on her arm, "glad to see you're all right."

Almost as if he could sense her being comforted, Doctor Vaughan floated into the room, scanning his kingdom. His eyes paused on Dorothy and Curtis a bit longer than on the other patients.

"Look," Curtis continued, "I'm sorry, but I wasn't able to get to Randy. They put the entire wing on lockdown every night. You weren't the only one stuck. We all were."

She didn't look at him, but just sat quietly. She flinched as Doctor Vaughan sidled up to her and Curtis where they sat.

"Dorothy. Curtis," Doctor Vaughan greeted the pair, eliciting nothing but a cold stare from Curtis. Dorothy, on the other hand, looked at him timidly.

"Hello, Doctor Vaughan."

No sass. No snark. Now Curtis was concerned.

Doctor Vaughan kept his gaze on Dorothy as he reached into his coat and slowly, and quite dramatically, pulled out her prized book from his pocket.

Dorothy's eyes betrayed a look of genuine shock. The malevolent little grin it evoked on Doctor Vaughan's face was equally real.

"Tsk, tsk," he chided. "You know unapproved reading material is not allowed in Camview. I mean, we have to keep the patient's best interests in mind, do we not?" He paused, waiting to see if she'd respond, but she was gazing at the book in his hand, tears in her eyes. "Don't you worry, I'll have Stan dispose of it for you. I know you wouldn't want to break any more rules."

Seemingly out of nowhere, Stan was suddenly at his side, taking the book from Doctor Vaughan's hand. He gave Dorothy an unsavory look as he walked away.

But... that only leaves two options now, and Randy's watch hasn't been panning—

"Oh," Doctor Vaughan interrupted her rumination. "I almost forgot. I thought you'd like to know just how committed I am to helping you continue along on your road to recovery. Your disruptive little friend claiming to be one of the Four Horsemen of the Apocalypse, um, Pestilence wasn't it? Yes. Well, I had him transferred to Westmoreland Psychiatric for more 'intense' treatment. In fact, he was shipped out yesterday."

Her last resource gone, Dorothy started to cry quietly.

Doctor Vaughan smiled.

"I knew you'd be thrilled," he said with relish before walking away.

"Dorothy?" Curtis asked.

She looked up at him, then over at Doctor Vaughan where he stood observing them from across the room.

Her gaze shifted back to Curtis as she muttered something quietly. Curtis leaned in closer, paused, then moved to touch her shoulder. Dorothy shrugged him off violently.

Vaughan smiled to himself. Things had gone better than he'd imagined.

Curtis leaned toward her again, and she once more muttered something back to him. He gave the slightest of nods, almost imperceptible, then reached out to try and comfort her again.

Dorothy slapped his hand away and jumped to her feet.

"Just leave me alone! Why can't you just leave me alone!" she cried out before turning and running off down the hall to her room, leaving Curtis looking distraught and alone.

Later that night, the majority of the residents were just starting to gather in the rec room for movie night. Tonight was everyone's clear favorite, *The Wizard of Oz*.

Dorothy, though now free to join the others, had elected to stay in her room, away from the throng. Given what she'd gone through, no one on staff thought it unusual in the least.

Every so often, thunder would rattle the windows as the storm outside intensified.

At one such rumbling interlude, Curtis stopped outside her door, casually squatting as if tying his shoe, though they all had slippers, and slid a small note under the threshold before continuing on to the screening.

Dorothy rose from her bed and picked up the paper. A small bundle of cash was tucked inside. More important were the words hastily scribbled in her friend's handwriting.

"Westmoreland Psychiatric, 1223 Bates Drive."

Pestilence. She allowed herself the smallest of smiles. *Curtis came through.*

The duty nurse was about to dig through the pile of DVDs on the table for *The Wizard of Oz* case, but to her surprise, it was conveniently resting on the top of the stack. Curtis watched her intently from across the room as she opened it, not even bothering to look at the disc as she inserted it into the player. He smiled.

Had she looked closely, she'd quite possibly have noticed the DVD in her hand was not the plain *Wizard of Oz* disc but rather one Curtis had substituted on the sly. A disc he'd shoplifted several months ago.

One Flew Over the Cuckoo's Nest.

A film about riots in a mental hospital was not likely something Doctor Vaughan would have put on the approved entertainment list. Oblivious, the nurse slid the disc into the machine, pushed play, and walked out of the room as soon as the FBI warning flashed on the screen.

Movie night was the rare moment the staff could actually leave the patients unattended and get a little time to themselves. While it was against regulations, there had never been an incident yet.

Curtis's smile widened as the movie started, bouncing in his seat with excitement.

He'd been looking forward to this for a very long time.

Back in her room, Dorothy lay quietly under her blankets. She heard quiet footsteps approach her door. Larry the buzz cut orderly quietly opened her door. He poked his head in the room. Seeing Dorothy in bed, he stepped inside, closing the door behind him.

"So, you're not going to the movie tonight?" he asked as he moved closer. Dorothy didn't respond. She just lay there. "Aww, you feeling a little down? Well I've got something that'll cheer you up." He reached a calloused hand down and began unbuckling his belt as he leaned over her still figure.

"Oh yeah, you're gonna love this," he leered.

With a quick motion he yanked back her blanket, his pants halfway down. Much to his surprise what he discovered was not a pajama-clad victim, but rather Dorothy fully clothed in her outside attire.

Including her boots.

"What the—" was all he managed to say before she lunged, kicking him square in the balls, dropping him to the floor in a writhing heap.

"Sick son of a bitch," she spat as she swung off the bed to her feet. "How many women have you pulled that on?"

Several additional kicks gave her a surprisingly enjoyable rush of satisfaction.

Dorothy walked to the door and peeked out. Satisfied no one had heard anything, she turned her attention back to the unconscious would-be rapist and gave him a long, cold stare.

One thing was for sure, if Doctor Vaughan could see her now, he'd realize the wool had been pulled over his eyes, and Dorothy was not so timid and broken after all.

With movie night in full swing, a poor orderly named Dean was the unlucky one who drew the short straw, having to leave the impromptu staff poker game to go check on the patients.

It should have been a simple thing, really. Just pop down the hall, poke your head in to see the loonies all drooling and watching tin men and scarecrows merrily skipping down a yellow brick road, then get back to the game. Dean was annoyed. He had been doing well at the table and didn't want to mess up his streak of good luck, but as he approached the rec room, he heard uncharacteristic hoots and hollers.

The nutjobs loved *The Wizard of Oz*, but this sounded like something different.

"Hey, guys," he said into his walkie-talkie. "You might want to get down here. Something's going down."

"Copy that, on our way."

With backup en route, he put his hand on the knob and pulled the door open. Inside, he found a chaotic scene.

Patients were up on tables, furniture was upturned, the bowls of pretzels and popcorn, left for them to snack on during the film, were flying through the air like edible confetti.

"Hey, what's going—" He didn't make it any farther before being broadsided by a hysterically laughing patient. Curtis saw the takedown and heartily approved, adding his own Nicholson flair with a favorite quote from the film.

"I must be crazy to be in a loony bin like this!" he cried out, then beat his chest like Tarzan, let out a whoop, and started flinging pretzels into the crazed throng.

Doctor Vaughan had been at home, shoes off, listening to the steady patter of the storm as rainfall landed on his windows. It wasn't often he'd break out the good stuff, but today was a good day, and he was thoroughly enjoying a tumbler of his precious and pricey Midleton whiskey. A little reward to himself for finally successfully putting an end to his most pressing troubles at Camview.

Sure, things would always happen to throw things out of whack, that was expected, but Dorothy had been a whole new level of problem, and one that had been bringing increased scrutiny from the board, and that simply couldn't be allowed. It was a good thing he now had that situation under control.

Or so he thought.

Standing in the aftermath of the movie night mayhem a short while later, Doctor Vaughan was most certainly not amused.

He had only just taken his first sip of whiskey, savoring the heat and subtle flavors, when his phone had rung, the panicked cries of his staff abruptly jarring him from his happy place.

As fast as he could get there in the pouring rain, he was back at Camview, storming down the hallways as his staff wrangled the last of the patients back into their rooms.

He surveyed the mess they'd made of the movie room. Another expense he'd have to creatively cover discreetly from his budget if he wanted to keep the board of directors off his back.

This was not good.

Things like this didn't happen at Camview. Unless...

"Come with me," he growled as he spun off down the hallway, the few staff not hauling people to their rooms following in tow.

As he approached Dorothy's room, Big Stan appeared from the other end of the hall, soaked from the rain and dressed in a T-shirt and jeans, having rushed in from his night off. He hastily trotted over to meet the doctor, leaving a small puddle beneath him as water dripped off his hulking frame.

"Open it."

Dorothy's door swung open, the orderlies moving aside as Doctor Vaughan stepped into the room.

Larry, the would-be rapist, lay tied to the bed, pants down and bound with sheets, gagged with a sock and his own belt.

Doctor Vaughan erupted.

"Find her!" he yelled, and his staff scattered, searching every nook and cranny of the building.

But Dorothy was long gone.

CHAPTER 26

The storm had developed into a full-blown downpour. Howling wind whipped rain sideways along the dark streets as the gusts redirected it as it buffeted off the darkened buildings.

A solitary figure in black forged ahead, ignoring the elements as she made her way toward the warm glow of a welcome place.

The door to the diner swung open with a bang as the wind seized it from Dorothy's hand. She pulled it shut behind her and strode in, dripping wet.

The diner was empty. Not surprising, as it was the kind of weather you had to be either desperate or crazy to be out in. Angela stepped out from the kitchen when she heard the door, expecting anything but what she saw.

"Oh, honey," she said to the soaking wet girl. "Where have you been all this time?"

Dorothy ignored the question, intent on her purpose.

"Where's Randy?"

"He's not here, hon. Oh, look at you, you're soaking wet. Here, I'll get you some nice hot coffee and a towel." She turned to pour a cup, the sound of the door swinging open and shut behind her.

"Dorothy?" she said as she turned, but the girl who thought she was Death had already gone.

Dorothy wasn't the only one out in the elements that night. Thoroughly warmed by his anger, Big Stan also stalked the dark streets, soaked to the bone as he looked high and low for their troublesome patient. He was not happy spending his night searching dark alleys. The pounding rain steamed off his bald head as he turned down another alleyway, searching for the escaped girl.

The beginnings of bedhead had shaped Randy's coif as he slept, leaving him with an interesting look, the kind that some trendsetters would probably pay a stylist good money to recreate. He flipped on his foyer light as he trudged to the door, clad only in boxers and a T-shirt.

"All right, all right, I'm coming," he grumbled. "Just a minute." Shaking the cobwebs of sleep from his head, Randy turned the knob.

Standing there, soaked to the bone, was Dorothy, shivering and wet, an intense gleam in her eyes. He was shocked, and any remnants of sleepiness quickly gave up the ghost.

"Dorothy, what the fuck—" he began.

"I have to tell you something," she interrupted. "It's important. No lies, no holding back."

He wiped the last of the sleep from his eyes. "Are you going to come in?"

"Just listen to me," she cut in. "I am an escaped mental patient. I just broke out of a psychiatric hospital tonight, and I need to tell you the truth about me."

"Look, I know you've had some problems, and I—"

"I am Death, Randy. And no, I'm not crazy or depressed or on drugs. I really am Death, and I really am trapped like this, in this form. I've been trying to find out how to cross back over, how to get back to do what I was created for. I even thought I might have found a way, but then... well then you had to come along." Her eyes misted up, a tear mixing with the rainwater dripping down her face.

"Look," Randy said, "if this is your way of saying you don't want to see me anymore, you could have just come right out and—"

She grabbed him by the shirt, pulling him tightly to her, and kissed him.

Hard.

"Uh..." He was at a loss for words. "Or that works," he finally managed.

Dorothy grabbed him, surprised at the surge of lustful heat that flooded her body. By how much she longed for his touch. Their mouths fiercely mashing together as they staggered into his apartment, Randy kicked the door closed behind them. They knocked over everything in their path as they moved, stripping off Dorothy's soaked attire on the way to the bedroom, leaving puddles of wet clothes in their wake, and not caring one bit.

They tumbled through Randy's bedroom door, landing on his bed in a writhing jumble of limbs, their long-building connection finally realized fully as a white-hot wave of passion surged through them both.

It would be many, many hours before they'd untangle from their lovers' embrace, wrapped in the warm haze of joyous exhaustion as they finally succumbed to sleep's siren song.

The clock read 9:17 a.m.

The storm had cleared, leaving clear, blue skies in its place. A ray of warm sunlight shone through the parted curtains in Randy's window, illuminating the lovers wrapped in a jumble of sheets.

Dorothy slowly roused, opening her eyes and taking in the room. She noted the trail of clothes leading to the bed, her eyes crinkling in amusement. The bedding was a jumble, condom wrappers haphazardly flung on the floor. Even in the heat of the moment, Randy had somehow had the presence of mind and self-control to pause to be safe, she recalled, and what a night it had been.

Wow, she marveled. *So, that happened. Not what I was planning, but...wow.*

Turning her head, she gazed at the sleeping man next to her, a flush warming her face, and regions a bit lower as well. With an utterly contented smile, she rested her head on his chest and curled back into his arms as they instinctively wrapped around and drew her close. He cracked his eyes open, a smile of such warmth focused on her that it made her heart nearly skip a beat.

"Hey, you," was all he said. The look in his eyes conveyed the rest.

"Hey." She smiled back at him, locking eyes with the man she realized she adored, his watch faded to an afterthought. He drew her closer still, his hands gently exploring her body. Not frantic like the previous night, but relaxed and at home.

And that was exactly how Dorothy felt.

At home.

A few hours later, Dorothy sat comfortably on the living room couch, coffee in hand as she replayed the prior night's events in her head, still amazed at the turn things had taken.

Randy, plates in hand, walked over from the kitchen.

"Sorry, this is all I've got at the moment. I wasn't exactly expecting company," Randy said as he put a plate of toaster-waffles on the coffee table. "We can pick up some real food later."

"This is fine," she replied as she took a bite. The sheer joy of carbohydrates and sugar flooded her system, recharging her body, weary from the night's exertions.

"So," Dorothy said, wiping her mouth with a paper towel.

"So," Randy replied.

"Look," she began, "last night was wonderful. And so was this morning, but I realize this is all really sudden, and I appreciate your taking me in. I can stay in Sam's room if you want. I don't mean to be an imposition."

"Sam's room? I haven't even finished painting it, and it won't have a bed until she moves in this summer. Besides—"

"I can sleep on the couch. I don't mind," she interrupted.

He looked at her like she was a madwoman.

"Seriously? The couch?"

"Well..." She didn't know what to say.

"I appreciate the concern, but just stay with me in my room. I mean, we've pretty much bulldozed any boundary issues, so why not?"

"Are you sure?"

"Of course I am. I was wondering, though, what about Curtis?"

"Yeah,... he's not really my roommate," Dorothy confessed. "He's actually a mental patient, like me."

"Why doesn't that surprise me?" Randy laughed.

"By helping me escape, he's sure to be under lockdown again. And here I am, staying with you. Are you absolutely sure this is all right?"

"We've got to figure things out before summer, but for now it should be fine. My folks might have an issue with me shacking up with a woman my daughter hasn't met yet, but Sam doesn't move in for a few months. For right now, let's take things day by day, at least for now. Sound like a plan?"

"I like the sound of that," Dorothy grinned. "Do you have a dryer?" she asked, looking at her soggy clothes strewn on the floor. "I really didn't plan this very well."

Randy kissed her on the forehead and went to gather her damp things.

"Yeah, I'll toss them in. But you can't wear the same thing every day. When you finish your breakfast, I'll take you to pick up a few things."

"But I only have a couple hundred dollars to my name."

"Don't worry, I know a guy, one of the collectors from the gallery. He'll hook us up, and if for some reason we still go over, I'll cover the difference and you can pay me back later. I think you're good for it. Oh, he's going to love you."

The afternoon sun arced high above the city as the pair entered a rather trendy-looking shop.

Fausto Designs in a stylish foil-embossed script greeted them from above the doorway as they entered the hip clothing store, conveniently just a few miles' walk from Randy's place.

The store was owned and managed by Fausto Fornaciari, an Italian clothing designer who happened to run in Randy's art-world circles. When Randy had called him asking for a favor, he was more than happy to help his nice young friend.

"Oh, honey, just look at you," the slight man with a huge presence commented as he gave Dorothy a once-over with a sympathetic gaze. "Oh, but these shoulders, these legs! You have excellent bone structure! Don't you worry, we'll fix you right up." He cast a snarky glance at Randy.

"Really, Randy?" he chided. "You take your lady out like this? I am horrified!" Randy blushed slightly and shrugged helplessly.

He had provided some sweats and a shirt for Dorothy while her things were in the wash, but they were several sizes too big for her slender frame. It was the best he could do, given that she had quite literally nothing to wear other than the soaked clothes he had scooped from the floor where they'd fallen the night before.

"Can you work your magic on her, Fausto?" he asked the gregarious little man.

The Italian smiled. He had taken an immediate liking to the girl, and, deciding she was to be his project for the day, he led her to his fitting area.

With a flip of the wrist, he pulled back a curtain, revealing three old Greek women at a sewing table. Their workspace bore a weathered little sign that read, "Moira's Alterations."

The three women looked up from their work, genuine puzzlement forming on their faces almost simultaneously when they saw their unexpected guest.

"Ladies, this is Dorothy," Fausto said with a gleam in his eye. "She is a special client, and is in need of your talents!"

Klotthie, the somewhat serious woman working a spindle, eyed Dorothy intensely, looking her up and down from toe to crown repeatedly. The poor woman seemed a little bit confused.

"I don't think we know you," she muttered.

"This is Dorothy," Randy chimed in. "She hasn't been in here before."

"No, we definitely don't know you," she confirmed, truly perplexed.

"How can we not know her?" her sister, Atroppie, asked from her seat at the far end of their work station. "That cannot be."

"She's new to town," Randy replied.

Lakhie, the more gentle-natured of the three sisters, approached Dorothy and looked her over carefully. Gently, she took the young woman's face in her soft but weathered hands, examining her with her remarkably sharp eyes for an older woman.

"Such a pretty girl," she said, then turned from her and began looking through the myriad threads on her table. "You look cold. We have this beautiful thread. We could knit you a nice sweater."

"I'll get my shears," Atroppie offered with a grunt.

"No! Not for this one," Klotthie said, a surprising intensity coloring her voice. "Fausto, you still have the samples from Milano, yes?"

"Of course."

"Good. She has the right frame for them. We will work from those. For now, anyway."

Lakhie took her by the hand. "Come, we will measure you," she said, leading Dorothy off to be fitted. The three women were fussing over her like mother hens, but the sisters all seemed unsettled by her presence, Randy noted curiously.

Fausto was back in a jiffy, carrying armloads of outfits to the odd seamstresses. His load delivered, he then joined Randy while the old women worked their magic.

Fausto looked on approvingly as his obviously smitten friend watched the slender girl step from behind the curtain to show off the various outfits he had insisted she simply had to try on.

Of course they look good, he thought with pride. Fausto had impeccable taste, after all, and with her lithe build, much of his sample stock was in the girl's size, or close to it. Oh yes, he would make her look *wonderful*.

It was indeed a productive visit, with several flattering outfits acquired. After several cheek kisses, they bade the gregarious Italian and his Greek associates farewell and headed back home to drop off their packages. They had acquired enough clothes to easily get her through the week, which wasn't a bad start.

"You look amazing. Simply amazing!" the Italian had said as they left his store. "You must come back next month. There will be some new arrivals that will look amazing on you. But your shoes. Oh honey, those will not do. Go and stop by Jovan's on Sixth. He'll take good care of you. Just tell him Fausto sent you."

As the pair strolled home, Randy noticed that every once in a while there would be a subtle shift in Dorothy's mood. Despite the fantastic day they were having, she would suddenly become self-conscious, glancing around almost as if she expected something bad to happen.

He wasn't wrong. She was increasingly on-edge. Every time she would see a bearded man of a certain build and age, or if she happened to catch a glimpse of a large, bald man, she'd tense up a little.

We're miles away. They wouldn't have come this far, would they?

She was paranoid, but given her recent circumstances, Dorothy felt justified in her caution.

She stopped suddenly as they passed a group of pedestrians. Without warning, she pushed Randy into a doorway, kissing him passionately, all the while keeping her back to the street. When the suited man with a beard walked by, she released her embrace.

Randy enjoyed the unexpected show of affection, but he also noted that she had studied the man as he passed, then relaxed when she saw that whoever he was, it was not whom she'd thought.

What's going on with her? he wondered. For the time being, he decided to let it be and not pry. Besides, Randy was quite happy to be the victim of a kissing ambush, so he smiled and went with the moment.

Little did either of them know, Doctor Vaughan and his minions were indeed out looking for Dorothy. Fortunately for the lovers, the searching eyes of Camview, while leaving no stone unturned, were currently combing the streets and alleyways miles away, far across town.

They finally arrived back at Randy's place in the early evening, arms loaded with the final items they'd picked up.

Not having a car limited their outing somewhat, but Dorothy was grateful for it in a way. Randy had spent a lot on her, and even with his friend's generous discount, she was acutely aware she had no means to repay him.

Randy did it because he wanted to, and he truly seemed to take pleasure in helping her out, but it nevertheless made her a bit uncomfortable, being so dependent on another person.

"Hey, give me a hand with this," Randy called out from the bedroom.

Dorothy walked to the bedroom, where she saw a sizable pile of clothing strewn on the bed. He was clearing out part of his closet for her.

"Wait, you don't have to do that."

"Can't have your new things getting all wrinkly, now can we? Besides, you said you just busted out of jail."

"Mental hospital."

"Even more impressive! Point is, you're staying with me for the time being, and I want you to feel comfortable here."

"I'm sorry, Randy," she said, a note of guilt in her tone. "I really didn't plan this out very well. I don't mean to be a burden."

His eyes flashed briefly to a small picture of his folks with his daughter, but he shifted his attention back to Dorothy.

We'll have to figure that out before Sam comes. Plenty of time before that, though.

"You're no burden," he said, then put down the parcels and replaced the clothes in his arms with the girl standing in front of him. "For the time being, mi casa, su casa." He then proceeded to alleviate her concerns, one kiss at a time.

CHAPTER 27

They both rose early the next morning to the sound of Randy's alarm clock. Though they'd have rather slept in, he had a meeting with a new client across town, and Gary was sparing him the hell of multiple bus transfers at rush hour.

At a quarter to nine, a full fifteen minutes early, there was a knock at the door.

"Shit, he's early," Randy said as he trotted to the door.

"Hey man, you ready to go?" Gary asked with a smile as he invited himself in.

"Yeah, just give me a minute. You could have just called, you know."

"Well, I *could* have, but then I wouldn't get to meet the new lady friend. Where is she?"

Hastily dressed, Dorothy emerged from the bedroom. Gary beamed his widest smile.

"You must be Dorothy! So glad to finally meet you. I'm Gary."

"Nice to meet you, Gary. Randy's talked a lot about you, it's nice to finally put a face to the name."

"All nice things, I hope."

"Mostly," she chided. "So you two are heading all the way across town?"

"Yeah. Don't worry, I'll bring him back in one piece."

Randy grabbed his friend and ushered him to the door.

"Come on, enough of your banter. I'll meet you downstairs in a minute."

Gary flashed a "nice going" look to his friend and stepped out.

"Nice meeting you, Dorothy. I hope to see you again soon!" He turned and walked down the hallway, the echoes of his footsteps fading as he went.

Randy turned back to Dorothy.

"Okay, I'll be back before dinner. You sure you'll be all right?"

"Yes, just go," Dorothy chided. "I'll be fine. I've got the key, don't worry about me."

"All right, then. When I get back, we'll grab something to eat. Any preferences?"

"I don't know. Maybe Chinese?"

Randy smiled. "Cool. I know an awesome place. Okay, you've got a key and some cash, so I guess we're good to go." He leaned down and gave her a kiss.

"Okay, see ya."

"Bye."

The door shut behind him, leaving Dorothy completely alone for the first time since her escape.

She took a moment to just be, sitting on the couch, thinking about everything, but also about nothing at all.

"Right. I should clean up my mess and get organized."

Dorothy rose and walked to the bedroom closet. Within a few minutes, she had re-arranged her new clothes in a more logical manner. *There. All in order. Oh yeah, I have stuff in the dryer.*

She went and retrieved her formerly soaked clothing from the machine and laid them out on the bed to fold. Her shirt went in the drawer Randy had cleared for her, while her pants had a similar space ready for them in the closet.

Dorothy froze when her fingers brushed a crumpled wad in the back pocket of the pants she was folding. Her heart pounding, Dorothy carefully took the crinkled paper out and smoothed it on the dresser.

"There's still a chance," she gasped, a surge of adrenaline flooding through her veins. She put the note down and quickly got dressed.

Dorothy was going out.

The paper had just one thing written on it: *Westmoreland Psychiatric, 1223 Bates Drive.*

Finding the address was relatively easy. A simple bus ride and short transfer had taken her to a bus stop a mere block from the imposing glass and concrete facility. Westmoreland Psychiatric was the polar opposite of Camview: a beacon of modern medicine, housed in a state-of-the-art facility.

Bright, warm lights shone invitingly from the lobby, and the staff milling about were all clothed in starched and ironed uniforms.

Dorothy steeled her nerves and walked through the front door. There was a pause as the double-door system cycled her into the building, the door behind her locking before the one in front of her opened.

"Hello, may I help you?" a smiling woman asked from behind the reception desk.

"Yes, I believe my friend may have been transferred to your facility. I'd like to see him, if that's possible," Dorothy replied in the most calm voice she could manage.

The woman turned to her computer. "All right, let me check our system. What's your friend's name?"

"He goes by Pestilence."

"Pestilence?" the woman flashed a perplexed look.

"Yes, um..."

Shit! What did Stan call him? Jerry something?

"What I mean is, he suffers a delusion that he is a Horseman of the Apocalypse. Pestilence, to be exact."

"Well, I need a name to look him up. You do know his name, don't you?" the woman asked, a hint of probing curiosity in her eyes.

"I knew him from outreach we did... um... at the bus depot," Dorothy quickly covered. "Food for the homeless, that kind of thing. He never did tell me his full name. I believe it was Jerry something."

"Hang on, let me see if I can find him in here," the woman answered, turning back to her screen.

Dorothy glanced around nervously. This was not going as smoothly as she'd hoped. High on the wall, she noticed the surveillance cameras monitoring the area. Several, actually.

No way to dodge that. Just stay calm. Everything is normal here. No one will ever even review the videos, there's nothing out of the ordinary going on here.

Then she noticed it.

A bulletin board behind the desk.

Most of it was covered with flyers about the importance of hand washing, emergency protocols, and a few department-specific notices. Also on the board, were several sheets with missing patient information and mug shots.

One of them bore the name Dorothy Maitland.

Shit! Dorothy forced herself to breathe slowly. *She hasn't noticed, just act normal.*

The woman turned from her computer. Something was familiar about the woman at her desk, but she couldn't quite place it.

"Okay, I see one patient transfer that looks like your friend, but I can't let you in without prior written approval since he's in a high-security wing. What you need to do is fill this out, then bring it back to me with two forms of photo identification. My supervisor will review it and log you into the system. After that, you'll be cleared for a visitor's pass."

Dorothy took the form from her and put it in her pocket.

"Excellent, I'll get right on that. Thank you so much for all your help." She turned and walked to the door.

The handle wouldn't budge.

What? She began to turn, ready for the inevitable sight of orderlies rushing to take her away.

"Hang on, I need to buzz you out," the woman called out to her.

Dorothy breathed a sigh of relief. There wasn't an orderly in sight. The door buzzed, and a few moments after that she was safe on the street outside. Safe, but also unlikely to ever see Pestilence again.

She quickly strode away from the building and caught the first bus heading remotely the direction she wanted. The most important thing at that moment was to get as far from Westmoreland Psychiatric Hospital as possible.

The bus ride was an uncomfortable one, and not due to the sweaty crowd. Dorothy's nerves were in a jumble, and a feeling of dread hung over her like a cloud. She disembarked, having traveled a bit off-course from her original destination, and found herself walking a familiar-looking street as she followed the bus driver's directions toward her transfer stop.

Her heart began to pound when she saw the store right there in front of her. She'd never seen it in daylight. For that matter, she'd only seen it once before.

This can't be coincidence, she told herself as she stepped into the old book shop.

It looked the same as it had the night she'd visited it with her friends, but in daylight it seemed to lack something. A feeling she'd had that night. The young man at the counter looked up from his cell phone.

"You need something?"

Dorothy approached him. Indeed she did.

"I bought a book here a few months ago and was hoping you might have another copy. An occult book the older gentleman who works the night shift found for me."

"Night shift?" the man said, confused. "We close at eight."

"But I was here. He got it from those shelves, right over there."

"I'm kinda new here, but no one ever told me the place had been open nights, and I don't know any old guy on staff. You remember his name?"

She thought a moment.

"I never asked it."

"Huh, well, I guess it's possible maybe he left just before I started. Anyway, let's see if we've got what you're looking for.

It took some searching, but less than ten minutes later, Dorothy exited the shop with a brand-new, crisp-spined copy of her missing book in her hands. She rushed to the bus stop, anxious to get home and begin the lengthy process again.

Fortune smiled on her once again as she walked the final blocks home. A trio of young girls were playing hopscotch on a chalk-drawn sidewalk, right in her path.

This is too convenient to be coincidence.

"Hey," she said as she approached the girls. "Can I buy that chalk from you?"

The girls looked at her like she was nuts.

"You can just go to the store and get some, you know," the one closest replied.

"I know, but I'm kind of in a rush. Tell you what, I'll give you a dollar for it."

"Well…"

"Okay, how about five?"

"Five?" the girl asked, shocked.

Moments later, Dorothy was on her way, chalk in pocket and book in hand. Less than five minutes later, she was back in the apartment, anxiously pacing the living room.

Okay, it's still early. I have time to start, but where?

She scanned every room, looking for an inconspicuous nook to begin her runes again. There wasn't one. Distracted, she nearly tripped over the edge of Randy's area rug that had bunched up ever-so slightly.

A light bulb went on in her head.

Carefully, she moved the chair and coffee table to the side and rolled the rug back. Plenty of space for what she had in mind, and entirely out of sight.

A feeling of calm embraced her as she sat on the floor and opened the book. It was going to be all right. All she had to do was recreate what she'd already done before.

Only, there was a problem.

Wait a minute, this isn't right. This chapter is all different, and half of the runes from this section aren't even listed.

She quickly flipped to the imprint page and scanned the tiny text.

There it was, printed plain as day in black-and-white. While the book title was technically the same, the edition was new. New and *revised*.

It's not all there, she lamented. *I'll have to fill in the blanks from memory. If I even can.* Frustrated, she sat staring at the space she'd cleared on the wood floor until, finally, she made a decision. *If the watch doesn't pan out, this is the only option I've got. I have to at least try.*

Slowly, she began the lengthy task of re-drawing her rune circle.

When Randy walked in the door later that evening, bags of Chinese takeout in his arms, Dorothy greeted him with a kiss. His rug, and everything on it, were all back in place, nothing amiss.

"Sorry! We ran late," he said apologetically. "I figured you'd probably be pretty hungry by now, so I went ahead and picked us up a few things."

"Mmm. It smells good. I'll get us some plates," Dorothy offered.

The two sat down for a relaxing dinner, and Randy happily proceeded to fill her in on the events of his day.

"How about you?" he asked between bites of chow mein. "You do anything fun?"

"Nope," she answered without hesitation, her eyes darting briefly to the area rug. "It was a pretty uneventful day."

CHAPTER 28

"Hey, sleepyhead," Randy called through the bedroom door. "Come on, get up. We're going on an adventure today!"

Dorothy stirred and stretched out on the cozy bed. The clock said 8:30 a.m.

She could smell a pot of coffee brewing in the other room. Not the diner's rocket fuel blend, but something smoother, with a rich aroma. Randy didn't make coffee at home often, but when he did, he preferred the good stuff.

Mmm, that smells wonderful, she thought as she wrapped herself in his robe and walked to the kitchen. *But what's this about an adventure?*

"Hey, you," she said, flashing a sexy grin.

He turned from his food prep and took in the sight of her with a hungry smile.

"There she is," he said with a smile. "You want some coffee?"

"Sure," she replied.

"Cream?"

"You know how I like my coffee," she said with a smile.

"Of course, what was I thinking? You like your coffee like you like your magic. No cream for you, then," he laughed. Dating a girl who thought she was Death certainly had its moments.

"Ha-ha, very funny," she said with a chuckle while Randy added a liberal amount of cream and sugar to her coffee. "So, what's this adventure of which you speak?" Dorothy asked as he handed her the steaming mug. Like a welcome, floating spirit, the divine aroma of caffeinated happiness wafted to her nose, gently elevating her consciousness.

"Urban picnic," he said cheerfully. "I'm packing a basket, and then we're going to go wherever you wish. Just pick a bus line and off we go." He dumped a handful of bus tokens on the counter.

"Fate is our guide, adventure our goal."

"You're a madman," she chuckled. "Has anyone ever told you that?"

"Maybe once or twice, but coming from you, I'll take it as a compliment."

She laughed, a bright and cheerful sound Randy was quite fond of.

"Baby, you're the peanut butter to my jelly," he said, leaning in and kissing her neck.

"Um, thanks?" was her confused reply, not exactly sure how she should react.

He raised an amused eyebrow.

"Peanut butter and jelly sandwiches," he explained. "You take one part or the other and you've got nothing special, but put them together and it's magic!"

"When I was a boy," he continued, "my mom wasn't always around. Both of my folks had to work. It was tough making ends meet, so they really didn't have a choice. Anyway, I was on my own a lot, but every Monday, Wednesday, and Friday, my mom would pack me a peanut butter and jelly sandwich with the crusts cut off. Man, I loved PB&J as a kid." He smiled at the memory, almost getting misty-eyed. "That's how I knew she cared, even if she wasn't always there. And cutting off the crusts? Now that's love."

Dorothy leaned in and kissed him sweetly.

"That's a beautiful story," she said, letting a little laugh slip out. "But I'm wondering, do I have to be the peanut butter, or can I be the jelly?"

"Baby, you can be whatever you want," he replied, then drew her into his arms for a warm kiss. "Okay, now get dressed. I'm gonna grab a quick shower, and then we've got an adventure to get underway!"

He stripped as he walked, excited for their outing. Moments later, Dorothy heard the water running.

Now's a good time, she decided.

Quickly and quietly, Dorothy padded across the bedroom and

picked up Randy's old pocket watch. The fine metal lines inlaid in the blue enamel seemed familiar, but random at the same time. She opened it and examined the glass face.

Nothing.

She then held it to her forehead, pressing the cool enamel into her skin, trying to sense something, anything that might explain her situation.

Again, nothing.

There has to be something to this watch.

She had an idea. Very quietly, she whispered the incantation she'd learned from her book. The old book, not the new one.

"Eeanay Sudominey Vorghalisi Nictu," she intoned.

Wait, was that something? She scanned the air around her.

"Eeanay Sudominey Vorghalisi Nictu," she said again, focusing her mind on the watch in her hands. She couldn't be sure, but she thought, for just a second, that maybe there was something. A tug beneath the skin of reality, but she couldn't be sure. Dorothy concentrated harder and said the words once more.

"Hey, babe. You say something?" Randy called from the bathroom. The water had stopped running.

Quickly, Dorothy put the watch back in its place.

"No, I didn't say anything," she called back. "Just getting ready."

The couple enjoyed the nice weather as they leisurely walked a few blocks to a bus stop. Randy's picnic basket, Dorothy learned, wasn't actually a basket, but rather, a well-organized backpack with Tupperware containers neatly stacked. There were also bottles of water and a pair of single-serving wine cups. He slung the bag over his shoulder as they boarded the random bus Dorothy had selected, setting off on their impromptu adventure.

"I wonder where we'll wind up," she pondered as they took their seats.

"Doesn't matter," Randy chimed in. "I'm sure we'll have a ball."

The doors closed, and they rolled on their way.

When they stepped off the bus a little while later, Dorothy felt the area looked somewhat familiar, but she couldn't quite place it.

Why do I know this place? she thought as she scanned the building façades, not recognizing anything.

Randy took her hand in his, snapping her out of her daydream. They headed off down the street, taking in the sights as they discovered more of the nooks and crannies of the city in which they lived.

A few blocks later, Dorothy and Randy found themselves at a busy intersection.

I swear, this looks familiar.

"Come on, we can totally make it!" Randy said, taking her hand and bolting across on a flashing *Don't Walk* signal.

He was right, but only just.

They barely made it before the light changed, laughing as they laced their fingers together and continued on their way, oblivious to the one spectator watching their progress with rapt fascination.

Madame Bavmorda had just arrived at her storefront when something caught her attention. She stopped and turned, doing a double take at a young woman running across the street toward her.

"No, it can't be," she muttered to herself as she squinted her eyes, trying to get a better look at the familiar-looking girl. She watched Dorothy and Randy grow closer as they strolled and was suddenly sure she wasn't mistaken.

The crazy girl she'd kicked out of her shop a few months earlier seemed to have gotten her shit together.

As they passed, Dorothy noticed the woman staring right at her and glanced at the store's façade. A light bulb of recognition illuminated in her head.

Dorothy flashed her an amused little grin and a wink as she and Randy passed.

"Well, good for her," Madame Bavmorda said with a little laugh and an approving nod, then stepped into her shop, the neon "Open" sign flickering to life moments later.

It was in their fourth week together that the inevitable finally occurred. The loving couple had their first fight.

Exhausted and a bit irritable after dealing with a particularly difficult client, Randy came home early from work to find Dorothy sitting on his living room floor, rug pulled back, covering the old oak boards with chalk designs.

"Jesus! What the fuck are you doing to my floor?" he yelled.

Dorothy nearly jumped out of her skin.

"Shit! Randy, you're home early."

"Ya think?" he growled as he surveyed the sprawling design. "What the fuck, Dorothy? I'm out busting my ass working and you're sitting at home messing up my floors? My kid doesn't even do that anymore."

She quickly tried to put his mind at ease.

"It's only chalk, Randy. It'll clean up. I just needed a big enough space to work on. It's not permanent, I promise. See? It'll wipe up when I'm done."

He was pacing. Angry. Trying to keep his temper, but only just managing.

"It's not about the mess," he began. "Well, it's that, but also, you don't have any aspiration. You stay home all the time. You haven't even once talked about looking for work. I mean, I'm glad you're here, but this..." He struggled to find the right words. "Look, you know this has to be a home my folks are comfortable with if they're going to let Sam move back in, and I don't know how they'll take it if I suddenly have a live-in girlfriend who doesn't even have a job."

Dorothy's patience finally wore thin.

"What would you have me do?" she snapped. "I don't exactly have a great and varied resumé, you know."

"Oh, come on," he countered. "It doesn't have to be some big, full-time job, just something to make a contribution. Hell, pick up some shifts at a coffee shop." Randy took a deep breath. "Look, anything you can do to at least show you're trying would be great."

She paused, digesting the point he was trying to make. Trying to understand where he was coming from. *A place of fear,* she realized. *Fear that I might get in the way of his little girl coming home.* Dorothy forced herself to relax.

"So you're not mad about the floor?" she asked, shifting the subject.

"Of course not," Randy replied, calming down as well. "It's only chalk. I just wasn't expecting to see my place turned upside down when I walked in the door is all. You want to make chalk mandalas, or whatever that thing is, have at it. Just promise me you'll look for a job too, okay?"

Dorothy's pulse slowed.

"I understand your concern, Randy. Really, I do. Samantha is your priority. I get it, and tomorrow I'll look for a job."

He moved close to her, the anger melting from both of them.

"Thank you. It means a lot." He held her close, breathing her in. "I'm sorry I flipped out on you. It was a shitty day, and this all surprised me—"

"No, you had good reason. I just hope I can find somewhere that'll hire me."

"You think about the morgue?" Randy joked.

"I only deal with people *before* they're dead. You know that. Besides, it'd be a pretty slow job. People aren't dying like they're supposed to these days."

"I don't know, I still see stuff in the news."

"Yeah, but those are catastrophic events. Everyday deaths are slipping through the cracks. The slack is being picked up, somehow, but the ones they're missing are piling up, and pretty soon it's going to reach a tipping point."

"Well, you're here for now, so it's not your problem, right?"

She stared at him a long moment. He still didn't *really* believe her.

"Yeah, right. Not my problem," she lied. "Besides, it'll be at least a hundred years before there are any irreversible problems."

Randy laughed. "We'll be long gone by then anyway. Come on, get your shoes on and let me take you out for an apology dinner."

"Really?"

"Yeah. Gotta fill up that tank. You're gonna need your energy for that job hunt."

Having trekked all over town, it turned out getting a job wouldn't be nearly so easy as Dorothy had hoped. Rejection after countless rejection turned her mood sour, and after a full day searching for a job, she realized an under-the-table gig was likely to be her best, and only, bet.

It was by sheer luck that she happened to stop in a hole-in-the-wall coffee joint halfway across town before heading home from her unproductive day.

The girl in dark makeup behind the counter who had served her didn't make small talk, but was nice enough. Dorothy found her pour-over coffee more than adequate as she rested her weary feet in a threadbare wingback chair.

She was beginning to decompress when the constant din of the somewhat crazy man at the counter finally cut through her calm. Despite the girl's polite refusals, the man wouldn't stop harassing her.

"Come on, just one cookie. You know you can spare it. You'll just throw them out at the end of the day anyway," he whined.

"For the last time, no, I'm not giving you free pastry. Now please leave me alone."

"Don't be such a stuck-up bitch!" the man yelled. "I oughta show you—"

Before he could react, the slender woman in black crossed the tiny space, getting right in his face.

"You really should leave now," Dorothy said, sharp ice dripping from her words.

Something in her tone, along with a dangerously cold look in her eyes, made him agree.

"Your cookies suck anyway!" he spat, trying to save face as he stormed out and slammed the door.

The barista reached into the display case.

"Hey, thanks for stepping in. I really appreciate it. You wanna cookie?"

"Sure."

"Cool. I'm Nadine."

Dorothy shook her hand.

"I'm Death—I mean, Dorothy," she quickly corrected.

Shit.

"Ha! I love it. Nice to meet you, Deadly Dorothy," Nadine laughed, embracing the moniker.

The two women started talking and hit it off, the surly barista and the girl who thought she was Death bonding over mutual dislike of the idiots who seemed to fill the city. Their conversation eventually touched on the subject of the misery of job hunting, and by the time she left to catch the bus home, Dorothy had landed her first part-time coffee house gig.

Randy was thrilled, not to mention impressed she had managed to find work so quickly. When she replayed the circumstances of her hiring, all he could do was laugh.

"That is so you," he chuckled. "So when do you start?"

Dorothy breezed through training, mastering the machines in a day. Nadine was impressed and felt quite satisfied her new co-worker had her shit together. She penciled her into the schedule for a few shifts starting that weekend.

"Don't worry, I'll be working with you the first few weeks until you really get the hang of things," Nadine assured her.

Come that Saturday afternoon, Dorothy found herself enjoying the casual camaraderie behind the counter. Nadine, being a rather surly barista, shared her morbid sense of humor. Thus, the two actually got on quite well.

"It's official now, you're part of the team. So, there's one last thing you have to do," Nadine informed her.

"Oh?" Dorothy asked, intrigued.

"Every employee gets to create a drink. See that one, 'Brew-ha-ha'?" she said, pointing to the chalkboard. "That's mine. Triple shot with almond milk foam, a dot of salted caramel syrup, and a bad joke."

"A bad joke?"

"Yeah. I've got a whole book of 'em, so don't worry. If someone orders it, just look at the cheat sheet I taped up on the register."

"And people order this?"

"Mostly for the coffee," Nadine replied. "But some like a joke in the morning. Anyway, be creative and have fun with yours. It's just coffee, after all."

"I'll give it some thought," Dorothy mused. "I'm sure I can come up with something interesting."

Fortune smiled upon her, and the rest of her first day went smoothly, especially as the weekend crowd tended to be a bit more laid-back than the frantic workweek morning rush.

By the time she returned home, hands fragrant with the caffeinated tinge of work, despite several washings, Dorothy was more than ready for a relaxing evening of nothing more than take-out and a movie, and Randy happily obliged.

Just a few days later, when Dorothy stepped off the bus and walked the few blocks to work, she opened the door to see a new menu item had been chalked on the board behind the counter.

Coffee of Death, a cold-brew iced coffee with an additional double shot of espresso made with a cinnamon/cayenne blend mixed in.

"It will touch your soul, but watch out, you might get burned!" Nadine quipped with a chuckle. Of course she liked the name. She was the one who had helped come up with it, after all. "Hey," she said as she pulled her sketchbook from her bag, "you wanna check out my new tattoo idea?"

Over the next several weeks, with the employment speedbump smoothed over, Randy and Dorothy hit their stride, really thriving as a couple, despite having been thrown together into a completely unexpected cohabitation situation. The widower, and a girl who thought she was Death.

Dorothy also found her paranoia about being recaptured and dragged back to Camview was finally easing, at least a little.

Working a few days a week helped, giving her a surprising sense of structure as well as extra cash, some of which went to acquiring more books on the occult. Unfortunately, no matter which store she visited, no book she found contained the wealth of information of that first tome. The one taken by Dr. Vaughan.

Eventually, after another futile attempt at a gateway incantation, Dorothy had to accept the very real possibility that her weeks and weeks of chalk-work and study was for naught.

All these runes. I've learned so many of them, tried every combination, but I'm no closer to home than before, she grimly realized, sitting cross-legged on the floor of their living room. *If these really won't work, then the only other option has to be the watch. I just don't know how.*

She looked at the time. Her shift started in a couple of hours. Carefully putting the rug back in place over her sprawling maze of runes, Dorothy got ready for the bus ride across town to work. *Well, it should be a pretty relaxing day, at least,* she reasoned. *I have to thank Nadine for putting me on afternoons this week.*

Calm and content, Dorothy locked up and headed off to work, happily settled into a satisfying routine, at least for the time being.

Despite whatever comfort level Dorothy had found, one person was quite the opposite, and still had his escaped troublemaker firmly in his mind.

Every day, Doctor Vaughan would still habitually scan the streets in hopes he'd catch another glimpse of the woman he'd come to see as the sole reason for his troubles and woes. She'd been gone long enough that he simply couldn't cover it up, and news of the escape had finally reached the board. He still had a job, but was desperately clinging to it with only his fingertips. To him, she was worse than just an institutional nemesis. She was quite possibly the death of his career.

He couldn't paper over things this time, and besides the wrath of the board, he was under scrutiny from the state regulators as well. Desperate to save his job, his nerves were on edge constantly. Doctor Vaughan had just picked up an afternoon cup of coffee and muffin from the shop around the corner from Camview, allowing himself a rare break, when his cell phone rang.

"Yes?" he answered, weary, but still determined. "No, I don't care," he snapped into the phone. "Keep looking!"

Doctor Vaughan ended the call and sighed. He needed a break. A moment to gather his thoughts, so instead of heading straight back, as was his usual routine, he took a seat on one of the vacant chairs in front of the establishment and watched the throngs of humanity flow by. The act of sitting, just for a moment, to zone out a little, allowed him a brief moment to decompress, even if just the slightest bit.

His phone rang again.

"Yes?" His shoulders slumped ever so slightly as he listened to his caller. "I see. Tell him I'll be there shortly. Of course, we can use the conference room. Um, exactly how many members of the board came with him? I see. Very well, I'm on my way now."

He took a deep breath as he rose to his feet, steeling himself for the browbeating he knew he'd receive when he returned.

"They have no idea what I have to deal with," he muttered as he stepped out into the human traffic and headed to whatever fresh reprimand was awaiting him.

CHAPTER 29

It was a beautiful morning down at Lafayette Park as the lovers stood in the shade of a large oak. It had all started off as a bit of friendly banter the night before, but when Dorothy answered Randy's innocent question, he was shocked.

"You mean you really haven't? Not ever?"

She had shaken her head no, and Randy had declared that simply would not do. It was a basic a rite of passage for everyone, and this horrendous oversight would not stand. The next morning, they were about to remedy that.

"You ready?" he asked.

"I don't know. I mean, is this really necessary?"

"Trust me, you'll get the hang of it," he said, then gave her a shove.

He ran alongside her, hands planted on the bike's seat as they gained speed.

They may have looked a slightly odd pair, the two grownups running through the park, one on a bike, wobbling side to side, the other yelling encouragement, but odd as they seemed, their exuberance left a smile on the faces of everyone they passed.

"Keep pedaling," Randy called out. "You've got it!" And she indeed did.

He let go of the seat. Dorothy wobbled a bit, but the centrifugal force of the wheels kept her upright, and as anyone who has learned to ride a bike knows, everything suddenly just seemed to click. She pedaled a wobbly, wide loop that finally brought her back to her waiting fella, coming to a somewhat off-balance stop in front of him.

"Piece of cake!" Dorothy crowed, throwing a triumphant, lopsided grin his way.

He gave her a congratulatory high-five.

"Yup. A natural. That's my girl, everyone!" he shouted. "Made of awesome, this one right here!"

"Shut up!" Dorothy blushed.

"Make me," he laughed.

"If you insist," she chuckled in reply as she leaned in and gave him a kiss.

A few loops around the park later, they returned the bike to the rental kiosk and found a nice spot at the foot of a small rise, where they could people-watch the park-goers to their hearts' content.

Randy gave Dorothy a quick kiss, and rose to his feet.

"I'm gonna grab us a couple of hot dogs," he said. "You want a root beer?

"It tickles my nose."

He cracked a smile.

"I'll take that as a yes, then," he said, then trotted off to fetch their afternoon snack, taking a quick glance at the time on his pocket watch as he walked to the vendor's cart.

A funny thing had happened in the time she'd been living with Randy. While she was still actively working on her mystical rune gateway and fretted about crossing back, she also noticed that she'd sometimes get so caught up in life that she'd forget to be worried about it for days at a time.

So, it's not a total catastrophe. At least not yet, she rationalized. *I mean, people still die, it's just at a lesser rate. The big question is whether the gateway will work. If I don't get back, it'll only be a matter of time before the ripples grow and start having a serious effect.*

She decided it was too perfect a day to ruin with worry and made a conscious effort to think of more pleasant things, at least for the time being. As she surveyed the people lazing in the park, her eyes fell upon an old man sitting in the shade on a bench just up the rise. Squinting, Dorothy realized, much to her surprise, that she recognized the ornate cane in his hands.

It... it can't be.

The failed suicide from her first moments awake in this realm. Dorothy rose to her feet, unsure.

Why here? Why now?

There was only one way to find out. Steeling herself for whatever may come, she slowly walked over to where the old man sat, lost in thought.

"Mind if I join you?" she queried.

He looked up at her from his iron and wood throne. She detected no glimmer of recognition from his eyes as he gazed at her. None whatsoever.

"Suit yourself," he answered with a Russian accent. It wasn't thick like a tourist, but rather had the sound of a man who had moved to the country as a young man and had made his way, learning the language and customs, but never really shaking the part of his old life that formed his early identity.

Dorothy seated herself on the bench next to the old man, her posture a bit rigid as she waited to see what would happen next.

Nothing.

"Um, isn't it a beautiful day?" she finally asked him, breaking the silence hanging thick around him.

He turned his sad gaze to her.

"Just another day, like all the others."

She recalled the small framed photo of his wife next to his bed. Much of that morning was a blur, but for some reason, that image stuck with her. The man tired of living. A man who had nothing left now. A man on his own.

A lonely man who simply wanted to die.

Empathy had never been Dorothy's strong suit. Hell, it wasn't even in her vocabulary until recently, but she found that today, it came easily.

"I used to feel like that, you know," she began. "Nothing was special, every day was just more of the same. Even when things were different, they really weren't."

"You're young," he replied. "You've got your whole life ahead of you. You don't know loss. You have no idea how tired you get." He looked as if he was going to continue, then fell into silence. After the brief surge of energy from conversation with another person, he seemed to deflate like a jostled soufflé as his depression slid back in its place.

Dorothy gently placed her hand on his arm, fixing him with a warm gaze.

"You know, for a long time I thought every human life was just a clock waiting to run out. No matter what they did, it made no difference. At the end of their time, no one was special, no one was unique, and no matter who they were or what they'd accomplished, they would all die, just like any other."

He turned, engaged by her tone, strangely comforted, though he couldn't quite figure out why.

"Do you know what happened?" she continued. "All of a sudden, out of the blue, my life was turned upside down, and I realized that I had been wrong. That every moment of every day was unique for every single person."

She looked into his eyes and saw much sadness, but she also saw a flash of vitality from this man who had lived such a long life. She glanced at Randy standing in line to buy their snacks and felt a surge of warmth in her chest.

"I realized that every moment is a gift that people should cherish. It's not just a greeting card line or cliché. It truly is precious."

"You say all these things, but you are too young to truly understand," the man replied. "When you get to be my age there is nothing more to enjoy. Life runs out. My wife..." He started to tear up.

"I remember."

"What?" he said, returning from his memories. "Anyway, I'm all alone now. I just wish it was over."

She fixed him with an ageless gaze and spoke with zero doubt.

"You'll see her again," she said. "But life is such a marvelous thing. You should enjoy every moment you have for as long as you can. It's what she would want."

"But I miss her."

"And you'll see her again."

"But it could be such a long time," he said, tears trailing down his face.

"Yes," she replied, looking deep in his eyes. "But it is also just a moment away." Dorothy held his gaze a moment longer, comforting him until his tears slowed.

"You'll be fine," she said, squeezing his arm as she rose to walk back to her post-bike lesson picnic.

"Spaciba, molodaya zhenschina," the man thanked her in his native tongue. "Thank you."

"Pazhousta," she replied, her Russian accent mirroring his.

Dorothy felt good as she strolled back to her little cozy spot on the grass.

He's going to be all right, she thought, smiling to herself, feeling so good that the unusual happenstance of a girl who thinks she's Death telling a man to enjoy life was lost on her.

She passed a man with a familiar styled beard as she settled back to the grass, and for the first time since her escape, the fact that someone looked quite a lot like Doctor Vaughan hadn't even fazed her.

Randy returned, hot dogs and root beer in hand, just a few minutes later.

"Sorry for the delay, m'dear," he said as he took a seat next to her. "The woman in front of me was ordering for her whole family, and apparently they all like the works. Whatcha gonna do? So, did ya miss me?" he chided.

"You know, for the millisecond you were gone, I actually did." She beamed.

"Right answer," he said as he leaned over and kissed her forehead before trailing down to her waiting lips.

Hours later, as Randy enjoyed a relaxing, post-picnic shower, Dorothy hung her little surprise on the living room wall. It wasn't much, compared to some of the paintings artists had gifted to Randy over the years. Just a simple, yet amazingly realistic, trompe l'oiel painting of a chunk of gray rock that had caught her eye.

The street artist, who frequently sold his wares on the sidewalk near her work, had somehow made the flat panel look as if it housed an actual piece of stone. When she first saw the new piece on his stand, Dorothy stopped in her tracks and found herself almost reaching out to see if it was real.

The artist was pleased.

"Tell you what," he said, "I'll cut you a deal."

"Why would you do that?" she asked. "You don't even know me."

"I see you working in the coffee shop. That makes you what I call a 'friends of the neighborhood' customer. Besides," he said with a wink and a smile, "you strike me as someone who understands that things aren't what they always appear."

Dorothy was on the fence. She'd only just begun working, and paying her own way was something she found surprising satisfaction in. Spending money on art was something she saw as frivolous, despite living with a gallery director. That said, she couldn't take her eyes off the man's beautiful artwork.

"Well…" she began.

Sensing a sale hanging in the balance, the man struck a bargain.

"I've got an idea," he said. "Half off, but you hook me up with your employee discount on coffee and pastry. Does that sound workable?"

When Randy, freshly showered and smelling of soap and cleanliness, walked into the living room, he stopped in his tracks. Something was different.

Dorothy held her breath. She had slowly been adding little touches to the apartment, but this was big. This was Randy's realm. This was art.

He stood there, silently studying the piece.

"So…" The tension was killing her. "I hope you don't mind, but I really liked it, and—"

"Where did you get this?" he interrupted.

"I'm sorry," she said, dejected. "If you don't like it I can take it down."

He looked at her like she was crazy.

"Like it? Babe, I fucking love it!"

"Wait, what?" She breathed a happy sigh of relief.

"Oh, yeah. Seriously, this is really impressive work. Where did you get this? The artist is amazing."

"Just some guy who sells them on the street by work."

"Oh my God, a true unknown? When you see him, give him my card. If the rest of his work is this good, I'll to talk to Gary about putting him in a group show. Just a guy on the street?" He flashed a happy smile. "You, my dear, may have just scored me an exclusive new artist for the gallery."

That evening Randy had a fair bit of paperwork to get in order for an upcoming gallery event, and so it was that Dorothy decided to try another new thing. She was going to cook dinner all on her own. Since she'd moved in, Randy had been doing the majority of the cooking, as well as bringing home take-out on busier days, so this was her first chance to play chef solo.

It didn't exactly go as planned.

The fire department wasn't called, at least they had that going for them, but her noble attempt had led to the windows staying open for most of the evening as they let the apartment air out.

Dorothy had actually done quite an admirable job assembling the ingredients, but then, as it was cooking, Randy took a break from his work and they both became... distracted.

By the time she and Randy had stumbled back to the kitchen, sweaty and disheveled, the noticeable acrid smell of something burning had begun to fill the air.

"Shit! Dinner!" Dorothy cried out as he yanked the oven open, releasing a cloud of smoke that set off the smoke detectors. Randy grabbed a towel and dumped the dish on the counter. He quickly put the lid on it, snuffing the smoldering meal and limiting further smoke release. Despite the destruction of her attempted meal, Dorothy couldn't help but smile, the corners of her eyes crinkling as she tried not to laugh.

"It's not funny!" he lamented. "That was our dinner!" He flung the windows open, then climbed up on a chair to disconnect the wailing smoke detector. When he stepped back down to the kitchen floor, Dorothy threw her arms around him and kissed him with a smile.

"We can always order take-out," she said with a giggle, then snuggled her face into the crease of his neck with a happy sigh, sending a ripple of goose bumps down his arms.

He looked at her, flushed, and suddenly felt hungry for something other than dinner. The look in her eye told him in no uncertain terms that she most definitely felt the same.

"Ah, screw it," he said as he tossed the potholders on the counter and swept Dorothy up in his arms, practically falling into the bedroom in his haste to savor his lover's delights again.

The bus was crowded for the duration of the long ride to work, but Dorothy didn't mind. She'd actually become rather fond of watching the broad assortment of people stepping on and off as they crossed the city. Mobile people-watching, of a sort.

She stepped to the sidewalk and turned toward work. Plenty early and in no rush, she took her time, enjoying the stroll.

A man in jeans and a sport coat bumped her as he hurriedly walked past, engrossed in some drama on his cell phone screen. Dorothy watched him, annoyed by his lack of situational awareness. Sure enough, he bumped two more people in his haste, before tripping over a drunken bum sleeping on the sidewalk.

The inebriated man sat up, startled.

It took a moment, but Dorothy realized it was the same drunk she'd briefly encountered when her ordeal had only just begun.

The oracle.

It's him! She felt her heart race. *He can tell me what I'm missing. The key to—*

"Hey," the drunk slurred loudly at the man who'd tripped over him. "Watch it, you jerk! Yeah, that's it... a watch!" he droned on. "You need it or you'll be blue like me. Blue! I'm so blue," he started to lament, then regained his zeal. "You have to find it!" he carried on. A passerby took pity on the vagrant and tossed a dollar to him.

"Get yourself something to eat, okay?"

"What? Yeah. Wait… but it's a question—no, a quest! Yesssshhh, that'ssss it!" He collected the money and took a swig from the bottle ensconced in a dirty brown paper bag next to him, then rolled on his side and fell back asleep, not even noticing Dorothy was there.

She didn't know how to react.

He isn't…? She was mortified. *But that means… it means he's just a crazy old drunk talking nonsense. He might not have even been talking to me that day. He might not have even known I was there. Randy, the watch… they're not be the key to anything at all.*

Dorothy stared at the slumbering man as she walked by. The rest of her way to work passed in a blur as she soaked in the enormity of what had just happened.

"Hey, you okay?" Nadine asked her as she stepped behind the counter.

"What? Oh, yeah, just an off morning is all," Dorothy said, covering.

The rest of the morning went smoothly, though Dorothy was working on autopilot for most of it. Standing near the storage room in the back washing mugs, she almost didn't notice the Camview orderly enter. Only at the last moment did a tingling on her neck make her turn to look.

Larry, the orderly she'd tied to the bed.

He was looking at his phone, texting.

Shit! Dorothy ducked behind the partition. Nadine, her sixth sense kicking into high-gear, stepped away from the counter for a minute.

"Hey, what's up?" she asked her friend. "You okay?"

"The man at the counter. He's…" Dorothy didn't know what to say.

"Ex-boyfriend?"

"No. Shit, listen, there are things I haven't told you about me. Let's just say there's a really bad man looking for me, and that guy works for him."

"Did he see you?" Nadine asked, concerned.

"I don't think so. If he did, this whole part of town would be off-limits for me."

"Okay, let's think this through. He ordered for here, so it'll likely be a while. Only one thing to do. End your shift early and sneak out."

"But what if he—"

"I'll cover you. Run a distraction."

Dorothy hugged her friend.

"Stop the hugging, you'll make me mess up my mascara. Now be ready when I block his view."

Dorothy peered out from behind the partition as Nadine poured a large iced specialty coffee. She looked at her friend and nodded.

Carefully, Dorothy stepped from behind the partition, angling her body to face away from Larry. As casually as she could, she started walking toward the door.

"Yes, I'm serious. Send them ASA-fucking-P, and tell Doctor Vaughan I found her." Larry noticed the movement and saw her edging by. "Hey! Stop right there, bitch!"

He jumped to his feet, lurching from behind his table, but before he could reach her, he inexplicably tripped, face-planting onto the cement floor.

"Go!" Nadine mouthed to her friend as she pulled her extended foot back. "Oh my God, are you okay?" she said, kneeling over the fallen man as Dorothy bolted for the door.

"Look out, you fucking idiot!" Larry shouted, pushing her as he scrambled to his knees.

The cup of iced coffee in Nadine's hand fell, not unintentionally, right across his face, flooding his eyes and nose with the dark brew.

Larry hit the ground, writhing in pain.

"Jesus! What the fuck did you do to me! It burns!"

Dorothy paused at the door. She shared a grateful smile with her friend, then took off running as fast as her feet would take her.

Nadine looked down at the coffee-soaked man on the floor.

"I'm so sorry," she said, unconvincingly. "It must be the cayenne pepper."

"Who the fuck puts cayenne in coffee?" he wailed in agony.

"Oh, it's a specialty drink," Nadine replied with a wicked little grin. "It's called Coffee of Death."

By the time she exited the bus ride home, Dorothy had managed to lower her heart rate to something resembling a normal level. Nonetheless, she was still quite discombobulated.

What do I tell Randy? I mean, this won't jeopardize Sam moving back, but he still might freak out.

By the time he came home that evening, she had decided that a toned-down version of the day's events would be the best choice. Over dinner, maybe after a couple of glasses of wine.

"It was a pretty eventful day," Dorothy said between bites. "There was a bit of craziness at work."

"Ah, coffee house drama," Randy said as he sipped his wine. "Now that brings me back a few years. So what happened?"

"Well, there was an issue with one of the customers. He was aggressive, and things got a bit out of hand."

Randy quickly sobered up.

"Do I need to do something about this?"

"What? No. I'm perfectly capable of handling things, Randy. I appreciate the protective instinct, but I'm not a child."

"Sorry, I just... it's a dad thing."

"Apology accepted. Anyway, since I've been working under the table there, this could be a big problem for them, so I had to be let go. But I'll start looking for another job tomorrow, so don't worry."

Randy got up, walked to her, and gave her a hug.

"Don't worry about it, babe. Take a few days and relax. I know you liked that place, and you really put a lot of effort into contributing to the household. A little break is well-deserved."

"Really? You're not worried about your folks?"

"Nah, I think it'll be okay. They know we're living together, and they know you've been working hard to help me finish Sam's room for her to move in. I haven't told her about us living together yet, but I will soon. She knows I've been dating, but this? I'm still a little nervous about it. More than my parents, even. I think they've gone from cautious to hopeful. You know how parents get when their kids finally meet someone."

"All right, then." Dorothy said as she took a deep breath of relief. "If you're really okay with it, I'll take a few days off. Maybe I can finish that last coat of paint in her room before I start the job hunt again."

"Excellent idea," he agreed. "So, you up for a post-dinner game of Scrabble?"

Dorothy flashed a come-hither smile.

"Make it strip-Scrabble and you're on."

A few days passed, and the beautiful blue skies were dotted with little puffy clouds. Happy little clouds, some might even say. It was a perfect morning outside, but Dorothy was indoors, wrapping up her painting project rather than out enjoying the sun.

The seasons were finally changing, the air growing warmer as winter was well on its way to becoming a thing of the past. She liked it that way. Warm was good.

Randy sat comfortably on the couch doing a crossword puzzle, sipping his coffee, relaxing a bit longer before heading to the gallery. Dorothy, meanwhile ,was bustling about in the kitchen, cleaning paintbrushes and rollers.

"Kick ass paint job, babe. Her room looks great," Randy said appreciatively.

"Thanks. I'm really happy with how it turned out. I think she'll love it."

A pensive look formed on Randy's face.

"You know, summer break's coming up in a few months," he said. "It's weird, I've been looking forward to it for so long, but now I'm nervous about it. What if she freaks out when I tell her?"

"You're her father, she'll want you to be happy," Dorothy soothed him.

"It's just that I... well, I haven't dated anyone since her mother, and now here I am..." He was briefly at a loss for words. "When I visited her last month, I did tell her that I was seeing someone, and it was serious, but I still have to broach the whole living together part of it." The concern clear in his eyes tugged her heart strings.

"Don't worry." Dorothy kissed his forehead, then headed back towards the kitchen. "I won't come between you and your daughter," she said. "Not for a long time anyway," she added under her breath.

She thought about her life and what it had quite surprisingly become, and decided she was okay with it all.

A minute later he turned his head at the sound of her soft footsteps approaching.

"Here, I made you something."

She handed him a plate, and on it sat a peanut butter and jelly sandwich. With the crusts cut off.

Randy took the plate, his eyes shining from the gesture they both knew was far more than just a snack. He leaned over and gave her a kiss, resting his forehead against hers for a moment, savoring the closeness, then took a bite of the sandwich.

"I got you something too," he said as he put the sandwich down. He went and retrieved the box he'd hidden in the hall closet.

"What is it?"

"That's the fun part of opening it, now isn't it?"

Dorothy took the long, flat box in her hands and slid it open. Inside, wrapped in delicate tissue, was a beautiful, deep red dress with a black lace overlay. She had commented on it during an outing weeks earlier, even going so far as to try it on, but had ultimately handed it back to the store clerk.

She felt tears rush to her eyes as she hugged him. "Oh Randy, it's beautiful!" she exclaimed as she squeezed him tight.

"I'm glad you still like it. Actually, I was hoping you'd wear it tomorrow night. I want to take you out for something special."

She kissed him, pupils dilated and cheeks flushed, as the two of them slid down to the couch.

"So," she asked, her voice a husky whisper as she latched her lips to his ear, "how much time do we have before you have to be at work?"

He responded by gently sliding his fingertips across her collar until he cupped her face in his hands. His pulse was pounding so hard in his chest that she could feel it as he held her close.

"We've got time," he said as he drew her closer, kissing her with an intensity that overwhelmed them both as they melted into one.

With Randy at work, Dorothy took a quick walk up the road to Fausto's. She greeted the Italian warmly, then made a quick beeline to the alterations experts.

"Ladies, I need your help."

The three sisters looked up from their work.

"We know you," Klotthie said, fidgeting with her spindle.

"Yes, I was in with my boyfriend a few months ago," Dorothy replied.

"You're right," Atroppie muttered. "We *do* know her."

"What's changed?" Lakhie wondered. "So interesting. So unusual!"

Dorothy cut to the chase.

"I have a new dress, but it needs fitting. Do you think you can help me? I need it by tomorrow night."

The three women circled her, examining her as they did.

"Do we run the thread out?" Klotthie wondered. "Something is different."

"Different is uncomfortable. I say we cut, while we can," Atroppie posited. "I'll get my shears."

Lakhie stayed her sister's hand.

"No." She studied the young woman for several moments, taking her in, head to toe. "At least not yet. But soon? Perhaps. First we have much to understand."

Dorothy had no idea what the three old Greek women were on about.

I hope they can get my alterations done in time.

"Yes, we can," Klotthie's eyes sparkled.

"What?"

"Your alterations. We can have them by tomorrow afternoon."

How did she know what I was thinking?

The three women smiled.

"Come," Lakhie said. "Let us measure. You will look beautiful on your big night."

"I still say we cut."

"Atroppie," her sister muttered.

"Fine, we measure. Always the measuring, never the cutting. You're too sentimental, Lakhie."

Ten minutes, and a great deal of fraternal bickering later, Dorothy headed for the door.

"It will be ready anytime after twelve, tomorrow," Klotthie called out to the departing girl. "It is a big day for you. Trust us, you'll look wonderful."

CHAPTER 30

Dorothy stood alone on the dark corner, a vision in a beautiful deep red dress, flashing its color when a passing car would flap her long, black coat aside in its wake.

What's taking him so long?

She'd been standing there for several minutes, waiting. Randy was being mysterious this evening, full of a barely contained nervous energy. Fortunately for him, that just made him all the more charming in her eyes.

But even charming only went so far when you were left hanging on a lonely street corner.

Well, at least no one's propositioned me, she thought with a smile.

Yet.

Dorothy thought she might wind up regretting that last thought as a shiny black Mercedes sedan glided to a stop in front of her, its powerful engine thrumming in quiet rhythm as it reflected her image back to her in its deeply polished flanks.

The driver's door opened, and Randy stepped out.

What the...?

"M'lady," he said with a bow as he came around and opened the passenger door for her. "Your carriage awaits."

"But you haven't driven since—"

"Special occasion," he interrupted her. "No buses for you tonight. Nope. Tonight, my girl travels in style."

Dorothy wasn't about to argue, so she slid into the soft leather seat. Randy closed the door after her, then trotted back to climb into the driver's seat and buckle in.

"And away we go!" The excitement in his voice had her curiosity piqued. Soon enough she'd learn their mysterious and special destination.

Really? she thought. *This?*

Having shed her coat, Dorothy was resplendent in her beautiful new outfit, not a hair out of place, and certainly the best-looking woman in the establishment by a long shot.

"So this is our special night out?" she said from the confines of their familiar vinyl booth. The diner was only moderately busy, but she was still acutely aware of just how out of place they both looked. "I mean, I like it here, don't get me wrong, but you were really hyping things up, Randy."

Randy didn't even notice the other diners as he shifted nervously in his seat. His every sense was fixed on Dorothy with laser intensity. Finally, he spoke in carefully measured words.

"Do you know why this is special? I mean, why it is so special to me?" He looked deep in her eyes as he spoke, his pulse strong under his collar as his heart beat hard.

"It's special because you blew me off in this booth. This is where we first met. And while it may just be some booth in a diner to anyone else, to me, it's the most important place I can think of."

Well, mister, flattery will get you everywhere, you know. She smiled at him, and was about to verbalize the thought, when Randy unexpectedly started to rise.

Wait, are we going already? We just got here.

Before she could voice a protest, Randy's stance took an unexpected turn as he went from two feet to quite the opposite, dropping to one knee on the polished linoleum floor, deftly popping open the small box hidden in his hand.

"Look, I know this is kind of out of left field, but when you know, you know, and... well, the thing is... Dorothy, will you marry me?"

Dorothy touched her cheeks. They were wet, she found, as her unplanned tears of joy welled forth.

"You know who I am. What I am," she said as he took her hands in his.

"Angel of Death, or crazy lady from the nuthouse—the thing is, whoever you are, I love you with all my heart, and there's nobody else I can imagine wanting to be with for the rest of my life. Baby, if you'll have me, I'm yours."

He held his breath as he awaited her response.

Could I? I mean, could I really? She was amazed to find herself actually considering it. *Famine and the others seem to be doing a good job picking up the slack without me,* she reasoned, weighing the likely repercussions of her choice. She looked at Randy's loving gaze, waiting for her answer. *You know what? I think I can live with that just fine.*

Dorothy slowly raised her hand for him.

"I'd be honored, Randy."

His face looked like it would split in half, he was smiling so broadly as he slid the delicately crafted ring onto his fiancée's finger. She looked at it glistening on her hand, admiring the vintage-design swirl of sapphires and rubies.

Angela glanced over at what was happening and nearly dropped the plates she was carrying. Fortunately, she managed to toss them on the counter before screaming with joy as she ran over to congratulate her friends.

"Oh my God! Congratulations! I can't believe it! This is amazing!"

"Well, it's largely thanks to you, Angie. If you hadn't pushed me that night... well, thanks for kicking my ass into gear." She laughed, then hugged them both, mascara running down her cheeks.

"Listen, you two, don't go anywhere. I have to take care of the family at table twelve, but then I'll be right back. This is so exciting!" She dabbed her face with a napkin, leaving it looking like a somewhat Goth shroud of Turin, then hurried to the waiting guests.

"So, what do you say?" Randy asked. "Shall we grab a bite? I know I must've just burned a whole week's worth of blood sugar worrying what you'd say."

"Baby," she said, "you've really outdone yourself." She then leaned in and gave him a tender kiss.

An hour later they lounged in the booth, full from a hearty meal and relaxing in the glow of the evening's events. Randy had left his pocket watch on the table along with his phone, and Dorothy picked it up as she'd done so many times since they'd met, absentmindedly fiddling with the ornate design on the case.

As she traced the inlaid metal lines, sitting with the man who wanted to be with her forever, a warm sense of calm washed over her.

Now this was a good day, she thought as she basked in a happy glow. *An actual life,* she marveled at the possibilities. *That means we have, what, fifty or sixty years? The world will be fine for that, and besides, really, it's just a blink of the eye.* She smiled at Randy as she imagined all the good times in store.

"I think this calls for a celebration beyond our celebratory pie and coffee, wouldn't you agree?" Randy asked.

"What did you have in mind?" she replied with a mischievous smile, her eyebrow raised in a manner that left no doubt what she was thinking.

"Well, I just so happen to have a lovely bottle of champagne chilling at home. I had to disguise it as a case of Budweiser."

"Now I know why that suddenly showed up."

"Well, I knew you'd never touch the stuff, so—"

At that moment something clicked in her hand. Dorothy wasn't even thinking about her movements as she absentmindedly traced the design of one of the runes she'd learned with her finger. To both their surprise, the enamel gave way as a small piece of the case slid aside under her finger, the back of the watch popping open with a soft ping.

"Hey, how'd you do that?" Randy said, surprised. "I've never been able to get it open. I guess you must have the magic touch."

"There's an engraving," Dorothy noticed.

"What does it say?"

She opened the case fully and read the ornate text.

"Forever is today, but forever."

A little smile blossomed on her lips as she closed the case and handed it back to him.

"Hmm, kind of anti-climactic, but sweet nonetheless," he mused.

"I think it was perfect," she said. "And fitting for our celebration."

"Speaking of celebrations," Randy added, a sexy smile in his eyes, "we have more celebrating to do back home. Allow me to fetch your chariot, m'lady. I'll be right back."

He rose to his feet, kissed his fiancée deeply, then stepped out into the night, walking on air as he headed to retrieve the rented luxury car from the nearby parking garage.

"Congratulations again!" Angela said as she wrapped Dorothy's slender frame in her arms and gave her a massive hug. "I'm so happy for you two! Now go home and celebrate!" she said with a mischievous wink.

"Thanks, Angie. We'll see you soon," she replied as she stepped out into the cool night air.

Dorothy paced down the street a bit, aimlessly pivoting on her toes, stretching up in a bouncing gait, a physical manifestation of her excellent spirits. She was downright glowing with happiness as she waited for Randy's return, perma-grin firmly plastered to her face.

With no warning, out of the shadowy alleyway beside the diner, a huge hand broke her trance as its owner roughly dragged her into the darkness around the corner.

Big Stan.

"It took me months, but I finally found you, you bitch!" his deep voice rumbled, his fingers digging into her arms as he held her firmly in place.

"We're clear across town, Stan," she said, "and nowhere near Camview. I'm out of your hair. Why can't you just let me be?"

"Doc said to bring you back. One way or another." His smile was unnerving. "I'm kind of hoping for 'another,'" he said, the threat clear in his tone.

"Hey now, let's not be rude on her special night," a familiar voice said from the shadows.

Curtis stepped forward into the light, sizing up Stan as he gave a little smile to his surprised friend.

"Curtis?" she uttered his name in shock.

Stan rolled his shoulders and cracked his neck, his attention turning to Curtis as he shoved Dorothy into some boxes and out of his way. He eyed the AWOL nutjob like a lion eyeballing a juicy steak after a long fast.

Today, the lion was hungry.

"Oh, little man," he growled, "I'm going to enjoy this."

The ever-present smile slowly slid from Curtis's face.

"No, Stan," he replied. "No, you aren't."

The huge man was taken aback by the escaped mental patient's demeanor. Curtis was actually being serious, and he was never serious. And hang on, had he actually just challenged him?

Stan lunged at his much smaller adversary, but his swinging fist met with empty air as Curtis deftly dodged out of the way. All this did was make him angrier.

"All right, no more messing around," Stan bellowed as he charged, confident in his sheer size overwhelming his prey.

Curtis paused for a millisecond, then his posture shifted, ever so subtly, and for the first time since she'd known him, Dorothy watched her friend unleash violence.

And oh, what violence it was.

I don't believe it. I had no idea, she marveled.

To her great surprise, her jovial and previously harmless-seeming friend moved with the speed and skill of a master martial artist, easily avoiding the pawing swipes of his much larger opponent as he ducked clear, then lunged in, landing devastating combinations of knees, elbows, and kicks before deftly sliding back out of range of Stan's counterattacks.

In short order it became very clear that Stan was horribly outmatched, and as that unsettling realization flashed across the huge man's shocked face, Curtis allowed himself a little smile, locking eyes with the lion, who had now become the prey.

Stan's eyes betrayed a glimmer of fear, but before he could fully realize that thought and wrap his brain around the fact that someone had actually scared him (which hadn't happened since well-before his teenage growth spurt), Curtis was upon him.

My God, he's so fast, Dorothy thought as she watched her friend lay into the man once more. She could tell this was the coup de grace, as Curtis sprang into an even faster burst of action, his flurry of brutal blows raining down on Stan like a relentless hail storm, pummeling him with granite fists until he dropped to the damp pavement with a thud.

Stan may have only been unconscious, but he certainly wasn't going to be getting up anytime soon.

Curtis was breathing hard, a slight sheen of sweat glistening on his brow, his body tense and ready for a fight.

Dorothy stared at him, not sure what to make of her friend.

And then, as if he'd simply flipped a switch, Curtis gave a little roll to his shoulders and his posture returned to its usual relaxed and casual state as he loosened his muscles and stood up straight. He sighed, letting the tension slide from his body as easily as shedding a loose coat.

With one last neck roll, he looked up to the sky.

"God, that felt good," he said, a faint smile on his lips.

He shifted his gaze to Dorothy, eyes glinting with happiness at the sight of his friend. She didn't hesitate, running up and giving him a huge hug.

"Curtis, that was amazing!" she gushed. "How on Earth did you—and hey, where have you been? It's been months!"

"Well, there was a big lockdown after you left. Plus, I kinda figured you two kids could use some alone time." He glanced at the vintage ring on her finger and smiled. "Guess I was right."

"But how did you get out? How did you know that Stan—I mean, what were you thinking?"

"Hey, I have my ways. Besides, I told you, someone has to look out for you." He kissed her on the cheek and gave her a warm look, then turned to walk away.

"Wait, where are you going?"

"Why, back, of course. It's movie night, and I'm missing out on the free popcorn."

"But you should stay."

He smiled at her kindly, looking unusually wise for a goofy jokester.

"You're going to be fine," he said before walking away. He stopped and turned back one more time. "Go on now, go be happy," he called to her, then with a final Cheshire grin, he vanished down the dark alley.

I really don't know him as well as I thought, Dorothy pondered as she dusted herself off, still unsure what to make of her friend's hidden talent.

She looked at Stan lying prone in the alley. He was going to be a problem if she didn't do something about him.

I'll call in an anonymous tip to the police when we get home, she thought. *Say there was a mugger in the alley. That should give me enough time to think of a more long-term solution.*

She walked out of the alleyway to the street where Randy was waiting for her in the sedan. He saw her, his face brightening as he stepped out of the sleek Mercedes.

"There you are!" he called to her, smiling at the sight of her, though it had just been a few minutes. "I didn't see you when I pulled up, thought maybe you got cold feet and changed your—"

The silver sedan really wasn't even speeding that much when it drifted across the lane and smashed into Randy as he closed the driver's side door.

At the last second the driver had hit the brakes, the screech of tires desperately grabbing for traction coming far too late as his alcohol-impaired reflexes had no chance of preventing the impact.

Randy's body flew through the air, arms and legs flapping this way and that as he tumbled off the hood of the car and rolled to a pile in the street.

Dorothy stood there in shock as Angela rushed out of the diner and sprinted to Randy's side.

"Call an ambulance!" she yelled to the lone patron who had followed her outside.

"I've got 9-1-1 on the line," the man replied. "A man has been run over..." he began into the phone.

Standing stock-still on the sidewalk, Dorothy stared, frozen in place.

That's odd, where did that car come from? And what's that noise?

She didn't realize that noise was her own screaming as she slid deep into shock.

The inebriated driver managed to stumble from his car with a lurch.

"Is he okay?" the man asked, then slumped drunkenly against his hood.

If Dorothy had her wits about her, she might have recognized him from her nightmares. Andy, the man whose soul she'd failed to take all those months ago.

"Dorothy!" Angela yelled to her. "Dorothy! Snap out of it! Come here and help me! Dorothy!"

Finally the fog seemed to lift from her brain, and Dorothy forced her leaden legs to shuffle forward. She gazed at Randy, bloody and unconscious, and slid to the ground at his side, taking his hand in hers as she sobbed.

In the distance, the blare of sirens could be heard approaching, their steady wail echoing the agony in Dorothy's breaking heart.

CHAPTER 31

Dorothy stood in the doorway of the hospital room, looking down at the man she loved as he lay immobile in his bed. A mass of tubes and wires ran from his body to the myriad machines that flanked him on either side, monitoring his ever-so-faint vital signs.

Her eyes were red from crying, her nose pink and raw, as she wiped it absentmindedly with a tissue clenched in her hand. The antiseptic smell of the room had briefly triggered the memory of her own stay in the hospital, and, for an instant, she found it grimly amusing that Randy had been more successful than she ever had when it came to being run over.

This can't be happening. Not him. Not now.

She felt tears welling up again and pushed off from the doorway, willing her exhausted legs to walk down the long corridor.

I just need somewhere to think.

No one else was in the chapel when she entered and took a seat.

It was a modest room, designed for use by any faith, and over the years, a great many people of all backgrounds had taken shelter in the small space, seeking whatever answers they hoped for, and whatever solace they could find.

As Dorothy quietly sobbed, oblivious to the discomfort of the wooden bench, a clean-shaven priest in his mid-fifties quietly approached her. She didn't even notice his arrival. He stood over her, quietly, looking down on the distraught woman with an expression of kindness, love, and pity.

Finally, he sat next to her, his presence suddenly registering on her radar.

She looked up at his kind face, then dropped her gaze to the name tag pinned to his chest. "Father McKenzie."

"Can I be of help, child?" he asked in a soothing tone. "Can I be of any comfort?"

"Nothing can comfort me, Father," she sneered, her anger surging up through her sadness. The priest simply took it in stride.

"Perhaps," he began. "But comfort can be found in many places."

"Well, not today!" she snapped, then turned her attentions skyward, angrily ranting to the air.

"This isn't fair! This is *my* domain! It's *my* job!" she wailed to the ether. "Haven't I always done what you wanted? Haven't I taken them all, young or old, without questioning you even once? Why do this to me? Why torment me like this?"

The priest quietly waited for her to calm and take a breath before interjecting.

"Child, the Lord works in mysterious ways."

"Don't toss clichés at me, holy man. Save your breath."

"What I am trying to say, is that oftentimes a loss does not seem fair. This is simply the way things are. You must accept His will."

"No, not me." She glared at him. "Me? I'm different. I'm being punished. He's making me suffer, when all I've ever done is exactly what he created me to do in the first place! Is he trying to teach me a lesson? What the hell have I ever done wrong?"

Father McKenzie's expression hardened ever so slightly as he listened to her angry outburst. He thought for a moment, choosing his words before replying.

"You say these things, but I hear the same from countless people every day. 'Why me?' 'It's not fair!' 'What did I do wrong?'" He paused and waited for her to meet his gaze before he continued.

"Do you really believe you are the only being who has ever felt such pain? This is a part of human existence. Every single day mothers ask why their child was taken, husbands mourn their wives, children bury their parents, yet the world goes on, and though it is difficult, they ultimately grow as people for it. That very delicacy of humanity is what makes life so beautiful. What makes it so precious, in the first place."

She sat quietly as his words slowly began to sink in.

I've been so callous...

"They—they all felt this. And I was the cause," she murmured, staring meekly at the floor. Her eyes glistened, not from her own pain, but as the enormity of the realization truly hit home.

"They all hurt, and I didn't care."

The priest watched her processing for a moment, then reached out and lifted her chin, gazing into her eyes as he took her hands in his.

His skin is so warm.

"Every life is precious," he began, watching her, gauging her reaction as he spoke. "Some people will go an entire lifetime without realizing that." A sparkle flashed in his eye. "And for *some*, it can take quite a bit longer," he added with a little grin.

Dorothy had stopped crying, soothed by the priest's presence and his calming words in spite of herself. Wiping her eyes, she looked at his warm, smiling face not with annoyance, but with gratitude.

"Thank you Father. I-I always played my part, did what I was made to do, but I never really..." She looked away briefly, almost ashamed at herself, before meeting his eyes once more. "I get it now," she said, holding his gaze. "I get how important it is."

"Good," he said, beaming like a proud father, the warmth of his smile relieving her doubts and soothing her heart.

Dorothy rose to her feet and slowly walked to the door, when the priest spoke to her once more.

"Child."

"Yes Father?"

"One last thing." He sized her up quietly for a moment.

"Remember, a person does not always need to have done something wrong to need to be taught a lesson. Many lessons, though often difficult to endure, can be a gift. Even a reward of sorts. But most importantly, sometimes the lesson itself is the entire point. People learn and evolve over time, it's the way of things, but, occasionally, they might need a little nudge in the right direction."

A final smile was shared between them as she stepped out of the chapel, thankful for his counsel.

She paused in the hallway, feeling pretty good. Surprisingly good, actually. Better than she'd felt in a while. Something had changed.

She stood there in front of the chapel for a minute, trying to focus on what it was that felt different.

"Can I help you?" a passing nurse asked. "Would you like me to find the priest for you?"

"No, that's all right," she replied. "Father McKenzie already spoke to me."

"Father McKenzie? We have a Father Jacobs here, but I don't know a Father McKenzie on staff."

A light bulb flashed in Dorothy's head. Spinning on her heel, she rushed back into the chapel. The door she had passed through was the only way in or out, and no one had exited behind her.

The chapel was empty.

Ah, I see. She smiled to herself. *Of course.*

She rolled her neck slowly and stood tall, shoulders back, as she finally tuned in to what had changed.

Surprising how something so familiar to her had become so foreign.

She stretched her hands as she moved, a faint ripple of power thrumming over her being as she turned from the chapel and exited back into the hallway.

She looked different. Calmer. Standing taller, confident. She turned toward Randy's room and started walking with measured strides.

"You!" she heard a startled and angry voice call out from down the hall. Doctor Vaughan was there, his huge lackey standing right behind him. Even from that distance, Dorothy could easily make out his black eye and broken nose.

Ah, yes, I forgot to call in to the police about Stan, she realized. *Curtis certainly did a number on him, though.*

Doctor Vaughan stormed down the hallway, anger radiating off him in waves as he barreled toward her.

"You've caused me a lot of headaches, and once you're back in isolation—"

She calmly raised her hand.

"No."

This time it worked.

Doctor Vaughan stopped in his tracks, his eyes going wide as he clutched his chest. He looked at Dorothy with surprise, which quickly turned to disbelief as he struggled to catch his breath, his face betraying his fear, while hers showed nothing but calm as she watched him collapse to the floor.

"He's having an MI—get the crash cart!" the nearest nurse yelled to her co-workers.

Staff fluttered about in a hurry, trying to save Doctor Vaughan as he lay on the cold tile, writhing in pain and staring at Dorothy, in shock.

A faint smile bloomed on her face, which only added to the dying man's alarm.

Dorothy slowly held up her empty hands, showing him the bare palms and bare backs of them. Then, while staring him square in the eye, with the slightest of twitches, an old silver coin appeared between her fingers.

His coin, Doctor Vaughan realized.

The amateur magician knew there was no way she could have possibly done that trick. The coin was in his office, and her hands hadn't even moved.

"It can't be…" he gasped.

Dorothy gave him a cold smile and dropped his coin to the ground as he watched helplessly. Then, after a moment, her gaze snapped from the dying man to the one still standing.

A damp spot slowly spread across the front of Stan's pants as his bladder let loose. Somewhere deep in his subconscious, the man so used to being an apex predator suddenly realized the horrifying reality. He was nothing more than the tiniest of fish in a deep and dark sea, and something huge and deadly had taken notice of him.

Damp with a terror-sweat, he slowly backed up until his foot felt the flat of the wall become the angle of a corner. Not daring to break eye contact, the terrified man slid backwards until he rounded the corner. The moment he was out of sight, he turned and ran faster than he'd ever moved in his life.

Go ahead and run, Stan. I'll be seeing you again soon enough.

Her attention shifted, her eyes finding a familiar face smiling at her from the end of the hallway. Curtis, wearing an amused grin, leaned casually against the wall. Watching.

Watching over her, like he always did.

The friends shared a knowing smile, then the madman slowly started to glow a warm golden amber as his wings unfolded from behind his back.

Well, he did say he was my guardian angel.

Curtis chuckled, as if he could hear her thoughts, and who knows, maybe he could.

"Go on now," he said. "Click your heels together." A loving smile flashed across his face, then he winked at her and was gone.

Unconscious and alone, Randy lay in his bed, monitors beeping steadily as they tracked his every vital function. A battery of IVs dripped various solutions into his battered body as the doctors did their best to keep him alive.

Dorothy stood at the doorway, though if you asked anyone if they'd seen the slender young woman in black, they'd all have answered in the negative.

Gone was her beautiful red dress. Dorothy, her skin a slightly cooler tone once more, was clad in her traditional attire as she sadly looked upon her unconscious lover.

A small crease furrowed on her brow, then softened. The monitors suddenly cried out in unison, their shrill alarms sounding a sad distress call.

Randy found himself standing beside Dorothy, observing his own body as it lay in bed, while doctors and nurses rushed into the room to tend their dying patient. They frantically pushed drugs into his IV as a defibrillator was quickly rolled into the room and charged.

He stared at himself lying there a moment longer, still unsure exactly how to process what he was seeing, then turned to Dorothy and looked her up and down.

Though her skin was cooler, all the fire and warmth remained in her eyes.

His fiancée, the Grim Reaper.

"Holy shit. It was true," he said, amazed.

More staff rushed into the room, but no one paid the slightest bit of attention to either of them. *Of course not,* he realized.

"He's flatlined," called out the lead nurse.

"Pulsox is dropping," added another as she jabbed a syringe into his IV line.

Staff swarmed his body, injecting more chemicals and prepping him for the defibrillator. Slowly, Randy turned back to Dorothy.

"So, I guess this means it's time to go," he said.

She shushed him with a pale, yet shockingly warm finger to his lips. Sadness and love burned in the depths of her eyes.

Death removed her finger and leaned in to her lover, kissing him as intensely as she ever had. An intensity he returned, holding her close, running his hands through her hair as he held her to him.

She finally broke the embrace, a tear dripping from her eye.

"I love you," was the last thing he heard her say before the world turned upside down as he jolted back to consciousness, the machines suddenly roaring back to their normal, rhythmic beeping.

The doctors stopped charging the defib paddles, unsure what had just happened, while a nurse began examining the machines.

"Wait, hold the defib. Rhythm is normal. It looks like it must've been an equipment malfunction."

"But all of them at once?"

"I know, it's weird, but what else could it be? Better have everything swapped out, and get the techs to run diagnostics."

"Doctor, he seems to be conscious," a nurse noted.

"Well, this one certainly seems determined to beat the odds," he said, then leaned over his patient, checking his pupillary reactions with a light.

"You're doing good, Randy. Keep fighting."

The staff gathered their equipment and began filtering back out of the room, leaving Randy to rest and heal. What no one had noticed was Randy's intense gaze at his hand.

There, between his fingers, were a few strands of Dorothy's dark hair.

CHAPTER 32

Over a week had passed since the accident, and Randy was getting stir-crazy, confined to a hospital bed as his body slowly healed. Though he was mending faster than doctors had anticipated, he still couldn't leave. Not just yet.

"She still hasn't been in?" he asked, though he was pretty sure he knew the answer he'd receive. "Not even once?"

Sitting next to him on the bed, Angela fed him another bite of the blackberry cream pie she'd brought to the hospital.

"Sorry, hon," she said. "I haven't seen her since the night of the accident. No one has."

He remembered what he had experienced in the ICU that night clearly enough, but Randy had chalked the strange out-of-body experience up to his severe trauma, along with the massive amounts of pain killers flooding his body playing tricks on his mind.

If not that, what else could it have been?

Randy chewed glumly, barely taking any pleasure in his treat as he sank farther into his bed and his depression. Though a few close friends had visited him and kept him company, he hadn't called his parents, not wanting to cause a stir and disrupt Sam as she neared the end of her school year. Instead, he focused on healing and getting back to his new life, but as the days crept by, Dorothy was nowhere to be found.

A week later, he had healed enough to convince his doctors to allow his return home. Though still heavily bandaged and walking with crutches, they told him that hopefully he'd be using just a cane within the month, and ideally would be off of any walking aids within three.

Randy finally contacted his father by email and told him that he was swamped with work, so he'd be off-radar over the next several weeks. He felt bad, not being forthcoming with his father, but his world was spinning, and he felt desperately in need of some quiet alone time to process things.

Gary gave him a ride home upon his release, saving his friend the misery of riding a bus on crutches. Randy made a single request.

The pair found themselves hobbling through Lafayette Park. Randy looked high and low, just in case he'd catch a glimpse of Dorothy, Gary following close by, helping when the exertion got to be too much.

He would have chided his friend for being excessively obsessed, but he knew it wouldn't make a difference. It was better to say nothing. He just quietly trailed his friend as he hobbled across the uneven ground, hoping to find his love.

When they finally gave up and left the park, Randy looked over his shoulder one last time, then gingerly slid into Gary's car.

He felt a gut-twisting surge of sadness flood his body. Not having her in the hospital was one thing, but now, out in familiar places, well, it was more than a little unsettling.

His world felt that much emptier without her in it.

"Listen, you take as much time as you need to get healthy," Gary told him. "The job ain't going anywhere, and you already booked the next four months, so I'll just get Jamie to come help me hang the shows until you feel up to coming back."

"Thanks. I really don't think I could schmooze with anyone at this point."

"I understand. Give it time, man, things'll look up. Now let's get you back to your place. It'll do you good to sleep in your own sheets."

Homecoming was a bit overwhelming at first. Everything had taken on a memory or familiarity associated with Dorothy, and none of them more than their shared bedroom.

Other things had meaning, but that space, well, it *smelled* of her, and every time Randy would inadvertently brush up against one of her things, the whiff of his missing fiancée would threaten to drag him farther into a depressive spiral.

Some days the sadness would win. At least the pain medication would help take the edge off.

When things got particularly bad, Randy would find himself sitting on the couch with a bottle of wine and one of her shirts, occasionally holding it to his face just to catch another faint olfactory reminder of her. On those days, the shirt would often wind up wet with tears, a few drops of spilled wine, or quite often, both.

The days turned into weeks, and Randy slowly, albeit reluctantly, began to accept that Dorothy might really have left him for good. The realization cut deep, leaving a pain that wouldn't go away as he became ever more miserable in his loneliness.

He often went unshaven since her departure, and in his increasing depression, he lost his appetite, only picking at the takeout he ordered, and even then more out of habit than hunger.

On top of that, since he had stopped visiting the diner (the quintessential "them" place), where his mama hen Angela would force him to eat, he'd begun to lose weight as he fell into the habit of forgetting to eat at all some days.

Randy eventually slid so far into his depression that he once more started revisiting places he and Dorothy had previously enjoyed in their shared past, desperately feeding the hungry beast of slim hopes that he'd see her again, perhaps catching a glimpse of her playing mini golf, or flipping through used records.

Logical Randy knew it wouldn't happen, but since when has love been logical?

A shock came one evening when he stopped in at Dante's Books. He ever-so-briefly experienced an adrenaline-rush moment of hope when he spotted a dark-haired woman of a similar build, but when he had excitedly grabbed her arm and spun her around, calling out, he nearly got a face full of pepper spray before blurting out an apology to the terrified young woman he didn't know.

The weeks slowly clicked by, one after another, and Randy

spiraled into an alcohol-soaked funk of epic proportions. Nothing mattered to him anymore.

His home was a mess, his hair and shaggy beard unkempt. His rumpled clothes had taken on the stale smell of his sour, malnourished sweat.

Crying himself to sleep, usually with a bottle in hand, had become the only way he could find solace from his misery, until one night, it finally piled up to the point where he couldn't take it anymore.

It had just gotten dark outside, and he was yet again foregoing dinner. It was the time of day, he grimly recalled Dorothy mentioning, that was something associated with mental disorders. Sundowners they called the people who experienced major mood shifts as the light changed. He supposed he could understand why, to some degree, but his misery was based in something far more substantial than how many hours of sunlight there were in the day.

The bottle of vodka on his coffee table was nearly full, having replaced the now-empty one he'd finished off earlier in the day. Next to it sat an ominous, little childproof bottle.

Randy stared at them both, sunken eyes bloodshot from crying, skin gray from lack of proper nutrition or sunlight. After several painful minutes of deliberation, he finally made a decision and opened the small bottle, dumping the pills out into the palm of his hand.

It would be a painless way out, he thought, and this misery would finally end, and maybe, just maybe, he'd see her again. Randy knew he wasn't thinking clearly, but he felt powerless against the riptide pull of his own depression. It was a choice between bad or bad, so what difference would it make?

With a shaky hand, he reached for the vodka, nearly jumping out of his skin when his landline phone unexpectedly rang.

No way he was going to answer it, he thought, as he shakily poured a tall glass of vodka one-handed.

"Hey, Daddy!" a gleeful little girl giggled, as the answering machine clicked on. He'd forgotten to turn the volume down, and now his daughter's joyful voice filled his living room.

"I sooo can't wait until next weekend! Spring break is gonna be totally fun. Grandpa said to tell you we'll be there at four on Friday. I said we should get pizza! He said we'd have to see. I don't think Grandma likes when he eats pizza, because he kind of farts a lot." She laughed into the phone. "Okay, anyway, I can't wait to see you next week—what? Oh, I've got to go. Love you, Daddy!" She hung up, leaving the bright essence of her childlike demeanor filling the stale air of his home.

As if waking from a trance, he shook his head, then looked at what was in his hands and started to sob.

Randy was disgusted with himself.

Rising to his feet, he grabbed the remainder of the pills and vodka and walked to the sink, dropping them into the disposal and pouring both the full glass, as well as the bottle of vodka, after them, flipping the switch on his wall and grinding it all away. But he didn't stop there. He then collected every bottle of alcohol in his house, each of them meeting the same fate.

Randy splashed some water on his face, took a deep breath, and started the long process of cleaning his unkempt home.

CHAPTER 33

The old man, gray hair gently blowing in the breeze, slowly trudged along the grassy knoll with his giggling grandchildren as they chased the bubbles he was blowing from a bottle of soapy water. Where the youngsters had boundless energy, their grandpa, after all the exertion of the afternoon, found himself more than a bit worn out.

"Okay, okay, I'm all tired out. You kids go play with your folks for a while. Grandpa's going to rest for a bit here in the sun."

Randy sat his aching bones on the soft grass, letting out a sigh as his throbbing feet and knees immediately felt some relief.

His daughter rose from her picnic blanket and walked over to where he reclined.

"You all right Dad? Don't let them wear you out."

"I'm fine, honey, just a bit winded. They are energetic, that's for sure. Just like their mother was." He laughed, and to his delight, his daughter leaned in and kissed his cheek.

"You know you wouldn't have it any other way."

"No, no, I wouldn't," he agreed with a smile.

"Love you Daddy."

"Love you too, honey," he said, beaming at her. "Now get along, the kids are waiting for you."

She grabbed a bundle from the blanket and chased after her children. "Who's up for flying kites?" she asked as they jogged off toward a more open part of the park.

Randy looked at his family lovingly as they ran off to play, wincing as he turned his head to watch them go. He grabbed his left shoulder as a twinge of pain shot through it.

A flash of fear hit him, but then as quick as it had come, the pain was gone.

"Whew, had me worried there for a minute," he said to himself, then reclined back on the grass, enjoying the afternoon's warmth.

A lone figure walked up in front of him, silhouetted as they blocked the sun, a bright aura of sunlight framing them where they stood. Randy squinted up, the rays of light blurring his old eyes.

A slender arm reached down to help him to his feet, and after pausing a moment, he reached out to take it.

He had just closed his fingers around her hand when he noticed the unusual, vintage sapphire and ruby ring she was wearing. His eyes clearing as he stood, Randy saw the woman he'd been missing for more than half of his life.

Then he noticed his body didn't hurt.

He looked at himself and realized he was the exact age as when they'd last seen one another. He didn't bother looking behind him on the grass. He knew what he'd see.

Instead, he happily gazed at the woman standing in front of him, barely keeping her own happiness in check. She looked absolutely radiant in her joy at seeing him. Somehow, they both played it cool.

"Been a long time," Randy said, casually.

"Yes," Death replied. "But it's only been a moment."

He paused, still holding her hand as emotion swelled in his chest.

"I missed you," he said.

"I missed you too."

They stared at one another a moment longer, then finally, and with the utmost tenderness, he cupped her cheek in his hand, caressing her temple and brushing the hair back from her face as they kissed.

A rush of warm energy flowed between them, and both were reluctant to break the embrace. Eventually they did, and laced their fingers together tightly, sparks flying between their eyes as they shared a loving smile.

Randy glanced across the field at his daughter and grandchildren playing in the sun.

"It was a really good life," he said, a slight sadness tinting his words.

"It was," Dorothy agreed. "You lived long, and raised her well."

"I'll miss them."

"But someday, if you wish, you'll see them again, you know."

"I know. And sooner than I think, right?"

She flashed a dazzling smile.

"Now you're getting the hang of it."

He watched his family play a moment longer, then felt a light tug on his hand.

"Come on, lover, we've got a lot to catch up on."

"Indeed we do," he replied, falling into a slow stride beside her.

"So," she queried, "anywhere you want to go? There was a big earthquake in Guatemala."

"Oh, that's just morbid."

"Hey, you knew you were dating Death. You can't say I didn't warn you." She laughed, and Randy couldn't help but crack a smile and join her as, hand in hand, they walked off into eternity.

Thank You Dear Reader!

Reader word of mouth is an independent author's lifeblood. Your ratings and reviews really help indie authors gain visibility, so if you enjoyed this little collection of odd stories and have a spare moment, if you would leave a rating or review, or perhaps share with a friend or two, it would be greatly appreciated.

Thank you!

~ Scott ~

Be sure to check out Scott Baron's oddball short story collections:

The Best Laid Plans of Mice (anthology)
Lost & Found
Worst. Superhero. Ever.
The Queen of the Nutters
Lawyers vs. Demons
The Tin Foil Hat Club
Snow White's Walk of Shame

About the Author

A native Californian, Scott Baron was born in Hollywood, which he claims may be the reason for his off-kilter sense of humor.

Before taking up residence in Venice Beach, Scott first spent a few years studying abroad in Florence, Italy before returning home to Los Angeles and settling into the film and television industry, where in addition to writing, he has worked as an on-set medic off and on for many years.

Aside from penning books and screenplays, Scott is also involved in indie film and theater scene both in the U.S. and abroad.

CPSIA information can be obtained
at www.ICGtesting.com
Printed in the USA
LVHW040234231120
672447LV00003B/100